The Creator State

The Creator State

A Novel

Sandra Walter

iUniverse, Inc.
New York Lincoln Shanghai

The Creator State

Copyright © 2008 by Sandra Walter

iUniverse books may be ordered through booksellers or by contacting:

iUniverse
2021 Pine Lake Road, Suite 100
Lincoln, NE 68512
www.iuniverse.com
1-800-Authors (1-800-288-4677)

Because of the dynamic nature of the Internet, any Web addresses or links contained in this book may have changed since publication and may no longer be valid.

This is a work of fiction. All of the characters, names, incidents, places, organizations, and dialogue in this novel are either the products of the author's imagination or are used fictitiously.

ISBN: 978-0-595-45237-8 (pbk)
ISBN: 978-0-595-69561-4 (cloth)
ISBN: 978-0-595-89548-9 (ebk)

Printed in the United States of America

Preface

A friend of mine said artists can talk about art all day, perform all night, and then go out afterward and talk about art some more. This may not differ from other professions, but when it comes to the topic of art and its purposes, I am guilty of such chatter. The conversation of art is a perpetual dialogue and I love to contribute every chance I get.

Current events prompt me to enter the conversation again with a twofold purpose: a need to document this age of uncertainty and the challenges of the artist within it, and to explore ways to utilize our unique gifts as creative persons. The desire for a better, more respectful, and more peaceful world society is not a new topic. Neither is the desire to create antidotes to the madness of hate and violence which infects so many. But if the research supporting this novel has taught me anything, it is that any small contribution to positive action is not lost in some void of existence. There is no void. On the contrary, there is a unification of all knowledge, all action, and all thought that has ever been or ever will be. It continues to grow with each moment. No thought is left unnoticed or unused by the collective consciousness. As we add our thoughts and actions to this ever-expanding body of history, we are woven into the fabric of its being. We can shape the future toward an improved world community. Regardless of immediate results, it seems actions for positive change are less impractical than the chaos which surrounds us.

This book engages a jump in logic between creating a temporary reality for an audience and creating a new reality for the world. It's not as far-fetched as one would think. Quantum physics has revealed many enlightening mechanisms, including the Zero Point Field, upon which the more scientific portions of this story rest. For every idea and question proposed, there is an answer residing somewhere in the Field. Connecting these ideas to their justifications is remarkably simple, if one is open to the exploration. Proof, as with so many things, rests within the heart of the thinker.

A sincere note of thanks to everyone who read the early drafts of this novel. I truly appreciate your comments and support. For more information on this book or my other writings, please visit www.sandrawalter.com

All the best,

Sandra Walter

Everyone has within them all of the answers they will ever seek.
In the absence of doubt, we are all God.

—Sandra Walter

1

We continually search for divine intervention, seeking higher sources greater than ourselves to guide, answer, and enlighten. When we finally realize this power exists within ourselves, our faith in each other will be more than enough.

—*The Magic Mobile*

Alex lay awake in bed and stared at the glow-in-the-dark stars on her ceiling. On each illuminant she penned a desire; a galaxy of dreams to wish upon. Creativity. Enlightenment. Love. Brilliance. Purpose. She focused on them before nodding off to sleep and sent energy to her aspirations. But insomnia visited her more often than slumber as of late, and that morning she gazed at faded stars, their light drained by hours of nighttime darkness. She extended a hand over the alarm clock beside her. It buzzed expectedly at 5 a.m. and she tapped it into silence again.

The details of her Chicago apartment slowly appeared in the pre-dawn light. Her Melrose Avenue studio was a small vintage room, painted white a hundred times. Two large windows faced the back of a Lake Shore Drive high rise, which provided a lovely view of the pricey units across the way and a parking lot full of equally pricey vehicles. If one leaned out the window and bravely tested the limits of the ancient sill's edge, yacht masts from the nearby harbor could be seen past the high rise. Before this panoramic view stood a sprawling ivy named Cleo, Alex's prized possession and confidant. Beside Cleo a lopsided radiator swelled the plaster wall behind it with its ghastly heat in the winter months. Alex dubbed the fixture "Fahrenheit 451" after it fatally scorched her copy of *Catcher in the Rye*. A dumbwaiter on the opposite wall was converted into a closet space, but the mute service button remained next to its door, over which Alex painted "Ring for Assistance." She pushed the buzzer several times per week, despite the absence of an attendant. A black and white photo of Alex from a stage play hung next to her door, under which she placed her keys. She aptly named the photo "Keeper of the keys," for it was during that production when Alex first encountered a startling out-of-body sensation; a deeply connected feeling she would crave in her performances thereafter.

Prior to the Melrose studio, Alex stayed at a decaying dump known as the Crandall Hotel. Only a few months had passed since she moved out of the transient hotel in the heart of Chicago. The dismal flophouse provided a backdrop for a very unusual personal event in Alex's life. Without warning, incident, or accident, she began to hear internal voices just before she dropped off to sleep. When her mind relaxed and the city noise fading, she heard a fuzzy static, as if someone were turning the tuning dial on an old cathedral radio. Blippits of conversation came and went, in and out of audible range. It both startled and intrigued her. After a few weeks, the static broadcasted singular voices which spoke of artistic purpose and creative inspiration.

Certain passages of time seem mystical in their enchantment. The commencement of the messages would remain a touchstone memory for Alex and her artistic growth: a time when sleeplessness began, words flowed from unknown sources, and strength came from deprivation. It was romantic for her to dwell in that terrible Chicago dive, in the dead of winter, as classic blues records wailed from the room below. Late into the night, Alex wrote about the magic of art, and felt well-placed despite the roaches that wandered across her desk.

She welcomed the nightly voices and diligently scribbled the passages of creative inspiration into a journal. After a few weeks of this activity, she decided to record them on her cell phone voicemail for her colleagues to enjoy. The daily message ended with a request to text in the numerals 2539, which spelled "Alex" on the telephone key pad. This let her know people were listening, without acquiring a slew of voicemails to retrieve. The Crandall's dingy atmosphere strengthened her voiceover skills to sound calm, centered, and purposeful despite her circumstances. The messages eventually gathered a few fans, with several 2539 texts coming in each day. This is how her first creative child, *The Magic Mobile*, was born. After a few months at the hotel, Alex manifested enough acting work to afford her Melrose Avenue studio. She left the Crandall with an education in survival, a dedication to a new inner purpose, and a lifelong addiction to Bessie Smith.

Alex loved her new apartment on Melrose, but her clairaudience was not quieted by the new enclosure. The voices began to break into her thoughts during the daytime, which forced her to carry a pen and journal wherever she went. Everyday conversation was interrupted by the messages, and she politely excused herself to write them down. Her friends didn't seem to mind the eccentricity, or at least they were kind enough not to criticize. While her sleeplessness delivered hours of fragmented quotes, it was her morning run which clarified the words and brought them to her journal afterwards. She rolled off of her daybed, wrestled into her running clothes, and tumbled out the door for a morning jog.

She emerged from her apartment building into the damp lakeside air and headed for the waterfront. Chicago was a peaceful haven just before sunrise, and the quiet accompanied her footfall as she lightly drummed along the sidewalk. Her physique cut a graceful silhouette against the dawn. She had the build of a dancer, but it was the theater which served Alex's passions. Her smooth voice and sharp wit complemented her patrician countenance, and blessed her with a long resume of leading roles. The *Chicago Tribune* christened her an "excellent and complex performer," a review which encouraged her to expand her skills even further. She moved toward the growing light on the running path and reached the lakefront trail.

As she worked along the water's edge, her gaze volleyed from the emerging sun on the lake's horizon to the opposite cityscape. Vivid corals washed the soaring facades of Lake Shore Drive as the June sunrise dappled the water's complexion with pastels. The town appeared less intimidating in that subtle light; it was momentary solace for a city girl. Birds and breezes played in the trees, and the rhythm of Alex's footsteps calmed her chattering mind. Her sleeplessness combined day and night into a dreamlike experience. But as inconvenient as the insomnia was, Alex felt she was meant to be awake during this stretch of time.

She padded along to the footbridge, up and over Lake Shore Drive, and into the refuge of Lincoln Park. Bronze statues of Chicagoans past chronicled her progress as she glided by them. Her reflection traced the edge of the park's pond. She surprised a great blue heron who lifted into the air and circled a wide spiral over the water until he pulled out of sight. She entered the gates of the Zoo and jogged to its north end, where a gangly black-and-white gibbon anxiously awaited her morning visit. The zookeepers released the ape into his outdoor habitat at sunrise. She dashed back and forth alongside the giant cage as he raced inside, each trying to beat the other to the opposite end. After a few laps of this activity, she waved to him and departed. He watched her exit with a longing gaze, as if expecting her to reconsider and return to him.

She exited through the northwest end of the zoo, ran past the ageless greenhouse where lush greens flourished regardless of the weather, past the statue of Shakespeare to whom she always blew a kiss, and along the Lakeview neighborhood sidewalks toward her Belmont Harbor apartment. Words tumbled in her mind from her sleepless night, and she quickened her pace to meet the morning message at the journey's end. After a quick stretch on the front stairs, she returned to her studio, anxious for the day's missive to unfold. She slung a towel around her saturated neck, gulped a glass of water, and sat down at her kitchen table with her journal. A message came through which foreshadowed the day. It spun out of the scratched words in her notebook, darting out of the twist of her consciousness. It read:

This is the playing field; this is where the collective consciousness explores the spirituality of art in our church of humanity. This is the place where we succeed and fail, challenge and defeat. Step onto the green, announce your entry to the game, and be welcomed by the team.

Alex recorded the passage on her cell phone and didn't question its motives. She considered herself a messenger, not a preacher. Many artists mentioned the synchronistic timing of the *Mobile* messages in their lives, so she let the words fall where they may.

During projects of the heart like the *Magic Mobile*, the mind often interrupts and requests a next step, a way to utilize the momentum. Alex closed the blinds on her Melrose windows and dropped to the floor to meditate on the path her life was taking. She meditated in her own style, surrounded by symbolic objects, as incense curled around her thoughts and candles flickered light across her eyelids. She listened for answers rather than inspiration for the world. Her phone began to ring. She interpreted it as a response to her meditation's request for a next step. It was unusual to receive a call so early in the morning, especially since the bulk of her friends slept their mornings away. An unfamiliar number displayed on her cell phone, but she returned the call promptly. The line jingled once, and a male voice answered.

"Andrews Theater."

Her heart leapt to attention as if she were taking off on a run. She recognized the voice immediately; it was David Cooper, a local off-loop theater owner. David was a talented but chauvinistic director who utilized his position to feed his sexual cravings. He kept his predatory nature hidden behind the guise of professional artist, but the path behind him was littered with actresses who had fallen to his appeal. She speculated if he was calling about the summer production. It was early June and prime time for next season's auditions, perhaps he wanted her for a fall role. Her performances and *Magic Mobile* missives granted her some cache in the local creative circuit, so she calmed her anxieties. She attempted to sound cheery despite the fatigue of sleeplessness. "This is Alex Davis. I'm returning a call?"

"Aleeex." David sounded amused. She waited for his introduction. "This is David Cooper. I want to talk to you about working for me. You've been highly recommended by a friend of mine. Can you swing by my theater today?"

She examined his statements. "Working for me" must mean the summer production. She wondered if she would have to do a monologue today, and why he sounded so flirtatious. If the owner of the Andrews calls at 8:00 a.m., something unusual was on the agenda.

"Give me a time, and I'll be there!" She reprimanded herself for sounding so excited.

He prompted, "Nine okay?"

She agreed and quickly got off the phone.

The call carried a weight, as if it changed the course of life events. She knew it was her next step arriving, just as she requested, and yet she felt inner resistance. A twitchiness deep within her sensed danger. Her mind toyed with it for a while: when something occurs as a response to a request, can you decide to avoid the event, or will your travels just bring you back to the same point? If a tough life lesson is about to unfold, can you put it off, or is your avoidance of the lesson still part of the plan? If you sidestep a change that may or may not be good for you, is the result the actual lesson in spite of your diversions? Alex let her mind reel and then avoided further questions. Too many answers would take all the fun out of the adventure. The journey interested her more than the finish line, or at least that was her way to cope with hearing voices and missing sleep.

She prepared for the meeting as the voices chattered away in her head. *We gain our future by living our dreams in the present.* In the shower: *We empower ourselves to recognize our own worth.* While eating breakfast: *Battles of wits and wills are played, not fought.* And again while selecting her clothes: *Weed out the false growths before they take root.* The morning energies zipped around like overheated bees. She spilled the phrases onto paper, some barely legible thanks to her long night, and headed out just before nine.

The morning rush was well under way as she strolled onto Belmont. Alex sported her usual style, clothed in what she referred to as "the uniform": black A-line skirt that landed at the knee where her black boots began, a dark gray cotton v-neck sweater with a black tank camisole underneath, all topped by blonde choppy hair that made her look torch-like. As she walked through her neighborhood, she examined the sharp business-folk who hurried off to work, dressed in their own uniforms of gray and blue. Her perception made her feel transparent and disconnected from the population. She felt invisible and invincible, as if she only existed on stage. Nothing seemed substantial to her except the creative endeavor; the mimicry of so-called reality. Despite the distance between Alex and her fellow citizens, she knew her performances enriched their lives, and they patronized the arts in return. Art and audience provided an amiable circle of support which had endured for centuries.

As she approached the Andrews Theater, her heart quickened. The flirtation in David's voice had her anxious about their meeting. She promised herself once again that she would not flirt to land work. Her personal vow proved difficult on a few occasions, when a carefree fling could have provided easy career advancement, but she stayed true to her oath. Frustrations with the flirtation game flurried in her mind until a sight abruptly stopped the storm. Mounted high atop of the Andrews were five silver metal stars which once surrounded a cross. The cross had been taken down as part of the building's transformation from church into theater venue, but the stars remained for theatrical significance. At that moment the stars bounced the morning sunlight directly into Alex's eyes, and she felt a tellurian blessing in the well-timed glare. Her mind quieted and she gave the Andrews a long look.

The Andrews Theater overshadowed its surrounding city block landscape. Stretches of gray limestone and tall Gothic arches alluded to its previous existence. The inside of its elaborate stained glass windows were shuttered to block out the light, but the exteriors remained faithful to their original purpose with dazzling, swirling colors. Two giant oak doors guarded the entrance from the street. The mass service sign was utilized as a "coming attractions" display. Alex pressed the intercom button at the front door, an obvious addition to the original structure, and waited. A loud clap of static answered from the box, and a buzzing sound growled near the door's handle. She pushed the weighty door open and entered. It took her a few moments to adjust to the dark Andrews' interior, despite her bat-like backstage vision. She saw nothing but blackness until after some active blinking, when shapes began to appear.

The lobby floor was covered with antique carpeting, which was pummeled to a near-threadbare red sheet. Carved oak began to materialize and climbed the walls and doorways, with the distinct smell of myrrh still emanating from its ornate curves. A display case honored the previous tenants, albeit amusingly, with an antique nun's habit and priestly garb. These were surrounded by leather-bound copies of plays, which pointedly resembled prayer books in the dim light of the lobby. It was a clear message to the patrons: theater would be the only religion worshiped here. Four words were painted above the main entryway to the house: "In Theater We Trust." Alex appreciated the company's sense of humor.

She subscribed to challenging the audience, and the Andrews pushed the envelope for ten years and counting.

Alex concluded David must be upstairs, so she opened the inner door to the house. Light spilled into the room through a single uncovered stained glass window. The constant lift of dust in the air highlighted the shaft of daylight which landed on the pews-turned-patron-seats below. It made the space feel downright sacred. She considered how similar their two worlds were. Theatre created a world of fantasy by blocking the light from the outside world; the original church filtered it with mystical images in its windows. It wasn't so different from their religion of theater.

"It's still a church in many ways." David entered behind her.

She calmly started in where her thoughts had taken her and spoke to the stage with her back to him. "Our traditions aren't that far apart. We create a space for something special to occur, lining people up in rows so they focus on the show, trying to touch their hearts through stories and devices. It's not that different from mass, is it?" She lit a smile and turned to meet him.

They had been introduced several times before, most recently at a screenplay reading a few months ago. David attended as many film events as he could, anxious to get his screenwriting career off the ground. Alex presumed the boys club at the Andrews was impenetrable, so until his phone call that morning she had forgotten David altogether.

In his element, in his house of worship, David seemed softer and less intimidating. They reintroduced themselves with handshakes, and for what seemed like a lengthy pause, measured each other's gaze. David had a square superhero face, complimented by wavy brunette hair and pale green eyes. He exuded the proper "successful theater owner" elements: talented, fit body, fit mind, attractive, and well-positioned in the off-loop scene. He carried some clout as one of the only theaters in this section of the city which made money. David discovered very early in his career that he didn't have the desire to perform on stage, so he spent most of his years perfecting his directing skills. Recently, he tried to develop screenplays in order to direct his own films. Not bad for thirty-seven. He accomplished more than most could without attaching themselves to a larger commercial organization. Alex admired him but remained guarded.

She smiled nonchalantly. "Can we cut to the chase, David? Why am I here?"

He chuckled and offered her a seat in the pews. Alex eyed the benches. Each seat was lined by a thick red velvet-covered cushion. She ribbed, "Guess this wasn't a Catholic Church." He laughed again and sat down. Alex sat in the row in front of him with her back to the stage, turning on the relaxed, confident attitude that made her attractive to men. Although she was only thirty-three, she had an air of indifference about her. It was as if she lived this life already and repeated it for the amusement. Both of them had a good fire glowing beneath the surface, which made their meeting even more potent.

David leaned back and folded his arms, which was unmistakably to show off his biceps. "I need someone to manage the theater while I'm attempting to get my film picked up in L.A., and I thought you'd be a good candidate, Alex. You have a good work ethic, you're smart, and I trust you would do a good job while I'm gone. And I'd love it if you would be in the summer show, too. I'd pay you for both the management position and the performances, and if you're sick of it by the time the fall comes, you can quit when I get back."

She released any apprehensions about romance. This was all business, and she felt relieved with the idea of a day job and a summer show. The joy of opportunity rushed in her blood.

"Wow, that sounds perfect." Alex twitched at her enthusiasm. "I'm flattered that you would ask. How do you know I'll be any good at managing?"

"Your name came up a few times. Plus you seem to have your act together, and you're a damn fine performer. Even if you screw up the marketing, the summer show will do okay. Your good reviews will make people come out in the heat. Not to mention, I've got the only theater in the area with air conditioning."

They laughed together and David offered a quick tour. The inviting theater space held three hundred patrons in its long-rowed benches before standing room crowded the back walkways. Above the lobby hung the choir loft, reborn as the lighting and sound loft, which also served as a hideaway for nerve-ridden directors as their creations unfolded below. From the bird's eye view of the loft, David pointed out the renovations that had been made, the most noticeable being the stage itself. The main platform extended deep into the original seating area, allowing for a good-sized backstage hidden by long, dramatic black drapes which matched the wing curtains. The interior walls of the Andrews were a deep rust color, and a dark blue carpet ran up the center aisle. Long stained glass windows framed the stage area, but were no longer graced by natural light. They were only admired during preshow and intermission, when gold bulbs glowed from behind their elegant designs. For the size of the space it had remarkable acoustics, noted by the actors who were lucky enough to break into the cliquish company. A few steps were installed left and right of the stage's apron, so actors could maneuver through the house. David smugly described how he surrounded the audience with action, as if he were the first to think of the concept.

As Alex glanced around, she noticed the space held no traces of religious memorabilia. There were no grand candelabras, no paintings of saints looking heavenward, no suffering souls, no shining infants or halo-crowned colleagues. Anyone who searched for crucifixes or sculptures of the Madonna would be disappointed, as David had them removed and donated to different charitable causes. Whether he did it to eradicate the religious connotations of the space or out of generosity was anyone's guess. But the space still held a distinct spirituality.

David's tour came to a close and he announced that he had to get to a meeting. He offered a set of keys, which Alex accepted as confirmation of their agreement. One summer of service, then she could decide to stay or go when David returned. She would start tomorrow morning.

As she stepped back into the street, Alex squinted in pain at the daylight. She took another look at the Andrews, testing to see if it looked different with her new relationship to it. It did indeed, and she whispered a thank you to its rooftop stars. "I'll take good care of you, and you do the same for me, alright?" They twinkled acquiescence.

With one day of freedom left, she jolted down Belmont and used the deafening roar of the passing L train above her to mask a gleeful shout of joy. She had a theater job to occupy her daytime, another role lined up, and a steady paycheck as icing on this delicious cake of a day. It called for a celebration Alex-style. She paced home and considered the best way to thank her answered meditations. Her head repeated: *Express your thanks by sharing your gifts.*

Alex reviewed her journal for a few good messages, and wrote them out on colored paper. With this pile of words in tow, she strolled to the park where the wayward people gathered during the day. She tucked the messages into sleeping pockets, handed them to those who would accept, and left them for pickup near the unapproachables. These people, at least the coherent ones, might have recognized her from her long walks or painting or running or photography or whatever she may have explored in her free afternoons. A few poetic words might brighten or change the course of their day, but at the very least they were a moment's attention from a kind stranger. To Alex, any creative action held reward.

That evening Alex arrived early for her performance at The Crown Circle Repertory Company, a.k.a. "Circle Rep." Circle Rep made its mark in the ever-growing Andersonville neighborhood as a solid theater venue and a magnet for talented actors. It was well-supported by the surrounding businesses, who reaped the rewards of its large audiences before and after the shows. The Circle Rep Company grew very close after their three-year tenure in the space. The resident directors found good roles for the actors to tackle, and the actors in turn did their best work for them. Alex decided to wait until after the show to announce her good news. Traditionally a few cast members hung out in the theater after the patrons dissipated, and tonight would be no different. Most of the cast lagged behind to get stoned, a habit which Alex sidestepped but tolerated in her friends. When the last of the crew members finally dispersed, the actors propped themselves on different parts of the set, and Alex broke the news of her new opportunity.

Thomas reacted first. Primarily because he was the first one to take a hit of weed, partially because he had nothing good to say about anyone as of late. He exhaled from his full lips and tossed his long wave of dirty blonde hair, grown specifically for his current role, out of his eyes. "David is so fucking lucky. Waltzes into a space with his uncle's money, throws the Lakeview hood a big marketing pitch with all of his 'challenging' productions, and now he's going off to L.A. to get a script reading. No offense, but I hope he gets his ass kicked out there."

"Pay no attention to the naysayer," Peter jumped in. "This is an excellent opportunity for you. Not to mention that we'll now have another place to hang out." He inhaled deeply on the joint and half-choked as he laughed at his own remarks. Peter had a stately air to his lanky stature. In spite of his drug and alcohol abuses, he remained a stabilizing force in this circle of friends because of his own ineptitude at getting his life together. A non-threatening friend in the theater world is a good friend indeed. Alex absorbed the commentary from a front-row seat. She looked like a director, the fabled passion of all actors.

Susan chimed in with her opinion in her customary tone, emphasizing the "*I*" in "*I* think" at all times. "Well *I* think it's great." She yanked her frizzy brown hair into its post-show knot on her angular head. "*I* think you should go in there, kick ass all summer, and teach those Andrews boys what good female leadership can be like." Susan was never short on words when it came to her view on anything, the blessing of an only child with excessively supportive parents. She had been to the best classes at the best schools with the best instructors, and had spent a fortune on private lessons, head shots, and agent-wooing. Alex liked her in spite of all of that.

Supportive words escalated for Alex's next adventure. Matt and Mark, a set of slender twins known as the "Brothers Slim" were excited for her, and regretted that they would miss the whole adventure as they were booked out of town with a summer stock show. Lisa seemed unenthusiastic and turned down the joint as it made its second pass around. She sat in a deep slump beneath her mane of highlighted hair, a posture unbecoming to her 5'9" stature. Something was bothering her these days, so Alex let it go. She knew Lisa was much more approachable after her first cocktail.

Thomas sucked down the last hit and hid the crushed paper butt in the set's tea pot. He fueled a secret vendetta against Phil, the prop master who denied him liquid to pour out of the teapot during the show. Each night, Thomas mimed pouring hot tea with nonexistent fluid, because Phil had borrowed the perfect little antique from his grandmother's china cabinet without her permission. Phil claimed that dark liquid of any kind would stain the interior if left standing each night. So Thomas poured imaginary tea during each performance with a smile, knowing Phil's grandmother would smell the unmistakable odor of marijuana emanating from her china collection for the rest of her days. Thomas thought it was perfect revenge, and emphasized the *pot* in teapot every time he mentioned it in the play.

Peter proclaimed himself sufficiently high and ready for a drink, so the group gathered themselves to traipse up the block to Jimmy's. There had been a shift in the dynamic of the group when Alex announced her good news, something which landed between concern and jealousy. Alex knew her position at the Andrews might alienate her from this crowd, so she made a private pledge to get them all involved in the summer production. Alex was the last to file out of Circle Rep and she turned to the stage, whispered a "thank you," and flicked out the lights.

Jimmy's was an old Chicago-style hangout, in the classic formation of a long room lined by a long bar on one side, with tables stuffed into any remaining floor space. Elaborate woodwork surrounded its liquor shelves and bar, making an elegant first impression. It only showed its age by daylight, when distressed floors were revealed and cracked mirrors caught the light. But in its nighttime display, Jimmy's was one of those dark places which provided a timeless safety zone for conversation. It always smelled of beer and cigarettes, even when no one was smoking or drinking. The odor latched onto clothing, even after a short stay. Many customers used the phrase, "Jimmy-ed," as in, "My coat's been Jimmy-ed," to describe the lingering aroma. But the place reeked of character as well, and you couldn't find a better place for artists to get together.

On the weekend the bar was shoulder-to-shoulder by midnight, but on a Wednesday it held only a smattering of patrons: a few stray casts and neighborhood alcoholics. Susan made her standard grandiose entrance, and planted a big kiss on the aging bartender. Ray was as much of a fixture in this neighborhood as the bar, and true to his gentlemanly demeanor, he blushed accordingly every time Susan landed one on his lips. She always earned a first drink on the house, regardless of her transparent behavior. Matt and Mark headed for the pool table in back, while Peter exchanged paper dollars for quarters to dominate the juke box. He knew more about classic rock than most, and insisted that respect be paid to his favorites. The group spent many a night at Peter's apartment, entertained for hours by his extensive collection of LPs. Vinyl was a safe outlet for his addictive personality. Alex often speculated what he could accomplish if he explored music rather than theater.

Lisa claimed a booth, threw herself legs-out into a seat, and roughly tossed her bag on the table. Alex glided into the opposite seat and left a space for Susan to join them. Susan blurted Alex's good news to Ray, and he responded by serving the trio a round of martinis.

"For my favorite girls, you're all treasures; jewels in the Crown Circle," announced Ray. He presented the drinks with the panache of a forgotten era. Alex admired his perfect wave of silver hair and enduring handsomeness. He had a winning style that made grown women swoon like school girls. He proclaimed the drinks were on the house, winked a sparkling blue eye, and tapped the table twice with his knuckle as if to end any further discussion of his generosity. Ray swung back to the bar as Susan glimmered at the drinks. She raised a glass to propose a toast. Lisa followed suit without uprighting herself, elbow propped on the table with glass in hand. Alex lifted and smiled.

Susan gathered the best compliment she could deliver. "To Alex! I think you are on your way, girl." They clinked all around and downed a first gulp. Lisa shuddered as the vodka warmed its way down her throat.

Alex watched the Brothers Slim bend their stick figures over the pool table like some kind of geometric performance art. Peter settled in for his long stay at the bar. He riffled his cigarettes from his breast pocket and searched for the matches which never accompanied them. He and Ray customarily talked for hours, the perfect partnership of trusty barkeep and loyal customer. Alex wished she could join them tonight, but she had to deal with Lisa's negativity first. It was a burden to Alex, who was riding a fresh wave of creativity, finding joy and purpose in everything she experienced. Lisa remained quiet, stared down into her drink, and waited for Alex to ask her what was wrong. Susan saw their conversation approach and invented a way to get the hell away from it.

"I think I forgot to ask Thomas about something," she said, and scurried away to the bar with her martini. Alex turned to see if Susan would give her an "I'm sorry, I can't deal with Lisa tonight" look, but Susan didn't flinch and joined Thomas at the bar.

Alex expected Lisa's usual tirade of problems. Complaints about men, money, show business, the government, politics; you name it, Lisa had it in her repertoire. Lisa sipped her martini as she sat back in the booth, looking like an exhausted child with her legs stretched out on the seat, back crumpled against the wall. Alex considered a gentle approach, but was too frustrated with Lisa's demands on her good fortune. She blurted out, "What the fuck is up with you, anyway?"

Lisa snarled at her, shocked at her insensitivity. "All these fucking messages you write every day and the leading parts you get and now the Andrews thing falls into your lap? I'm pissed off about all of it, okay? You say all these beautiful things every day on the *Mobile* about strength and individual morality, and then you go and take a job from David fuck-everyone Cooper? What the hell is going on? You were my hero, Alex. But now you have me doubting everything I believed about you. I saw you as a genuine artist, someone who could really make a difference in this profession, and now you go to work for the biggest ass of the neighborhood? It pisses me off! And I intend to stay pissed off for a while!"

Lisa stopped her rant, retreated to a full slouch, and gulped her martini in distress. Alex censored her immediate impulse to defend herself and collected her tongue. She thought the Andrews position would challenge her to stay above the drenching current of David's manipulations. She wondered if she would be used as so many before her. Her mind leapt to the messages. For six months she heard voices, recorded the *Mobile*, changed her acting style, and let her true creative forces come through. Would it endanger her progress to work at the Andrews? She calmed herself and took a breath.

"Lisa, for a while I thought the *Mobile* was a separate issue, this weird clairaudience thing of mine, and I don't expect you to believe any of this, but hear me out."

Lisa hiked herself up in her seat at Alex's sudden intensity.

"About half of the messages that I hear," Alex began, "I write down and use on the *Mobile*, but lately something is changing in them, something is changing in me. I don't want to sound too dramatic, but something new is coming through, and it's waiting until I'm on stage, in the middle of the deepest, longest monologues to reveal itself. I feel something coming in, or maybe I'm going out, reaching out for whatever it is; some answer, some kind of purpose to all of these strange things that have been happening to me. And I can't figure out if I created it, or if it's creating something new in me, but it has me wondering where all of this is leading."

Lisa listened intently and waited for how this involved David. Alex sensed her line of thought and responded. "The ideas about being an artist and expressing ourselves freely, being open to all of this seemingly new-age idealism that I've been spreading with the *Magic Mobile*, needs a next step on the path to wherever this leads. This morning I asked for it in my meditation, and I was answered with David's call."

Lisa shifted, not buying it yet.

"I know what you're thinking about this," added Alex, "but this is happening for a reason, so I'm just going to see how it all plays out."

Lisa dropped the David accusations, embarrassed that she brought them up. The girls had recently recovered from an uncomfortable snag in their friendship. A few months earlier Peter and Lisa had been flirting up a storm when Peter became distracted by an intimate on-stage scene with Alex. It temporarily suspended the flirtation, but Lisa forgave Alex when nothing happened outside of the play. Lisa held on to the incident in her emotional Rolodex nevertheless. She cautiously questioned her, since Alex hid more internal duress than she let on to. "Well, what do you think is going on?"

Alex's knitted brows expressed more than her words. The clairaudience had strengthened its foothold in her life, and she was concerned it was a madness she shouldn't have welcomed so easily. She relished being more challenging, insightful, spontaneous, and on top of her game than ever before, but the personal price of it all was steep.

"*I* think," Alex began, prompting a much-needed giggle at Susan's expense, "that I'm doing the right thing. After all, what is the point of life if you can't allow fate to aim you in a new direction? But lately it's different. I can't sleep, I'm hearing these voices all the time, and last night I was struck by this out-of-body feeling during a scene in Act Two, like I was connected with the whole universe; like a rush of light flew through my character. It was overwhelming and fascinating and ..." Alex checked Lisa's expression for an approval to continue, and it was granted. "More present than anything I can imagine."

Lisa contemplated her friend. Alex had always been a little out there. She had a choice to make. Acknowledge her pal's observations, or walk away, run away, from this total freak of a friend who sat before her. She folded her hands and rested her mouth on them, so she wouldn't speak too soon. She searched her mind and found no passage, no message of her own to enlighten her friend or ease her circumstances. All of the admiration she had for Alex turned to concern for her friend's mental health.

Alex sensed her dismay. "It's a lot to hear, I know. But it isn't the first time I've felt this thing. I wonder if anyone else is having the same experiences." She made a sober request. "I want to find out what's happening to me. I'd like to explore it within the safe haven of my friends. You're the first one I've told, so be kind, okay?"

"Right." Lisa released her hands and let the information soak in. If anything would relieve her artistic boredom, it would be a new way of performing or aspiring to a higher level. Lisa was addicted to the new, just like Alex, and she welcomed anything out of the ordinary. It may be her only source of excitement this year, and to write off Alex as nuts might be premature. Lisa playfully raised an eyebrow. "David's going to be gone all summer long, isn't he?"

Alex returned her elevated spirit. "Yes he is."

"Well then we'll have the Andrews all to ourselves, won't we?"

"Anytime outside of performances and rehearsals, it's ours to use."

Lisa raised her glass. "Let's take advantage of the situation, then. Let's see what trouble we can get ourselves into, eh? Seize the summer, explore the unknown! I'll stop by the Andrews tomorrow and we can chat about it."

"I don't even know how to start talking about this thing," Alex confessed.

"Sister, you already have." Lisa clanked her glass into Alex's and downed the last of her beverage. For the first time since their conversation began, they heard noise tumble in from the group at the bar. Lisa slung her arm around Alex as they crossed to their colleagues. Alex was energized by the possibilities ahead and ordered a round for her friends. She paid Ray, gave Lisa a wink, excused herself from her friend's company, and caught a cab home.

Back in the sanctuary of her studio, anxieties surfaced about the day ahead of her. Another sleepless night would ruin her first day at her new job. She had to sleep. On occasion she would escape her insomnia and indulge in sleeping pills. They weren't always effective, but when they worked she referred to it as "plastic sleep" due to their unnatural effect. She prepared for bed, slid the pills down her throat, and tucked herself in. As her head rested on her pillow, her anxieties dissipated. Her ceiling stars slowly began to fade beyond heavy eyelids. She felt her body shut down for the night, as if the security guards made the last round and shut off her brain one bank of hallway lights at a time. One by one the passages of her mind snapped into darkness, until at last she slept.

2

They are older than Stonehenge, these pursuits of the soul. They endure millenniums of entities, and slowly seep their messages to the curious nature of man. We hear their voices and transmit their secrets as our unrecognized senses are empowered.

—*The Magic Mobile*

The sun broke over Lake Michigan and found Alex running off the fog of false sleep. Her face remained expressionless beneath her flamboyant hair. Sunrise corals reflected off her disorganized strands of gold and glowed on her damp cheek. She stared ahead in deep thought: she would have to be at the Andrews by nine, which left a few hours for her habitual morning activities. The schedule pressured her to find a message. Perhaps the voices would honor her conversation with Lisa from the night before, or provide strong words to christen her new agenda: day-jobbing by light and exploring by night.

Her feet fell quietly beneath her as her head rambled on. She looked to the sunrise-tinted clouds above her and tuned into the calm morning sounds. Waves slapped the concrete wall next to the path; seagulls began their day-long dialogues; Lake Shore Drive awakened with commuters; leashes jingled on dogs out for their morning walk; masters grumbled commands between sips of coffee; distant music hummed from muffled headphones. Somewhere in this symphony resided a peace which could only be found in the early morning. Alex breathed it in and settled her mind.

Her peripheral vision caught something on the path. She looked to the pavement and jumped simultaneously as she leapt over a small green creature beneath her feet. She halted and turned to investigate. It was a praying mantis, bright green and lit by the sunrise. It faced the rising orb as if performing its morning meditation. Alex glanced down the path and checked for oncoming harm, but found herself alone with the creature. Its bizarre appearance was made stranger by its unflinching stance. It seemed to be unaffected by her inspection. It stared into the morning light, arms permanently bent in prayer. She didn't know if she should chase it into the grass or let it remain fascinated with the dawn. She chose the latter, trotted down the path, and threw a smile back to the mantis which remained hypnotized by the coral daylight.

As she jogged, she tried to find a reason for this encounter. Everything held a connection for her these days, everything had a purpose. Spotting a praying mantis at the lakefront was unusual. She considered her new job. It was in a converted church; perhaps the praying mantis symbolized worship of nature, a principal which Alex held dear. Perhaps it was a subtle reminder to hold onto her personal rituals as she worked in a space built for a different kind of worship. Perhaps the mantis was a sign to remain true to herself in the upcoming months. Alex laughed at her interpretations and simplified them: perhaps she almost squashed a bug.

She focused on the physical challenge at hand and powered up the stairs of the North Street overpass. Her legs burned and her breath quickened as she worked over the bridge and carefully down the park side stairs. In the green of the park, her spirits lifted and she searched for a *Mobile* quote of the day. She observed the trees, the grass, and the birds bathing in the water fountains. She began to play with the images passing by her, and saw their connection to the art world; a symbol in each bird, a suggestion in every living thing which surrounded her. What endurance nature had; what unconditional love in its continuity. Nature seemed inexhaustible.

Then a message came to her. *Life imitates art.* Rather than the standard "art imitates life," the voices had flipped the words. She contemplated which execution was true: all of these fascinating creatures had to be created, just as a performer creates a role, or a painter creates a painting. If the original creator was likened to an artist, and the creation followed afterwards, then wouldn't it be true that life imitates art? Life would follow the inspiration to create it. Whether flawed or brilliant, the idea replayed in Alex's mind as she quickened her stride to get home and write it out. She raced her mind through the park, the zoo, the gardens, and finally home. She snatched a pen upon entry to her studio, crashed to the floor, and scratched the ideas into her journal. She recorded her message of the day with a bright voice.

The creative impulse spawns creation. The creative vibration causes everything we know of to manifest in our reality; art is the source of our existence. It is not our purpose to mimic, but to design. Life imitates art.

Pleased with her words, she checked the time: 7:30 a.m. She had enough time for a quick thank-you meditation, and then had to get ready for the Andrews. She had almost forgotten how it felt to have a day job; the camaraderie with her fellow citizens which her night-owl existence hadn't provided in over a year. Alex was a good employee for others in the past; organized, reliable, and hard-working. Although David and Alex knew each other by communal association, she still considered his turnover of responsibility to be an odd move. He seemed to be a decent businessman, but she questioned his trust in her. She searched her memory for their few encounters. They were first introduced about five years ago when he came to see her perform Hedda Gabler. After the play he came backstage to meet her, which created a stir in the dressing room. He never visited actors after a show, and gave Alex a generous amount of compliments. Since that evening they had crossed paths at a few readings, auditions, a few parties, nothing outstanding. She discerned the reason behind her sudden employment wasn't important. The purpose of this turn of events would be revealed in time.

She walked with enthusiasm toward the Andrews. Her phone hummed 2539s at her waist, and she apologized to the appliance as she turned it to silent mode. A sight in a gallery window stopped her progress. A giant painting of a praying mantis glared at her from behind the front glass. A mural in vivid greens and yellows portrayed a gleeful creature in mid-air, about to leap off the canvas. Alex broke a wide smile at the sight. She shortened her admiration of the artwork and moved on quickly, as she had a schedule to keep. It was the second mantis of the day; one more and she would have a "three."

Alex noted a recurring pattern in her life, where synchronicities occurred in threes. She interpreted three similar events, within a reasonable amount of time, was evidence of universal gears in motion. It was fun to track the threes, and this unusual symbol of the mantis intrigued her. Rather than push the issue, she waited patiently for the third moment to surface, and invariably it always did.

She paced quickly down Belmont and peered ahead for the stars atop the Andrews. They came into view and were now warm and familiar. They welcomed her as a family member rather than a guest. The front doors were locked and she remembered the keys David gave her. She jiggled one of them into the ancient door and heard a grand thunk as the bolt retracted. A rush of air pulled into the space as she opened the door, and the darkness inside indicated she was the first one to arrive. She felt around for a light switch and discovered one that mercifully lit the lobby. The warm glow illuminated the details of the room and she felt a familiar sensation: the immediate comfort level she shared with theater spaces.

It made David's absence a bit easier to take. As she entered the house, she spied a few benches and a dim aisle. The same stained glass window was left uncovered again, and now she knew why. The shaft of dusty light guided her across the room. She drifted toward the stage, and turned around to observe the loft. The office remained dark. She considered David might like the dark, or maybe he attempted to save on the ComEd bill by keeping the space dim during the day. She gave out a yell but her hello found no reciprocation. She ventured upstairs to investigate, only to find the office vacant.

Smoky incense had lingered at the Andrews for so many years that the space had its own signature perfume. Alex breathed it in, delighted by its charm, and surveyed the stage from the loft. She gave herself permission to greet the space, authorized by her aloneness, and spoke a favorite *Mobile* message to the empty house.

"Welcome to the feast table of creativity! Here, take a goblet of inspiration. We dine on the bounty of the universe. And if you never leave full, all the better!" The space warmed to her voice and welcomed her. She knew this employment was her destiny, but David's absence seemed odd. She walked back to the tiny office, tripped over a coil of sound cable, and caught herself on a very unstable chair on casters. It skidded with her touch and she almost fell face-first into a light fixture.

"Jesus!" she squealed, then raised her eyes to the ceiling and shrugged, as if to apologize to the former tenant. She discovered a note taped to the office door with her name penned across its surface. She removed it and lit a tiny lamp at the sound table.

Dear Alex,

Thanks for starting today. I had to take off early for the airport, wanted to beat the traffic. Sorry for the short notice. Glad I gave you a key. There's an envelope on my desk that has cheat sheets on everything, along with additional keys you will need. I'll call you when I land to go over it all. The computer has a login and password taped to it. Please check my e-mail. I also started an e-mail account for you to use.

The current show closes in a week. Joseph (our Tech Director) will have the set strike under control, and the rest of the crew will clean up or break down as necessary. You'll then have three weeks to prep for the next show, which will be plenty of time to take care of publicity and marketing, and to learn your lines of course! Everything is programmed into my Outlook, just open it and all dead-lines, tasks, and contacts are there for you.

Talk soon,
David

Alex lowered the letter, relieved with David's organizational skills. All one had to do was follow a little direction, and she had plenty of experience doing that. She entered the dark office, flipped on the computer, and checked for immediate tasks. Since nothing was pressing, she decided to commune with the space before anyone wandered in. She followed David's lighting cheat sheet and snapped on the work lights. She descended into the empty house and studied it from center stage. Her eyes scanned from floor to ceiling and searched for anything that hinted at its history. But rather than lingering prayers or hymnal choruses, there was a different kind of echo: that of performances. Monologues and moments were imprinted in the air. The trials and tribulations of humanity's joy and suffering vibrated in the walls. Creativity stirred in the aura of the house, coloring its mystique. As she surveyed her new turf, Alex had the impulse to ordain the space as her new creative home. She needed a place to experiment with her new discoveries and this could become a safe refuge. She spread her arms wide and raised her hands and voice, grinning at the priestliness of her stance. "I ordain this space for creative brilliance! Everything I have been working on, everything that has led me here will come to fruition in the months to come. The purpose for my messages and my creativity shall be revealed here!" She hesitated, then added, "Thank you!"

Alex lowered her arms and waited for biblical repercussions. Instead of penance, a silent blessing hung in the air. She smiled and whispered another "thank you." The phone suddenly jingled in the office, and she dashed up the stairs.

"Andrews Theater, Alex speaking."

David's greeting held a belittling tone. "Well, don't you sound professional."

"David, your baby is safe, don't worry. Thanks for all the notes and reminders, it's making this a lot easier than I anticipated." Alex rolled her eyes and knew he would like the idea of her worrying about the job.

"Oh, you're gonna be great, kiddo. Don't let Joseph push his weight around. I'm sure he's still pissed about not getting the job. But he's a hell of a techie." Alex listened intently as the Andrews office politics unfolded. David continued, "Keep an eye on Lucas, too, the Sound Op. He may want to linger and spin records half the night. He's been doing that a lot since we bought the new sound system. Let him play if you like, but feel free to kick him out if you don't."

"Anything else I should know about these guys?" Alex realized she was the only female employee at the Andrews, evidence of David's irritation with females in the business world. She wondered if this was the reason for his immediate departure after his last-second hiring of her. Maybe he left town in order to side-step any confrontation. Alex shook off the notions running in her head, and tried to pay attention to the conversation.

"Well Alex, you have your hands full with my team. You know, you can use the space after hours for rehearsals or whatever. Just show it respect and every-thing will be cool. And don't think you have to be there all day, take enough time to do your show right. Joseph can lock up the Andrews at night until your Circle Rep show is done. Hey I gotta go, but send me an e-mail if you need anything."

"Will do." Alex emphasized, "Thanks for the opportunity, David. You won't regret it."

David's voice lifted with gratitude. "All right then, talk to you soon!"

For a few moments after the conversation, Alex sat behind David's large oak desk, a remnant of the original church. She imagined how similar it must have been for a priest to carry on his small tasks, waiting for the opportunity to per-form for his congregation. A daytime mass during the week, a few more on the weekend and the rest of the time spent in preparation. She pulled the heavy black drape aside of the office window and a shock of light beamed into the office. Alex pondered her circumstances as she stared out, her body slung in the leather-cov-ered swivel chair with her feet resting on the cold radiator. This is where she would spend her days for the summer. She contemplated the best way to take advantage of her position. There were a few factors to consider: access to rehearsal space, a new show to begin in a few weeks, a new audience to perform for, and a chance to prove herself as more than just an actor. All of those benefitted this arrangement, but something bothered her.

She stared at the sidewalk below and let her mind ramble. Her messages usu-ally held appropriate instruction for her, so she flipped on David's speaker phone and dialed the *Magic Mobile*. She rolled her eyes as if shy about her own voice in the presence of the Andrews. Her words filled the office and echoed into the loft and beyond, where the stage strained to catch a few words. The "life imitates art" message lectured from the speaker, then ended peacefully with a request to "punch in a 2539 for the faithful." She laughed at using the term "faithful." The Andrews must have been on her mind that morning. She resisted texting herself, re-dialed, and listened to the message again.

She turned up the volume, wandered out to the loft, and surveyed the theater from above. The phone broadcasted her words loudly. The message bounced off the walls, down the aisles, and to the back of the stage. Suddenly her voice became many voices, doubling each time they hit a wall or ceiling arch. The echo of her words coming from all directions felt like snow down her collar. She ran back to the office to end the call.

She mulled over her conversation with Lisa and hoped she wasn't premature in sharing her mid-performance encounters. A little summer experimentation would be exciting for Lisa, but failure might loosen Lisa's frail grip on theater life. Alex knew her friend had been disgruntled with the theater for a few years now. If Lisa wasn't able to experience the same thing, it could mean losing her for good.

Alex quieted her doubts and restlessly walked down to the stage again. She jumped up on the deck and turned to the empty seats with her arms folded as if inspecting the atmosphere. The ominous aura of the old St. Andrews architecture was hard to ignore. But the building's latest incarnation sustained a curious, lighter tone. It craved delicious drama, good dialogue, and healing laughter. Its expectations caused Alex to freeze for a moment as she let the Andrews vibration sink into her. A face-off occurred; both Alex and the Andrews seemed to be waiting for the other to make the first move. A buzz came from the back of the house and distracted her. As she dashed to the lobby, she noticed a peephole which spilled light through the front entrance, a blessing on the monster of an oak door. With her eye to the light, she beheld a fish-eye Lisa on the sidewalk. She sighed a thank goodness for some company and let her inside.

Alex gave her guest a quick tour of the theater. She suspected Lisa might be curious about the place. It felt like sneaking into the boy's bathroom after hours; women rarely got a glimpse of the little men's club at the Andrews. Lisa wanted to get to last night's conversation. Alex avoided the subject and rattled on about the Andrews at every turn. After a plethora of sidesteps and sidebars, Lisa finally coaxed her to get to the topic of her experiences. They settled into the seats for a chat. Alex's eyes worked the deep blue carpeting as she spoke.

"I'm unsure how to begin." She looked like a child who had been caught in the act: guilty, apologetic, and miserable.

"Okay ..." urged Lisa. "Then give me the do-re-mi version, start at the beginning."

Alex chuckled at her friend's kindness. "It started before the *Mobile*. Wait, it's hard to say, they are both so intertwined with each other that the *Mobile* may have initiated it, but I'm not sure." She sighed. "Sorry, this is a clumsy start."

"Just tell me what happened. When was the first time?"

"It was during *Streetcar* last year. I was really getting into the part and its poetic connections. Remember how much script work I did for that role? One night during a rehearsal, I was really letting all of my inhibitions go, just went full-out. It was an emotional scene; remember the part when Blanche is on the ground dialing Western Union?"

"Yeah. The 'caught in a trap' part."

"Right. Well, I hadn't really let my defenses down until then. So I decided before the scene to release all of my fears and see where it took me. I figured that's what rehearsals are for, to explore the best and worst of myself." Lisa gave her a nod and Alex pressed on. "So I was really opening myself up to let the character live through me, and suddenly it felt like my body unzipped. Honestly, it felt like my soul or my spirit just blew wide open. This went on and on. I was still delivering the words of the play, and still performing at full speed, when an out-of-body feeling suddenly overcame me. Like a light was shining from my own soul all the way up to the stars. A few moments later I settled back into my skin as the scene ended."

Lisa tried to rationalize this information quickly. "Did anyone else experience this, or see that you were behaving differently during the scene?"

"No one else said anything. The director praised me for connecting with my character, and Thomas told me how good I was after the rehearsal. That's about it. No one else shared the moment." Alex studied Lisa for a minute, watching her friend's mind whirl. Regardless of Lisa's imminent counterpoint, Alex felt absolved after confessing her experience. She patiently waited for Lisa to digest what she had told her, and offered a route for their discussion. "That play was the first time this thing occurred. There have been other times when the same thing, or stronger, came through."

Lisa snapped, "What do you mean 'came through?' Isn't this just a release of inhibitions? An escape from your own boundaries? Deep down, we all just want to escape reality. Maybe your diversion feels stronger than most. Maybe this is just something you needed to tackle in order to be a better actor. Don't tell me that it's mystical, Alex, I'm not sure I can handle that."

"What the fuck?" Alex chastised. "Last night you claimed to be open to this thing, and I thought it would be alright to tell you about it. Don't make me regret it now! You're the only one I've told, and I thought you of all people would be sympathetic after all of your preaching about yoga and meditation. Shit, you're the one who suggested I start meditating in the first place!"

Lisa toughened. "Well I didn't mean for you to do it on stage, and don't get pissed at me, I'm trying to grasp this as best I can, okay?"

Alex released a laugh of disbelief. "I am not meditating on stage! I have these moments, these flashes of connection or ... something ... I don't know what they are! But I thought talking about it would help me understand what is going on. If you're just going to sit there and judge me, then forget about it. But I wish you would hear me out first. You're best friend, can you give me a break here?"

The noon sun trailed through the stained glass window and crept away from the bench where the pair sat in silence. Alex traced the ceiling arches with her eyes and deliberated if she was in the midst of a test of wills. She questioned why she confessed to Lisa; lately all they did was argue. Alex also knew conversations in the glow of Jimmy's sometimes dissipated with the daylight.

Lisa sensed her own hypocrisy: a betrayal of Alex's confidence was unacceptable. She broke the silence. "Let me hear it. Honestly, just let me have it. I need something new, I need to hear something I haven't heard before." She looked aside. "I'm so fucking bored, Alex. I don't want to argue anymore. How about we agree to not argue anymore, can we at least do that?"

Alex lightened to her change of heart. "Absolutely."

"So tell me what you think this thing is, and dumb it down so I can understand." Lisa sat intently in her seat and tried to cover for her shameful behavior a minute earlier. Alex gazed at her. Lisa looked very smug in her too-cool Urban Outfitter getup, too empowered by her position as close confidant. Alex explained despite her friend's attitude.

"I've felt the connected thing about a dozen times now, when I'm deep into my performance. Each incident becomes more lucid than the one before. It's a kind of expansiveness, like being everywhere at once; like a good meditation. But the words keep coming and I'm still performing. On occasion it has felt like another person has stepped into my spirit and is expressing themselves through me, within the context of the character."

Lisa interrupted. "Peter always claims to feel possessed when he's really into character, is that what you mean?"

"I understand what he means. I've felt that possession before, but this is something different. The expansiveness of it is so incredible; it feels unique." Alex repositioned herself on the bench and explained. "When I re-read the *Mobile* messages, a lot of them mention a 'new era' of creativity, and the release of any doubts along the way. I wasn't sure what they meant until I started thinking about these episodes I've been having on stage. Here's what I wonder: if we can attain a level of performance where we completely surrender to the life of the character, wouldn't we be able to let pure creative energy live through us, even if it's merely for the length of a monologue? Or for the length of a show? What if this expanded consciousness is not my own expansion outwards, but a channel opening for something to come through?"

Lisa tried to stay on track. "But that's the possession-thing, a surrender to the character."

"But what if it's surrendering to another consciousness, like the creative consciousness that creates life? If we eliminate fears and the self-conscious ego while surrendering to the creative force, then we could open up to the same forces used by …"

Lisa caught up to her conclusion and spoke with her.

"God."

They looked intently at one another. The idea clicked through Lisa's mind and Alex could see the pieces fall into place. Lisa understood what she was saying, so perhaps the idea wasn't as crazy as she thought. Alex composed her darting mind.

"Do you realize what I am proposing? There's always been talk of artists letting God shine through them or work through them." Alex took a breath for emphasis. "I'm saying that we, as artists, are fellow creators. Our artistic abilities enable us to use universal creative forces, thereby making us creators as well."

"Not just creat*ive*," Lisa offered. "But creat*ors*."

"Right. Our natural creative talents."

Lisa stretched out on the bench, as if flattened by their discourse. She spoke from that position, overwhelmed by the possibilities which unfolded before her. "So the wide-open feeling that we experience isn't just a high from performing, it could be our creator skills coming into play?"

Alex amplified her enthusiasm. "Something like that, but not merely the rush you get when things are going well. It's the moments when your ego steps aside and you let the character live through you. Complete surrender without the censorship of the mind."

Lisa remained horizontal. "But how does the connected feeling fit into it?"

"I'm just hypothesizing of course," Alex started. "But perhaps when we reach those moments of complete openness, our true nature as creators is available to us. Our true talents are revealed. That consciousness where possibility is endless, where we channel creative forces to make something unique, is the state of consciousness where all creativity resides. The same state of consciousness that creates everything we know of."

The two sat in silence for a moment. The Andrews surrounded them with a protective barrier from the noise and distraction of the outside world. There in the sacred womb of the theater, Alex sowed her theory. She felt an affirmation when she spoke the words aloud; this was to be her life's purpose and path.

Lisa sat upright and spoke. "I see only one way to do this thing." She raised her eyes to meet Alex's. "We have to start asking around, see who else is feeling this, get our group together, talk to other artists, get a movement going."

Alex recoiled from Lisa's suggestion. "Wait a second, there's no movement here, it's not like I can teach or preach this thing."

"But you can't just hold onto it, what if this is happening all over town? What if we can tap into some hard-core energy here? Everyone's struggling to get audiences. What if this becomes the next big thing and we help out artists in the process? And you don't have to teach or preach. Just ask around, find out what other people think, and see what happens."

"Tell you what," Alex bargained. "Let's get the Circle Rep group together tonight. We'll come over here and have a theater-warming, welcome the new space, and turn the conversation to my experiences after everyone's comfortable."

Lisa brightened. "Yes! Then we can ask if anyone else has felt this. I can't wait to hear what Thomas and Peter have to say!"

"Hey!" Alex cut her off and pleaded. "Let's be chill about it for tonight, alright? Ease them into it. I'm not ready to discuss this thing yet. Deal?"

They gave each other a look. Deal. Suddenly their attention was drawn to the black drapes which covered the back wall of the stage. Slowly they began to swell, seemingly without a source. The curtains danced eerily towards center stage. Both of them gasped and Lisa let out a "Christ!" The drapes swirled wide and released a big, muscularly built man who evidently had a key to the back door. Both girls breathed relief and laughed at their fright.

Alex announced, "Joseph Bancroft, ladies and gentlemen!"

The Technical Director entered, instantly irritated by her. Joseph was pointedly stoic and didn't joke around unless surrounded by a room full of male techies. Alex's introduction set off his immediate dislike for her and her comrades.

"You must be Alex," he responded flatly. The girls looked at each other and chose the higher ground. Alex properly introduced herself and Lisa with professional handshakes all around. She thanked Lisa for "stopping by to check out the space." Lisa exited quickly. Joseph went upstairs to stake his claim in the loft. Alex took a breath and made a silent wish for strength before she ventured upwards. By the time she reached the loft, Joseph had already cleared her bag off David's desk and planted himself firmly in front of the computer to review his e-mail. He had also redrawn the drape over the office window and clicked on the corner floor lamp. As territorial as it appeared, Alex found his blatant display of insecurity endearing. She reminded herself to be sympathetic to his situation despite his bad behavior. She took an effective, albeit manipulative, approach with Joseph. She asked him a few simple questions which made him feel knowledgeable. This made it clear she would treat him as a partner rather than an employee.

To Alex's surprise, Joseph was swayed for the time being by this method. He offered the details of his history with the Andrews. He designed and installed all of the lighting and sound equipment in the space, which took him months to complete due to the antiquity of the church's original systems. Everything was rewired and updated, and he did the work gratis as a favor to David. In exchange for this favor, Joseph was given the title of Technical Director, which apparently entitled him to a small salary and even more work on David's behalf. Joseph was a grumbling workaholic, but very committed to the Andrews. His despised Alex's new appointment as manager, a position he felt he earned more than a few times over. He carried his accomplishments with self-righteous pride, and his arrogance won him few friends in the theater community. After thirty minutes of conversation, Joseph still remained behind the manager's desk. Alex decided to take a foothold on the imminent turf war.

"Well if I could get in there, Joseph, I'd like to get familiar with some of my duties."

He leaned into the screen and spoke gruffly to it. "I'm not done with my e-mails yet."

Alex considered this a power play, but spun it to her advantage. She was casual but unapologetic. "What time is your crew called tonight?" She knew her statement would land in two ways. It said, "Hey, I notice you are abusing David's absence by using his computer during the day," and secondly, it clarified Alex would truly be a manager. Joseph heard both sides of the question and immediately fabricated a reason for his early presence.

"Uh, yeah, typically call is at six, but there's a dimmer that's been fucked up for a while that I have to fix today." He logged off his e-mail as the broken dimmer suddenly called to him, and crossed to the doorway. Alex allowed his ego a little room on the way out. She waited until he was gone before she jumped into the chair victoriously. She called after him, "Let me know if you need anything." It was an unnecessary comment, but it was one he should have offered to her as a newcomer. He was being an ass and she wanted him to know it. When no reply came, she settled behind the desk and tried to shake his ambient negativity. The quiet reminded her that her phone was off, so she fished it out of her bag and turned it on. The screen lit up with twenty-three calls, all 2539s except for one voicemail. She called in and was surprised to hear Peter's languid tone.

"Yeah, Alex ... hey, 's Peter ... Good message today ... yeah ... hey, I know you just started over there at the Andrews, but I was thinking, y'know, we should initiate the place tonight, y'know, like after the show, get some classy wine, y'know, get away from Jimmy's for the night." He sighed heavily. "Jimmy's ... man, that place is getting to me. Anyway, y'know, I'll see ya tonight." When it seemed he stopped talking, he added a high-pitched Alex imitation, "Punch me for the faithful!" and hung up quickly.

Alex grinned and listened for signs of Joseph. A distant clanging of metal indicated his whereabouts. Her thoughts turned back to her conversation with Lisa. With the group gathered tonight, they could have a round of wine and casually get into a chat about loftier subjects. She decided to clarify her thoughts on paper, for she knew her friends would challenge every loophole. She yanked twice on the desk's tight top drawer before it opened, which revealed a stack of legal pads. "David L. Cooper" was monogrammed across the upper edge, which made her snicker. She revisited the drawer for similar objects of amusement. Behind the pads was a Post-it cube imprinted with "From the desk of David Cooper," which made her laugh out loud. She stifled her giggle and listened for Joseph, then went back to discover more materials in the second drawer. David had a collection of monogrammed supplies that rivaled an egocentric socialite. Stacks of imprinted envelopes, pens, and note pads hid in the shadows of the drawers, in an apparent attempt to hide them from misuse.

She forgot about her note-taking and investigated the rest of the desk. The bottom drawer was full of printer paper. The center drawer held writing instruments, most of them monogrammed with David's name, and some imprinted with "The Andrews: In Theater We Trust!" The left side of the ancient desk had traces of water damage squiggling down the larger front panels. Files hung inside in neat, well-labeled pockets. She wondered what revealing treasures the rest of the office held, and scanned around for more clues to David's daily activities. A high bookcase packed with scripts towered against the far wall. Framed posters from David's productions hung on both sides of it. Boxes of archived playbills and memorabilia hugged the walls, all well-labeled with dates and show titles. A short bookcase stored bulk mailing supplies, while an aging coat rack leaned toward the door in anticipation of David's entrance.

Alex glanced around again. It didn't make sense to her. If David had been there for ten years, where were all of the personal touches, the history of David? It seemed too neat, too boxed and proper. Not what she expected from an infamous swinger like David. She considered that he may have tucked things away for his summer absence. The dynamic David Cooper wouldn't work in an office this boring, unless it was a rouse. Perhaps he posed professionalism on the surface to attract the unsuspecting prey, then came in for the kill. She thought about this a bit, until her eyes landed on a box labeled "Auditions." Alex felt her heart quicken. She fought her conscience about opening the box: she didn't have to see his private notes on every actor in town. But it was likely he kept his audition notes somewhere else. She thought he must have a secret stash of the "real" David at another location, because the office was as revealing as a Russian fur coat.

She considered her title: she was manager now, which should include free reign of the place. She might want to familiarize herself with the next cast before she started working with them. She justified a peek, but decided to check for Joseph first. She walked out to the edge of the loft. Joseph was gone, and his over-size bag was absent too. A lighting instrument lay in a few scattered pieces on the stage. She called out to him and her voice echoed back unanswered. She shrugged and went straight to the audition file.

The box held files on everyone who auditioned at the Andrews, including those who left town for bigger and better, or moved on to other careers. The box was in alphabetical order, and she plunged in to find her own file first. Each actor's photo had an audition sheet attached, complete with notes on their performances by the man himself. She could hardly believe this gold mine of information at her fingertips. She carefully slid her file out and grimaced at her old head shot. It had been a long time since she had long hair. She flipped the page over and flew to the notes section. David's handwriting read, "Strong personality, hot, good monologue, summer deal."

Alex re-read "summer deal" a few times over. She hoped the note meant the summer show, which could mean consideration for the regular troupe. It was difficult to get into the company, but once you were in, you stayed in. The only way out of the troupe was banishment, and several had been ejected by the wrath of David Cooper. She analyzed why he kept his space so exclusive, then dismissed further consideration of David's psychological problems and went back to the notes.

"Hot," she said aloud, and affirmed the little stroke to her pride. David threw around a lot of machismo, but she was still flattered when some of it landed on her. She loved and hated the exploitations of a thriving theatrical career. Alex knew how to get what she wanted, but her principles maintained a steady pulse beneath the sexual politics.

Alex's stomach rumbled and she checked the clock: 3 p.m. She thought it was odd that the office phone didn't ring all day. The Andrews was awfully quiet. She grabbed a sandwich from her bag, returned to the audition file, and looked for her friends. She found Susan first. Her completely retouched head shot gleamed, with no possible flaw for the eyes to land on. Her skin looked like porcelain, all creases and freckles were painstakingly retouched, and her usually crinkled hair was sculpted straight with a perfect sheen. Susan's page contained only two notes: "Snob" and "Friend of Alex." Alex laughed out loud at the "snob" comment and searched for Lisa's file. Her friend's photo revealed a shy smile which hid a dislike for her career choice, and a long wave of freshly highlighted hair. Lisa's notes read: "Weak monologue. Lacks confidence. Decent tits. Friend of Alex."

She hoped no one else had an Alex connection marked in their notes. She checked Thomas: "Friend of Alex." Then she reached Peter's, where she discovered the most unnerving note: "Have to use him for summer show with Alex." She mused why David would bother to write "Friend of Alex" on each file. Suddenly her new opportunity seemed like a conspiracy. Knowing who her friends were wasn't confidential information. Most of this corner of town hung out at Jimmy's. Everyone knew who played together. She grew suspicious of David's intentions. Her discomfort urged her to take a walk, get some air, and consider this with some perspective. She lidded the box, replaced it on the floor, and headed out after scribbling a "Back at 5:00 p.m." note for Joseph, just in case he returned before the evening call time.

Daylight-blinded as she paced down Belmont, she dodged shadowy oncomers as her mind reeled on the subject of David. Question after question arose: why would he care about her associations? Had he been considering her for the management position before the annual auditions? Why the secretive notes scrawled on head shots? Why did he disappear on her first day at work?

The scent of sea air drifted up from the harbor, which was still many blocks away, and beckoned for Alex to pay a visit and lay her troubles on the glistening lake. She was about to answer its call when her eye caught someone waving madly from behind a storefront window. It was Thomas, desperately in need of distraction from his copy store tedium. Thomas worked at Kopy Kat for years. His access to copiers allowed for bootleg script duplication, but his bad mood was never healed by the place. She waved back brightly and continued to walk out of sight, then backed into his window again with a "just kidding" smirk. Thomas cracked a rare smile of appreciation as she entered.

"What'd ya lose the Andrews already?" he quipped. She searched her pockets in jest and received another smile. Thomas looked different by the light of day.

His blue uniform softened his pessimism. He played his day-life well, because he knew he could escape to a different reality each night. Thomas loved gossip and stored a lot of nonsense about everyone in town. He also had a deep, seething resentment of David. She avoided talking about her audition note discoveries.

"Well, I had the pleasure of meeting Joseph Bancroft today, and David called this morning from L.A. He's gone already, left me to my own devices." She anticipated that Thomas would take a stab at David, as he always did, and maybe reveal something new that would give her some insight. Instead, Thomas looked at her directly, an action he usually reserved for the stage. It was uncharacteristic of his day-life to lock eyes with anyone. She read his gaze: he knew more than he was about to vocalize.

"Watch yourself over there, okay kiddo? They don't make a move without good reason. David may be out of town, but his prick minions are still on the scene. How was Joseph with you?" Thomas delivered the question with a serious tone. She resisted feeding into his drama.

"Joseph was fine. He checked in during the day to fix a lamp and I'll see him before call tonight. Nothing exceptional." Alex watched Thomas consider the circumstances.

"David's in L.A. already? Well that was quick. How convenient that you were hired the day before he left."

"It's too convenient. Something is up."

Thomas agreed that Alex was a strange choice for the Andrews, but he wanted to find out the real story on his own. He distracted her with a personal question.

"What is it like to have all those voices roaming around in your head? I've wanted to ask you about that. Maybe your new job has something to do with the *Mobile*."

Alex studied his delivery as if it was a set-up for a joke. He might mock something she cared about for a laugh. His attitude was confidential, though. She tried to disarm any witticism he prepared.

"I don't see how the *Mobile* could be connected to David. He's too self-involved. While I'd like to think he's just using me for the summer show, my intuition says there's more at stake here. I just don't know enough about it yet. I discovered his audition files this afternoon and every one of my close pals has 'Friend of Alex' written on it. Every single one. What do you make of that, Thomas?"

A bell rang as a customer entered behind them. Thomas would have to let the conversation go for now, but his thoughts churned over this apparently new information. "I'll catch up with you later. Don't sweat it. He probably just wants to get up your skirt." The comment visibly offended his customer, and he gave a quick shrug of apology. He waved goodbye to Alex and she was out the door again.

A shift in the infamous winds stole the sea scent from the breeze, so Alex headed home to collect her things before her long evening. She was surprised Thomas knew nothing about the audition notes, because he made it his business to keep a watchful eye on David. In the past Thomas attempted to get the Andrews closed, or at least fined, by reporting their fire code violations. He secretly informed the City of any supposed neglect, and cited a few regulations which shut down other venues in the same district. Expensive repairs and upgrades drove many a small storefront theater into bankruptcy in the past few years. The City Council had gentrification on their agenda: they wanted to install income-friendly businesses which would attract higher rents and wealthier tourists. The days of innovative rag-tag theaters were disintegrating, and Thomas wanted the Andrews on the hit list. His efforts were rejected by the City, as David's uncle was an affluent member of the City Council. Evidently Uncle Cooper made it clear to his City associates to keep their hands off the Andrews. Thomas thought everyone theater should have the same chance at survival. But as other theaters collapsed under the financial burden of upgrades, the Andrews stood sound as a grand monument to nepotism. Thomas might expose David's shifty under-the-table deals eventually. Alex hoped it didn't occur while she worked there.

Alex entered her apartment as her cell phone hummed with text messages at her waist. She flopped into her daybed. It would take some time to adjust to her new schedule. For the moment she had an hour at home. She closed her eyes and relaxed into the comfort of being in her studio. As her mind eased, a feminine voice crept into her thoughts. *The absence of art would be a dull existence.* She sat upright and the voice continued. *An artist who doesn't honor their spirit blocks their own happiness.* She grabbed her journal, jotted the words down, and listened as her writing caught up with the message. *And the opportunity to right the world and population which surrounds them. You must live the gifts.*

"Live the gifts," she said aloud. The message energized her. She tossed her things together for what might be an exciting evening. She stood in her doorway, blew her studio a kiss, and mimed it tossing one back to her cheek. She ordered any worries to take a rain check as she darted down the hallway. "This will be a magical night!"

3

○ ○

I found myself floating in a sea of self discovery. When sharks began to circle, I realized they were nothing but my own fears. They could sense my trepidation and would feed on me unless I saw them as they actually were: toothless and blind, and I could swim much faster.

—*The Magic Mobile*

The front door of the Andrews was unlocked when Alex returned. She heard men laughing in the loft, and detected Joseph's voice among them. Apparently he called the crew in early on her first night, in a transparent attempt to dominate the space. Alex prepared herself for first introductions and contemplated Joseph's position. He appeared to be a difficult personality, and unhappy with her presence at his theater. She didn't appreciate his attitude, but she did understand confrontation might make him feel threatened. Alex decided to allow him some illusionary power for the moment, as long as it didn't interfere with her work. She could eventually find a way around his bad behavior.

Her arrival at the top of the loft stairway silenced all conversation. She faced a group of men who obviously had been briefed on Joseph's politics. However, politics are often set aside when a pretty face appears. The standard Andrews crew consisted of three men, all of whom worked with David since the theater's inception ten years ago. Lucas, the Sound Operator, was the first to break the ice. The resident hipster and brilliant audiophile composed original music for David's productions. His ever-present headphones hugged his neck like a pet. The brushed silver orbs clung to his translucent pale flesh, which was made even paler by his nocturnal lifestyle. Lucas extended a hand from his alabaster forearm and crossed to her with a streetwise swagger. His West Side lingo and coy glances intrigued Alex as they made introductions. He complimented her performances and *Mobile* messages, and flattered her with phrases like, "You are stokin' it." A friend passed the *Mobile* number to him that spring and he was hooked. The

33

other members of the crew followed Lucas' lead. Joseph remained pointedly aloof during the intros, and made no effort to participate in the meet and greet session.

While Lucas ruled the kingdom of sound, Miles served as Stage Manager. Short, strong, and spectacled, Miles was a true "people person" and often referred to as an angel. His ability to handle the personalities of this arena, especially David and Joseph, was legendary. In his years at the Andrews he never allowed an actor to miss an entrance, never caused his employer any stress, and never expected any reward or kudos short of a paycheck. He was a theatrical Godsend, and Alex liked him instantly. He introduced himself and flamboyantly complemented her outfit; a nice ground-breaker and direct indication of his sexual status. Alex smirked at his desire to out himself immediately, and it made her like him all the more.

The last member of the trio was a raven-haired, impossibly elegant House Manager named Chris Caldwell. He had a winsome air which suited his position, the ever-gracious maître d' at the front door. His voice was smooth and deep, an obvious voice-over talent, and he made a striking first impression in his dapper attire. Alex surprised herself by glancing at his left hand for a ring, but discovered unembellished fingers flowing from his starched cuffs. She felt a tinge of embarrassment for her monochromatic uniform, but Chris gave her a gaze of approval during their conversation. With everyone introduced, the men disbursed to their separate stations. As she watched them go their own ways, she recognized David had assembled a good team, each a proper fit for their duties. She wondered if she would live up to the Andrews standard.

She had to wish Joseph a good show before she went uptown to her own performance. They exchanged niceties as he preoccupied himself with the light board, and she stopped short before blurting out a "see you later." She didn't want him policing the place, so she let him think she wouldn't be back until tomorrow. After a round of goodbyes and nice-to-meet-yous to the crew, she headed out and blew a kiss to the house as she left. Miles noticed her farewell to the space. He seemed to be amused with her personality, and she modestly exited the building without acknowledging his surveillance.

She stripped off her sweater as she jogged to the L stop, which exposed her black tank and received a whistle from a passerby. She ignored him and hustled to the sound of the approaching train. Once inside the air conditioned L climate, a refreshing chill wafted over her flesh. It was a welcome break from the evening's growing humidity. Surrounded by bodies, she grabbed hold of a passenger rail and steadied herself for the trip north to Circle Rep. The gentle rock of the train temporarily calmed its rush hour guests. Alex examined the crowd present: frazzled Mom with three kids in tow, yuppie commuters on their way home much further north, a few princess types who spent the day shopping on Michigan Avenue, a gay couple who spent the day shopping in Lakeview, an obvious crack head whore, a rent-a-cop in a limp uniform who leered at the crack head whore, and employees and employers of every shape and size. The city swayed in the windows as Alex evaluated her own journey.

As an artist, she carried everything she needed within her. Self-directed spirituality brought a new effect to her life this year. Each day seemed purposeful and energized. Time felt as if it had been lived already: present day and memory all at once. It swirled and wrapped around her, sometimes with clarity, sometimes as a watery blur. She felt like the future Alex, looking back and reliving her year of discovery with the unknowing wonder of the present. In that moment on the train she knew that tonight's events would alter the course of her life.

Familiar murmurs stirred in her head. *Artists make their own morality.* Her mind churned behind eyes fixed on the passing high rises. The tranquilizing effect of the L lead her into a meditative zone, as her voices swam in the languid pool of her thoughts. She daydreamed about where she was headed: if life imitated art as she wrote that morning, what was in store for the performance that was her life? Perhaps the messages would lead her to a higher truth. *There are no final plans for our lives.* Regardless of what the future held, Alex thought this evening would be an experiment in trust. *Change brings fresh passions to our work.* Her instincts told her it was time to discuss her thoughts outside of the *Mobile.* Her protective shell of anonymity would have to be sacrificed for the larger purpose of her ideas. She reviewed her plan. First, she would share her discoveries with a select group of friends, then ease herself into more exposure. She considered it strange that she could stand emotionally bare in front of hundreds each week on stage, and yet speaking one-on-one with friends brought her waves of anxiety. *Nothing to fear. It is our ever-changing perspective on the world that heals those who remain constant.* The station announcement broke into her thoughts. "Wilson Station." Doors hummed open, humid air rushed in, and Alex hypnotically exited onto the platform. She morphed into the crowd and headed to Circle Repertory.

She arrived earlier than her coworkers and sat center stage with eyes closed for several minutes, until Peter tried to sneak up behind her. She heard the light shuffle of his Converse sneakers but remained motionless. A slight twitch of a smile lit her face as he crept closer. He would soon break into their nightly game of faux-kickboxing with a loud "Eeeyah!" Every play had its ceremonial antics, and the nightly ritual of goofing around was hard to resist before preparing for the show. Peter's initiation came, and Alex sprung into a karate stance as she whirled around. Peter stood in a similar pose, but he had a hysterical blonde wig atop his head. She recognized the wig from the daytime children's show, and she crumpled in laughter before she rose again to meet her opponent.

Peter remained in the pose. "Laugh now, sister, 'cause I brought my posse!"

The Brothers Slim jumped on stage in similar wigs and whirled like inverted floor mops. The battle which ensued included several near-misses on Alex, as she miraculously kicked all of their butts simultaneously. This went on and on until Thomas entered the theater, sighed at the familiar sight, and shouted out his copy store miseries with a loud, "Cut the CRAP, ya damn freaks!" All enemies bowed to each other honorably. The men dispersed to their dressing room, and left Alex alone again on the stage.

Her pre-performance routine might have appeared rudimentary to an out-sider. There were stretches and vocal warm-ups typical of any actor, but before the house opened she sat center stage awash in the work lights and meditated. She exhaled her own attitudes out of her aura, and breathed her character into her body. Tonight her thoughts wandered to post-show discussions. How would she describe the purposefulness she felt in these new experiences? Would she have any viable answers if they questioned her? Would they think she was deluded? Alex hushed the questions which interrupted her pre-show magic, and concentrated on her character.

It was the last week of a month-long run of *Dylana*. A strong cast supported leading roles for Alex and Thomas. She portrayed the title role, a Victorian era painter with a philandering and abusive husband, played by Thomas. In the course of the play, Dylana escapes her undesirable reality through her paintings, eventually living in the world she creates on the canvas. It was a poetic, beauti-fully woven story, and Alex's commitment to it remained steadfast throughout the run of the show. The character of Dylana revealed many layers of depth, and Alex enjoyed embodying her each evening. On many occasions during the run, Alex felt her connected sensation during a particularly dramatic monologue. Until this afternoon she hadn't confessed her experiences to anyone in the cast. But her colleagues recognized a truth in her performance of Dylana, and an unin-hibited naturalness which deserved imitation.

The Stage Manager cautioned opening of the house, so Alex exited to the dressing room. She quickly donned her costume, makeup and wig, and slipped into the darkness of backstage where she waited for the show to commence. The pre-show lights faded in with gentle colors, and transformed the set with that magical grace which is the theater. Music began as the house opened to the public. The low moan of a mournful cello piece clung in the air like light smoke lingering in a humid room. Chattering patrons filtered into the seats, and their dialogues escalated as the house filled. Alex eavesdropped on their conversations as she stood in the dark. One or two familiar voices peaked here and there, identifying friends who had come to see her. In the backstage shadows, Alex banished her post-show anxieties and centered herself to perform. A few moments later, the cast joined her.

They circulated and silently touched fists like warriors about to take the enemy camp. Alex leaned in and whispered to Lisa, "Take no prisoners," and Lisa repeated the same to Thomas. Peter silently mouthed his lines, as he had a particularly long monologue in Act One. Superstition forced him to repeat the entire monologue before each performance. He wasn't alone. Susan, with all of her specialized training, still ran her lines prior to the show. Thomas found a passage or two to feed his superstitions as well. The cast stood backstage in the half-light. Emotional emphasis darted softly across their faces and they mumbled silently as if praying to the theater Gods for appeasement. The house lights dipped and warned the start of the show. The actors swelled with anticipation, shook their hands at their sides, jumped in place, and stretched their necks and mouths. The House Manager welcomed the crowd out front, and the lights dimmed to a smattering of applause. The actors entered the stage in blackness, felt for furniture pieces, and searched the floor for glow-taped opening positions.

The lights rose on *Dylana* and enveloped the audience in the world of a woman trapped in a reality which didn't suit her. The performance received appropriate laughter and tears, and two hours later, emphatic applause accompanied the final curtain call. Afterwards the cast mingled with their friends in the house, while Alex retreated to the dressing room to strip away the evening's illusions. Her anxieties weren't revealed during the show, but after the final bows her heart quickened. It was the hour she worried about all day. She fought to gain some ground on her self-confidence before the night unfolded. *Everything you need is within; it won't be taken away if they disapprove.* She knew there was no need to be self-conscious now; the greatest rewards came from the greatest risks.

Lisa entered the dressing room and grabbed Alex's shoulders like a boxing coach. She rubbed them vigorously and attempted to psych her up for the evening. "It's gonna be perfect, you're gonna be perfect. Everyone's going to head over to the Andrews. Matt's going to drive the guys, and Susan will take the gals and Peter."

Alex stared at Lisa in the dressing table mirror. "Why isn't Peter going in Matt's car, doesn't he want to get stoned?" She observed Lisa's reaction and saw a secret dash across her friend's face. Lisa turned away to hang up her costume and hide her guilt.

"No, he wants to be straight for this one."

Alex wheeled around to face her. "Did you tell him what we were going to talk about?"

"Well, yeah." She iced her response with enthusiasm. "I mentioned that you have been having some breakthroughs and that we might talk about them tonight, kind of round-table it in the new space."

Alex quickly replayed their conversation from earlier in the day. They agreed to keep all of this under wraps until the right moment tonight. She moved to chastise her confidant, then remembered her promise to herself. They were all going to hear about it sooner or later. She should have known Lisa would spill the conversation ahead of time. Maybe that was why she told her first: Lisa would spread the word and indicate how the evening was going to unfold. Peter sidestepping an opportunity to get high was nothing short of eventful. His interest prepared her for the task ahead. "Okay, that's cool," Alex said at last. "I'm glad they're coming over."

Lisa looked relieved. Before the show, Peter inquired about her visit to the Andrews. Lisa relished locking eyes with him for a while, and eventually gave in to his questioning. Between her flirtation and his curiosity, the talk with Alex was revealed.

The actors finished their post-show routines and dispersed for the Andrews. Susan babbled on about a friend who had come to see the show, a New York actress who hadn't worked in over a year. Susan planned to move there in the near future, and wasn't pleased to hear about her friend's misfortunes in the Big Apple. Lisa and Peter led an animated conversation on Susan's behalf, saying she was far more talented than her colleague, and needn't worry about unemployment. They actually disliked Susan, and indirectly urged her to leave town. Alex was amused by this display, and hid a smirk as she pensively gazed out the window of the car. They arrived at the Andrews and lingered on the sidewalk as they waited for their colleagues in the Brothers Slim car.

The moon was out, a shining perfect crescent hung in filmic perfection behind the silhouetted stars of the Andrews. Surrounded by the activity of city nightlife, the Andrews remained poised as a silent observer. If not for the floodlight bathing the front doors in a wash of amber, passersby wouldn't notice it at all. The group waited in the shadowy glow until the Brothers and Thomas arrived, then Alex proceeded to let them into the theater. She kept the lobby lights off to discourage attention to their entrance from the street. She left her friends in the dark and she darted upstairs to the loft light board.

By the light of the moonbeam through the uncovered window, the group wandered around the space like schoolchildren. Their excitement with the new space was evident. They tripped on fixtures, stood on seats, and checked out the acoustics. Alex brought the work lights up to half level, a nice intimate glow for her impending monologue. The light calmed the group down. They settled around the stage and first row in their classic post-show formation, laughing and one-upping each other with humorous quips. Alex sat in the front bench to avoid a stagey delivery of her experiences when the right moment arrived. These people were accustomed to drama, and she wanted to separate her topic from any histrionics. Thomas had charmed a bottle of wine out of the Circle Rep House Manager for the occasion. He divided it into clunky plastic cups salvaged from Matt's car. Thomas raised his glass, flipped his hair back, and toasted Alex's new position.

"To the Queen of the Andrews, long may she reign. Or at least not screw up for the length of the summer." They thunked glasses all around and drank. Peter joked that Miles was the real Queen of the Andrews, which led to a good guffaw followed by a long silence.

Alex asked, "Twenty minutes before or twenty after?"

Thomas checked his watch. "Eleven-twenty, how'd you know?"

"Old Irish thing. When there's a sudden silence in the conversation, it's usually twenty minutes before or after the hour." The group grunted and nodded. Obviously it was time to spark the conversation. Alex was about to speak when Lisa beat her to the chase.

"You were really on tonight, Alex," she started. "Remember that performance you had last Friday? Such strong moments. It's really impressive the way you do that."

Peter jumped on the bandwagon. "Yeah, man. Y'know, I'm about ready to start meditating before the show myself. You rock." He lifted his glass again, took another swig, and hoped his contribution would lead her on.

Alex looked at her friends before beginning. The Brothers Slim sat on the stage, looking like human tinker toys. Susan fussed with her hair and clothes, primping herself for nonexistent admirers. Thomas showed post-performance burnout, vapidly sipping his wine and waiting for a topic he could complain about. Peter and Lisa glanced about the room with bright eyes, eager to move the night along. The whole scene made Alex chastise herself for being nervous; this group was not intimidating. She decided to get to the point, and pointedly.

"You guys, I need to talk to you about some things I've been experiencing lately." Alex got their attention with her change of subject. "I've been having these episodes, for lack of a better word, during some of my performances. It's happened before, a few times during other shows, but recently these episodes have been more frequent. I want to know if any of you have felt the same thing, or something similar, and could help me out with what's going on."

Lisa jumped in. "Tell them what it feels like."

Thomas shot his gaze between Alex and Lisa, and observed their previous discussion of the topic. He was irritated with their confidentiality. "What the hell are we talking about? How long has this been happening?" Thomas liked to be the ultimate source of information, and was insulted that they kept him out of their chats. Alex tried to smooth things over.

"I mentioned it to Lisa this morning, and she suggested I talk it over with you guys." Thomas relaxed at being only a few hours behind on the information, but he was still injured. Alex started again. "I knew this was going to be difficult to express to you, considering my other eccentricities. I'll completely understand if you write it off as Alex nonsense, but I have to find out if anyone else is feeling this thing. I had this breakthrough during a performance, when I felt so at-one with my character that it was as if I had channeled another soul into my body. That presence is something most of us are familiar with, yes?" She received nods of confirmation. "That connection is addictive for me, and I've aimed for it since that first occurrence. Then another event happened. During a passionate rehearsal one night, I felt as if my body was opening with a bright energy. It felt expansive, like being everywhere, and as the scene neared its end the energy retreated, and I was back to normal."

Peter questioned, "The play kept going, I mean, y'know, you were talking during this whole episode and nobody noticed anything?"

"No one noticed. As wild as it sounds, the whole three minutes of it went undetected, except for a compliment from Thomas on how good I was that night."

Thomas' spine straightened as the memory dawned on his face. "Holy shit, that was during *Streetcar*, I remember that night! That was the first time it happened? Why the hell didn't you tell me about it? Jesus, how many times since then? Why wouldn't you say anything?" His temper flared. "What if there was something medically wrong with you? You don't even tell your friends? What the fuck!?" He stopped his outburst, marched to the back of the stage, and lit a cigarette to ease his frustrations.

Peter tried to keep everyone calm. "Okay, wait a sec. Let me get into this for a moment. I have gone on record saying that often I feel 'possessed' when I'm really into character. And I do, I honestly do. But what you're describing Alex, I honestly don't see the benefit of something like that. Possession, sure, it's like being taken over. Getting really into your character's head and life? Yeah, why not, it enriches everyone's experience if you can do that. But feeling all up-in-the-clouds, what's the purpose of that? What good is it?"

Alex scanned the Brothers, who looked confused by the subject matter. Susan lay back on the stage and indicated exasperation. "Well Susan, let's hear from you."

"Jeez, I think I should have come here in the stoner car." The group tittered at her comment. "I think I need more information. I haven't ever felt possessed or anything close to that kind of feeling. I think I may be missing something. I feel left out on a secret, like I should relate to what you've experienced and be able to get what you're explaining, but I don't. And at the same time, I'm not sure if anyone is going to, Alex. You know, you're a little out there to begin with. I appreciate your sharing this with us, but I really can't support it. No one has experienced it, so maybe it's all just in your head?"

Alex lowered her eyes and a silence passed over the group, the silence of isolation which Alex had feared. Some secrets were meant to be shared, and some were best kept to oneself. She worried she had gone too far. But she believed art was about communicating everything, all the facets of life, the entire range of the human repertoire. Susan's words lingered in her head: no one else felt it.

From the shadows of the stage, Thomas flicked the butt of his cigarette onto the ground, crushed it with his heel, and emerged into the dim light with his hands stuffed deep into his pockets. He stood center stage, drawing focus to himself. He had an announcement to make and wanted to make it poignant. They all waited. He flipped his hair out of his eyes and looked to the top of the house with a dramatic pause. He took a breath and sighed.

"I've felt it. I know what you're talking about. I've experienced the same thing, to the same degree, about three times in the past few months." The circle sat agape in anticipation. He had more to say. Alex felt her heart jumping in her chest.

Thomas began again. "I don't want to hear about the hypocrisy of me wanting to know everything and criticizing Alex for keeping this a secret, even though I have been keeping it from all of you. I don't want to have that discussion. But I have felt the same thing, and I have some personal ideas about what it means, and when the time is right, I'd like to share them with you. Right now, I'm just a little sideswiped by the fact that someone else had the same experience. I need to digest that before I can get into reasons and purposes for whatever it is."

Thomas brought his confession to a close and refilled the group's plastic cups, as if a silent oath of trust was about to be demanded from all of them. They offered their cups willingly with an air of honor, toasted silently, and drank for a moment. Lisa looked like she wanted to speak, which surprised Alex. She thought Lisa would remain true to her typical form: cheerlead by day, then clam up when the game started. But this was different for Lisa; she felt empowered by her friendship with Alex and sat on the edge of the stage to address the group.

"You guys know that I've been a bit disgruntled with the theater lately." She watched Peter for a humorous response, but he was respectfully still. "Nothing new has happened for me in a long time. My work has remained the same: same auditions, same techniques, same kind of roles, same rejections, same B.S. that bores the hell out of me lately. Well, I've been looking for something new. I don't want to abandon my craft because audiences are dwindling or head shots are getting too expensive, because none of that really matters to me. All that has ever mattered to me was performing. The art was all. You know I don't give a damn about celebrity or good reviews, and this group wouldn't be as close as we are without all of us feeling the same way. Fuck the critics, we're here to create and explore our craft. Am I right?" All gave a nod, and Peter added a "hear hear." Lisa was strengthened by the sound of her own convictions. "So we're presented with a new opportunity here. When Alex told me about this, I took it with a grain of salt." She turned to Alex, "Sorry girl, but you're kind of weird sometimes. No offense."

The group giggled and Alex responded, "None taken."

Lisa continued. "When I hear that Thomas, our dear grumpy doubting Thomas, has had the same thing happen to him, and he had the balls to admit to it, well that's more than a coincidence. And the way you guys explain it, it seems like just the thing that I've been looking for, something to rejuvenate my love of performing. So I want to know if you would like to explore these experiences. There may be a lot more to them than we expect, or maybe we'll find nothing at all. But I'd like to try, and I know there's safety and strength in numbers. What do you say? Can we try?"

Thomas retreated to a bench during Lisa's speech and folded himself into a protective crunch. Alex mimicked a similar twist in the front row. They waited for the others to decide the fate of their friendships. Everything would change if the group chose to reject their confessions. Peter supported Lisa's proposal, shook his head in agreement, and looked to the others to voice their opinions. The

Brothers Slim shrugged at each other and nodded to Peter. Thomas was about to speak when Susan rose abruptly and grabbed her bag.

"I don't need this." She spoke as if defending her choice. "Sorry guys, enough is enough. It's been fun hanging out with you, but I'm going to New York sooner or later and I don't need to get caught up in some flaky touchy-feelie bullshit." She darted down the aisle, stormed through the lobby, and out the front door. The friends watched the door slam closed behind her. The echo of it hammered in the voluminous space. No one spoke until the sound ceased.

Then Peter said, "No ... Susan ... wait ..."

The group burst into laughter, surprised that none of them had attempted to keep her from leaving. Apparently she was not the class favorite. Alex joined in with a half-hearted giggle and looked at Thomas. He raised his eyebrows and glanced away quickly, revealing a shyness she hadn't noticed before. She regretted underestimating him; there seemed to be more to learn about Thomas.

The laughter died quickly and the group turned their attention to Alex. In that instant she realized she would be a guiding force in this collaboration. No matter how enthusiastic Lisa was, no matter how supportive Peter appeared to be, Alex would have to drive this caravan through unknown territory. She sensed their election and spoke.

"I don't blame Susan at all, this was hard enough to deliver, let alone digest." Alex looked to Thomas, who smiled weakly. "Since Thomas and I are the only ones who have encountered this thing, I guess we should try to explain what we feel during these episodes." She remembered a strong moment that might help them understand. "Remember when we were doing Richard II at the outdoor summer festival?" The group perked up at the mention of the play; they all enjoyed Shakespeare, which is why Shakespeare is high on the list of actor's playwrights.

"Before the farewell scene I was standing backstage in my Queen Isabella robes under that beautiful starlit sky. The scent of the night breeze transported me. I thought of all of the women who had played Isabella before me, and the legacy of the play. I listened to that wonderful speech before the farewell scene, when Richard has his monologue, 'Let us sit upon the ground and tell sad stories of the death of kings,' and I was at once overwhelmed. The loss I felt as Isabella, knowing that I would never see Richard again and being a stranger in an unfamiliar country, not knowing what would happen to me, the whole sadness of Isabella encompassed me. I looked up at the stars again and it was as if the whole universe watched me relive the moment. My soul felt borderless and connected with the divine purpose of the lessons within the piece. Each night I would start the play over from a point of innocence, without anticipating what would happen. Each time I approached with the intention of being absolutely present, I felt that connected feeling. I kept having these episodes." She stopped, frustrated with the description. "I can't keep saying, 'episodes, encounters, experiences.' What are we going to call this thing?"

Lisa tried to assist. "This morning you described it as creativity itself, like tapping into creation. The moment when that happens, let's name the moment." Thomas' eyes alighted with Lisa's words. Excitement rose in him, and he spoke directly to Alex.

"You think it's creation? Like tapping into a source?" He looked astonished. "I had the same kind of reaction to it. Like being in the place where all characters are made, where all art is born." Thomas fidgeted on his bench and tried to feign casual after his outburst. His discomfort with expressing himself outside of a play was evident. He dragged his fingers through his mop of hair, leaned his head back on his clasped hands, and stared up at the graceful arches high above him. He was both excited and exasperated with this new emotion.

Alex measured her words for clarity. "I think these moments are a glimpse into a kind of creativity that is more than art. It's not interpretation or imitation. It is pure creation." Alex heard her voices swell. *This is where all of the answers are held. This is the seat of creation. This is the Creator State.* She opened her mouth and repeated it aloud. "It's the Creator State."

The moment the words left her lips, Alex felt the world whirl around her. A gust of purpose blew through her and across a new landscape: the world and her purpose within it appeared vast and wide. All of the voices, messages, and directions forced her to the helm of her life. She tried to return her attention to the room, which appeared liquid and distant.

While Thomas studied the ceiling and yearned to escape through it, Peter and Lisa discussed a way to explore the newly dubbed Creator State during the summer months. The Brothers Slim offered their support, even though they were booked out of town for the summer. No one noticed Alex's momentary disconnection. She let the others continue their animated discussion and moved to the bench next to Thomas. He sensed her approach and cleared his throat to speak.

"They should paint the ceiling with murals like a cathedral. Only they should put playwrights and composers and literary giants up there: Shakespeare and Mozart and Yates." He flopped his head toward her and spared a smile. "Why didn't you tell me, Alex?"

"Right back atcha," she replied. "But now that I've put it out there, I'm motivated. I want to find more artists who have felt it. I want to know what it is and how to get there more often. I've been holding this for months now, but lately my intuition is giving me a sense of urgency." Alex expected a response from Thomas, but he grabbed his cigarettes instead. He offered one to her, which she declined, and lit one for himself. Alex waited patiently for him to speak again. After a few drags, he sat up and turned to her.

"How long have you been acting?"

"Forever. Since I was eleven."

"Me too, since I was a kid. I always wanted to be an actor. I never considered the reason why. I knew I loved it and wanted to be good at it." He raised his eyes from below his hair. "I didn't expect it to be anything more than small theaters and small paychecks. And I was prepared to accept it as that, nothing more." His hand quivered on the way up to his mouth to take another drag.

"Go on, Thomas. It's just me."

They recognized their friendship. Sadness fluttered in Alex when she realized they let five years pass without acknowledging their bond. This conversation was gold though, and she allowed the richness of it to overcome her guilt.

Thomas witnessed her attitude and reciprocated. "We've known each other for a while now, Alex. I trust you, probably now more than ever. You know I'm uncomfortable with these things; I've never been a religious or spiritual kind of guy." He laughed at his own expense. Typically Thomas did not reveal his soulful side, but people change, and he was changing right before her eyes. "The absolute power I felt in those encounters; I can't brush it aside. I have to know more about it."

The conversation at the foot of the stage escalated. Peter and Lisa expressed their pent-up sexual emotions with attempts to outwit each other. The Brothers tried to get involved, but ended up as enthusiastic bystanders. Thomas was momentarily distracted by the behavior down front.

"Whadya think they're gonna have? Two, maybe three kids?" He sucked down the last of his cigarette, exhaled harshly and crushed the butt on the tile floor. Alex watched and reminded herself that she'd have to ask him not to smoke in the theater. That night all seemed fair, so she saved her reprimand for his next visit. She politely laughed at his joke and got back to the subject.

"This afternoon you asked me what it was like to be me. How could you say that with what you've revealed tonight?" She watched Thomas shrink as she spoke. "I have to admit, Thomas. I haven't trusted you as much as I could have. You're always digging for information. I realize as actors we have a natural curiosity about people, but I'm not sure what your motivation is at times."

"The motivation for my question this afternoon was simple. I am genuinely curious what it's like to hear voices in your head all day long." He prompted, "Quick, what do you hear right now?"

She rolled her eyes at his amusement with her ailment, listened for a second, and said, "The weight of martyrs is no longer needed." She revised, "Only it's w-a-i-t of martyrs."

Thomas sighed and refused to interpret the passage. "I had no idea you were experiencing the same thing on stage that I was, but now that I know, you're in for a lot more questions."

"Don't you see that the *Magic Mobile* is the same as performing?" Alex had his attention. "I treat my characters the same way as I treat the voices. Just let them work through me. If I fought the voices, or examined why this happened to me, I would have wrecked the experience and the opportunity. Does that make sense?" Thomas agreed without verbalizing. She pushed on. "The same principle works with painting. I start and see what happens. I surrender to the act. Same with photography. If I see a glimpse of inspiration, I follow it, but I try not to dominate or examine it, or place guidelines on the inspiration. I try to have patience, trust the instinct, and the moment of payoff usually arrives soon thereafter. This is why I think creative activity is a microcosm of the original creative force. It uses the same openness, the same sense of possibility."

Peter and Lisa ceased their chatter and moved closer. The Brothers sat near as the group reclustered. Alex spoke to all of them, but directed her speech to Thomas.

"We study our technique too much. Perhaps the techniques surrounding our art forms have short-circuited the natural impulse, the natural flow of creation."

Peter interjected. "It's the same with religion. Our relationship to God is toned down by rules. We're told over and over that we can't understand God. As if because we're human beings we can't possibly imitate him. Or her. Or whatever, y'know, you think God is."

Alex agreed. "It's that conditioned control factor that holds us back. The denial of a natural state of being which we are supposed to experience."

The Brothers watched the ongoing discussion, heads pivoting from person to person, though they themselves remained silent. Lisa desperately wanted to enter the conversation and watched for an opportunity to jump in. Anticipation fidgeted in her body.

Thomas shed a layer of self-consciousness and spoke. "When I'm there, in the Creator State, it's only after I've allowed myself to step aside. My experiences started when I was doing comedies a lot. I had to forget about looking foolish or wise and just exist as the character. When I surrendered, it was freeing. Like I was getting confirmation from the universe for doing it right."

Lisa found her break and entered. "Releasing inhibitions is nothing new. We all know that we have to let go to be brilliant." She grabbed a seat in front of Alex. "What interests me is resisting the constant control of modern life. These days you can't go anywhere without some ad telling you what to do, how to feel, that your life would be better with a different product, a better lifestyle, a better God. We're so inundated with marketing efforts, how can we feel the way we're really supposed to feel with all of that around us?"

"That's our strength as artists," Alex responded. "No matter what influences claw at society, no matter what distracts humankind, we will always have our creativity as a guide, leading us back to our true selves. Because we study human nature, we have some perspective."

The group sat together and collectively reflected on her statement. Peter added, "So if creativity is a reflection of the natural order, then art can endure the way nature does. No matter what history brings to the table, art will endure, like nature does."

"Well there's some job security for you," laughed Thomas. A burden lifted deep within him and he thought clearly, openly, for the first time outside of a play. His life had arrived, and his mind raced to keep up. He rose to his feet, elevated by his lightened heart. "I'd like to explore some possibilities. What can we do with this information?"

Alex and Thomas wandered around the benches, since both of them thought better on their feet. Alex paused and proposed, "What if we can affect outer reality the way we affect our inner reality during performances?" Her question was met with silence, so she elaborated as she strolled. "I'm not sure about the details yet, but what if the same force that temporarily alters reality in art, for both performer and observer, is the same force that allows for creation of the reality around us." She looked back at the group. "What do you think?"

Peter shook his head in denial. "Nah, that's impossible. Y'know, think of all of those guru-types meditating and enlightening themselves all day. Man, if they can't alter reality, then we can't either."

"But they aren't artists," Lisa interrupted. "It's the creative connection that makes the difference. Just think: if you're experiencing brilliance on stage like Alex and Thomas, if you feel a real creative force breaking through, then what happens if you channel it into changing the reality around you. Like creating, I don't know, peace in your community or something. What if you get so into the Creator State that one night, zammo, peace is suddenly a reality."

Alex called across the seats to her. "Yeah, what if that's the key to creation, I mean *real* creation? What if you just stop listening to all of the influences telling you that you can't or shouldn't, and just do it?" She thought of how absurd this might sound to an outsider stumbling by that night. She lightened the conversation. "Did you just say 'zammo'?"

The group cracked up. Thomas waited for the laughter to lower a bit, a device of his comedic training, and started to speak when the giggles were at forty percent. "Experiencing more on stage is going to interest a lot of people. You know how actors latch on to any new technique or promise of a higher level. We'll probably have to be careful with this thing for a while. So we should keep our mouths shut until we figure out what's going on. How about we start with a simple inquiry on the Artist Exchange site."

Alex agreed. She and Thomas started "The Artist Exchange" Web site the previous year as a place to post creative ideas, rants and events. The point was to fuel each other's creative projects by exchanging ideas. The popular chat board would be a decent place to start looking for similar encounters.

Peter strengthened the shift in topic. "Let's call it a night, eh? This is a lot of new information for all of us. Best thing to do is to part ways and sleep on it. We'll see each other tomorrow night at the show."

Heads nodded all around, so the group gathered their belongings. Alex shut down the lights, blew the stage a kiss, and thanked the space for its hospitality. The friends divided paths at the front door toward their homes. Their conversation evaporated into the damp night air and dispersed to find sympathetic spirits. Alex took the jaunt home on foot, and suspended her thoughts in a cautionary silence as if to honor the night's events. One voice crept in. *Limitless possibility awaits our unification.*

4

Artists raise the awareness that there is more in song, dance, theater, literature, film, art, and music than can be interpreted with our human senses. Art can be a medium to whatever God source or order which may be in the universe. Expansion is felt within divine moments of inspired art. This is the essence of the universe and the channel to transport consciousness.

—The Magic Mobile

Despite a sleepless night, Alex wanted to prove she was a worthy manager on her second day at the Andrews. She confirmed marketing deadlines, sent copy to the ad designers, and prepared the contracts for the upcoming show. She invited the cast and crew to a welcome meeting the following week, so everyone could be properly introduced. Alex predicted things would go smoothly with Joseph if she demonstrated some dedication. She longed to collect evidence of the Creator State to support her experiences, but that would have to wait until the evening hours. Her first priority was to establish herself at the Andrews. It was a wise decision. Her reputation from the *Mobile* colored her in a strange light. She had often overheard conversations at Jimmy's discussing her daily missives. The subject habitually drifted from the message to the messenger, when her sanity was questioned. Those random comments inspired her to flaunt some professionalism in her new position.

With meetings in place and rehearsals scheduled, she broke for lunch. She strolled to the lakefront to revive her spirit with a nice sea breeze. When she arrived at the edge of her sparkling companion, she found no stressful thoughts to discard. Unlike the anxiety she endured before discussing the Creator State with her closest friends, she was now calm, as if her true mission had commenced. Last night seemed prophetic to her. It was the inception of purpose for her life. Her voices whispered to her. *The time is here when we must step into the roles we have created for ourselves. It takes a great deal of strength to live out one's intentions. When we realize the powerful changes that our self-designed destinies deliver, mediocrity simply cannot be encouraged.*

Alex scribbled the words into the *Mobile* journal she kept in her bag. The voices were second nature to her now. When her clairaudience first began she considered not telling anyone, as she feared being perceived as completely crazy. Many of the passages were unexplainable. So she chose to reveal her mysterious voices, and keep the spirit of the *Mobile* quirky rather than preachy. Listeners digested the messages more easily from an unknown source than a colleague. She questioned what it would be like when the voices left her; she knew it was inevitable that they would move on someday.

The breeze came in sticky gusts and foreshadowed a stifling summer. Alex inhaled a last lake view before she returned to the Andrews. She mused how David's script was holding up with the Hollywood types. She tried to picture pale, dark-haired David surrounded by palm trees and expressionless botoxed faces. She didn't know what his screenplay was about, or how he got a high-profile producer to listen to it. Their paths were very different, and yet they both assisted one another. She thought it was almost too well-played. Her trepidations with David's audition notes began to surface, so she suppressed them and headed back.

Alex stopped by the Kopy Kat and discovered Thomas had called in sick, which was a rare occurrence. His boss stood before an agitated crowd at the counter five persons deep. She exited quickly. Back at her desk she disputed whether or not to give Thomas a call. She never realized how sensitive he was until last night. Apparently his armor of negative humor sheltered a trembling heart. If he went to the length of faking illness, he must be sorting things out from the evening before.

Thomas was downright brilliant on stage. It was obvious he had a deep well to draw from. He made performing look effortless. Evidently his cynical side was just a rouse to keep fellow performers at bay. The Thomas persona threw people off the trail, as if to demonstrate that whatever he did on stage was just performance, and not a clue to his inner workings. Alex deliberated his defense mechanism: make believe the emotions you portray on stage are just acting gimmicks in order to conceal your true emotions. She didn't agree with his choice to deny his true nature in order to protect himself. She accounted it to self-preservation, respected his space, and let him be for the day. The phone interrupted her thoughts. An exhausted David was on the line, checking on his beloved Andrews. He sounded as if he didn't care if the Andrews burned to the ground. He was deep into his screenplay work, and obviously had not slept since landing on the West Coast. He attempted politeness.

"Hey Alex, just wanted to check in and make sure all is okay. Any questions? Problems?"

Alex sympathized with his lack of sleep and attempted to ease his mind. "Everything is fine, David. Don't worry about anything. We're striking the set on Sunday and everything is in place for next week." Joseph crossed through the loft and approached the office door. He suspected it was David on the other end. She flipped the phone to speaker so he could listen in. "Everyone has been good to me." She continued. "Don't feel like you have to check in. We're fine." An embarrassed Joseph lowered his eyes.

David rushed to tie up the conversation. "Okay then, call if you need anything ..."

Both Alex and Joseph cried, "Wait a sec!" He stayed on the line. Alex asked, "How is the screenplay going?" Joseph added, "Yeah, man, are they gonna buy it or what?"

Their enthusiasm flattered David. "Hey, Joseph, I didn't know you were there. Yeah, they're gonna take it. I think. I don't know. There are a ton of formula blockbuster B.S. rewrites. They're complete Hollywood stereotypes. They don't even realize how ridiculous they are. Well, I don't want to speak ill of my possible employers. Take care of my place. I may be back sooner than we all think."

Joseph responded. "No way, man. Just keep your story intact and don't let them fuck it up with all that movie crap. Keep it real."

David laughed at Joseph's lack of perspective on his Hollywood situation and signed off. "Okay guys, I'll talk to you later in the week."

After the call, Joseph lingered in the office for a while and made small talk. Alex took it as a sign that she did a good job that morning. He held a copy of the rehearsal schedule and contact sheets in his hand, and it looked like there was something on his mind. At first she suspected he knew about her late-night gathering, but he abruptly changed the subject.

"I read David's screenplay before he left," Joseph started. "He doesn't know that I read it. He left it out one afternoon and I read it before the show started." He paused to see if Alex would chastise his snooping, but received no such reaction from her. "Honestly, I think it sucked and I can't understand why he got called out there. It's a really boring script."

Alex replied flatly, so as to not show any disapproval of his actions. "What was it about? Maybe they latched on to a part of it, or a concept, and will make him rewrite the rest. Is there an exciting section they could work with?"

"Hell, no," Joseph stiffened. "It's a romance. A schmaltzy romance about a director who falls in love with a leading lady who ends up ruining his life."

"He wrote a redemption piece? A penance for all the horrible things he's done to actresses?" Alex laughed out loud. "That's hysterical!"

Joseph didn't see the irony, and frowned at Alex's outburst. She added, "That's probably just the kind of thing they love out there. I can just see all of those Hollywood guys thinking they've found the next 'Fatal Attraction' or something."

"Yeah, the script may be lame," Joseph proposed, "but they have people to fix that. Or rather, they have people that can fuck it up even more to gain box office appeal."

Alex laughed again. Joseph raised a corner of his mouth and gave a hint of a smile. She saw a spark of possibility in him, the possibility to be a friendly guy. He noticed her detection and his attitude shield went up. He excused himself to the light grid which he had been unable to repair the day before, grabbed a wrench, and stormed downstairs.

Alex sighed at his needless shift in behavior. She turned to the street beneath her window and watched the Friday afternoon traffic flood the streets. She avoided her cell phone all day because she expected post-conference rebound from her friends. She checked the display and found all 2539s; no phone numbers or voicemails to retrieve. She propped herself in the office window and reviewed last evening's departures. No one besides Susan seemed offended when they left. It struck her that she may have alienated herself from a circle of friends which took years to form. Friends like that were uncommon. She decided to call and see how things looked to them by the light of day.

She chose Lisa first, and dialed her office day job. Lisa had called in sick. Not surprising, as Lisa was a genius at inventing ways to get out of work. She tried Peter next, and discovered that he too had called in sick. Either a rampant flu bug was on the loose, or her friends were playing hooky after their late night at the Andrews. She called Lisa's apartment for an answer and found one. Peter answered the phone.

"Hey!" Alex tried not to sound surprised, but her tone gave her away. "Peter! What's up? I've been looking for you guys, everyone's staying home today. It's weird that I'm the only one at work."

"Uh, yeah," Peter replied cautiously. "Well, y'know, I crashed at Lisa's last night so she didn't have to drive me home to Wicker Park."

Alex grinned at his slip-up. He never could lie well, a surprising characteristic for an actor. She toyed with him. "A ride from Lisa? Hmm, that's funny Peter, because Susan was the only one with a car besides the Brothers last night." She paused and heard guilty silence. "Gotcha."

"Ah man. Okay, we finally hooked up. But you can't blame us after all that wild creator-talk. We cabbed it back here and drank, and, y'know ..." Peter trailed off as Lisa shouted something from the shower. He shouted back, "It's Alex!" and then apologized for yelling near the mouthpiece.

Alex avoided talking about them. Everyone knew Lisa would eventually convince Peter to sleep with her. It was just a matter of time before she broke whatever code he had about relationships. Alex accounted Lisa's desire for him to genuine love, or at least genuine lust. She could have argued that Peter was not the right pursuit for Lisa's restless soul. He was a stationary man, tried and true, but not the type to attach yourself to if you were looking for new experiences. Alex and Lisa had different views on relationships: Alex was pointedly against the tradition, and Lisa desperately wanted the comfort of it in her life. Peter wanted to discuss their new topic.

"There's so much to talk about. I have questions, problems, issues. I've never been a religious guy, so I'm a little lost on the God-talk. We'll have to get into that, and you'll have to speak slowly so I can grasp it." He gave a self-depreciating chuckle. Lisa interrupted and grabbed at the phone. He protested, but she won the phone war and attempted coolness. "Hey, how is your day going?"

Alex snickered. "Well, I'm relieved to hear that I wasn't the only one up all night." They laughed girlishly. Lisa shooed her new lover to the kitchen so the ladies could speak privately.

"Hey listen, I don't want you to think that last night's talk was just a tool for me to get Peter. We're both serious about our interest in the State."

Alex sighed to herself at the comment: were they already calling it "the State" for short? It was brand new and it already had a nickname. She questioned if the whole experience would be shortened into quotes and sound bites by the end of this journey. Everything these days seemed to be served in bite-sized bits of information. It was as if no one could concentrate anymore. If you wanted people's attention you could have it, but no longer than a few seconds at a time. She remembered something she had been told in a monologue workshop: directors decide whether they like you or not in the first fifteen seconds. Some argued it was even shorter, that they knew a few seconds after you entered the room. The

American way had no patience, and Lisa demonstrated that characteristic frequently. Bedding Peter was no exception. Lisa grabbed her opportunity before he could process the situation and make a wise choice. Alex accepted the weak apology and knew her own impatience got the better of her choices on occasion.

"Don't sweat it, Lisa. I just wanted to make sure that you were okay. Thomas called in sick today, as did you and Peter, and I was concerned." Alex realized "concern" was the wrong term. Quiet enfolded the people around her. She reviewed the day while Lisa chattered on about her night with Peter. Thomas had called in sick for the first time in recent history, an unusual move for him, as he approached managerial status at his daytime dwelling. Next up was Lisa and Peter, the long-awaited union that finally came to fruition. These events would have been insignificant on their own, but to Alex they seemed synchronized. Lisa's one-sided monologue was winding down, so Alex switched her attention back to the conversation.

"This is an important union," Alex advised. "The two of you getting together is no mistake. It's important." Lisa was silent, as if her previous chit-chat about her sexual encounter had belittled what Alex was about to say.

"You and Peter finally got together, and Thomas called in sick today."

Lisa gasped in disbelief. "Thomas called in sick? Thomas, the bawdy preacher of zero time off? Man, something is up with him if he bailed on work. His boss must be livid. They don't even have backup for him anymore, he's been so steady."

"Yeah, I know. Between Thomas, you, and Peter, that's my three."

Lisa appreciated Alex's notation of the power of threes. They had fun sharing their little synchronicities with each other. When the threes showed up, something exciting was in store for them. Even if the girls disapproved of each other's actions from time to time, they remained steadfast in their creative sisterhood. The world was magical to Alex, and a sympathetic companion was a true treasure.

Lisa questioned, "Are you going to call Thomas before the show?" They both recognized how off-balance he seemed last night. Alex thought to leave Thomas to his own devices today, but the concern in Lisa's voice prompted her to change her mind.

"Okay, I'll call him at home. He's probably felt alone on this subject long enough." Alex let Lisa get back to her house guest.

She returned her gaze to the sidewalk below. Her intuition told her Thomas was just fine. His sick day might be a sign of independence, a sign that he was breaking out of the mold he had fashioned for himself. She called him and anticipated the best case scenario. Thomas' phone rang twice. Alex waited patiently for him to pick up. She knew he had caller ID, so if he didn't answer he was either out or avoiding her. After four rings his machine answered. She hung up. He would see she called. It was four o'clock, so she worked until the crew arrived, and then headed for the door. Thomas was on her mind and she grew worried about his disappearance.

Last night's sleeplessness began to blur her day as the haze of insomnia thickened. After a polite chat with Miles she exited the office, and spoke briefly with Chris when she reached the house floor. His shoulder-length waves played with his collar as his words fell around her, muffled and distant. She had to get to the L, to Circle Rep, and clear her head before the show. It was the second to last performance of *Dylana* and she wanted to be ready for it. She excused herself from Chris' company and dashed to the lobby, where Lucas caught her before she could leave. His demeanor radiated anticipation. He looked like a pale schoolboy about to ask his crush to the big dance. Alex veiled the sweetness she found in his appearance. Lucas avoided her eyes and delivered a request to the air around her.

"Hey, I'm spinning on the top floor of Club Zen tonight. I'll leave your name on the guest list if you're into the scene." He met her eyes after the invitation left his mouth, wide-eyed and waiting for a positive response. Alex enjoyed his warm smile and offered him hope.

"Sure. That would be cool Lucas, thanks."

He grinned and spun around to exit with forced nonchalance. Every inch of him was adorable to her. The incident propelled her out the door with a smile.

Alex grabbed a seat on the train, rubbed her eyes, and tried to give her mind a quick rest. She asked the woman next to her to nudge her when they got to the Wilson stop. The strange woman grunted and surveyed Alex with an annoyed glance. Alex closed her eyes and drifted into a mediocre nap, her body aching for a much longer rest. Her mind drifted to her schedule: just two more shows and then she had a day off. She reviewed her opportunities for rest: the cast would want to go out tomorrow, so maybe she could slip out early after they started drinking and get home to bed. Then she could attempt to sleep in on Sunday, since she wasn't required to be at the Andrews strike. Even if she couldn't sleep, the idea of being home was enticing enough. A whole day of rest would heal her.

The L train lurched to a stop and Alex's head slammed into the pole beside her. The strange woman sneered at her. Alex rubbed her throbbing temple and turned to look at the station sign. Wilson. She grabbed her bag, ran for the door, and threw a bitchy look to the woman as she exited. As the train pulled away, the indignant stranger gave Alex the finger until she was out of view. Alex saw the insult, but let it go and hustled for the theater.

Alex finished a hasty preshow routine without any kickbox interruptions. New romance kept Peter in the dressing room, which put the Brothers on edge due to the new dynamic backstage. They attempted some karate antics with the House Manager, but the man had closing week melancholia, and droned on about their enjoyable performances. The Brothers patiently listened to his flattery. Their handsome identical features never ceased to endear them to people. When he finished, they scampered to the dressing room before another crew member could approach. Alex giggled as they bolted backstage and she checked her watch. It was seven o'clock and Thomas still hadn't arrived.

Thirty minutes later the cast and crew gathered to distribute Thomas' role. Matt stepped up as his understudy, and the ranks filled in below him. The actors quickly ran the lines of the opening scene before time ran out, and the lights dimmed in the house. In the black of backstage, a cast of fluttering hearts stood silent. They listened to the House Manager as he welcomed the crowd and announced Thomas' last-minute replacement. Matt quivered upon hearing his name as the lead. Alex kept her eyes closed and wondered why this would happen with two final shows to perform. The most important part of the show was to show up. She silently wished him to appear and relieve the cast of a night of tension. Applause capped the end of the welcome speech and the stage faded to black for entrances.

Alex found her starting position in the dark and took a deep breath. Her first long dialogue was with Thomas' character. It would be a much longer conversation if Matt got off track. The lights came up and she blinked at the mirage before her. Thomas stood there in costume and delivered the first line of the play. He was cool, unruffled, and showed no signs of a last second entry. She thought she was hallucinating. He couldn't possibly have made it on stage during that last moment. Her mind questioned if her insomnia took its toll and she dreamt all of this. Had she actually fallen asleep on the L? Thomas spoke directly to her. She glanced at Peter for some confirmation, but he was too busy exchanging a flirtatious smile with Lisa during Thomas' lines. That demonstrated present time. Thomas made it to the show. Another glance back at Thomas revealed a spark behind his character's guise. It was a spark that said, "How could you think I'd miss a performance? Let's have some fun." She returned the look, and they commenced their best performance of the run. By intermission, Alex knew they could reach the Creator State by the end of the show.

They kept silent during the break. Act Two began, the play churned along, and Alex arrived at the point where she had previously experienced the Creator State. She opened herself to the creative energies and started her monologue.

Dylana flowed through her body. A pinpoint of energy grew in intensity within Alex, until she felt surrounded by a vibrant field of energy. The effect lasted longer than any of her other encounters. The second she thought of the monologue coming to a close, the feeling subsided. She delivered the last of her lines and the Creator State left her. The scene ended as whispers from the audience complimented the beautiful performance.

Thomas delivered the next bold passage, and Alex watched from the wings. The anticipation of it electrified the air. Wise theatergoers attended closing week; it always held brilliant performances from this kind of company. Thomas crescendoed to an apex of emotional height. He released every pent-up, fed-up, isolated expression within him. Alex beheld his catharsis and dropped to her knees in the wings. Whatever Thomas had been through that day had changed him, and he sped full-throttle on the new energy. She watched closely for his crossover to the Creator State, but she couldn't detect it. She wondered if it was visible to the outside observer or completely internal. Thomas delivered the last lines of the play as the ambers faded above him. A pin-drop silence followed. The audience drank the moment in, and then broke into grateful applause and bravos. The cast filtered on stage for curtain call, then joined hands for a dignified bow to the standing crowd. Three bends later, the actors were on their way to the dressing rooms.

In the flurry of visitors and bustling crew backstage, Alex lost track of Thomas. He disappeared again. She thought he might be outside smoking, trying to get away from the chaos. The Brothers took a dose of worship from patrons in the hallway as she snuck by them and popped into the men's dressing room. She walked in on Peter and Lisa, who were wrapped in a deep block-out-the-world kiss. She backed out without disturbing them. Realizing she had an opportunity to sneak out and get home to rest, she quickly grabbed her bag, gave the house a thank you, and headed out the back alleyway door undetected.

She turned the corner to the alley and spied two silhouetted men, one of whom she recognized as Thomas. He smoked and talked with a man who appeared to be a patron. As she moved closer, Thomas stepped forward. The second man followed, and the light revealed a stylish urbanite with black rimmed glasses who introduced himself as John. Alex gave Thomas a look which demanded a reason for his tardiness to the show. He explained quickly.

"I went to the Library to post a message on the Artist Exchange site, to ask if anyone else has been experiencing the Creator State." Alex glanced toward John, who evidently had been informed about the State. Thomas beamed. "It's cool. I met John at the library and we struck up a conversation about creativity. You'll never guess what he teaches."

John pushed up his glasses and answered. "Physics."

Alex stared at him, not knowing how this related to theater, and turned back to Thomas. "Well, you guys have a good night," she responded, and aimed to walk away.

Thomas ignored her plans. "Let's get to Jimmy's before it gets too crowded. You'll enjoy John's conversation." Alex gave Thomas a warning look. He was not off the hook for scaring the cast earlier that night. She agreed to accompany them for a short while. Thomas sped ahead and left Alex to pair behind with John. He complimented her performance as they walked and she sensed he was trying to warm her up. She wondered what brilliant things this man had to say that would make someone like Thomas be late for a show.

Alex's curiosity about John fueled a third wind in her. With one more performance of *Dylana* to go, the relief of a job well done approached. She was amused by John's compliments, which seemed somewhat passé now that the show was almost over. He obviously wasn't a performer or he would ask her about her next gig. His naiveté lightened her spirits as they approached the bar. It would be fun for her to talk about something other than acting. She managed to get John talking about himself.

John was flattered by her inquiry. "I graduated with a degree in physics, but I ended up teaching science in human culture; science as it applies to history. Lately I've been obsessing about finding something a bit more meaningful."

They slowed to a stop and hung outside for a moment. The noisy interior of Jimmy's blasted each time a patron opened the door. Their conversation was soundtracked by this ebb and flow of noise from within. Alex studied John as he spoke; she searched for a sign of purpose, which she realized was her own obsession. She considered the circumstance of it: what happens when a science teacher obsessed with finding something meaningful meets an actress obsessed with creativity? She smiled to herself and returned her attention to John, who detailed his personal history. She hadn't heard a word of it.

Alex interrupted him mid-sentence. "I'm sorry John, I have a confession. I didn't sleep well last night so I completely zoned out just now. Can we go in, get a drink and start this conversation over?" She watched him for a reaction. He seemed stunned that she hadn't been listening. Perhaps his teaching occupation had him conditioned to speaking and being heard. Alex took the lead and entered Jimmy's before he had a chance to object.

They crushed through the Friday night mob toward Thomas, who waved to them from a booth in the back. As they passed the bar, Alex locked eyes with Susan. Her ex-pal seemed to be curious about the new guy who was following her. Alex gave her a quick smile and struggled across the floor. She looked over her shoulder and discovered John had been swallowed by the sea of people waiting for a drink, a typical Jimmy's phenomenon for a Friday. Alex grabbed his arm, yelled a few words to the surrounding crowd, and the pack released him. They finally reached Thomas and scooted into the sanctuary of the booth.

John looked overwhelmed by the activity of the bar. "I typically don't go to places like this." He faked a smile that revealed he was quite uncomfortable with the atmosphere.

Thomas sympathized to calm him. "The first time I came in here on a Friday I thought all of Chicago had been invited. I got stuck in a corner and couldn't escape for two hours. I just stood there, sandwiched against the wall, waiting for a break to get out. It was terrifying!" They laughed and he explained. "I'm not kidding. I didn't even get a drink that night. I had to smoke upwards, toward the ceiling!" Thomas mimed his humorous tale as John grinned in appreciation.

Alex felt an uneasiness surface. She accounted it to her discomfort with the impending conversation. It was obvious they wanted to talk about the Creator State, and she wasn't in the mood to explain herself for the second night in a row. She would have to get used to talking about the State, but Thomas' good-looking new chum tested her patience. She watched John as he and Thomas babbled on about their bar experiences. It was a topic Alex had no interest in, and it tested her patience even further. As she watched John attempt to entertain a master entertainer, she felt sad for the non-creative population. Maybe John had talent in his own profession, but he tried to outwit Thomas and one-up him in the presence of the new girl. She resented his tactics. Thomas, who had dedicated a lifetime to understanding and portraying human nature, dumbed it down to help John feel more comfortable. At one point Thomas shot a look to Alex that said, "Give this guy a chance."

She posed interest and gazed at John's watchable face. He had flawless ebony hair that rivaled Chris Caldwell's, and a complexion of pinkish silk. She noticed a flash of silver chain cutting the corner of his neckline. Some kind of amulet dangled deep in his shirt, but she couldn't get a glimpse of its shape. The longer she watched him, the more she admired his hands. Their smooth texture evidenced his cerebral occupation as they subtly emphasized his words. They jutted from his lengthy open-cuffed sleeves, which was a fashion fetish she enjoyed. She appreciated intelligent types, and John's hipster facade gave him a dichotomous quality of brains struggling with beauty. After several minutes of barely-heard conversation, Thomas snapped Alex out of her stupor. He glared at her, insulted by her blatant attraction to their guest, and dragged her into the conversation as punishment.

"Alex writes messages on creativity every day," Thomas interrupted. "She records them on her voicemail for people to listen to. It's called the *Magic Mobile*." John turned to Alex, instantly curious. Thomas gave her a toothy smile behind his back. She warned Thomas with her glance, and then attempted to downplay the *Magic Mobile*.

"It's really more like poetry. I find things to inspire me, then share them with other artists. Kind of like the Artist Exchange site that Thomas and I have. Everyone posts their ideas just to see what happens." John considered a reply but she beat him to it. "It's a good creative exercise. My voicemail just happens to be an available outlet."

John looked like he had more cooking in his mind. "That's cool, who calls? Can you see who calls? How do they get your number? What do they say?" He wanted more data. He tried to pace himself, so he wouldn't offend his new acquaintances. "I'm sorry, I don't mean to drill you. What are the messages like? Can I hear one?"

She leaned back in the booth and shifted uncomfortably. "You know what? I'm going to get us all a drink first, then we can talk *Mobile*, okay?" She rose, darted toward the bar, and was quickly swallowed by the mob and out of sight.

Thomas covered as John watched her depart. "No worries, she's just a little antsy this evening. Last night was the first time she told anybody about her experiences, then tonight I was late for the show, and then I brought you around. She's just a little freaked out."

The comment made John concerned about his inclusion on Alex's stress list. He scanned the bar and said nervously, "I hope I didn't offend her."

Thomas wanted to turn the conversation back to their daytime topics. The two men had discussed every subject they could get their minds on: philosophy, religion, art, politics, physics, and creation theories. It had been a stimulating day for Thomas, the best day off he spent in a long time, and he was primed for more vivid conversation. He tried to soothe John's discomfort. "It would be hard to offend Alex, she tends to let things slide. That's one of her better qualities."

"You make it sound as if she has a few bad traits?"

"Well, nobody's perfect." Thomas noticed John's interest in Alex. "She's been through a lot, so she doesn't dwell on the insignificant stuff. Out of all of my friends, she's probably the coolest in the bunch. Definitely the smartest." He bent an eyebrow. "The most talented, too." He seemed perplexed, and John inquired about his distraction.

"What's the problem?"

Thomas checked the crowd for any sign of Alex, and leaned in. "I probably shouldn't tell you this," Thomas began. "But I figure I can trust you, after all of the talking we've done today." He spoke confidentially. "Alex hears voices. I mean, she calls it clairaudience, but with all explanation aside, she's hearing voices in her head. In my experience that's always indicated that the person was a little cuckoo."

John brushed off the wisecrack. "I've read about clairaudience and clairvoyance in my studies. There are viable explanations for its existence. Some people are more sensitive to the inner workings of the world than others." He saw that Thomas was unhappy with his response, so he attempted to sympathize. "But if you think your friend is mentally unbalanced, then perhaps you could suggest she get some help."

"No, you're misunderstanding my point. I don't think she's crazy, I think she's connected to something I've been searching for my whole life."

John cocked his head and guessed. "A more creative voice?"

"No, it's more than that. It's a kind of live-for-the-moment attitude that I'd like to be bold enough to try. I just don't think I have it in me. But the older I get, the stronger the urge becomes."

"Urge to do what?"

"Be the complete man that I would like to be." Thomas avoided his companion's gaze and knew he provided too much personal insight. He laughed. "Sorry, it's been a strange day. I'm just in a funk about my lifestyle."

John held up a pale palm. "No no, I understand completely. I've been questioning my motives for getting involved in science for a while. I've had the same ideas circulating in my brain for the last year. Where to go with myself, how to live, what to explore, and what to run away from. I've made some subtle exterior changes, but the interior is still reaching for higher ground." He gave a self-depreciating laugh. "It may not be creativity I'm after, but it's definitely more than teaching. The idea of regurgitating other people's work for the rest of my life is less than desirable."

"Yeah, maybe it's the same for me. I can't see myself performing other people's plays and ideas as a lifelong career." He felt a surge of enthusiasm. "Maybe that's my issue with Alex. No matter where those messages of hers are coming from, they're fresh words every day. Maybe not new ideas, but that doesn't matter."

"What do mean 'not new ideas' ... do you doubt their originality?"

"The messages have a quality of old wisdom, like a combination of poetic observation and good creative advice. Some of them have an ethereal mood. Those are the ones that intrigue me. They seem to predict things we haven't experienced yet, but from a conclusive viewpoint. The statements are delivered as fact, like the voice is in the future throwing little scraps back to us poor fools in the present."

John straightened. "Technically there is no future, or present, or past. Time doesn't really exist, if you can even define existence. It's all happening at the same instant; it is our perceptions that keep our reality intact."

After a slight pause, the two men chuckled at the course of their conversation. Thomas browsed for Alex and spotted her navigating the crowd with three beers crushed in her hands. He motioned to John that she was on her way back. When John saw her struggle, he promptly came to her aid and helped her carry the pints back to the table. Thomas remained seated and realized that his own relationship with her didn't warrant such chivalry. He also noted her surprise with John's assistance; she was unaccustomed to such manners from her usual crowd. The thought of such a great gal getting less attention than she deserved saddened him.

Alex slid into the booth next to Thomas and started downing her beer. She tried to make a quick getaway, which Thomas recognized but didn't mind since he enjoyed his conversation with John. After a few gulps, she announced a forgotten appointment.

"Well guys, I have to make an appearance at Club Zen tonight, so if you'll excuse me for the evening." She mentally mapped out the fastest route to her daybed, and smirked at the thought of her "day" bed. She considered if it worsened her insomnia; her attempts to sleep in a bed named for daytime. John smashed into her sleep-deprived train of thought.

"May I go with you?" John imposed. "I haven't been there since it reopened."

Alex was astonished that her quick escape was brought to a halt. She tried to be polite. "What did Club Zen used to be?"

"Club Chaos," Thomas quipped.

"It's the old Blitz warehouse." John brightened to the idea of spending more of the night in Alex's company. She perceived that his excitement would not wane, so she gave in to a quick trip across town.

"Well if you like that sort of thing, come with. My name's on the list, so it should be a nice brief visit." She emphasized *brief*, which caused Thomas to titter. He knew she wanted to get home. She tried to rope him into going along, but he refused.

"I hate places like that." Thomas directed the line to John, then whispered into Alex's ear, "and so do you." She gave him an elbow in the side to shut him up.

"It can be bearable, especially if you have good company." John smiled wide at Alex, and she ate up his handsome attention. Thomas recognized he was suddenly odd man out, and sunk a bit in his seat.

Alex downed the rest of her beer and got up to exit. John followed suit and rose as he finished the last of his drink. They offered Thomas a last chance at accompanying them, which he refused, and bid him good night. They bumped through the crowd and received a last bit of surveillance from Susan before they reached the door.

Thomas watched them go and hoped he did the right thing. He allowed one of his best friends to leave with a man he just met. It made him feel guilty for not being more protective of Alex, but he absolved his conscience. Alex had seen much worse than the likes of John and Thomas knew she could handle herself. Thomas sipped his beer as he considered his relationship to women. He noticed four girls watching him as he sat alone. They smiled at him and began to approach his booth. He sat up, flipped his long bangs out of his eyes, and played cool. One of the girls leaned on his table and said hello. She allowed him to look down the deep v-neck of her shirt at her bulbous breasts. He curled a crooked smile at her and said hello. The girl looked back at her friends, then back to him as she opened her frosted mouth to speak.

"There are four of us girls out tonight." She fluttered her lengthy jet lashes at him. Thomas was immediately intoxicated with the idea of being surrounded by four beautiful women for the rest of the night. The girl smiled sexily at him. "Can we have your booth?"

His stupefied grin fell and he forfeited his seat to the girls. He sulked to the bar, plopped down on a lone stool, and proceeded to get drunk.

5

○ ○

There are a few who enter our lives with a kindred peace and embrace our passions and missions with unconditional acceptance. Their presence confirms that all of our lofty ideas can become reality.

—*The Magic Mobile*

Some evenings are remembered in detail; each word and moment magically imprinted on the memory. Alex would remember her first night with John for the rest of her days. At one minute to midnight she exited Jimmy's with her escort. Sleeplessness throbbed in her veins as her voices began to echo around their conversation. John beamed at her, far too anxious and far too enthusiastic for her energy level. She thrust a hand into the air and a cab answered. It didn't occur to her that John might find this emasculating, nor did she care. After downing her beer so quickly, the world was off balance and she needed to sit down again. John trotted to open the cab door for her, and she dove into the vehicle with him close behind.

In the muffled interior of the taxi, Alex felt the full force of John's presence. She chastised herself for getting into a date-type situation with a total stranger. He vied for her complete attention and nervously talked on, as if he had something to lose if she didn't approve of him that night. Their auras crushed against each other in the back seat like over-inflated balloons. She felt claustrophobic and began to doubt if the trip to Club Zen would end well.

Alex inhaled slowly to calm herself, and was infused with the scent of John. He smelled clean, like fresh laundry or fresh-cut grass. It soothed her and she secretly took another hit of it. He spoke about his last experience at the old Blitz warehouse, a gathering for the birthday of a colleague, but she didn't hear it. Behind seemingly attentive eyes, her mind carried on a completely different dialogue; another skill gained via her stage career. Her voices nagged her like impatient children, and she tried to quiet them. She adjusted her body language and angled herself toward him. She placed her arm on the back of the seat and gave

John the impression that she listened. When she tried to focus on his words, the volume in her head increased. She finally gave the voices the attention they demanded. She cut him off for the second time that night and searched her bag for her journal.

He stopped speaking and looked wounded. "Don't tell me I'm boring you again."

"No, not at all, I've just got to write down this message idea or I can't concentrate on what you're saying." She found her utensils and wrote furiously. John sat back silently, looked at the sneering driver, then turned to watch the nightlife whiz by his window. He waited patiently for Alex to cease her scribbling in the half-light of the cab, and strained a glimpse toward the words which had interrupted his story. Alex finished with a flourish that ran her pen off the page. She exhaled relief and apologized for the interruption.

"Thanks, I just, um, have to strike when the impulse is there?" She smiled faintly and waited for repercussions.

John locked eyes with her. He softened into a slight smirk and reached out his hand. "Let's see what the voices have to say tonight."

Alex dropped her smile. Evidently Thomas told John about her clairaudience. Personal confrontations about the mysterious sources of her words made her uncomfortable. Hundreds of artists knew where the *Mobile* came from and she was fine with it. But an outsider like John, and a scientist to boot, made her feel exposed and about to be judged. She looked to his outstretched pallid palm, illuminated by the passing street lights. It flashed like a separate entity, a symbol of passage to a new phase of her life. She would have to share these creative thoughts and accept the consequences. She passed the open journal to him. He held it gently in the light of the window and heeded Thomas' warning about Alex being shy about her work. He regarded the page carefully. Alex held her breath and hoped the moment might help her self esteem. It might prove she could take immediate feedback and didn't need to hide behind a cell phone voicemail. The seconds played out in slow motion. His lips parted to recite her words and he began, softly and carefully.

"Remember when the stars floated around like fireflies on a hot July evening? The world was wide open and unpredictable. As hearts hardened and theories were written in stone, the stars slowed to it; paused to listen for glimmers of consciousness. A mere moment to the milky way, but lifetimes of fixed stars for us."

He didn't raise his eyes from the page, but read the words again, as if letting them sink into his skin like a warm bath. He seemed consoled by them, but Alex waited for his review nonetheless. He turned to her after the second reading and said earnestly, "This is beautiful, Alex."

A well of tears surged to her eyes and she repressed them immediately. John noted her reaction and lowered the book to his lap. "Breathe, Alex, it's good stuff. I'm not just being nice." Alex laughed nervously, obeyed his order, and enjoyed his fragrance again. Her vulnerability was on display, but rather than her aloof defense mechanism, she allowed him some leverage.

"Thank you," she said quietly. "My shy side doesn't support me very well." She recovered from the anxiety and wanted to turn the topic back to the message.

John caught on and addressed the journal still resting on his leg. "I like the idea of the stars slowing down to search for similar consciousness. What seems a blink to the universe is millennia of steady constellations to us here on tiny planet Earth. I like the concept. It gives my science a bit more soul." He registered that she was paying attention. "Can you imagine what it was like, all of those eons ago when everything was so malleable and chaotic? How thrilling it must have been for the universe." John was stimulated by the idea and felt his skin tingle underneath his clothing. He raised a floppy-cuffed hand to his collar and adjusted his shirt, which revealed the slash of silver at his chest. The outside light streaked along its length, and repeatedly traced the serpentine links from his neck to his chest. Alex wasn't sure how much detail Thomas gave John regarding the message sources, so she kept her cards close as she responded.

"This compares perceptions of time as well." She offered. "What seems so important to us in our lifetime, these present tribulations, appears trivial in comparison to the vastness of time. It saddens me when I consider my life as a blink to the larger workings of the universe. It's difficult to think that the stars wouldn't hear me, wouldn't find my consciousness interesting enough to listen to."

John looked at the message again. "But perhaps the pausing, this slowing of the stars is caused by our presence. Maybe they are listening right now, maybe that's why they've been stationary for so long." He raised an eyebrow, which he held up until she could witness it when the next streetlight darted through the cab.

"Well said," Alex confirmed.

John returned the book to her and agreed on her message's behalf. "Well said."

She stuffed the journal back into her bag and glanced out the front window. They approached Club Zen, where a long line trailed down the block waiting for entry. Clubbers of every type lined the sidewalk and posed their best attitudes to sway the selection of the bouncers. Two giant men shirted in Club Zen t-shirts held clipboards and kept the unwanted element at bay. A third Zen man surveyed the lineup and searched for eye candy who would satisfy the atmosphere inside. People waited in line for hours to get in, and Alex despised the entire concept. The cab slowed at the entrance as she scanned the crowd. Unease grew in her stomach. Scores of leggy model-types in tinier-than-thou clothing pouted next to their chiseled male counterparts; a sea of fashion extreme and desperation. Alex reviewed her choice of apparel and had second thoughts about the entire adventure. John displayed some of his own angst as the cab came to a halt.

"Christ, what a pathetic sight." He thrust the fare at the driver before Alex could donate her half and opened the door. The building thumped with the heartbeat of overamplified music inside, which heightened the restless atmosphere on the sidewalk. Alex stepped out of the cab into the glare of floodlights and ruffled her hair while John had his back turned. She wasn't clear on his take of the scene, and wanted to know where his comfort level was with this kind of place. She shot him a remark.

"It's going to be wall-to-wall attractive blondes and their hunky escorts in there."

John put an arm around her and guided them toward the door. "Good, then we'll fit right in."

Alex flashed him a smirk of appreciation as they boldly charged up to the largest guard with a clipboard. Alex shouted her name to him. He checked his list, threw a thumb over his shoulder, and granted them entry. John looked delighted with the easy access and waved back sarcastically at the long line waiting behind the ropes.

Unlike the wall of people at Jimmy's, Club Zen opened into a wide carpeted area of cocktail tables, stocked with the pick of the line from outside. The thunder of dance music was deafening at first and muffled conversation as the eardrums adjusted. Alex felt her ribs shake within her chest with each thump thump thump of the beat and looked weakly to John for a sympathetic reaction. He scanned the scene, but his confused look indicated he had difficulty with the volume as well. Conversation was not the modus operandi here, it was a place to be seen and pair off into like-selves by 4:00 a.m. Alex hoped their evening wouldn't take that turn. Her exhaustion turned the atmosphere into a dreamlike whirl.

To Zen's credit, the decor was worth the price of the ego slam to get in. A span of cobalt-glossed wood covered the dance floor and enticed even the meekest of dancers to its inviting surface. Fog machines misted knee-high clouds which dissipated as they rose and gave the effect of a pre-sunrise rainforest. Giant trees of sculpted iron and brass grew out of the glowing blue haze and twisted up to the three-story ceiling, while a waterfall coasted down a slate wall which dominated the south end of the club. Movement was detected in the wall of water; a transparent elevator rose gracefully behind it to the upper floors. Choreographed lights hypnotized patrons with shafts of amber, crimson, and purple. Holographic images of spiritual and inspirational figures appeared on the dance floor; anyone from Jesus to Gandhi or Martin Luther suddenly materialized within the crowd. Cirque de Soleil style acrobats entertained the crowd from high in the cavernous ceiling above, where a web of jungle vines and tree branches supported their efforts. The attractive wait staff wore semi-transparent white linen, and served drinks in clean-lined glasses accented with sprigs of exotic fresh herbs. It was a cacophony of amusements, and held its Zen theme intact.

From within her cloud of insomnia, Alex peered out at the view. Fleeting milliseconds of unconsciousness taunted her with sleep, but she concentrated on the night before her. She would have to find Lucas, and quickly. John claimed a table near the edge of the dance floor and she followed, not that he would have heard any objection over the music. They sat on slender barstools and leaned in to the small shiny cocktail table between them. Alex tilted her head up as her eyes climbed the three stories of club. The second floor held more tables, with a same-level view of the acrobats. Up above the tree vines was the third floor which held Lucas. Treetop level looked quieter, and Alex longed to get there as fast as possible.

"Hey," she shouted to an attentive John. "I have to check in with Lucas and let him know that I showed up. He's on the third floor."

John looked heavenward and turned back to her. "I'll see if I can get us some drinks while you're gone."

Alex wasn't sure why he wouldn't go with her, but his absence would grant her a way out with Lucas. She could look down and show Lucas that John waited for her, and have an easy escape from the third floor. Afterwards she and John could down a quick drink, decide it's too loud to talk, and be on their way again. Alex excused herself and headed for the elevator behind the waterfall. A sculpted man in linen pants kept watch at the lift and she mentioned Lucas' name to access a ride to the sky. Once inside the Lucite box, the sheen of falling liquid blurred the club into an acid-like vision. It was dynamic to behold, and Alex enjoyed the experience of it on her sleepless high. Transported to above tree level, she entered an open room smelling of sandalwood and sage. The floor was covered in a sand-like carpet, with suede pillows grouped to provide seating. A distinctly cooler vibe of music complimented the distant throb from below. Cloudy light illuminated the upper branches and webbed vines. It felt Godlike being up there, literally above it all. She felt eyes on her and turned. Lucas waved to her from the D.J. booth on the opposite end of the room. She cautiously wove through the guests reclined on the floor and entered the box where he worked. He removed his headphones and surprised her with a warm embrace.

"Alex, you showed! This is righteous! I'm spinning trance tonight." Lucas had one hand on the turntable and apologized. "Hold on, let me hook this one up." He mixed in a new track which would give him an opportunity to step out for a minute. Lucas looked divine in this element. He had traded in his t-shirt and jeans for the Club Zen uniform: a linen shirt open to the waist which exposed his taut little musician's chest, matching pants, and a leather neck rope with a jade Z pedant. His golden hair was appropriately mussed and glossed in all the right places, and his enthusiasm for his beloved hobby gave him a vibrant glow. He led her to the edge of the rail which overlooked the scene downstairs.

Lucas grinned. "I didn't think you'd come."

"It isn't every day I get into Club Zen without a hassle. That line is harsh. It was a pleasure to slide in below the radar."

"Nah, you'd be rushed in without the Lucas tip. Did you bring someone? Don't tell me you're playing it alone on a Friday night. Crime if you are."

Alex smiled at his flattery, but wondered why he thought so highly of her when they had just met that week. She accounted it to *Mobile* interest or actress lust. "I'm here with a friend." She looked down and found the table where she left John. He was still there, but a dark-haired girl stood next to him and laughed at his commentary. The girl was trying to join him, or maybe John was trying to convince her to take a seat. From the third floor, it didn't look good either way. "That's him, in the white shirt, dark hair, glasses, talking to that brunette."

Lucas glanced briefly, but he was interested in Alex's reaction to the view. "Are you like, *with* him? Is that chick working your dude?" She looked up at Lucas and her head reeled behind her eyes. He saw that something was wrong. Her look could have been interpreted as jealousy. He feared she was attached to the man below, but sensed more was going on that night. "Alex, you all right?" He grabbed her elbow and guided her down to a pillow behind them. Once seated, Alex realized she was on the ground, and Lucas gazed at her with concern. "You look kinda pale, and that's coming from me, the king of pale." She half-laughed politely and silently begged for a last wave of energy to bring her to the moment. It arrived and she apologized to Lucas.

"Sorry, I haven't eaten a lot today and I drank too fast tonight. I'm okay now." She looked around to change the subject. "This place is cool. Nice vibe up here, it's like the lounge of the Gods." She brightened to convince him of her wellness. He shook the incident off and described his side of Club Zen, from the loneliness of the booth to the unique opportunity of spinning in a cutting edge club. Alex watched him speak and heard only half of his words over the dizziness which flurried in her head. She wanted to be unconcerned that John was being picked up by another woman, but she felt injured by the last glimpse of him talking to a stranger. She considered that they were strangers themselves; he tagged along to the club and could do as he pleased. Lucas was so thrilled with Alex's presence that he didn't take notice of her distraction.

"So Alex, how do you like the Andrews so far? Everyone treating you right? You just let me know if I can help you out. Anything you need, come to me." Lucas saturated his gaze with intent and caught her complete attention. "I have to give you props for the *Magic Mobile*. It's so true. I've never met anybody like you, so willing to just let it fly. Respect to you. Honestly." He had more to say, but he paused.

Alex felt the full force of the night upon her. She drank it in; reclined in the heavens while a linen-shirted angel admired her. She played directly at Lucas' momentary crush and seized the fleeting opportunity. His intentions were obvious, and she gave him permission to act on them. She gazed sexily at him. "When are you going to kiss me, Lucas?"

He didn't blink and rushed his lips to hers immediately. He knew he would have to cut his actions short when the record ended. One lengthy unwavering smash of a kiss later, Lucas ran to the booth to mix in another song. Alex righted herself on the cushions after he dashed away. She tried to break free from the erotic atmosphere's stranglehold on her late-night indiscretions. Lucas shuffled through his vinyl for the next track, in anticipation of a lengthy interval away from the booth. It took him a while; just long enough for Alex to change her mind about continuing their heavenly make-out session. She rose as he approached.

"You're wonderful, Lucas. But I should go. I really need to get home." Alex squeezed his hands and he stole a last kiss before she wished him a good night. Lucas watched her descend in the elevator until she faded into the watery haze. He sighed with pleasure and returned to his music.

Alex anticipated the scenario upon her return. She decided if John was deep into his pick-up, she would play it cool. The crowd spilled out of the elevator and scattered. Alex observed the table area. John sat alone and she watched him for a moment. He enjoyed the music, or at least pretended to, and acted as nonchalant as possible at a table with two cocktails. The dark-haired girl was long gone and the door was left open for Alex. She took inventory of her emotions before approaching. There had been a tinge of jealousy at the sight of him flirting. The wave of anxiety from that vision made her lip lock Lucas impulsively and she felt guilty. Her insomnia brought carelessness, but she concluded that the kiss was worth it, and let it go. She surmised the atmosphere once more and felt energized by the night. The voices started in again, but she ignored them. Boldness swelled within her. She swooped over to John, grabbed the sculpted dressing out of her cocktail, took a giant gulp of her drink, and invited John to the dance floor. He mimicked her guzzling, grabbed her hand, and led her into the swirling blue mist.

John displayed his excitement for her return in his dancing. They whirled in the mystical fog until the beat morphed into a sexier mix. She eyed him appropriately and he answered by moving in close. They intertwined and became a shape-shifting duo. Eventually they were mouth to mouth in the surreal haze of Club Zen. Alex took in his scent, made pungent by his body heat, and delighted in his kissing skills. A few cycles of song later, they agreed it was time to go. John wove them through the crowd until they emerged into the cool, quiet night air of the street.

The sidewalk contained smatterings of smokers and cab-seekers, the latter of which were unsuccessful at this late hour. The empty block attested to their futile search; a collective of clubbers stood stranded in the skanky guts of the far West Side. The dark street was intimidating, and Alex retrieved the sweater out of her bag to shield her exposed flesh from the neighborhood. She wrestled into her gray knit as quickly as she could. As she pulled the neck of it over her head, she heard the unmistakable sound of skidding sneakers sweeping by. They swooped up her bag from beneath her and dashed down the sidewalk in a rush of efficiency. Instantly she jerked to the chase and sprinted after the blur who stole her bag. As she pounded after the figure, John turned around and was stunned at the immediacy of her action. His eyes flashed at the sight. A low-crotched teenager ran with Alex's bag flailing for release under his arm, with Alex hard on his heels. John sprung after them. He reasoned her bag wasn't worth the chance of getting hurt and called after her to stop. Alex had other demands working her legs as she huffed down the sidewalk. Her only copy of the *Magic Mobile* journal was in that bag, and she wasn't giving it up without a good fight.

The teen darted down an alley which pulled both of them out of John's view. When John turned the corner, he found an empty corridor. At the far end was an open gate, and he dashed for it yelling Alex's name. She didn't back down and gained on the perpetrator. The teen tossed expletives over his shoulder as he ran, nervous that he was being pursued.

"Give it up, bitch, or I'll stop runnin' and blow your fuckin' head off!" The boy turned to see Alex in hot pursuit, and he laughed at her as they sprinted. "Girl what the fuck is in this bag? Must be good, if you still runnin'." He looked back again with wide eyes and taunted her. "Ain't no way you gonna get it now!" He sped up and headed down another alley with Alex right behind him. She huffed rhythmically and knew endurance would have to get her through this.

She yelled, "I'll let you have all the cash and cards, just let me have my book, it's the only copy of my words that I've got!" She noticed he listened. "I swear, man, I'll let you have it all, just let me have the notebook that's in there. Just throw it back and I'll stop running!"

They dodged down another alley and she noted John followed about a half a block behind. She took inventory of her situation and noticed the street sign as they turned another corner: Milwaukee. She knew where she was at least. Soon they'd hit a more populated area, and it seemed that the teen knew it, too. Evidently he wasn't bright enough to stop and fight, or pretend that he really had a gun, or dodge into a questionable area where the folks behind him wouldn't go. He kept running, but appeared to be considering a move. His gait evened out as if it were a race rather than a chase. Alex called out again, now only twenty yards from him. "Just give me the notebook, man!"

The boy hung the bag out to his side as he ran and dug into it with his hand. He plucked out the closest thing he could find to paper and held it up for Alex's review.

"Yes!" she shouted. "That's it! Please, just throw it!" Alex was closing in on him, near enough to smell the wake of his cheap adolescent cologne. "C'mon, man, do it!"

He threw the notebook rebelliously into the street and kept running. He cackled, "Fuck you bitch!" as he darted away.

Alex dove after the journal in relief. She rose with it and saw John streak by, still pursuing the teen. She called out after him, "Wait John, I have what I need!" But John was in hero mode, and he ran full-out after the unsuspecting boy.

The teen slowed after he tossed the notebook, so John gained on him quickly. Alex gasped for air in the street, winded from her sprint, and witnessed John tackle the boy football-style around the upper legs. They crashed to the ground and John wrestled the bag out of the stunned boy's arms. John punched him squarely in the face. The boy stumbled to his feet. John curled an arm around the bag to guard it, and his other arm retracted for another blow. The boy looked back at Alex, who stood stunned with her notebook protectively crushed against her chest. He realized his defeat, gave her the finger as he cursed, and ran off. He disappeared around the next corner.

Alex huffed to herself. "That's the second time today somebody gave me the finger. One more to go." She approached a winded John, who looked very smug with his efforts as he recovered.

He presented the satchel to her and exhaled. "Your bag, m'lady." He brushed the street filth off his clothes. He didn't look at her directly, and kept the post-traumatic fear in his eyes hidden from view. As he gasped to regain his breath, he joked at their expense. "You know that kid probably needs the cash more than we do." John looked at Alex with a questioning gaze, flustered by the fleeting excitement they had just experienced. He wanted an explanation and saw the journal in her hand. "Is that the reason for this insane drama tonight?"

"It's my only complete copy of the *Magic Mobile* messages. I couldn't let it end up in a dumpster on the West Side." Alex smiled to reassure him. "Thank you for getting my bag back. You didn't have to do that. I'm glad you didn't get hurt." They slid into an embrace, both of them relieved as they recovered from the run. As they looked out over each other's shoulders, they realized they were alone on a strange block.

John slid back and looked around, still holding Alex's arms. "Where do we go from here?"

He said it innocently, but she heard her own interpretation of his phrase. Their dance floor make-out session seemed light years away after the traumatic chase. There was a bond between them now, initiated by the events of the evening. She remembered the street sign and oriented them toward the more populated nearby strip. They walked in silence for a block and let the night sort out in their minds. Headlights grew behind them and they spun to the light. An empty cab cruised down the street, headed for the strip. John riskily ran into the street and hailed it, practically throwing himself in its path. Alex laughed at his aggressive approach and joined him. The cab stopped. They dove into the back seat and revealed their circumstances to the driver. The cabbie seemed unaffected and waited for their destination. Alex gave her address to the man and he returned to his driving with a grunt. They sat in silence for a few blocks and let the safety of the cab calm them.

John looked to his clothing and waited for Alex to make the next move. He fidgeted with a giant smear on the side of his shirt, at the center of which was a small tear from his slide on the sidewalk. She watched his hands work at the cloth and then stopped them with her own. She wanted a kiss from him, a kiss outside of the mystique of Club Zen; something to clarify that there was more to the night than impulse. He interpreted the thoughts which twitched behind her eyes and half-smiled.

"Alex," he said gently, "I don't know much about art, or theater for that matter, but there's no reason for you to think that I'm just one of those guys who is momentarily fascinated with the artist stereotype." He smirked at his impending humor. "And even though I'm a hero, I want you to treat me like any other incredibly brave and good-looking scientist, alright?"

She grinned and nodded. A feeling of violation grew within her from the earlier bag-snatching. She knew she wouldn't sleep until after the sun had risen. Cruel for a Saturday morning, but at least she had the daytime to rest before the closing night performance. She wondered if John would keep her company without expecting sex if she invited him up to her studio. She considered her options quickly and contemplated a moonlit talk with him at the lakefront. It would be romantic, close to home, and a safe spot for a couple in the single digit hours. John was pleasantly surprised when she suggested it, and he redirected the cab to the Belmont Harbor. The driver grunted again and delivered them to the lake, then he displayed his hatred of romance by giving them the finger as he drove away. Alex laughed at being flipped off for the third time that day, and explained the threes to John as they strolled to the lake's edge.

The air was cool, with a slight humidity which kept it comfortable for 3:30 a.m. visitors. The two arrived at a vantage point where giant boulders were assembled for seaside viewing. The half moon gazed at itself in the lolling blue-black waves of the quiet night. The isolation was uncomfortable at first, so they made small talk. John finally ended their polite banter and carefully changed the subject.

"I know this may not be the protocol after such a fun-filled evening, but I'd like to ask you about the Creator State." He tested the subject so cautiously that she wondered what Thomas had told him. She wanted John to feel at ease with her. More importantly, she wanted him to stay with her until sunrise, so she opened up.

"It's happened to me maybe a dozen times altogether," she began. "I'm not really sure what to make of it, but knowing that Thomas felt the same thing certainly helps." She paused for his reaction but he was quiet. "There's a feeling of observing the scene and being in the scene at the same time. Only it's liberating, as if all restraints had been removed. It's as if my spirit is experiencing its natural form." He looked confused so she stopped. "I'm sorry John, it's hard to describe."

"Don't apologize. I'm getting a clearer picture of the moments. My brain is just rushing ahead to what the source is, or what rational reason there is for these experiences. I'm the one who should apologize for trying to compute the equation too soon. We're kind of running from either side of the yard toward the same problem." He smiled at his own remarks and looked out over the water. His scent intermittently drifted toward her in the breeze as he turned the subject to himself. "Alex, my rational outlook has always been my touchstone. No matter how violent the world gets, or what new problems I encounter, I can always retreat to observing life from a voyeuristic, scientific approach. I watch the world grow more and more twisted and privately chart the downfall of humanity. But lately I'm not sure that I can just examine life with a calculating eye anymore." John shifted and looked for permission to continue. She recognized his uneasiness and encouraged him.

"Maybe you've decided not to become numb to the world. Maybe you want to be a participant rather than an onlooker?"

"There's nothing wrong with observing. No matter how much one participates in life it's the recorded observations that endure. The people who actually do the fighting and the rescuing don't bother to write it down accurately. Their observations are lost or fade with time. It's the scientists who are taking the last revisions and final cut into the future. And we're doing it with an unbiased eye. There's nothing wrong with that. It's respectable to be ... reliable." John was visibly agitated, and knew that his tirade was not lost on Alex. "Wow. I almost convinced myself. Pretty good, huh?" They laughed together and he put his arm around her. "Obviously I have some issues with my profession."

Alex moved closer to him and studied his face. "John, if we're going to hang out together, you don't have to defend yourself to me."

John narrowed his eyes in question. "Can we do that?"

"Do what?"

"Hang out together. I haven't had a night like this in a long time, Alex. I really enjoy your company, gangster-chasing and all." John smiled in a way which stayed locked in Alex's mind for days to come. The smile held an acceptance of all that she was, without a glint of expectation, prejudice or need. He simply took her for the person that she was right at that moment, and won her over with his honesty.

"This has been an unusual night for me too." She felt the aliveness of the night surround them as they leaned in for a kiss. She committed it to memory and detailed everything she could. The dark sloshing waters below; the cool stone beneath her skirt; his moist tugging mouth; the perfume of him that hung in the humid air; the way he pulled lightly at her sweater as they kissed deeper. She cat-alogued all of these elements in her memory under John Mitchell, and noted her own observational tendencies in the interim. The flash of silver on his chest dis-tracted her and she asked him what hung around his neck. John reached into his shirt and pulled out a strange looking sculpted piece at the end of the serpentine chain. It glistened as Alex strained to see what it was.

"It's a praying mantis. It's very sentimental; we used to have them in my back yard when I was a kid. The pendant reminds me to keep my possibilities open, like when I was a child." He smiled. "I think they're cool creatures, so no 'geeky bug-collector' jokes."

Alex laughed. "No, they are cool. I saw one on the running path the other morning, and a painting of one in a Broadway gallery window." She humphed. "This must be my third mantis."

John looked impressed that he fit into her coincidences. "Well, the word 'mantis' means prophet in Greek. Maybe this is a good prophecy, this three." They kissed deeply and felt the magic of the night around them. John broke their kiss. "I do want to talk to you about the Creator State. I'm not just trying to sleep with you, Alex." She sat with lips interrupted and yanked him back into her. He cheerily added, "It can wait." The two remained intertwined until light began to grow on the horizon. The edge of the water glowed with anticipation as the birds began to wake. Alex avoided starting a discussion on the State at that late hour, so they kissed and made small talk until the sunrise. The coral ball of light slowly emerged over the waves as morning noises grew behind them.

Alex paid homage to her routine and recited the message she wrote down in the cab. John kept his eyes on the view before them as she spoke. She noted the orange glow on his skin, which reminded her of the praying mantis from the day before, or maybe two days ago. She couldn't remember. Insomnia blended her calendar again. She felt her body relax to the sun's appearance. The sunrise cued her to retreat to bed at last. Alex decided to call it a night before it turned into breakfast. She could handle John seeing her after a full night of dancing, thief chasing, and sleeplessness, but they weren't familiar enough for him to see her nod off into a pile of pancakes.

He escorted her home and made a final request at the lobby door. "I want to see you again. Soon if possible." Alex nodded as impending sleep weighed on her like a wet wool coat.

"You've got my number," she grinned.

"Who doesn't?" He beamed a smile and turned to walk away. She watched him saunter down the sidewalk, then she gave a thumbs up to the heavens and retreated indoors.

6

Sometime during the pursuit of science and the great quest for explanation, a floodgate of lost information from deep in the collective cellular memory opened wide. It revealed that reality is not based on cause and effect, a grand experiment or chaos theory. Rather there is a demand for beauty to be present; spontaneous and synchronistic creativity which is woven into everything we know of. This is reality. The universe is devised for it, lives for it, and grows with it, cleverly and subtly expanding its agenda.

—*The Magic Mobile*

Thomas deduced the night went well for Alex and John. It was a sunny Saturday afternoon and he hadn't heard from either one of them. He rang Alex's studio but she didn't answer. The *Magic Mobile* repeated itself and played the same message as the day before. He tried the Andrews, but he hung up quickly when Joseph answered the phone. He thought contacting John would be inappropriate, as they had only one day's camaraderie between them. Thomas sat in his loft window and smoked. He rubbed a clean spot on the glass to peer through. His neighborhood was busy on Saturdays. Everyone rushed about. They tackled weekend tasks, lunched with friends, shopped, strolled, scuttled around, and choked the streets with traffic. Thomas lived in the same spot for a few years. In that time he watched Wicker Park turn from a cool West Side hangout for artists to the latest place to be seen. The yuppies swept through and cleaned up his part of town, and eliminated its character in the process. Most of the artists moved on, priced out by soaring rents and condo conversions, but Thomas managed to stay put. His copy store salary supported a comfortable lifestyle, and he wondered if he would be the last artist standing by the end of the renovations. He couldn't help but see the parallels in his own life. As the need for financial stability crept into his priorities, his art was banished to threadbare venues in the nighttime hours.

He exhaled a long stream of smoke over the scene in his window and engulfed the throngs in a gray cloud. "Choke on it, motherfuckers," he ordered and checked his watch for the third time: 3:10 p.m. He worried about Alex traipsing off with a stranger and turned his thoughts to his new acquaintance. He didn't know much about him, but John made a good first impression. As Thomas examined the multitudes below with disdain, he lit another cigarette and reviewed the previous day's events.

Yesterday a surge of excitement filled him the second his eyes popped open. After he revealed his Creator State experiences to his friends, he felt empowered to change his behavior at last. He was on the fence about the lifestyle he lived for the past year: copy guru by day and vibrant artist by night. Frustrated with the mediocrity of it all, Thomas threw himself into his theater work and hoped an event would occur to allow him to live a more creative life. After he experienced the strange connected feeling during a few performances, he knew something different was finally happening to him. Until the conversation with Alex, he thought he was alone in his madness. Her confession confirmed his notions that this unique experience demanded attention. On Friday he awoke wide-eyed and purposeful; the impulse he desired suddenly arrived. He detached from his responsibilities and called in sick, even though it might mean termination. He surmised if they fired him for one day's freedom, he was merely a servant to the corporation. He gave himself one last chance at the artistic life he imagined before he forfeited to financial gain.

Alex planted several ideas in his life through the *Magic Mobile* messages, and it inspired him to surrender to his artistic drive. His recent experiences on stage brought excitement back to his performances, and he couldn't wait any longer to find out if more people were out there who felt the same thing. So he ventured to the library on Friday afternoon with the Artist Exchange Web site on his mind. He could have logged on to the Artist Exchange at a nearby Web café, but he had a grand affection for the downtown library. The giant stone fortress was a monument to learning and literature, trimmed with banners which declared Chicago as the "City of Big Readers." He often gazed up at the corners from the street and admired the sculpted stonework and giant owls which rose from its structure. The building appeared as if in flight, and it was a grand addition to the impressive architecture of the downtown landscape.

The interior held everything a thinking person could desire: books on every subject and whim that humanity could conjure, sheet music and recordings from every musical era and style, soundproof rehearsal rooms with pianos, a lively children's wing, and a graceful glass-roofed reception hall on the top floor. Thomas bee-lined for the computer tables. He posted his inquiry on the Artist Exchange site as John arrived behind him. John invaded his personal space by standing too close, and shifted impatiently as he waited his turn at the computer. He read over Thomas' shoulder and audaciously asked him about his posting. Thomas was annoyed at first, but then revealed his situation. It was a test drive for his desired persona and he spoke openly about his experiences. It didn't matter to Thomas if John thought he was nuts, he didn't know him anyway.

What surprised Thomas was John's reaction to the Creator State. John studied physics in relation to creativity, and was instantly fascinated with this new information. They sat at one of the heavy wooden tables and spoke in husky whispers, until the shushing from nearby readers chased them into the streets. They strolled up Michigan Avenue, charged by their good conversation and the fantastic structures which surrounded them. Thomas felt a tingle in his veins. Here was a new topic at last; the fresh air that his stale life needed to awake from its deep numbing slumber. He detailed his stage experiences, and didn't slow when John seemed unable to grasp what all of it meant. He explained how it made him feel and how it came into his life. Thomas was enraptured to have a captive audience for his personal revelations. John was transfixed as well, and took mental notes as he found connections to his research. Thomas turned the topic to Alex, revealed her troubles with insomnia, and proposed it might be a possible side effect of the Creator State. He saw that John was curious about Alex, so he invited him to *Dylana* after they had dinner. It was well into rush hour when Thomas feared he wouldn't get to the show on time. He and John worked their way uptown during the course of the afternoon, and the streets were jammed to a slow crawl.

Even though they made it to Circle Repertory with fifteen minutes to spare, Thomas hid in the back alley in his alternate costume. He tested his new defiance and toyed with his colleague's nerves. He knew everyone was a wreck inside, and yet he remained out of sight and snickered in the alley at his antics. When he heard the opening applause, he crept on stage in the blackout, grabbed a startled Matt, and tossed his wiry frame off stage before the lights rose. It was mischievous, and the look on Alex's face when the lights came up was worth the price of a good scolding.

Thomas laughed to himself at the memory of it and looked at his watch: 3:45 p.m. He unfastened the clunky timepiece, flung it at the sofa, and returned to staring at the activity outside. He spotted a black-cloaked figure with spiky yellow hair moving down the sidewalk and his body twitched to attention. Further observance revealed it was not Alex, but a young man with a similar anti-gravity haircut. Thomas chuckled at the mistaken identity and remembered his first encounter with Alex.

It had been five years since she arrived on the off-loop theater scene, a newcomer from the East Coast with an edgy air. She burst into the first read-through for *Three Sisters*, flopped down in the seat next to him, and propped her flimsy combat boots on the seat in front of them. She placed a shockingly cold hand on his and whispered into his ear if she could bum a smoke. Thomas was entertained by her defiant attitude, and they formed an unspoken attachment with their off-center observations. At first she appeared impulsive, even reckless, but he learned that she simply recovered quickly from the blows of fate. She moved to Chicago by way of a love affair and adapted by necessity. These days her smoking habit was kicked, her running habit warmed her icy fingers, her lengthy hair was chopped short, and her boots upgraded to Kenneth Cole. Thomas reviewed his own accomplishments in the same span of time and found nothing but a longer resume. As he reviewed their time together, an emotion swelled within him. His stomach reacted with sudden nausea, and his head felt light. Deep within his gut he felt a tugging, a sense of longing that rose up the center of his chest. Thomas got up, paced his hardwood floor, and tried to shake it off. He stopped pacing and put his hands at his waist in disbelief. He knew the feeling; he had imitated it for years on stage.

"Holy shit, I'm in love with Alex!"

With no one in the loft to debate, he talked it out with himself. "How the hell did that happen? It's impossible. Well, not impossible. Definitely crazy." He shook his head in denial and paced. "I'm just jealous of John for stepping in and sweeping down on Alex. Why the hell did I introduce him to her anyway?" Thomas walked around his new problem as if there was a solution.

"I can't be in love with her. She's a friend. She's a good friend. If anything was meant to happen, it would have happened already. It's been five years." He stopped pacing. "So why am I obsessing about where she is and why she hasn't called me today? That's a sure sign! It happens all the time in plays. This is so fucking typical of what happens." Thomas shuddered at the thought of playing into a common plot line and shouted to his high ceilings.

"Fuck, I'm in love!"

He rushed to the window, grabbed another cigarette, and sat on the sill puffing angrily. "Ridiculous," he harrumphed. "It's all this new connection crap. She's the only one who has felt something that really means anything to me. That's all it is." He reviewed his actions from the day before. "But I rushed to the

Artist Exchange to find more people right away. That means I don't want to be alone with her in this Creator State stuff. Fear of being alone with her is another typical reaction, another typical sign of love." He rose again. "Fuck!"

Thomas couldn't sit still with his discovery. He agreed with himself to go into renunciation, get out of the loft, have dinner, and get to closing night where he would avoid Alex as much as he could. He threw his well-worn backpack over his shoulder. The bottom seam gave way and spewed the contents onto the floor where they skidded in all directions. He yanked them together and raced against the impending doom of accepting his emotions. He stuffed the items inside the floppy pack and grabbed a roll of duct tape for a quick repair. He slapped the tape on with panicking hands and knew if he stayed any longer in the loft, he was bound to have to face his new dilemma in full force. If he got out of the loft, he could avoid this pitiful change of heart until after the show closed, when he could get away from Alex for a few days. The patchwork tape held and Thomas darted for the door. He turned and raised a hand to say goodbye to his loft, realized that it was a habit he had picked up from Alex, cursed loudly, and slammed the door behind him.

Thomas crashed down the sidewalk and threw himself around the oncoming throngs. He maneuvered from behind the lengthy wave of hair that covered his right eye. He flung it to the side with a jerk of his head every few steps. He cussed at it and vowed to chop it off the second the curtain came down that night. After a block of flinging his head to the side, he grumbled into a corner convenience store and bought the first available remedy: a bright yellow baseball cap imprinted with a large image of Sponge Bob Square Pants in tightie whities. He pulled back his shock of hair, smashed the cap over it, and exited again. He knew he would have to endure a few sideway glances from the crowds on Damen Avenue. Thomas was in no mood to tolerate pretense. He dodged an oncoming group of too-fashionable twenty-somethings and sharply turned the corner. As soon as he rounded onto North Street he stopped in his tracks. There were Alex and John, having an animated conversation and unavoidably moving in his direction.

John caught sight of Thomas and waved excitedly. Thomas blanched and wondered if he could whip the ridiculous cap off of his head without them noticing. But it was too late, they were too close. John greeted him with an outstretched hand, which Thomas shook with too much fervor.

"Hey guys," Thomas said enthusiastically. "Last big night o' *Dylana*. Don't be late now, Alex."

She shot him an unforgiving look for his antics the night before. "I'll be glad to put this one to bed." She paled and knew Thomas could easily turn her comment into a joke at her expense. He looked to the sidewalk and suppressed a crude remark. He glanced up again and allowed her to see that he would let it slide this time. Through the eyes of his new crush she looked amazing. She was clad head to toe in black as usual, but her clothes floated with femininity in the warm afternoon breeze. Her hair glistened, her skin glowed, every inch of her appeared electric to him. Thomas wondered if she had primped a little more for her companion, or if his vision was affected by his throbbing heart.

John was oblivious and continued the conversation without interruption. "We're headed for a bite, but I'm not sure where we're going. We keep talking so much that we'll never get to a decision." He discussed dinner plans as Thomas studied their dynamic and searched for clues as to what occurred between them last night.

He looked over John's clothes as they talked and noted his stylish ensemble. Thomas quickly inventoried his own appearance and felt the Sponge Bob cap resting on his head like a billboard for geekiness. The duct tape on his backpack didn't help, and his confidence shrunk in the shadow of John's coolness. Yesterday John was an average guy, but today his status escalated to icon. John stood atop Mount Cool with a torch and cast beams into the darkness where Thomas hid, revealing everything that made Thomas undesirable. Thomas' ego couldn't take much more exposure in the unfavorable light, so he decided to flee for the shadows.

He interrupted John. "Sorry, I've gotta get going. I wanted to, uh, check the Artist Exchange site for responses before the show." With that invented, he saluted them weakly and tore down the street before they could contest.

Alex watched him dash away and apologized to John for her longtime friend. "He's always this way on closing nights, don't take it personally." She about-faced to continue their migration toward the dining strip. John stared after Thomas and wondered why he was so cold after their strong debut yesterday. He let it go for the moment and caught up with Alex. Her attention had moved to her cell phone, which purred at her waist. "I have to answer, that's the Andrews number." John strayed to give her a little privacy and examined some books through a storefront window.

An excited voice was on the other end. Alex recognized it immediately and felt her voice catch as she tried to sound innocent. "Hi Lucas, how are you today?" She flipped through the responses she planned for him and hoped that fourteen hours had altered history. Music crackled in the background and Lucas shouted over its din.

"You recognize this groove, Alex? That's the vinyl I was spinning when we frenched last night!" He sang along with the lyrics at full volume. Apparently he was alone at the Andrews, or at least she hoped he was. She kept her eyes on John and made sure he didn't witness her uneasiness. Occasionally he glanced over at her, and she rolled her eyes as if the caller annoyed her. Alex had to cut Lucas off and find out what he expected. She stopped his serenade short and admitted she remembered the tune. He went on about how beautiful she looked last night and how happy he was to see her. Alex decided to come clean. She turned away from John and spoke clearly into the phone.

"Lucas, you are a nice guy, but I can't go out with you or anything." His sudden silence had her search her excuses again, and she chose a good one. "I'm Manager of the Andrews. I can't threaten my job, or your job, by dating a co-worker. Joseph would find out, and we'd both get fired. I don't want to lose this opportunity, you know?" Alex strained to hear a reaction to the scapegoat. It was true they could get fired, and she doubted he could find a better gig for himself. He finally stirred after some consideration, and replied.

"I thought about that, but when you showed up last night I didn't think you cared about work." Lucas swallowed his pride. He didn't regret his actions. "Hey, we'll always have Club Zen, right? It was an awesome kiss."

She smiled into the phone with relief. "It *was* an awesome kiss, Lucas." She twisted to return her gaze to the storefront, but John stood right behind her. He heard her last line, put Lucas and last night together, and was visibly shaken. She ended the call and waited for John to chastise her behavior. Whatever he said wouldn't compare to the tongue-lashing in her head. She knew she may have endangered their possibilities, and felt her spirit sink at the notion of losing him so soon.

John picked up on her guilt and spun it to his advantage. He grabbed her to him, planted a deep lengthy kiss on her, and pulled back. "Now *that* was an awesome kiss," he proclaimed. He yanked his mussed shirt straight again and extended a bended elbow for her to latch on to. "Shall we?"

Alex hooked his arm and gave a surprised smile. She glanced up at him as they strolled. He beamed victory, unconcerned with the details of Lucas. Part of her was agitated by his arrogance; he seemed sure that he won out over Lucas. Another part of her admired his attitude: perhaps the present moment was all that mattered. She looked up at him again and he gave her arm a squeeze.

As they walked to an early dinner, she was thankful John suggested they explore a daylight hour or two together. He respectfully waited until 2:00 p.m. before calling her. She slept deeply and was refreshed to discuss the Creator State with him. Alex hid a grin of pleasure at John's daytime appearance. She thanked the hair product gods for the messy pomade-laden style which enhanced many a good looking guy like John. She noticed their reflection in the windows; they looked well-partnered. They wanted to pick up Thomas on the way to dinner, but their brief encounter with him left them ungraced by his company.

Alex reviewed her status with John. On one hand, she valued his non-theatrical ear as a sounding board for her ideas. After he read the message in the cab last night, she considered exposing the *Mobile* to a wider audience. Anyone who could get her to feel more comfortable with her voices would be an asset. There was a sexual chemistry there, a quality which distracted her from her goals in the past. Relationships muddied the playing field, and she wanted clear turf to her new frontier. She wanted to play the game differently this time. There would have to be an understanding that if she felt restrained, they would be finished. Alex laughed to herself at the audacity of her inner monologue. John noticed her amusement and inquired about the source.

"Are your voices back for another round?" He asked the question with ease, another trait that was wooing Alex. Anyone who could be nonchalant about clair-audience received gold stars in her book. She tossed her head and laughed.

"No, not yet." She looked at him flirtatiously and dove in with the truth. "I was thinking about relationships and how bad I get when they stop progressing."

John pushed his glasses up and countered. "When the relationship stops progressing, or when you stop progressing in the relationship?"

She stalled a bit and acknowledged his accuracy. "Wow, are you as matter-of-fact about dating as I am? I may have met my match." Alex realized she overestimated their status. It was too early to assume they were dating. Her pride recoiled after committing another gaffe, her second of the afternoon. She checked John for which way he would lean on the issue. He surprised her by remembering an anecdote from their conversation last night. From the stack of information they exchanged, John pulled out the threes.

"That's two faux pas in less than an hour, Alex. I'll expect the third by the end of dinner." They approached Misfit, a North Street bistro which served outstanding vegan cuisine. He opened the door to the restaurant and gave her a smug pat on the back as she entered. Alex was not pleased with his statement. It implied that he was in control of their romantic destiny, and she resented that he wouldn't use that gallantry of his to make her feel better. She decided to swing the dinner conversation to all business and close the door to her vulnerable side before John could enter. By the time they were escorted to a table, Alex was primed for a good discussion. They settled in and ordered promptly since Alex had to be across town by six. She went straight to the subject.

"When I began experiencing the Creator State I was startled by it. I couldn't find any psychological or scientific explanation for what I was going through. So I turned to resources on the unexplainable, and did some research into new age theories on energy. That's the closest thing I could compare it to; a kind of energy. I found an article on universal vibrations, and how they affected Earth. According to studies in the past few decades, strong energies have been traveling through our corner of the universe causing changes in our world. These energies supposedly seeped into our consciousness and allowed for a worldwide awareness of suffering, intolerance, environmental abuses, and human rights. But the catalysts for these energies were artists. The population found new ideas and inspiration through the 'breakout' artists of these decades: rock and roll, folk music, poetry, modern art, anything that expanded awareness of our surroundings and fellow man. It wasn't just history unfolding, there were universal forces at work, which allowed for positive changes to be implemented on Earth." Alex paused and John cocked his head to urge her to continue.

"The idea of a universal creativity was beautiful to me," she explained. "As I linked the events of the twentieth century, it made more and more sense. It was as if our creative batteries were given a jump start. Artists seemed to be a natural catalyst and transmitted the need for change through challenging songs, performances, stories, poetry, films, and creative action. A lot of artists didn't ponder the source of their work, considering it 'divine inspiration' or 'brilliance' or 'a good day,' so I wanted to dig deeper and find out what it is that makes us do what we do."

John leaned back, crossed his arms, and considered her point of view. His body language displayed a need for distance. Alex shifted in her seat and thought she may have lost John with the new-age talk. He didn't speak right away, so Alex persisted.

"This is what I'm proposing. If creative people are able to be affected or energized by a universal source, and then translate that energy into works of art which motivate the population to care about each other and the Earth they live on, then artists could be a catalyst for an original source of creation." She waited for John to understand the point she made to Lisa earlier in the week. He silently digested her words. She worried if there was some kind of mid-table filter scrambling her words as they passed to his ears. She pushed the point more blatantly.

"John, what I'm saying is this: if creative people can channel a passing universal energy, then why can't we channel the original creative energies? What if we are able to transmit a godlike source of creation?"

John noted her agitation and assured her. "Yes Alex, I get it. I'm just trying to fill in the blanks. People can't just unknowingly create something and then claim it's universally inspired. At least not on my side of the fence. That's the whole problem with new age issues. In the scientific world, we have to see proof. Everything else is religion to me, and doesn't bear any value." John recognized his professional persona taking over, and repressed its hold on him. For years he had alienated others when the subject turned to science and allowed curt responses and a self-righteous tone to dominate his communication. He vowed to change, and exercised his commitment to it by apologizing. "I don't want you to think that I'm shutting you down. I find your imagination fascinating, and your desire for answers is something we both share. Let me change my perspective for the moment, and disregard all of my instinctual pessimism." He faked a cleansing breath and put on his best open-minded smile. "Okay. How does this relate to your Creator State?"

Alex wondered if she was wasting her time on John. Apparently it was a stretch for him to tolerate her art-speak. She didn't want to be perceived as a flaky creative type. She knew there was no denying the reality of her recent incidents on stage, and wanted an explanation for what was happening to her. If he could provide a few morsels to point her in the right direction, she would be satisfied. Alex looked directly into his eyes and made sure he heard her correctly. "Let's argue for the moment that creativity is an energy which goes unnoticed. Unseen, unheard, something intangible that makes us pick up a pencil and draw, write, or interpret life in some way. That drive must exist within us in order for us to utilize it. We use some kind of creative force buried within our cells. Then along comes a vast streak of energy, flying through the universe and cutting the corner of our milky way, filtering into our consciousness. Whether it's intentional or not, whether there's conscious source for this energy, we don't know yet. The everyday man and woman go to their jobs, take care of their kids, make dinner, the regular schedule. But the creative people start making waves: writing books and poems, whipping people into a frenzy with song, motivating people with rhythm and words, painting the world with new vision, making films, and performing plays that display a need for change."

She saw him follow her line of thought. "So the everyday folks start listening, opening up their own lives to the messages around them, and start taking action. Over the course of a few decades, these vibrations start motivating humans to be more aware of themselves, their neighbors, the environment, and the world population. While these energies travel past Earth, people try to make things better, try to understand each other." Alex was interrupted by the waiter, who delivered their dinner and made a showy display of the meal. They accepted his descriptions with flashes of thanks, impatient to get back to the conversation. He finally departed, and John led with a question.

"If all of these wonderful energies are flying around, then how do you explain the violence and political chaos in the world? This doesn't seem like positive change to me." John wore the smug look he kept for conversations like this; a look that Alex disliked.

"I'm going to have to default to the new age theories for a moment, if I may." Alex realized his high and mighty tone was rubbing off on her. She shook it off by removing her jacket, which revealed her lacy black camisole. It made her feel less stodgy to have her skin exposed. "It's going to take time, John, to produce the kind of positive changes that the world needs to recover from the destructive behavior of our ancestors. These energies were delivered across the universe to change the destructive path that our societies were taking. We were going to destroy ourselves and our Earth. The predictions of world annihilation have now been softened to the bad weather, political unrest and suffering that we currently encounter. It could have been much, much worse. But the transmission of positive energies has rescued us from this end." Alex stopped talking and let John absorb what she said. They ate in silence. He weighed the lightest way to disagree with her. His need to express himself sat in him like lead. Finally, he raised his eyes and looked ready to speak.

"Okay, the brown rice and kale I recognize, but what's the orange stuff?"

Alex quelled her frustration with his response and accepted his need to interject a few friendly comments into their dining experience. She answered politely.

"It's summer squash blended with tofu," she replied. "You're not a vegetarian, are you?"

John raised his eyebrows and laughed. "No, I'm not. But this stuff is not bad. I had no idea they made veggies taste like actual food."

Alex enjoyed the little break from their debate. "It is actual food! You ordered the macro plate, that's as real as it gets."

"Macro means big, and I was hungry, so I thought it was the best choice."

She leaned in to him. "Why did you choose this place if you're not a vegetarian?"

"Because you told me you were a vegetarian, last night at the lake." He grinned. "Did you ever notice that vegetarians tell people about their diet choice, but meat-eaters never announce, 'I am a meat-eater.' Why is that?"

She smirked. "Maybe it's not something you're proud of. There's not much point in announcing that you're mindlessly following the same diet as millions of others, throwing the world food supply off balance, needlessly supporting the slaughter of billions of animals each year so you can eat their steroid and disease-filled flesh, now is there?"

He gave her a victory. "Point taken." He raised a forkful of squash and toasted. "To the orange stuff!" She clinked forks with him and he gulped down the mouthful. He returned to their discussion. "Is that what it's all about for you, Alex? Saving the world?"

"What else is there?" She defended, then she relaxed."I should speak for myself only. For me, yeah, I want to help out the global picture as much as I can. I can't see myself settling into mediocrity." She paused. "I'm sorry, let me rephrase that. I can't see myself getting married, having kids, and doing shows until I'm replaced by a younger version of me. That long treadmill hike which leaves a lot of people feeling satisfied just doesn't work for me. So why shouldn't I try and solve a few problems in my time here?" Alex wondered what made John get up in the morning, or stay up all night. He read her face and offered his own take.

"Alex, I've been going through some changes of my own in the last few months. I'd like to say, 'I used to be a stuffy closed-minded analytical geek,' but I haven't shaken those stereotypes yet. I barely know what I'm doing these days. Teaching is tedious and my sideline research has stalled completely, so I started changing the things I could easily control. I got a new haircut, bought some new clothes, and started working out in an attempt to revise myself. But my reflection is still in the mirror; I'm still John staring at myself and wanting something amazing to happen."

He stopped and thought he was being too sensitive for a Saturday afternoon, but he saw a look in Alex's eyes. It was the same look he gave her at the lake last night. It was acceptance, and he welcomed the reciprocation. "I have to admit, in my search for some fresh air to blow the cobwebs out of my brain, I did wander to the new age section of the library. I thought I might stumble across something that would either point me in a new direction, or send me running back to my own corner with gratitude. A few of the books mentioned Web sites to visit, so I went to the computers to check them out."

Alex shrugged her shoulders. "So what happened?"

"I ran into Thomas." He smiled sarcastically and realized the chance meeting had ultimately brought him to Alex. "So there's a little universal energy in play right there, eh?" Alex returned to her food and gave him a comedic told-you-so look. John rolled his eyes at the performance, and they began to eat again.

The atmosphere started to mimic their late-night talk by the lake. Alex recognized the familiar dating dynamic; the challenge of demonstrating oneself as unique. But the conversation always cycled back to common ground to make both parties feel accepted. She appreciated John's quest to find himself. She knew he would loosen up if she teased him a little. "So are you going to counterpoint my earlier statements or what, science boy?"

John finished the last of his colorful meal and prepared for a long rebuttal to Alex's assertion. He pushed the plate aside, wiped his mouth with his napkin, and sat with hands clasped, ready to speak. Alex gave him her complete attention and slid her unfinished dinner to the edge of the table.

"I know there are a lot of things science cannot explain," he began. "What I like about science is that it gets revised as new discoveries are made. We correct ourselves. What seems right today may be unveiled as wrong in the future, and science is always open to the new. It allows me to propose a theory and pursue the facts, then say, 'Wow was I wrong!' later on."

Alex was anxious for him to get to the point. She had to dart for the show soon. "So why not take my proposal to heart, and prove it later? If it's wrong, I'll apologize."

John tiptoed to his point. "Alex, you're talking about unseen God-like sources. When it comes to God, there is no revision. Faith sells itself as above human understanding. Religion sets its principals in stone, and rejects everything that challenges it. You can't propose an explanation for creation without it turning into a religious discussion. Especially if you're talking about how the universe works. Anything outside of gases exploding and stars slamming into each other is religion. You're talking about a knowledgeable, conscious source. That's religion."

Alex struggled to validate her point. "I don't think I'm saying what you think I'm saying. Yes, I'm seeking a consciousness, I'll give you that, but it's more than just one conscious source. I think there is a universal substance of creation that tries, and succeeds, in maintaining its existence. I see it demonstrated in nature, in the expansion of the universe, in the complexity of humankind, and in the irrepressible quality of love. It's the desire of our universe for beauty and love to be present." Alex carefully circled back to his objection. "Religion eliminates possibility. It's self-righteous. The Creator State might let us see that everything is within our power. If we are made of the same substance as the universe, then we should be able to manifest anything that the universe can. If the energies of the universe whisper to us and we translate them into our reality, then we can do the opposite and whisper to the universe, because we are speaking the same language. Do you follow?"

He did, and tied the loose ends together. "So the experiences you have on stage, how does that fit in? Is this still residue energy from the sixties or …"

"If creativity is a response to a universal demand for creation, then we must be sympathetic to the source. Part of that source must exist within us. New energies wouldn't motivate us unless part of ourselves resonated with the same material, the same essence. When we produce a creation that seems guided by an unseen force, the true artist within us is activated; the ultimate artist which is the universal creative energy. We are tapping into the collective creative energy that exists in the universe. All of us contain the God we've been searching for. Artists just happen to have a better relationship with their creative skills, enabling us to channel creative brilliance."

John was intrigued. "Nature always aims in the direction of producing more of its own kind, strengthening the need for self-preservation. Hmph. Why wouldn't the universe try to grow some more company, some fellow creators? Maybe evolution is guiding us toward becoming our own source of creation. It's possible, but I'm not sure it's probable."

Alex smiled. "Oh ye of little faith."

They laughed lightly at their deductions and gazed at each other. Alex broke the spell and checked her cell phone for the time, then looked to him apologetically. He reached for his wallet and waved to the waiter for the check.

"I'm so glad you wanted to see me today, Alex. Last night seemed surreal for some reason. It was a long night for both of us. I hope I wasn't too impatient in calling you for a date today." John smiled broadly at his direct use of the term. He wanted her to know that they would be more than just buddies, if she was willing.

Alex recognized his subtle innuendo and grinned at him. "You just stole my three."

John raised his hands in surrender. "Maybe you're right. Maybe I have met my match." He bid her a good closing night and attempted to hide his desire to see her later on. He knew he would appear needy if he asked what they were doing after the show.

Alex noticed his struggle and contemplated the consequences of asking him to the closing night gathering. She knew her friends aspired to be open creative types, eager to experience new people and new ideas. Yet the circle hadn't provided any evidence of an open door policy. They were a tight group, and any visitors were treated as such: visitors. No one could enter the group unless they received a nod of approval from the collective. The circle would be polite, but they wouldn't allow entry without a lengthy initiation. One of the unspoken guidelines was to honor the sanctity of the closing night ritual. There would be a good deal of alcohol and other substances abused in celebration for a job well done. Tales of mishaps and perfect moments from the duration of the show would be told. Promises of future collaborations. Reflections on the long history of the Circle's endeavors. An outsider could visit, but the conversation set them at a distance. John would feel completely out of his element in the context of closing night, and that's precisely why she asked him to attend.

"If you don't have any plans, why don't you come to the show, and hang out with us afterward? Closing night is always a blast."

He was flattered that she was eager to see him again. "Well, I already saw the show last night."

Alex flinched at his rejection. "Haven't you ever seen a show twice?"

He scanned his memory. "No, I guess not. Why, is it different every night?"

"Yes! Especially on closing night. It's electrical. Everyone gives it one last kabang before the curtain comes down. It's magical. You can't get fired, so nothing is off limits." Alex realized her own enthusiasm got in the way of her perspective. John was not a theater person, and wouldn't want to sit through two hours of *Dylana* for the second night in a row. She laughed at herself and knew she encouraged him to attend for her own benefit. She offered him a solution.

"You don't have to see the show again, but maybe you could join us after." As the words left her mouth, she changed her mind about torturing him with the group's behavior. She hoped he would bail on the whole night. It wasn't his crowd, but it was definitely hers, and she wanted to partake in the post-show traditions without worrying about John's presence. She waited for him to decide the fate of the evening.

"I think I'll pass on tonight. You should celebrate with your friends and not have to worry about entertaining me." John hoped she would sway him to come, but Alex took his decision as final.

"Okay, you're probably right," she affirmed. "But let's get together soon. I really enjoy talking with you. Your unsympathetic ear is a good filter for my Creator State ideas."

John was disappointed by the response, but wrote it off. They exited Misfit and parted after a brief kiss and promises to call one another. Alex sped for the L train, anxious to begin her closing night. She glanced back at John, who had his arm outstretched to the approaching cabs. He turned it into a wave when she looked at him, and she felt a heart string tug in his direction. She waved back and whispered. "Oh Alex, be careful with this one."

He appeared to mirror the same response to himself, and she quickly turned away. She jogged up the stairs to catch the approaching train. She spoke aloud, "Shake him, girl. You got a show to do," and shivered her body to the command. It worked momentarily, and she boarded the L with *Dylana* on her mind.

7

○ ○

The game of fame is one long round of Red Rover, Red Rover.
Completely dependent upon personal wills, the whims of the callers,
and cheaters in the chain. If joining the line across the yard is your
goal; run hard, try to break through near a friend, and be prepared
to move on to gentler games if you keep getting thrown back.

—The Magic Mobile

Alex paused at the Circle Rep stage door and contemplated the mood that would greet her on the other side. When the production went well, closing nights were steeped in melancholia. *Dylana* was a great gathering of talents, and would be an emotional departure for many. Alex anticipated a wide range from the group: sadness from crew members who bonded with their coworkers, relief from the few who didn't get along, pride for accomplishing a good run, and thirst for the next venture. It was a stressful ordeal for the uncast. The old adage, "you're only as good as your next project," strikes with full impact during closing night gatherings. Except for Susan and the Brothers Slim, everyone would be in the summer show at the Andrews which relieved anxiety over when they would work again. Alex took a breath and entered the closing night milieu.

She tried to focus during her pre-show meditation and set aside thoughts of her whirlwind romance for a few hours. She felt eyes on her and snapped her lids open. An overly friendly Susan plopped down on the stage next to her and flattened herself into a stretch.

"Hey Alex, how about that hottie you left with last night?"

They hadn't exchanged words since she stormed out of the Andrews two nights ago. Susan's curiosity was notoriously unaffected by her own bad behavior. Alex knew this was the last night she would have to deal with her. Since Susan apparently wanted to spin it friendly, she conceded.

"Do you think he's hot?" Alex chimed back. "I can't tell. I'm no good with the rating system." She stifled a laugh at her girlishness. "He's got good hair though, doesn't he?"

Susan rolled her eyes playfully as she moved into another stretch. "Alex, I think he's that guy who used to go out with Christi from The Hysterics. Remember the guy she used to talk about? John, who talked about his work all the time? I'm sure that's him. Watch out for him, girl, he had like four girls going at the same time. That's why Christi called it off with him. He's a total player."

Alex found this new information unbelievable: how could her shy, brainy, just-learned-how-to-dress-myself guy be a player? Christi was another odd image to add to the overall picture of John. She was a leggy thing with flawless features and a drive to succeed that rivaled Susan's. She wondered why he seemed uncomfortable with the beautiful crowd at Zen if he was actually into that scene. Maybe he just wanted to add another actress to his collection. Her mind reeled as she tried to justify him, and Susan sensed Alex's turmoil.

"I hope I didn't say anything wrong. Just watch out for yourself, okay?" Susan switched to caring mode, and it annoyed Alex in light of the information she just revealed. Alex received enough of Susan's opinion for one lifetime, and ended their conversation. She jumped to her feet and attempted to cover her disappointment with John. "Thanks for the info. Let's have a great last show, eh?" She dashed to the dressing room.

Susan leered behind her and suspected Alex was upset by her new boyfriend's background. She continued to stretch, satisfied with her little victory. Thomas stormed through the house as his hair fluttered in the breeze of his own motion. Susan shouted a bright hello to him, which he returned with a thrust of his middle finger as he passed.

When Thomas reached the women's dressing room he paused at the door and knocked in an uncharacteristic display of respect for its occupants. Lisa came up behind him in the hall, mussed his long locks as she walked by, and mocked his sudden modesty. "Come on in, Thomas. All pussies are welcome." She pushed through the door, held it open for him, and announced his arrival. Thomas squirmed when he saw Alex getting into her corset in the mirror's reflection. A wardrobe intern tugged at her laces as she glanced up at him. He covered his trepidation and entered with vigor. He tossed his hair aside, raised one hand to quiet the cheering ladies, and raised the other hand which held several sheets of paper.

"I hold the fruits of my trip to the Library yesterday," Thomas proclaimed.

Lisa cackled, "I thought Alex was holding the fruits of your trip to the Library." She put her hand up for a high-five from Alex, but Alex scoffed at her instead. "Ouch," Lisa added, "Guess John's better than I thought."

Alex responded sarcastically. "I don't know, maybe we should ask Christi." She regretted it the second she allowed her irritation to surface. *Damn that Susan.*

Lisa picked up on the reference right away and put the ends together. "Holy crap, he's *that* guy? Wow, I heard he's a real player."

"Dammit, that's the second time someone has said that." Alex demanded, "You know what? Never mind about John. It's closing night, let's forget about John."

Thomas agreed. "Yeah, let's forget about John. Fuck John. Goddamn player sonofabitch John."

Lisa exclaimed, "There's your third *player!*" Alex threw a shoe at her.

Thomas waved the papers and started over. "Can you shut the hell up for a minute? I have e-mails from the Artist Exchange here."

Lisa sat at the makeup table and started to apply her face as Alex received the final pulls on her corset. Thomas thanked them for the quiet and read from the top page of the stack.

"Dear T-Power," he began, then explained, "That's my online name." Lisa giggled and got another shoe from Alex. He persisted. "I read your posting about the Creator State and I had to write. I am a musician, who has been having out-of-body type experiences on stage for the last several months which feel similar to what you describe. I'd like to hear more, please write me back."

Lisa and Alex exchanged a look of surprise. Thomas held his hand up to keep them from interrupting as he went to the second page.

"Dear T-Power." Thomas shot Lisa a glance to keep quiet. "I make Indie films here in Chicago and feel that sort of 'higher self' thing all the time, especially when I'm really dedicated. It's like I'm a vehicle for my art to drive around in. It comes in spurts, but has lasted for hours sometimes. I love that zone; it makes me feel like I'm not just some filmmaker, but a true artist."

Alex crossed to Thomas and read over his shoulder. He concealed his new crush as she stood next to him tightly laced up in her corset. He hesitated before he went to the next page, distracted by her cleavage which elegantly curved out of its pink ruffled container. She glanced up at him and caught his gaze.

"Stop staring at my tits and read another one, Thomas. How many letters are there?"

He fumbled with the pile, angry with getting caught. "They're not that impressive, Alex."

"The tits or the letters?" quipped Lisa.

"The tits," he grumbled. "If you don't want me to look at them, then cover 'em up."

Alex snatched the first letter playfully and jammed it into her corset to cover her chest. "May I remind you that you're in the ladies dressing room?"

Thomas frowned and went to the next letter. "Dear T-," he stopped short. "Blah blah blah ... I am a fellow thespian." He stopped again. "Man, I hate that term."

Lisa interjected. "Thespus always speaks highly of you."

"Yeah, tell him to stop calling me already." Thomas returned to the page. "I can't believe you posted this message. Just last week I had this major break-through during a monologue. I'm doing True West."

Lisa interrupted. "Who isn't?"

Thomas wrapped an arm around Lisa's back and planted his hand firmly over her mouth so he could continue. "I'm doing True West, which is a pretty intense show, and suddenly I felt this break in the ceiling, not literally, but as if someone unzipped the ceiling on my reality. My world opened up."

Alex moved in closer to review the letter. "Wow, that's the closest one yet."

Thomas dropped his hand from Lisa's mouth and read on. "There was a moment when I surrendered to it. I felt like I was floating around in the charac-ter. I think this is what you have described in your posting. Let me know if it is the same. I'd like to talk with you."

They nodded to each other and knew this was the same thing they experi-enced. Alex urged him to read another letter. Thomas shuffled the pile. "That's it for the out-of-body responses. Most of the others are the connected feeling. And then there are a few miscellaneous jokes and slams, but I expected that."

"Poor T-Power," Lisa mocked, then realized she went over the line and added an apology. Thomas was already unnerved from being in the same room with Alex. He lowered his papers in disgust.

"We know you're feeling left out, Lisa," he attacked. "But you might be expe-riencing the same thing someday. In the meantime, could you have a little respect for what's going on here, and keep the transparent witticisms to yourself?" He turned and stormed out the door.

"Geesh, sorry!" Lisa expected some sympathy from Alex. She received none, and Alex settled into putting on her makeup in silence. This irritated Lisa. "Now I get the silent treatment? On closing night? What is this about?"

"It's not about you, just chill for now. Let's get through this last show." Alex painted her face quickly, knowing Susan would come back at any moment. With that thought, Susan entered, busied herself, and avoided Alex's gaze. Alex took the high ground and tried to lighten the atmosphere in the tiny room. "We gonna rock this house tonight or what!?"

Lisa joined in. "Let the games begin!"

Susan cheered and the mood of the room transformed to celebration. She produced a bottle of champagne, which she flamboyantly placed on the makeup table. "A little something to look forward to after our last hurrah. For all of our hard work, and because this may be our last show together." Alex and Lisa turned to her in shock. Susan confirmed. "I'm moving to New York at the end of the month."

The girls jumped to their feet and embraced her with congratulations. Peter entered the room and watched with pleasure as the trio excitedly hugged each other. He shouted over their joy. "So this is what really goes on in the ladies dressing room. Yeah, baby!" They quieted a bit and he added, "Don't stop on my account. Please, don't stop!"

Lisa skipped over to him. "Susan's finally moving to New York!" She let him see that what she really meant was *thank goodness she's finally leaving.* Peter reached out a hand to congratulate Susan.

"Well done. Have anything lined up?" Peter saw from her reaction that she didn't, so he added quickly, "Oh, what the hell does that matter. You'll find a few agents in no time and blow them all away." He gave a look to Lisa and Alex and let them see his real intention. Lisa darted to her seat at the makeup table to stifle a giggle.

Susan appreciated his encouragement and shook his hand firmly. "Thanks, Peter." She looked around at them. "I think I'm gonna miss you guys."

After a beat of silence, Alex covered their lack of reciprocation and mimed a raised glass. "To the last show together! May we kick ass and have fun."

"To the last show!" They offered a pantomimed toast. They clinked invisible glasses, drank, and tossed the glasses over their shoulders. This nonsense stopped when the Stage Manager called fifteen minutes to places, which scattered everyone to get ready for the show.

The final performance of *Dylana* was a memorable one for both audience and performers. A full house added to the excitement. Last-minute arrivals sat on folding chairs which lined the back wall. Standing-room-only patrons stuffed themselves into the corners. The actors knew they had one last shot to be immortalized in the memories of all present. The crew attempted perfect cues and flawless scene changes as they seamlessly morphed their craft into the life of the play. The director witnessed the growth of his creation, as if observing his child at graduation. Opening night was nerves and crossed fingers. Closing night had a pleasure in it: one last shining attempt to achieve perfection.

During the performance a few dynamics were hidden from the audience. Susan was on her way out, Lisa and Peter fell in love, and Thomas denied any display of affection toward Alex in order to disguise his real feelings. The Brothers hammed it up and knew they wouldn't receive retribution, and Alex suppressed her disappointment with John and tried to get to the Creator State. The audience detected none of this, but the backstage stories would have easily entertained them as much as the show.

Alex and Thomas typically watched each other's second half monologues. Given the heights they reached with this piece, Alex knew closing night would be a knock-their-socks-off night. Relentless fun for the actors, and marvelous to watch. Partway through Act Two, Alex encountered her first spark of the Creator State. She allowed Dylana to be fully present, and the thrill of the State lifted her. As her monologue came to a close, she felt a rush of joy which gave her goose bumps. Afterwards, she squatted stage left to enjoy Thomas' last incarnation as her hateful husband. When the scene began, she noticed Thomas was distracted by her presence in the wings. After a few peripheral glances from him, she decided to leave and not impose on the last scene. She disappeared into the black of backstage and returned to the dressing room.

Susan sat at the makeup table and Alex joined her. They chatted at each other in the mirror and congratulated themselves on a job well done. Susan felt isolated since she announced her departure. While they had a private moment, she apologized to Alex for her comments about John. "I'm sure he's not always a cad. If you really like him, just be careful."

Alex was willing to bury the hatchet for the evening and cited Susan's uncharacteristic kindness as a sign of regret. She wanted to downgrade her attraction to John and say he was "just a friend," but she couldn't critique him just yet. Everyone deserved a second chance in Alex's world, and that included Susan. She tentatively inquired about her reaction to the State. "Why did you reject our experiences so quickly? We barely had a chance to explain and you were out the door."

"I don't need an explanation," she snapped, then put her bitchy tone in check. "Sorry. You know I'm conservative. I think artsy types who ramble on about lofty meaning-of-art theories are all losers in the long run. I think successful performers are the ones who try to get to the top as quickly as possible. I don't want to be held back by talking about *why* we perform. I just want to win the game as quickly as I can. I'm twenty-six, I'm already old in Hollywood. I think New York is my last shot."

"Last shot at what?"

"At being famous! Why the hell else would anyone get into this business?" Susan saw Alex's reaction. "Don't tell me you don't want it, because I'll know you're lying to me. Everybody wants fame, that's the whole goal of this absurd profession!"

Alex held her tongue. There were two camps in the theater world. Susan was part of the stairway-to-fame camp, and Alex was a card-carrying member of the do-it-for-the-art camp. The fact that Susan disregarded the art campers was another of her myopic attributes which Alex despised. She decided to keep the peace, let Susan have her opinion, and voice her view on the topic.

"Susan, people choose to do things for different reasons." Alex spoke calmly to assure her point was being conveyed. "Everyone is not the same, and there's a danger in presuming that everyone thinks the way you do. Everyone chooses their path for different reasons. It is a free country, despite the current leadership's direction."

Susan put her hands over her ears. "No politics tonight, please." She dropped her hands to her lap. "I think that artists want to gain attention. I think you can whittle down any excuse to that basic necessity."

Susan seemed so self-satisfied with her statement that Alex found it difficult to argue with her. Alex settled for being honest. "Your path is going to take you where you want to be, Susan. I'm sure you'll be successful." She leaned on the makeup table and looked directly at Susan, who avoided her eyes during their conversation in the mirror. "For myself, I see a different path. The changes in my life are pointing me in a different direction. Perhaps there's more to my theater work than performing. The things I am experiencing are foreign to me. So I can do one of two things. I can either chose to ignore them because I want a 'normal' path that may lead to starring in bigger productions and, maybe someday, a certain level of fame. Or I can follow a different trail that may lead to something extraordinary, or something new, or, hell, maybe something completely boring and useless. But at least I will have tried, you know?"

Susan lowered her head. "I think you're wasting your time, Alex. I think you're going to wake up one day and regret not trying to be famous."

Alex sighed with frustration and dropped the subject for the betterment of the evening. "Hey, it's almost the end of Thomas' scene. Where's that hooch?"

Susan retrieved the champagne from the mini fridge and launched the cork into the wardrobe rack. She raised the frothing bottle and announced with a contemptuous tone, "To the death of *Dylana!*" She took a foamy swig and handed it to Alex, who drank as well. By the time they had a few gulps down, applause trickled through the backstage speaker. They set the bottle down, shook the sticky liquid from their hands, giggled through a last look in the mirror, and darted toward the stage for the final curtain call.

One by one the cast entered and took a bow. They received a loud ovation, and the crowd rose to their feet for them. Thomas grabbed Alex's hand for their separate bow as the leading roles. He gave her a perplexed look because her hand was tacky with champagne. She leaned her lips toward his face and he froze. She playfully blew the long wave of hair out of his eyes before they turned and bowed together. They were delighted by the enthusiastic audience. Alex glowed in the bravos and extra applause, and turned a quick look to Susan as if to say, "Maybe the fame isn't so bad after all." The cast clasped hands for a final dip together, then exited with a flourish. The shower of applause dwindled to a sprinkle as they left the stage.

Backstage, in a flurry of flying costume pieces, the cast bid joyous farewells to their restraining corsets and period shoes. The cast and crew gathered in the ladies dressing room to finish off the champagne. They crushed into the tiny space half-dressed and delirious with accomplishment. The bottle was passed around, accompanied by congratulatory hugs and kisses. Thomas squirmed through the crowd and arrived at Alex for an embrace. She clinched him over the arms with a powerful grip. Before he knew what she was up to, Lisa aided her efforts and grabbed him from behind.

Peter held up a pair of scissors and yelled a quote from the play. "Remove the abomination!" The collected bunch cheered as Thomas realized what was going on. Peter grabbed Thomas' lengthy bangs with one hand and chopped them off with the other. Thomas' eyebrows lifted comically in their new forehead real estate. The crowd cheered again and the girls released him. He took advantage of Alex's proximity and gave her a peck on the lips. She grinned at him and turned to the gathering.

"Hey, listen up!" Alex waited for them to quiet. "This was a superb cast and we deserve a superb night together." Everyone hoorayed. "Our dear Susan has decided to follow her dream and move to New York." They hoorayed a second time, though it sounded more like joy for her departure. "So rather than go to Jimmy's like we always do, how about we join the closing night party at the Andrews and make it double trouble over there, eh?" Emphatic hoots and cheers answered and they all prepared to abandon Circle Rep.

As the actors hurriedly scrubbed off their makeup and tossed costume pieces to the laundry baskets, the crew scuttled around and tried to control the bedlam. While the wardrobe crew tamed the beast backstage, the deck crew cleared props and furniture on stage. The actors knew it was just a matter of minutes before Phil the prop master would find his grandmother's teapot stuffed with marijuana butts. They raced to make a clean getaway before it was discovered. Alex tiptoed to the stage to check on Phil's progress, and saw him approach the precious item. He beamed confidence and thought his teapot had survived the wrath of Thomas. With a self-serving swagger he picked the teapot up. He was about to remove the lid when Alex gasped and dashed to Thomas, who was exiting the men's dressing room. She grabbed him by the arm and dragged him towards the door. Thomas was about to question her actions when they heard a screech rise from the stage.

"Son of a *bitch*!" The phrase echoed through the house and backstage. It was unmistakably Phil, witnessing the final revenge of Thomas within his grandmother's antique.

Thomas ran with Alex as they slammed out the back door into the alley, with the rest of the cast right behind them. They hustled out to the street and down the block before they slowed down. Peter huffed and gasped for breath as he searched for a cigarette in his jacket. Thomas handed him one and they lit up together as they recovered from the short jog. Susan looked at them with disgust and rolled her eyes as she turned away. She caught up to the Brothers Slim, locked arms with them, and lead the group northward like a baton girl with flagpole bookends. Peter admitted to the group who marched behind that he would miss Susan's misguided arrogance. They all agreed.

When they arrived at the Andrews, the post-show celebration was well under way. Live music rumbled from behind the doors, generated by a gathering of Lucas' friends who lent their talents for the night. The Circle Rep crowd spilled into the lobby where Chris greeted them. His elegance seemed out of place at this hour. He endured a standing-room-only rush that night, and downed a few drinks afterward, but remained impeccably styled and pressed to his credit. Not one midnight lock or winsome word was out of place. He generously welcomed the Circle Rep collective to the party. Susan took advantage of one of her last nights in town and went straight to work on Chris. She playfully grabbed him by the arm and demanded a personal tour of the theater. He conceded politely and they strolled into the house. Lisa attempted to imitate her and grabbed Peter's arm flirtatiously, but he wanted to check out the live music. He lumbered into the house as Lisa clumsily trailed along. Alex gave the Brothers and Thomas an "after you" flourish at the door, and they entered the scene.

Approximately forty people had assembled inside, spread throughout the house in niches of conversation. One group clumped in front of the stage and enjoyed the band's efforts to entertain the entertainers. The band was an ethno-techno collective that blended modern and tribal rhythms. They provided a peaceful vibe; laid-back and good for the soul. Lucas beamed a hello to Alex from the stage, proud to have his musician friends winning the theater crowd. He was caught up in the music for the evening, and Alex was grateful for his distraction.

Joseph transformed the space for the evening and placed large cream candles throughout the house which glowed with a golden light. A sweet and filmy cloud of incense stretched above the gathering in horizontal wisps. He lit the stained glass windows which bordered the stage proscenium. It was an honor typically reserved for intermission, as the bulbs were in a difficult spot to replace. They framed the event perfectly, giving it a sacred and mystical allure.

At the back of the house, a folding table displayed a wide assortment of libations. Joseph resided behind it as barkeep, and he motioned Alex and the boys over for a drink. The Brothers reviewed the bottles and discussed concoctions, while Alex tried to ease the bitterness between Joseph and Thomas for the night. She reintroduced them and they shook hands for her sake. Joseph appeared less irritated than Thomas, who wanted to leave the vicinity quickly. After a few customary exchanges, Joseph turned his attention to the Brothers. They inquired about a batch of martinis, so Joseph offered them a shaker and jar of olives. Thomas rolled his eyes at Alex and whispered a crack about Joseph's pretentiously stocked bar. She warned him with a look to keep the peace tonight, and he wandered away to a bench near the back of the theater. Alex surveyed the scene and smiled at Joseph. He acknowledged his talents as a host.

"Cool, isn't it?" He boasted. "This is the last show of the regular season, and with David gone, I figured a little extra fanfare wouldn't hurt."

Alex nodded. He would need her approval in the future for this kind of display. She let it slide and pointed to the musicians. "They're really good, are they Lucas' friends?" She detected a glint in Joseph's eye. Apparently Lucas was the kind to kiss and tell. Fortunately the Brothers interrupted and asked for cocktail glasses. Joseph gave Alex a glance and discarded the topic of Lucas, but she knew it might breach later on. She took advantage of the distraction and scurried to join Thomas in the back bench.

Peter parked himself at the end of the stage, thoroughly engrossed in the music. Lisa abandoned him, unwilling to remain quiet at his request, and joined the Circle Rep bunch in the back rows. A few crew members arrived and were motioned over to the group. The Brothers served everyone a round of martinis and they began the official closing night service for *Dylana*.

As the group fired stories back and forth of the show's highs and lows, Alex let her eyes wander through the event. She noted there were only three women present, the three from Circle Rep. David was gone, but the remnants of his chauvinism lingered. A season of all-male casts and crews surrounded them, and not one of them had brought a female friend or significant other. She silently hoped more women would be around during her management. As the hypnotic beat cycled through the space, Alex felt sentimental about their little gathering. The incense, the music, and the week's events took their toll and gave her a glazed look. Thomas noticed and tugged at her sleeve to snap her out of it. "Hey," he whispered, "You okay?"

Alex wanted to step away from the *Dylana* storytellers, so they slipped out without disturbing the anecdotes. She climbed the loft stairs with Thomas following close behind. She stopped short when they reached the top and motioned for him to get out of sight. When Thomas lifted his head for a peek, he spied Chris and Susan at the back of the darkened loft. Susan leaned on Chris and tested the Caldwell waters for a warm, meaningless dip. Thomas mouthed an "ouch" to Alex, then elected to save the gentle House Manager from further manipulation. He grabbed Alex and lifted her beside him, walking freshly into the loft on a fabricated tour, and made bawdy small talk to interrupt the tryst.

Susan whirled at their entrance and gasped nervously, caught in the act. She hurriedly excused herself and trotted down the stairs. Chris mouthed a "thank you" to them and monitored Susan's progress from behind the loft railing. He waited for a chance to make a clean getaway. It arrived when Susan joined the band groupies at the front of the house. Chris saluted Alex and Thomas goodnight and slipped out unnoticed. Heroism swelled within Thomas, and he toasted his good work with the rest of his martini. He looked at his empty glass and motioned for Alex to drink up, which she obeyed. She examined the empty cups, tiptoed back to the office door, and slipped out of Thomas' sight. After a moment she reappeared with a bottle of vodka and padded back to a pleased Thomas.

"I found this in the bookshelf this week. I can replace it on Monday." She worked the bottle open and poured three fingers measure into each of their glasses. As she replaced the cap, she noticed him examine the volume in his glass. She justified, "Gotta keep those cab drivers in business."

Thomas concurred. "To the Hellcabs!" He sipped and tried not to embarrass himself in front of her. Alex jumped onto the tech table and invited him to join her. He did, and they surveyed the crowd below as they drank. She apologized for the all-male crowd. "Sorry there aren't any ladies present to make it more interesting for you." Thomas grunted disinterest.

As they sat side by side, Thomas repressed every romantic signal that Alex would pick up on. They were both accomplished interpreters of human nature, and his paranoia grew that she would recognize his new love for her. He bit back the urge to blurt it out, and tried to see her as he had the day before. He repeated in his head, *It's only Alex. It's just my old buddy Alex.* When she turned the conversation to the Creator State, Thomas gripped his glass firmly and took a long gulp of his drink. His body shivered as the vodka scorched the back of his throat.

Alex sighed, "I feel strange."

"You are strange," he answered flatly.

She punched him lightly in the arm, and his drink sloshed onto his hand. He shook it dry, toasted Hellcab a second time, and tossed back another mouthful. No shivers followed and Alex continued.

"I'm serious. I'm feeling exposed since I let my little secret out. I'm wondering if I spoke too soon. I'm not sure what this thing is yet."

Thomas looked to his glass. "I'm not sure what it is either." He saw that she was going to counter, and he held a hand up. "Wait, just hear me. You have to admit that the things you talk about are a bit hard to digest sometimes. Hell, most of the time." She moved to interrupt again, and he gave her another hand to remain quiet. "Personally, I have to know if there is more to my art than entertainment. That would make the whole thing seem worthwhile. If I could add something to the big picture, everything wouldn't feel so pointless. I want to reach people. Do you know what I mean?" He saw that she did. "I think you're feeling exposed because your *Mobile* is catching on, and now you're going to have to talk about the Creator State. Both topics are off-the-scale weird for most, not exactly casual conversation. Maybe the uneasiness you feel is the possibility of being labeled 'strange'?"

Alex sobered. "No, I'm fearful that I won't find more people experiencing this. It'll be a lonely world for me without the companionship of performers. It's bad enough with the clairaudience, but if the Creator State doesn't find company, then I'm just a deluded freak."

Thomas set his drink down. "Everyone is a freak to somebody. You're an artist. If you have a shot at making your artistic interpretation of the world mean something, then please, as a fellow freak, I'm begging you, please do it."

She stared at the layer of incense lingering over the crowd below. "I have visions like this during the State." Thomas looked through the cloud as she spoke. "The scene dissipates, like looking through that smoke below us. Only it feels clean and energized. I can still see what my eyes see, but there's another layer around everything, as if the objects and people around me are being energized." She checked Thomas' face for permission to continue, and saw he was paying attention. There was a deep look in his eyes she hadn't seen before, and she interpreted it as a longing to know more about the Creator State. She unknowingly spoke to his secret desire. "It feels so natural."

Thomas caught himself before his gaze could be examined and looked to his drink. It did feel natural to hang out with Alex after another show had ended. He pondered how many times they had done this in the past; how many times he sat next to her and felt nothing but companionship. The new emotion burned a hole in his stomach. He didn't want to ruin their friendship, but there weren't many love interests crossing Thomas' path. And it was awful timing. If he approached her now, there were factors outside of his control that would influence her reaction. Her new job at masculine central, the State, and her new involvement with John would block any ridiculous pass Thomas could conjure. The idea of professing his love seemed absurd, not to mention the competition involved. Suddenly he wanted to torture himself and ask her about John. He kept his voice from sounding too curious. "What did John have to say about all of this? When we talked on Friday he was spouting a lot of physics. But maybe he was just trying to impress me with his knowledge. What did you guys talk about?" He lightheartedly ribbed her. "Maybe I should ask if there was any talking at all?"

She took offense, which made him shrink with shame. He apologized immediately, and she recovered just as quickly. "We just talked. We were coming to get you for dinner when you left us on the street."

His chest lightened. He pressed a little further and hoped John had disappointed her. "What does he have to say about the State?"

"Well, John thinks that any time you attempt to explain creation without a scientific base that you're talking about religion or faith in a higher power. But I countered with my thoughts on an energy residing in artists that contains the original source of creation." Alex kept her eyes away from Thomas. She was uncomfortable expressing her recent ideas to someone who knew her so well. He noticed her hesitation and urged her to loosen up. She appreciated it and went on. "There are times when my intuition feels so right to me, when every question within me is answered with yes." She looked to him. "The idea of the artist as a creator is my answer. It's all 'yes' in my head. Something about this subject is giving me peace."

The dialogue in Alex's eyes said much more than her words. Thomas witnessed her longing to find a purpose for her unusual symptoms; her fatigued soul seemed to be wearing her down. Between the voices, the insomnia and these new sensations, Alex struggled to keep herself together. He also saw sadness, or perhaps that was just his own sadness reflected back at him. When she looked away, he thought his suspicions were confirmed. She denied him access.

"From what I hear through the grapevine, John's kind of a prick," she prompted.

Thomas swirled the last of his vodka in his glass and offered no remorse. "Yeah, the ladies have nothing good to say about him. But I'm sure you can handle yourself." He downed the last of his drink and noticed Alex consider if she could handle John. He nudged her. "Hey, I've seen you go through dozens of guys in the last five years. You can handle a Don Juan. Just keep him at arm's length."

"There's something different about him. Part of me just wants to pump him for information, sleep with him and let him go. But something makes me think I'll regret not giving him an honest chance."

Thomas felt his stomach burn, then realized it was his heart that was on fire. He surrendered, remembering that love lost and returned was truer than love captured. He used her own words on her and quoted the *Magic Mobile*. "Love and art take risk. Failure at either one is inevitable from time to time, but taking the chance allows us to know true love and true art."

A smile of thanks lit her face. She hopped off the table and held him. He wrapped his big arms around her and hugged her tightly. He knew he was letting her go; his own risks would have to wait. He resigned to let the future play itself out as necessary. Their squeeze ended with the sudden silence of the band. Applause echoed across the space as the musicians filed off the stage for nicotine and beverages. Peter spotted Thomas up in the loft and motioned to him. He used a peace sign to the chest signal, which was Circle Rep code to step outside and smoke pot. Thomas signaled back and excused himself from Alex's company. She watched him descend the stairs and debated if she should join them for a change. She quickly discarded the thought, and stuck to her decision to remain clean. It was three years since she quit smoking tobacco, including the wacky kind, and she wasn't about to ruin her personal record on a whim. Lisa waved up at her excitedly and invited her to join the Andrews actors. A group of seven men surrounded Lisa and Susan, all of whom beckoned for Alex to come down. She poured herself another sip of vodka and started down the stairs.

As she approached her friends and their actor harem, she straightened for a strong introduction as the Manager of the Andrews. Lisa announced, "This is the girl who writes the *Magic Mobile!*" and Alex's spine softened again. Handshakes extended to her, as well as wolfish curiosity that seemed irreparable. Alex saved face and reintroduced herself as the new manager and the summer production's lead, which immediately altered the situation to her benefit. The men shifted to shop talk, and the few who had seen *Dylana* complimented her performance. Susan wanted the gentlemen's full attention, so she burst into the *Dylana* conversation.

"Hey Alex, that guy you're seeing isn't the same John we thought he was. Christi was dating a different guy altogether, so it looks like your boyfriend is okay after all!" Susan beamed as if genuinely happy for her friend's welfare, but Alex knew her aim was to mention a boyfriend. It didn't seem to ease the men's interest in Alex, but Susan managed to divert the topic to New York City within a few minutes. Alex was relieved by the latest tidbit on John. She absolved him of any wrongdoing and hoped he was as good as he appeared to be.

As the conversation dragged on, Alex's thoughts drifted to Sunday. She would have the whole day to herself, and began fantasizing about the leisurely activities she could indulge in. As her second drink began to take hold, familiar tones echoed through her head. *How can they call us gentle artists? We plunge into the depths of human emotion with each performance, and each time from a point of innocence. None but the strongest could survive it.*

Alex hushed the voice as Derek, a regular performer at the Andrews, approached her. Derek was an established actor who carried an air of soon-to-be-star with him at all times. An instant success from the moment he walked on stage two years ago, it was only a matter of time before his agent found him the right film and whisked him away to L.A. His deep voice resonated through the small gathering and allowed everyone to eavesdrop. His self-confident gait looked good on his six foot frame. His perfect teeth shined at her and stood out against his coffee and cream skin. "*Magic Mobile* Gal!" Derek opened. "I liked the rant on life imitates art yesterday."

Alex twitched with the thought of Derek listening in on the *Mobile*. She straightened to his presence, and silently chastised herself for doing so. She gleamed a winning smile right back at him. "Didn't know you were a *Magic Mobile* fan, Derek."

He exhibited his comfort in the space. He sat on the back of the bench above her and defiantly placed his feet on the seat below. Derek knew he was infallible at the Andrews, but he wanted to play amiable with the new manager. He wouldn't be in the next show; it was beneath him to work in the city during the summertime. He was the type to escape to a beautiful wine-country setting with a summer stock company, while the rest of them sweat it out in town. He expanded on his *Mobile* compliment.

"I try to call in at least once a week. I have to admit, the messages do give me a lift, but sometimes I have to call back to catch what you said. I may play a lot of intelligent men, but I can be a little slow on the take in real life." Derek laughed at his self-depreciation. Alex was unsure if he criticized the *Mobile* as too lofty, or admitted his own stupidity. She took his comment as a sign that he wanted to buddy up to her.

"Nice work in the last Andrews show, Derek. That final moment at the end of Act One, when you discovered the letters? That was brilliant."

He glowed with her compliment. "I can't believe you noticed. Thanks, that means a lot to me." He smiled again. "You're very perceptive aren't you. I'm glad to have you here at the Andrews."

Alex heard the ownership in Derek's statement, but she enjoyed being the newbie. It gave her perspective on the little planets that made up the theatrical universe of Chicago. Everyone had their own rulers, dramas, and difficulties, but they were all similar in structure. Alex reviewed the choices for Circle Rep King and Queen, and realized it was Thomas and herself. From Queen to pawn, she thought, and let a laugh escape her. Derek misinterpreted it as a reaction to his praise, so she explained. "Sorry, I was just thinking about the hierarchies we create in our theater companies. Everything seems so important when you're involved, but when you step away, it all seems irrelevant. One step out of the kingdom and it disappears."

Derek considered which way to go with his response. If he agreed with her, he might be perceived as a kiss-up to the new manager. If he disagreed, he might create tension where he didn't need it. He wasn't sure how to read her. He didn't know if Alex was accusing him of being King of the Andrews. Before he had the chance to decide, Alex assisted with a direct response.

"There's nothing wrong with enjoying your position, Derek. It's good to be King." She added a compliment to smooth things over. "And you deserve it, you've worked hard." She knew it was a fib, but it had the proper affect. Derek broke his perplexed look and revealed his sparkling choppers. He anxiously turned the subject.

"You're going to kick ass in the summer show. That role is perfect for you." He knew the summer show was the only opportunity for women to grace leading roles at the Andrews. Alex was not the submissive type, and gave him an honest viewpoint despite his kingly status.

"The Andrews is a great space that has been under not-so-great management. David has been chauvinistic for far too long. I intend to change that during my stay here. If you guys are expecting me to just show up, play my role, and avoid female businesspeople all summer long, then you're underestimating me. This blatant discrimination ends this summer."

Derek stiffened and bent his salon-shaped brows. "He doesn't discriminate. Look at me, I'm Latino, and there were two black guys in the fall show."

Alex realized that Derek only heard what he wanted to hear. She didn't want to fight with him. She chose a better topic which allowed him to put on his artist persona. "Let's drop it. Tell me about the end of Act One. How did you come to that moment? Was that directed to you?"

Derek answered cautiously and grew uncomfortable as Alex drove the conversation. "That moment kind of happened on its own. It was one of those third week rehearsals when you stop thinking about the director's needs and realize it's going to be your ass up there, so you'd better make it good?" Alex nodded; she knew that part of the process well. He explained. "I was trying to loosen up, and all of the sudden that impulse just came to me. I picked up the letter that I wasn't supposed to find until Act Two, and let it drop again on the desk. I could feel the whole room gasp, and I knew I was on to something. I'm not sure where that impulse came from, but it didn't feel like me, it really felt like my character. We ended the scene and the director had me keep it. He said it gave a whole new layer to the play, with my character holding a revelation in his hand, and then just setting it aside." Derek stopped talking and looked like he had more to say. "Alex, all those messages on the *Mobile* about a higher purpose for art, is there anything to that or is the *Mobile* just talk?"

"How do you mean?"

"Do you really think there's a higher purpose, or are the messages there to make yourself feel better about your position?"

"What position is that, Derek?" Alex sensed he meant the position of an actor who would never be a star, but she gave him the benefit of the doubt.

"I mean acting. It's a stupid-ass profession. We're unemployed every four months and don't make much when we work. I thought maybe the *Mobile* was your way of justifying your choice to perform." He opened up with a heart to heart question and requested a purpose for his whirlwind success. "I understand what you're preaching, Alex. I felt it during that rehearsal. I feel it when I let myself give in to my art." Derek glanced around to assure their privacy. "What I want to ask you is, do you think I'm sacrificing being a really good performer by following the easy street that my agents are presenting to me?" He was visibly agitated. "If I stay on the path they're paving for me, I'll be in L.A. any day now doing films. After that, what do I have to aspire to? More films? An Oscar nomination? An Oscar? An Oscar curse? What if I'm missing out on the real stuff, the real art?"

"Derek, a lot of artists would agree that 'I would like to thank the Academy' aren't the sweetest words to be spoken. But if you have the chance to express yourself to a broader audience, please do it."

Alex realized Thomas told her the same thing that night. Derek recovered his persona and finished his drink, which gave him a reason to exit. "Thanks, Alex. I should take the chance. Sorry for the rant. I'm gonna get a refill. Hey, take it easy on the guys this summer." He was done with playing chummy.

She smiled as he got up to leave. "Have a good summer." He moved back to Lisa's group. She found something offensive in Derek's talk of higher art versus the path to stardom. He knew he was going to make it big, but wanted to maintain the air of a sensitive artist. As he morphed back into King Derek, Alex saw him roll his eyes for the benefit of the guys in his clan, which received a laugh at her expense. Susan joined in on the joke and leaned heavily on the very drunk Andrews actor next to her. She flirted mercilessly with the poor fool who had won her attention. From a distance, it appeared that Lisa was the only one who defended Alex. She got in Derek's face until he apologized. Once the argument ended, Lisa left to find Peter. Derek rolled his eyes again, this time at Lisa's expense. Laughs spattered from the group, but Lisa didn't flinch at the abuse which echoed behind her. Alex looked back to Derek, who glanced her way. He gave her a shrug for 'no harm meant' and she returned it. She sighed at the exchange. Derek's inner artist couldn't redeem his behavior. He had become what his agents expected of him: the handsome leading man without conscience.

The air in the house grew dense; a combination of humidity, candle wax and incense. Alex wanted closure on closing night and got up to make her goodbye rounds. She scanned for Circle folk and saw Peter leading Thomas, Lucas, and two members of the band toward her. Knowing that they were all high, she sat down and waited to hear what suddenly brought them back inside. Peter threw himself in the bench in front of her and leaned over with a fiery look in his eye.

"Alex! This guy, Rashan, he's been to the Creator State. He describes it just like you do. He's ..." Peter stopped as Rashan approached. He was a thirty-something dread-locked musician with deep tan skin, and a flash of white teeth that rivaled Derek's. They all looked at each other for a second, then Rashan grinned at Alex.

"You that *Magic Mobile* woman?" Alex nodded, pleasantly surprised by his smooth Jamaican dialect. Rashan had an attractive confidence which accepted all creatures around him, and his energy was satisfyingly calm. He laughed too loud and took a breath. "Well now, this is gonna be some fun. I been feelin' the same thing you have, sistah. You leave your body on stage and feel like the world is inside of you, kind of takin' over?"

Alex straightened and smiled. "That's sort of what it's like. It's euphoric."

The man laughed again and worked his way through the better part of his high. The group giggled with him, unable to stop themselves. He repeated it to emphasize her term.

"Euphoric? Oh yeah sistah, it's euphoric! It's like seeing the true connection to the art Gods. Some say sound created light, so I feel I got a way through the front door already. You know what I'm talkin' about?" Rashan narrowed his smile and spoke softly. "I think it's the only way to enter heaven, through the art, into the arms of God. Artists got it right, we all got the way in. You hear what I'm saying, my friend?"

Alex couldn't process his question. Externally she heard his words, but in her head the voices picked up speed and increased in volume. There was a message in her head, a second message in the man before her, and a third message in the moment. Rashan noticed the worry in Alex's eyes and gave her a hug. He promised they would talk at a better time. His gesture was without agenda, and it saddened her to think of the rarity of it. Someone shouted across the room for the band to play again, so Rashan rose to return to the stage. He looked at Alex and offered some advice.

"You gonna find a lot of friends with this thing, sistah Alex. Don't be afraid of it; don't be afraid to guide people. We know where this thing is goin'." Rashan pointed to the heavens with both hands; a very biblical move in a very biblical space. He laughed as he joined the rest of the band. "Let's have us some magic!" The scattered groups cheered throughout the space. The band kicked in for the duration and the Circle Rep group danced in front of the stage.

Alex was lightened by the encounter with Rashan. She enjoyed the band until she felt the drag of sleeplessness upon her. She knew it was getting late, or rather, getting early, and she would have to be alert to walk home. She surveyed the scene for her friends. Peter was drunk and hypnotized by the band. Lisa was about to fall asleep on his shoulder. Susan won the affection of an Andrews actor and they actively made out in a corner of the church. The Brothers Slim played borrowed percussion instruments and enjoyed their last party in town before their summer stock engagement. Joseph cleared away most of the bar and tried to clean up quietly without rushing his guests. The Andrews actors formed a mob in the back of the house, and laughed like collegiates at a pep rally. Everyone else had dispersed, and Alex noted Thomas slipped out without a proper goodbye. Exhaustion wrenched through her bloodstream and she breathed deeply to awaken herself before the venture home. A sleepy gal on the streets was an easy target, and she wasn't up for unsolicited intervention tonight.

Joseph saw her prepare to exit, and waved her over to check in with him before she left. His attitude was reminiscent of his earlier cranky self. He reminded her of Monday's staff meeting, which was unnecessary since she was the one who had scheduled it. Then she realized they were within earshot of the Andrews group. Evidently Joseph was making a last attempt to show the boys who was really boss. With that endured, she wished them all goodnight, and headed home.

8

When was this seed planted? These ever-expanding vines overshadow all other forms of life, and make all else appear to be in darkness. When was it planted in our veins? Why does it force other things to grow at such a distance? The radius of creativity needs vast room to survive, and consumes everything which surrounds it.

—The Magic Mobile

Oppressive heat blanketed the city as the summer progressed. Alex raced the muggy sunrise each morning and sped down the lakefront path in the cooler moments prior to daybreak. Her first month at the Andrews provided many interesting opportunities. David gave her the freedom to take on more responsibility, so she coordinated additional daytime events and after-play discussions. Public relations took a turn for the better; suddenly the Andrews had a pleasant persona at the helm. Her work did not go unnoticed. When the summer show reviews came out, the local papers recognized her performance offstage as well as on.

The residual effects of management trickled into her Creator State work and sharpened her organizational skills. The Artist Exchange turned up several reports of State-like connected experiences. Many people wanted to explore these sensations in the name of art. Peter suggested they begin weekly meetings to investigate the Creator State. Alex agreed and posted a call to action on their Web site. The announcement read:

Dear Fellow Artists,

Several artists have acknowledged a new feeling surfacing in their performances. Some are finding a level where an expansive, out-of-body condition is achieved. We call this connected creativity "The Creator State." We seek a pur-

pose for these new occurrences. Perhaps art is more than just a creative outlet? If you have felt this recent change, please join us post-showtime on Tuesday evenings at 11:00 p.m. at the Andrews Theater to discuss these experiences in confidence.

All the best,
Alex Davis
The Artist Exchange

The posting supplied an immediate turnout at the Tuesday gatherings as artists surfaced from all over town. Throughout the summer, Alex's friends remained steadfast in their support of the Creator State. Thomas became a tireless coordinator and kept in constant contact with the members of their new collective. His private explorations into the State raised more questions than they answered, but he never lost enthusiasm. Desperation lingered in him, as if the State was his last opportunity to push himself beyond his own limitations.

The call for exploration also prompted a wave of e-mails which accused Alex of being audacious. She ignored the nasty correspondence, as the accusers never stepped inside the walls of the Andrews to confront her in person. However, she wrestled with her anxieties before the first Tuesday meeting. Addressing a room of high expectations made her nervous. She anticipated a sea of demanding faces blinking back at her. Surprisingly, the group hit it off immediately. Invisible threads of common purpose strung them together from the start. Rashan and Lucas brought their musician friends to the meetings, and they pulled in a few professional dancers who shared their experiences with connected art. Kona Trent, a brilliant pastel artist, joined the group in mid-July. Coincidentally, it turned out that Kona was responsible for the large praying mantis mural that Alex admired the month before. The same day Alex leapt over a mantis on the running path, and the day before she discovered the same creature slung around John's neck. Alex enjoyed Kona's down to earth presence, and asked her to lure a few painters to join the group. By the end of July, the Tuesday gatherings were well populated with artists from many different mediums, most of whom experienced the State's sense of enlightened bliss during their work.

Peter and Lisa grew into the couple they envisioned a "good couple" to be. They moved in together, which surprised their friends. Lisa struggled with reaching the State, but forgave Peter when he found it so easily. He was so overwhelmed with his first State experience that he wept afterward. He collapsed onto

Lisa's lap while the rest of them congratulated him. Peter would refer to the moment, with much dramatic emphasis, as the most significant of his creative career.

To assure everyone felt the Creator State as the group defined it, John recommended they explore each art form individually. He structured the experimental aspect of the evenings and had the group focus on a different medium every week. Each artist shared their methods for entering the State, as well as their experiences within it. The musicians had immediate success. Their rhythms created the trance-like feeling associated with the State and guided them to the consciousness desired. Rashan and Lucas led the group in musical explorations, while Alex and Thomas taught the acting experience. Painters, performance artists, musicians, actors, dancers, and filmmakers all filtered in each Tuesday to expand their knowledge of what they loved most: creativity. In the blessed space of the Andrews, where air conditioning provided a cool haven, the group fertilized the seeds of a new approach to art.

John insisted they produce some theories to pursue. He reviewed his textbooks and found the intellectual connection he sought. He dominated more than a few meetings with scientific possibilities for the group's experiences. He began with a study which showed how particles were constantly exchanged in our world; how matter was used and reused throughout the years. A human body could contain particles which had once been in their neighbor or someone halfway around the planet; it was all the same material. While the embodiment of similar molecules mildly supported a physical experience, it didn't explain their feelings of purposeful connection. Then John revisited his quantum physics studies and came across his notes on a unified plane called the "Zero Point Field."

The Field connected everything that had ever been, and everything that would ever be. It was a field of perpetual energy which flowed through everything in the universe and connected all living things past, present, and future. All realties, all memories, all consciousnesses, every being on Earth to the farthest reaches of the galaxy were connected by the Field. John delved into his Field research and begged the group to put their efforts on hold until he could clarify a connection, if any, to what they were experiencing. His requests were met with resistance, and the first sparks of conflict ignited between Alex and John.

Their personal relationship remained amiable, while their ideas butted heads on several occasions. John finally ceased his objections at the group meetings and doubled his research efforts in private. Alex appreciated his cooperation. She struck upon a link between John's findings and her aspirations for the State. She intuitively tied the feeling of the Creator State with the realities of the Field, and found a possible way to connect them. If they could manipulate the field of consciousness which joined all living things, they may be able to create a subtle shift in earthly reality. She imagined they had to work in the same way the Field worked: with an element of fearless, questionless authority. The Field could create anything desired, because it knew all, saw all, and was ever-present in the active moment. She proposed if artists could create with the same unwavering truth as the universe, they could utilize the same force to create change.

John objected to her unsubstantiated proposal and found fault with her intuitive approach. She persisted despite his objections. She described to the group what she wanted to prove: artists were naturally connected to creative energies which gave them unique access to the genesis of creation itself, a unified creative field. Surrender to the creative spirit brought the connection. In the moments of inspired art when they arrived at the Creator State, they could access a channel to transport higher consciousness.

With her hypothesis in place, Alex gave in to John's need for an organized approach. The group convened to discuss how they would investigate these new ideas. Several members voiced concern about confidentiality. If their ideas leaked out of the Andrews, involvement with such an eccentric collective might affect their ability to get hired. Within the sanctity of the meetings there was elitism, but outside of the gatherings the theories might be scorned, laughed at, or rejected as madness by the general public. Alex gave an impassioned address to the group about the risks and challenges of art, which convinced them to share their ideas with their fellow artists. With everyone's consent, Alex summarized their discoveries on the Artist Exchange site. She knew there would be retribution, but the summer activities empowered her to express herself. She posted their proposal on August 13 for all to examine, and dubbed it "The Creator State Project":

Dear Fellow Artists,

A collective of artisans met regularly for the last two months in an effort to find higher purposes for creativity. Our discussions have led us to propose the following:

- *Creative artists have a special bond to a universal creative energy which may enable artists with a unique connection to universal consciousness.*

- *This connection may allow for new ways to bring about positive change in the world. Art has done this on some level throughout history, but perhaps we can go further than we previously anticipated.*

- *The purpose of artists may be more influential than we have considered in the past.*

- *An artist's understanding of the creative process and ability to enter the Creator State may enable them with a unique ability to create change on our earthly plane.*

- *When an artist yields to the power of creation, they create with the same boundless energy as the universe itself.*

We hope to receive feedback from our fellow artists. Please post your responses on the Artist Exchange forum.

All the best,
Alex Davis
The Creator State Project

Alex released the missive with a cautious click of the mouse. She slid back in the library chair, grasped its oak arms, and reviewed her words. The group championed the last point as the most brilliant. It was also the most difficult to prove: *When an artist yields to the power of creation, they create with the same boundless energy as the universe itself.*

She stared at the passage and carefully considered the words. She deduced if the group could utilize the Creator State for positive change, attempts at destructive creation wouldn't be far behind. Perhaps it was a step in promoting modern humanity to descend into the madness which ended many a past civilization. She rethought her negativity. Maybe it would be possible to start a movement which recognized this pattern of madness, and began to build a new world beneath the skin of the old. Perhaps the soiled and abused skin of the old world was about to be shed. Not in a dramatic display of world annihilation, but in a subtle alteration toward peace. She considered what would happen if the meek did, at long last, inherit the Earth, and what if those inhabitants were creators. Maybe it was the new order of goodness, brought about by the yearning of everything peaceful on the planet to survive.

Alex's head proposed questions as John approached behind her. He paused before he embraced her shoulders. He didn't want to startle her in the middle of the library since their relationship skated on shallow ice. They dated throughout the summer, but lately she politely turned down his invitations to get together. A lengthy conversation brewed between them, but the developments of the Creator State Project left little time for personal matters. John knew a playful move like sneaking up behind her might be unwelcome today. Since he could never predict her reactions, he tested it for fun. Alex saw his reflection in the computer screen before her, and decided to let him have his amusement. She remained unaffected until he grabbed her shoulders with a "Hey!" She invented a frightened jump and won a wide smile from him. He bent over and kissed her on the cheek, pleased with her welcoming facade. He raised his eyes to the computer and saw the Artist Exchange post glowing before him. Alex noticed her words reflected in his glasses, and wondered if her ideas would ever penetrate his head. He finished reading the proposal and sat in the chair next to her. This next move in the Creator State process would put another burden on their already wavering relations. Alex saw it was time for their big talk. John recognized it too and suggested they get some lunch, but her appetite was diminished by her preoccupations. She needed the comfort of some good art.

"How about we AC-hop to the Art Institute?" she suggested, and John agreed.

It was a common summer practice for many downtown dwellers. They moved from one air conditioned space to another during the day, and slept in the warm breeze of a buzzing fan at night. The sizeable drain on the electric company caused brownouts which plagued the city all summer long. This introduced skyscraper apartment neighbors to one another for the first time. Alex served as part of the candlelight guidance team in her building, and led tenants who returned home during the brownouts up dark staircases and down hallways. Other tenants sat on the sidewalks to escape the stifling interiors, which provided another chance for neighbors to introduce themselves. During one of the lengthier brownouts, John ventured to Lakeview. It had been powerless for over twenty-four hours, so he swept Alex away to the Drake Hotel for a luxurious respite from the darkness. In the perfectly controlled climate of the classic hotel, they made love all weekend on sheets of pristine Egyptian cotton. They ordered champagne and sustenance from room service, relaxed in their cushiony spa robes, and delighted in the habits of the other half. At the Sunday check-out hour they walked down Michigan Avenue to the Art Institute. Alex remembered the visit as they made their way to the museum.

It felt like returning to the scene of the crime. As they made the hot trot to the Institute, John silently vowed to try his damnedest to keep this lovely creature beside him. Alex caught him staring at her and he covered with, "You look beautiful today." Any skilled actor can accurately read a face, and she recognized the longing in his gaze. She grabbed his hand as they crossed the street, anxious to get to the museum where their conversation could begin. They climbed the stairs to the massive space, and Alex gave a respectful salute to the stone lions which guarded the front door. Sadness swelled in John with the possibility of his last adventure with the divine Alex. He wrapped an arm around her waist as they hurried inside and inhaled the rapture of cool air.

They strolled through Alex's favorite areas and silently admired the Renoirs and the Clifford Still collection, until they entered the room where Georges Seurat's *Sunday Afternoon on the Island of La Grande Jatte* resided. The painting filled an entire wall. It gave the illusion of walking into the waterside scene as they neared. Alex and John sat on the bench placed before it, some ten feet back from the park, and sat in silence for several minutes as they beheld the marvelous sight. John prompted some conversation.

"I want to thank you, Alex, for introducing me to this marvelous world of art. I look at everything differently now; I observe my life through your creative mindset."

John seemed to be summarizing her impact on him, and she kept her eyes on the painting. She took his statement as a last-ditch effort at flattery. He hadn't granted her much patience when it came to her Creator State work. She suspected his involvement in the art world was based on tolerance rather than admiration. Deliberations circled in her head and she jumped to the topic that bothered her most. "I'm not sure you truly understand what I'm trying to do, John. You say you're intrigued by the Creator State Project, but your fascination seems fleeting, as if it were entertainment for you. Your attitude changed when we disagreed about holding off on the meetings so you could do more research. You turned sarcastic, as if you were waiting for me to find out that my ideas are just dreams of how things could be, and that I'd eventually have to deal with the 'real' world. Is there any truth in my perception?"

John stared expressionless at the pixilated vision before him. He could agree with her. She saw that he didn't mirror her beliefs. But she had confessed to pushing people away when she became busy. He wanted a fair chance at staying with her and cautiously treaded forward. "I realize that I have a cold view of the world sometimes. If the human race decides to extinguish itself, I don't see why we should try to stop it. This may be the natural order of things. We burn ourselves out, the universe blinks, and we're a memory. Much of your peace-preaching is beyond my limit of care." He slowed his pace. "I also realize that you are very dedicated to your work. There is nothing wrong with that. I'm not expecting you to see things my way. And I'm not fabricating that your outlook has affected me. I wouldn't be here if it hadn't." John glanced around the room to assure their privacy and lowered his voice. "I see the commitment that you have to this Creator State thing. Quite frankly, it makes me jealous. I envy your interest in it, the time you spend with it, both in your head and in your days." She kept her eyes on the Seurat as he pleaded. "I don't want to throw this away because you can't balance work and a relationship."

Alex took her eyes off the park and looked at John. He cocked an eyebrow at her to emphasize that he understood her struggle. She returned her eyes to *La Grande Jatte* and let his words sink in. As her vision drifted through the landscape, she measured her response carefully.

"Sometimes a creative project has to be cut off from everything that surrounds it in order to be completed. It fuels itself on the energy of those around the creator and eliminates anything that gets in the way of its realization. It has a will of its own; it demands autonomy until it is manifested." John absorbed her words and anticipated a conclusion. Their eyes remained on the painting as she gently continued. "Look at this work before us. A billion blippits of color. It's madness to paint that way. The sheer volume of repetitive work involved is insanity to anyone outside of the artistic realm. But when you work without fear, knowing that creative inspiration can be trusted, look at what happens." Alex stretched a hand out to the painting. "A gazillion dots of pure color become this gorgeous contemplative place for humanity to escape into. Seurat created life. And just like looking at a living thing, when we gaze upon it, we are touched, moved; it elicits a reaction as real life does. Because he trusted his creative state; the place he had to go to in order to be a true creator."

John shifted uncomfortably, as he always did when Alex argued her side of the creative theory. He was prepared to hear her rejection of him next, backed up by the dedication she had to her work. She tried to make him understand what motivated her.

"I'm an artist, John. I've always been an artist, that's all I know how to do. When I can't perform, I paint, when I can't paint, I write. That's my way of dealing with the negativity in the world. While you say it's natural to let humanity crumble, I say why not see what we can do in our time here? If a few lives are made more enjoyable because of something I performed or created, I'll be pleased. I want to express myself and discover why I think the way I do."

Alex paused as a chunky man grunted by, unimpressed with the art which surrounded him. She spoke after he passed. "I'd also like to learn why non-artists think the way they do. I realize it's not black and white; there are countless variations of perception. But I'm curious about how I am able to do the things that I do and why I am driven to be an artist. And the deeper I get with the Creator State Project, the closer I am to finding my own truth. I'm not the type to settle down, have kids, become a Vice President of a company, or retire to a hefty pension. I have to walk my own path. If none of these adventures amounts to anything, that's okay. At least I will have tried. It's all part of creating my own life. We're all living our own realities. Maybe I am finding a way to make other people's realities a little bit better. Do you understand what I mean?"

John bent over and clasped his hands as he leaned on his knees. He looked like he was praying to the Seurat, begging it for the power to comprehend this woman he had become so attached to. "Alex, I had no idea that you saw my sarcasm as a threat to your beliefs. You're right about my practicality. Sometimes I do think that positive efforts are futile in this chaotic world. I don't see one person or a group of people making much of a difference." He shifted his eyes sideways to get a glimpse of her, and then looked to his hands again. "But I'm avoiding asking the inevitable question, aren't I?"

She braced and knew her answer would be inspired by the moment itself. Suddenly a tug pulled in her chest at the possibility of losing him. She tried to decide if she needed the convenience of his available companionship, or if she truly desired to share her life with him. His voice interrupted her over-processing.

"Tell me Alex, am I to be eliminated by the radius of the Creator State? Am I to be creative road kill?"

John saw the reply he didn't want circle behind Alex's orbs. He fought for his survival. "Before you answer, know that I understand you need the challenge of the Project. I know it's what matters most to you. I'm not asking for exclusivity, I'm asking for cohabitation. You, me, and the Creator State Project. I also have to know how far you see these proposals going. You've connected creative people with creation, which I can grasp. But where does it go after that? How do you plan on proving these ideas? Or is the proposal enough?" He saw Alex was fatigued by his questions so he summated. "Will you make room for me in that cluttered brain of yours?"

Alex smiled faintly and looked to the painting again. She wondered if other lovers quarreled like this at *La Grand Jatte*, while trying to keep their words confidential from those within earshot. She whispered. "There are a few things I want you to take note of before we agree on anything." John sat upright and heard some promise in her words. She faced him to make sure he heard her well. "I don't believe in God, so stop getting antsy whenever I mention the term 'original creator.' It's just a name for the creative substance that makes the universe grow. So don't cringe when I mention it, okay?"

John nodded, surprised by the critique. She persisted. "Secondly, I realize that in the past I've pushed people out of the way to allow my art to exist without interference. I'm not sure it's necessary to destroy one thing to create another."

John kept his eyes on the canvas and paced in the Sunday afternoon scene. He heard compromise in her words and knew a resolution was near. He listened politely and restrained the urge to grab her hand as they sat before the romantic landscape. She kept talking.

"I know you mean well with your suggestions for structure during the meetings, and your input has been priceless. I know you want to sort the reality of the experiences from the emotion. But for me, the reality *is* the emotion at times. I have to trust my intuition with these ideas. I have to pursue it in the same manner in which it came to me: freely, without outside regulations and guidelines imposing on its form. Wherever this is taking me, I must follow it without restrictions. I need to explore it without inhibition, without censorship or structure." She spoke to his profile as the tide turned for him. "John, I have to do this on my own. I'm very sorry, but that's what my mind keeps telling me when I question our relationship. I have asked often, believe me. I've toiled over this decision since we first met. Right now, my art demands my complete attention."

He couldn't look at her. His mind analyzed every time he imposed on the Creator State meetings and asked for a more scientific approach. His insides churned with regret, and he wanted to exit immediately. Then he found he couldn't move. He lost mobility under the crush of this information. He sat in silence as his stomach churned. He fought the urge to tell her he would change, that he would do better in the future if she would stay with him. But he surmised promises wouldn't matter now; at least he could escape with his pride. He tried to calculate an alternative way around the decision, but the fact remained stationary: they wouldn't see each other anymore. She got to her feet, touched his bowed head, and left John on the bank of the Seine.

Alex reached the front steps of the Art Institute and looked up. The blue sky was painted over with a mural of gray and black, with the familiar greenish tint of an approaching Midwest thunderstorm. She hustled to the L wrapped in the numbness of leaving someone she cared about. She gazed blindly out the train window on the way to the Andrews and wished the rain could flush the guilt from her heart. As the L approached Belmont, the storm kicked into full force. It drenched her to the skin during her three block dash to the theater. She wanted to be cleansed of her actions, the weight of her passions, and the filmy residue of her doubts. But in the downpour that evening, Alex was only relieved of dry clothes. She dove into the Andrews lobby with an exasperated yelp, then tiptoed dripping wet into the house. When she discovered it was devoid of actors, she sunk into the last bench and wept.

A groan rose above her sobs as another victim of the rain entered the lobby. When she tried to turn off her tears, they doubled, which forced her to stifle the sound of her bawling into her saturated skirt. The noise from the lobby produced Thomas, exactly the person she needed to comfort her. He offered a soggy embrace. She cried into his shirt and revealed the source of her episode. Thomas held her even tighter. Alex felt a safety in her friend's arms and unraveled her conversation from the afternoon at the Art Institute. Thomas listened patiently to her justifications for ending it with John and hoped she would recuperate quickly. Their private experiments were going well and he didn't want to sacrifice all of his efforts to the relationship gods.

He waited for her to finish, paused a respectful silence, then asked, "How green was the grass?" He heard a light laugh rise between her tears. They used this game in the past to distract each other from personal woes before a performance. By describing the details in a piece of art or a moment in a play, they could divert attention from a personal problem. It ordinarily worked like a charm. The more detail the troubled soul could provide, the more they released their worries and allowed the pleasure of expression to take hold. Alex answered from Thomas' shoulder and envisioned the park's shadowy lawn of green.

"The foreground forms a pool of deep sage." Alex searched for terms to soothe her soul. "Beyond the cool pond of grass, bursts of yellow glimmer through the trees and magnetize around the timeless beings imprinted on the canvas. Ellipses of gray stretch from each participant deeper and deeper into the park. The figures twitch and remain immobile all at once. It's the colors that dance; the people are forever transfixed in their delightfully simple universe."

Storm survivors clambered into the lobby which noisily announced the arrival of the cast and crew. Alex straightened and thanked Thomas for his kindness. She stood in the aisle next to where he sat. Her damp clothes clung to her skin and revealed curves Thomas still longed to caress. Her obliviousness to his desires annoyed him, but he repressed any seize-the-rebound attempts for the evening. She bent over and kissed his forehead, and swiftly exited to pull herself together for the performance. Thomas watched her go, and then turned back to the empty stage. He pictured the grass she described stretching over the floorboards. It called for him to stroll upon its magical surface. He saw himself walk barefoot through the Sunday afternoon, and felt the cool blades crush underfoot and between his toes. Clothed in a linen suit and waving a breeze from his straw hat, he approached a vision of Alex in a Victorian gown of cream silk. The full skirt flowed from her corseted waist. They walked to a secluded spot beneath a giant chestnut tree, her skirt rustling with each step. When they stopped, he leaned in to kiss her. Her lips waited in silent acceptance for him, the pink of her mouth radiant and welcoming. He was about to land his kiss when a voice cut sharply into his fantasy.

"Thomas, don't sit in the benches in your wet clothes please."

Chris Caldwell swept by on his way to the box office. Thomas abruptly got to his feet, apologized to Chris who was already out the door, and wheeled around to the stage again. He shook his head at his own nonsense and raised his hands high in surrender. The move attracted Lisa's attention on her way through the house. Thomas joined her and he mumbled, "Poor bastard died from exhaustion. All of that beautiful meticulous creativity." Lisa gave him an incredulous look and he added, "Seurat. Never mind, it's nothing." He laughed. "Did you ever notice that people gesture even when no one is looking? Who are we entertaining when we do that? Ourselves?" Lisa laughed with him as they descended to the basement dressing rooms. She replied, "The sound of one hand clapping."

Thomas darted into the men's dressing room. It was a quick move that made Lisa think something was going on. She stopped at the door of the ladies dressing room and found the source of the malaise. Alex watched her unattended tear tracks fade in the mirror, as if an effort to wipe them would be futile. When her gaze caught Lisa in the doorway, the tracks began to flow once again.

Lisa knew the reason. It wasn't the first time Alex dumped someone prematurely and regretted it, at least for a day or two. Rather than chastise her friend for a lesson repeated, Lisa chose to take it easy on her overworked companion. In years past, Lisa would have openly offered a wise crack or at least an I-told-you-so. But Alex's current position as creative leader and Manager of the Andrews made Lisa more cautious with her wording. Alex sensed her trepidation.

"What, no witty repartee? No wisdom to pour on my broken heart?" Her delivery was harsher than she intended, and she waved a hand for Lisa to forget about what she delivered. "John is a great guy. I just couldn't handle the Andrews, the Project, and him at the same time. It was too much." Alex looked at Lisa in the mirror and saw a conversation brewing behind her pale eyes.

"You know what your priorities are," Lisa responded. She had more to say but clammed up, which drove Alex straight into the conversation she wanted to have with her.

"A relationship is not top priority for me," Alex defended. "It is for you, but not for me, and definitely not now."

"It's never your priority. Your art always comes first." Lisa heard the words leave her mouth. "I didn't mean that the way it sounded. Of course your art comes first. But John excited you mentally, emotionally, and physically. That must have been a good thing to have in your life. I worry that you're giving up too much along this path of yours." Lisa kept her from interrupting. "I don't think he deserved to be treated like the other guys you've dated. You always complain about people stereotyping you. I think you may have done that to him. And while we're on the subject, I wish you would stop thinking of my relationship that way, too."

Alex sobered. "What way?"

"As if I'm involved in some common, going nowhere but kids and retirement kind of relationship." Lisa's eyes widened. "It's insulting to me and it makes it seem like you fear love."

Alex slouched in her chair and contemplated the idea. She thought she sidestepped having a boyfriend on behalf of her art. A relationship seemed to take up valuable time. She wondered if the true reason behind her treating men as sidekicks was a defense mechanism. Maybe it was possible that her work could be fueled by a relationship rather than drained. Considering a way to work harder made her chuckle, and Lisa softened to the sound of her laughter. Alex noticed her relax and took note of Lisa's attitude. Lisa feigned innocence and said, "What's wrong?"

They gave each other a long look and silently examined their five year friendship. They knew they were at a turning point, but didn't know if they would share the same path or go their separate ways. Alex bathed in the professional limelight as manager, and added the artistic limelight when she began the Tuesday meetings. She was higher on the artistic food chain because of her work that summer. Lisa could come along with her or step aside, but she had Peter to consider. He was very involved in the Project. She couldn't force to him to choose between her and the group, because she knew which side would win him over. The two women acknowledged their discomfort and dropped the conversation until later. It was time to dry off and prepare for the performance.

After the show, the cast and crew lingered in the lobby and delayed their exit into the post-downpour dampness outside. One audience member stayed behind and requested to speak with Alex, who was still in the dressing room. The spar-kling-eyed older man introduced himself as Bob. While the cast couldn't place his face, they saw an air of confidence in the well-groomed fellow which intrigued them. He made small talk with the lobby dwellers and sidestepped the purpose of his visit. No one inquired directly as to his business with Alex. Their curiosity entertained the man as they attempted to goad him to the subject. Eventually he excused himself from the group, ran his hand across his closely cropped hair, and nodded to indicate he had endured enough of their conversation. He sat aside of them and pensively read the evening's program until Alex emerged at last. Chris approached her, and directed her attention to the patient man. Bob was relieved when recognition washed over Alex's face. They shook hands vigorously and dis-missed themselves from the group. Alex escorted the man into the house where they could speak privately.

They settled into the back row and spoke in hushed tones. The man leaned in, aware that his smooth crystalline voice carried well. "Alex, I've been hearing rumors about your Artist Exchange meetings. People are talking about this little group, and the things they are saying about you … well, I had to find out for myself." His thin mouth curled into a smile which made him look fox-like. Alex wondered how often that smile had been used to charm. She interrupted his rou-tine.

"Going straight to the source, Mr. Clarke? That's good reporting I suppose."

His smile deflated. "I'm not here as a reporter tonight, Alex. I'm here as myself, just Bob who has taken in hundreds of performances in this town and is, quite frankly, bored out of his mind with it. I'm here because I'm hoping you have an alternative to the mindless tedium which has become my career. I'm hop-ing you have something new to share with us."

"'Us' being the readers of the *Chicago Tribune?*"

"'Us' being the population of people who publicize art. There are two camps in my world: the entertainers and the entertained. I consider myself a liaison between camps. Everyone benefits from open communication between the two. It's important that everyone knows about new developments in each other's camp." Bob's smile widened again and he oiled his approach. "Give me a glimpse of your camp, Alex."

She fought the urge to roll her eyes at him. "And what will you do, tell the other camp about me? I don't need publicity for our meetings and I get enough nasty e-mails already. Besides, I'm not even sure what we're doing yet. So far, we're just a group of artists getting together on Tuesday nights." She saw him take a mental note of the day. "Those gatherings are for artists only, Bob. No reporters allowed."

He tried another way in. "C'mon, Alex. I've always had flattering things to say about your performances. I'm a part of your success. I'm already in your camp, just let me take a peek at the action."

She gave him a flat stare which warned him not to use his theater reviews as leverage. He switched gears again. He sobered and his face dropped to appear serious. Alex admired his unique talent, a tool of his trade: the ability to manipulate a conversation to his benefit and acquire the story he desired. But as he attempted acting on an actor, he realized his usual tricks would not easily persuade Alex. He had to come up with something factual or this camp would be forever closed to him. He began again, this time with a request of purpose.

"I've been at my job for a long time. As endearing as the aging newspaper reporter persona may be, the reality is that the *Tribune* wants to squeeze me out. The paper business is changing. There's no respect for the old guys. It doesn't matter that I've been reporting for thirty years. My awards don't matter, my years of dedication don't matter anymore. Now they want the new style, the sexy topics, the titillation factor. And unless I prove that I can bring that to the table, I'm out of a job and my pension is cut to shit. I'm fifty-five now, Alex. I'm not going to find another good job at my age. Especially in the arts, and that's everything I am. For thirty years I've lived it, breathed it. It's my sustenance. But I have to find something new to talk about or I'm out of the game, and permanently." He lowered his eyes to elicit sympathy. She couldn't decide if this was a good performance or a genuine request for assistance, but she found some truth in his argument.

"Why bother with my group? We don't even know what we're doing yet."

He raised his eyes and looked into hers intently. "Yes you do, Alex. You know where this is leading. You know it's purposeful at least." He sat back and took a breath. "You sent me a collection of *Magic Mobile* quotes when I won my last award. The book was both a congratulations and a thank you gift. Congrats on my recognition, thank you for the good *Trib* reviews. You are the only actor who has ever sent me anything. After all these years of reviewing." He shook his head in disbelief. "After all the kudos I have doled out to the Chicago theatrical population, you were the only one to thank me. And with a very appropriate gift, your own thoughts on art. It moved me. It genuinely moved me that you thought of me as one of your own, a fellow artist. I guess that's what I really wanted, more than an award from my supposed peers at the paper. I wanted recognition from artists that I made a contribution, that I made a difference through my articles and reviews. Even when I criticized, it was only to make things better, raise the bar, and encourage audiences to expect more from our theaters." Bob realized he was defending himself and turned back to Alex. "C'mon Alex, help me out. If not as an artist, then at least as a friend?"

Alex's head swirled with the feeling of simultaneous past, present, and future. Robert Clarke sat before her: Robert Clarke, mysterious judge-all entity of the *Tribune*; Robert Clarke, who praised her performances; Robert Clarke, who needs her help to save his position; Robert Clarke, whose funeral she attends on a frozen January day, when the icy sheen of cemetery snow crunches beneath her boots. She felt all of her encounters with Bob, all of her connections with him rush through her life. She saw the future article he would write in her mind's eye. She reads the title over Peter's shoulder: "The State of Chicago Art." She snapped back to the moment, and agreed to let Bob attend the next Tuesday gathering.

"We meet at 11:00 p.m., come earlier if you like. Most arrive just after the curtain is down."

Bob relaxed with relief, or maybe it was victory. He thanked her and slipped out the door quickly. Alex stood in the church and watched the door close behind him. Something about his speedy exit felt crafty to her. Surely he could have bought her a drink if he was the friend he claimed to be. But it wasn't his style to hang around after the show. Besides, Alex's longing for a libation stemmed from her breakup with John. Sadness stirred around her heart and she darted for the door as she fought back the urge to weep again.

She entered the lobby and faced a grinning crowd. Thomas had told the cast and crew who the strange man was. A reviewer's presence was a very big deal under this roof. She revealed the *Tribune*'s interest in their meetings, which led them all to cheer. They jolted into the thick night air, electrified by the good news. The group reassembled at Jimmy's, where the Saturday night crowd spilled out of the bar into the street.

Thomas scanned the mob and shook his head. "I'm not in the mood for this tonight. How about Don's?" The group turned together and looked across the street. Don's, affectionately referred to as an "old man bar" was quiet, tame, and contained a minimum of patrons. Lisa agreed, "Yeah, let's keep this celebration tight."

They crossed the street and slipped into the timeless dank of Don's. Four men sat at different points at the bar, but only one glanced up as they entered. The bartender looked warily toward the group and recognized a few of them who graced his bar two weeks ago. He hoped they didn't have plans of luring over more theater types. This group he liked, but the rest of the crowd could stay across the street.

Peter approached the bar first, extended a hand, and utilized his natural bartender rapport. "Good evenin' to ya, Charles. Happy to be back in your fine establishment."

Charles shook his hand and made nice with the new clientele, probably because it included two beautiful girls. "Welcome, Peter. Have a seat up front, let's have some good conversation tonight." The group followed and filled in the west end of the bar. Peter quickly made introductions to put Charles at ease.

"Charles, this is Miles, Lisa, and you know Thomas and Alex." Peter introduced their host with a flourish. "And this is the irrepressible Charles Stanford."

The bartender tipped his head hello and began taking drink orders. Miles spotted Chris Caldwell waiting in the crowd outside of Jimmy's. He bounced to his feet and pranced to the door. "I'm going to rescue Chris!" This attracted the immediate attention of the four stoic regulars. Apparently it had been a long time, if ever, since they had an openly gay man in the bar. Charles avoided the glances from his patrons and shot a look at Peter.

Peter read the situation and tossed a diversion to the men after Miles exited. "Hey, you can take the boy out of Lakeview, but you can't take the Lakeview out of the boy!" After a beat, the men chuckled at the joke and returned to their beers. Charles gave Peter a "well done" look as he reached under the bar. He revealed an ancient bag of paper umbrellas, pulled one out, opened it, and planted it in Miles' drink. He proclaimed, "I've wanted to use these for a long time. Looks like tonight is the night." The regulars chuckled again at the sight of the frilly décor poised on the martini.

Alex wondered if Miles would return to some harassment. At the far end of the bar a hulky half-sloshed character got to his feet. The man raised his beer, pointed to his glass, and slurred, "Hey, bartender, gimme one of them umbrellas." The three remaining regulars raised their glasses in turn, and lightheartedly demanded an umbrella in their drinks. Charles plopped the paper embellishments in each of their glasses. Peter shouted, "Now we got ourselves a party!" The room filled with laughter. Miles sauntered in with Chris behind him and the room erupted again as the men raised their adorned glasses. One of them toasted Miles as they crossed to the bar. He sang, "Howdeedooo, Lake Vieeewww."

Miles looked a little stunned and checked Alex for confirmation that he wasn't about to get his ass kicked. She smiled and pointed to the umbrella in her glass, and he noticed the colorful display of them lining the bar. He picked up his glass and weakly toasted back. One of the men gave Miles a dour look and said, "Hey, you're breakin' the rules, son." Miles held his breath. The man added, "You're not supposed to enter a room before a guy who's prettier than you are." The group howled as Chris and Miles glanced at each other. Miles finally relaxed and threw back, "Age before beauty, my friend, age before beauty." The laughter resumed as Miles settled into his seat.

Thomas leaned into Alex, "Well that went well." She motioned to a table across the bar. They slipped away from the others as Alex panicked about their plans for the *Tribune*.

"Okay we need to discuss how to handle Bob's visit next week. I don't want to come off like some wacked-out theater troupe. How do I avoid sounding like a lunatic? I'm not even sure if I'm doing the right thing here. Should we divulge all?"

Thomas took a drink. "Well first you can do me favor and relax. It's not a review. It's an article about something he has no information on. Whatever we decide to tell him is what will end up in the paper."

She sighed because he was right. Bob's visit caused a knee-jerk reaction within her. His presence made her feel judged, as if everyone would read his opinion the next day. It made her simultaneously nervous and defiant. She wanted to damn the reviews and do her best regardless of his opinion. But this was a different situation. "If Bob is telling the truth about his position at the *Trib*, then he needs to exploit the edgiest qualities he can find in our activities. He's going to be looking for anything that sounds out-there; anything new or weird or sexy."

Thomas laughed. "Sexy?"

"His words, not mine. Actually, he may have said titillating."

Thomas shifted in his seat. "Did he flirt with you? I've heard he's relentless player."

Alex rolled her eyes. "You think everyone is a player, Thomas."

"No, but I said that about John and see what happened?"

"The breakup was my fault, can we drop it?" she snapped. Thomas noted her abruptness; it was just like her to move on the second things changed. He admired her ability to recover, but it saddened him. It seemed she didn't allow the pain to get in; she wasn't disappointed for more than a day when things like this happened. In Thomas' world, the elements of disappointment, pain, and struggle were a constant. He didn't know another way to be. Her view seemed a bit naïve to him, but he knew he missed out on a more joyful life.

Alex went on. "He tried every trick in his arsenal to get what he wanted. Let's be clear about what we want him to see, hear, and write about, okay? This man is manipulative. Let's try to stay one step ahead of him."

"Shouldn't we involve Lisa and Peter in this conversation?" He turned to wave them over, but Alex caught him quickly.

"Not tonight, Lisa is pissed at me for breaking up with John."

Thomas looked wounded. "Why would she care about John?"

"She thought he was good for me, I suppose." Alex took a sip of her martini. "Because of the way he helped us out, doing all of that research. She thought it was a sign of how much he cared."

Thomas ventured, "What do you think it meant?"

"I suppose he cared, but his approach to the State was too factual, always trying to prove that what we were doing had some kind of scientific explanation. As if the possibility of changing the world wasn't enough."

He broke away from her stare. Changing the world seemed to be the ultimate dream of every artist. The notion that somehow your work would touch the population and simultaneously heal centuries of despair with one piece, one poem, one performance; something they would talk about for years after you were gone. He didn't like the idea. It seemed too common. "Are we talking immortality? Are you going to be one of those artists who thinks they can change everything?" He kidded her in a sarcastic girlish tone. "Leave the world a better place than you found it!"

Alex hit her emotional breaking point. She had kept her breakup, her argument with Lisa and her exchange with Bob under control, but reached her limit when Thomas teased her. She felt tears well up, but rather than allow everyone to see her cry, she forced them back down again and gave him a pointed glare. "I expected more from you."

She got up, whisked out the door, and left a bewildered Thomas behind. She rushed down the sidewalk as the long day overextended its welcome. She negotiated through the throngs headed for the bar strip and avoided glances from Saturday prowlers on the lookout for their next one night stand. She wanted no advances, no flirtatious looks, and no contact with anyone outside of her own brain. A few blocks away from the bar, she slowed down and breathed in the night air. It was mercifully cooler at last. High above the dome of light which constantly emanated from the city, there were stars looking down on her. The only company she desired tonight was the quiet peace of the midnight sky.

Thomas' comments stirred within her as she walked. She wondered how he could demean their magical summer by calling it a need for notoriety. It was possible the *Tribune* column might grant them a bit of unsolicited attention, but it would provide momentary limelight. She worried the article might make the group appear trivial. As she raised her eyes to the glistening sky, she questioned her perspective: what if her fascination with the Creator State made her look like a nut ball? Alex laughed as she thought about her lifestyle; what part of it wasn't nut ball? She inventoried her day: voices, messages, long hours in a dark converted church, and the end of a good relationship for the sake of a personal goal. Alex stiffened her gait as she choked back tears. She didn't want to cry on the sidewalk. But the wells were full to the rim, and it was her first moment alone since she and John parted. She hurried down the block, then slowed again so she wouldn't attract attention. She turned her path toward the lake at the next corner, relieved to see an empty street before her.

She churned over her decision to leave John. She could smooth things over with him after the Project ran its course. She might even convince him to get back together. But in the interim he suffered, and it wasn't fair to him. He had no idea that she may want to reunite when the chaos had quelled. She felt manipulative. In the past she forgave herself for this kind of behavior as part of the process of being an artist. There were sacrifices to make, demands which had to be met. But this situation was different; she truly cared for John. Apparently she was changing, and as the idea of change came to her, she passed by a tiny corner market that held a donation box for the homeless mission. Written on its exterior was "Change for the Better." She soberly smiled through her weeping eyes and walked home.

Back at Don's, Peter sat down across from a puzzled Thomas and jested at Alex's speedy exit. "Lover's spat?"

Thomas raised his eyes to attack, and then realized he shouldn't appear sensitive to such a remark. Peter caught the glimpse and read it instantly. "Holy shit, Thomas. Is that why Alex broke up with John?"

Thomas straightened in his seat and hushed him. "No!" he whispered harshly. "No, that's not it at all. She has no idea. It's all me."

Peter leaned back in his chair and said nonchalantly, "Sucks to be you. How long have you felt this way about her?" By the look on Thomas' face it had been a long while, so he offered, "Ever consider, y'know, telling her?"

"What, and get my ass kicked worse than John's? No, I know her too well. That's the problem. I know she'd try it out, dump me, move on; I can see the whole relationship in one long painful blur." Thomas gulped the rest of his martini and raised the glass at Charles, who nodded and began to prepare another for him.

Peter shook his head. "You don't know how it would play out. You guys are friends already. That's how the good ones start. You share the same interests, have the same experiences with the State, and you're both equally neurotic when it comes to relationships."

Thomas smirked at him. "I don't have relationships, Peter. I haven't had a girlfriend in, what, three years? Nothing that lasted longer than a few months at least. I'm no good at it."

Peter leaned into him. "Neither is she. The numbers don't count, it's the results that matter, and both of you are zero-zero in the relationship department. What have you got to lose by giving it a chance?"

Thomas slowed the momentum of their conversation and paused. "Wait a second. You seem a little too prepared for this. Why are you encouraging me to try and hook up with Alex? Aren't you a little shocked, or surprised at least?"

"Man, I have known you for a long time. Gimme some credit." Peter chuckled. "I've seen you dancing around this thing for a while. It's so obvious you adore everything about her. And I wouldn't be surprised, if Alex stopped working for a second, if she felt the same way about you."

Peter kept talking as Thomas wondered if it was possible. His recent obsession with Alex existed in a vacuum in his mind. The whole crush felt like a fantasy; the idea looked different when outside light came pouring in. Peter's insight encouraged and surprised him; Thomas wondered what else he knew. Peter had drifted from the subject, bored with it already. Thomas interrupted. "You seem to be very perceptive tonight. What else do you know?" A smile twitched on Peter's mouth. Thomas demanded, "You know something!"

The smile cracked across Peter's face and he toyed with Thomas. "Yeah, well, y'know, I have friends in high places, some valuable information is entrusted to me. I can't just throw it around, Thomas." Peter took a slow sip of his drink and giggled. He let Thomas see that the bit of information he held was big. Big, fun, exclusive information. He loved holding it, but was about to spill. "You have to swear," he emphasized.

"Of course," whispered Thomas. "You got the goods on me. I expect you'll take that as ransom."

"Absolutely, because this is big, man. Really fucking big." Peter chuckled again, checked the room to make sure no one was listening, and leaned in. Thomas waited anxiously and mirrored the smile on Peter's face. Peter began. "You know my Uncle Jeff in L.A.?" Thomas nodded, surprised by the introduction. Peter continued. "He got David the script reading and the chance at shooting his lame-ass screenplay."

"Why the hell would he do that?"

"Because," he grinned, "I caught him naked at our family cabin last spring with a woman who was definitely not my Aunt."

"So what? Why would he help David?"

Peter unraveled the chain of events with delight. "When Alex started writing the *Magic Mobile*, she and I spoke about her ambitions for starting a new group in the off-loop scene. She really wanted to start something fresh, and she wanted to learn how to do it herself. I used to drink with the Andrews clique at Jimmy's, and one night, David mentioned his screenplay. I thought it would be a perfect barter. David gets a shot at Hollywood, and while he's gone Alex gets to manage his theater. We drank on it, and the rest, as they say, is history."

Thomas sat stunned. "So you got her the job at the Andrews?"

"Yep." Peter shrugged. "Honestly, I thought Alex would be miserable and decide that she didn't want to be a businesswoman. I think she's a great actor, and I didn't want to lose her at Circle Rep. I thought a taste of management would sour her desire to run her own thing. That plan seems to have failed."

Thomas considered David's reaction upon returning to Alex's "new" Andrews. "He's gonna be pissed when he gets back. She's turned the image of the place around. What is he going to do when he returns and everyone is raving about her? He's gonna fire her immediately."

"Nah, not as long as I can provide L.A. access. Plus you forget the marketing angle involved here. If Alex starts the 'next new thing' in the off-loop scene at the Andrews, David is going to reap the benefits of ticket sales, news coverage, publicity, you name it."

Thomas rubbed his hands over his face. "We might have a problem if Bob Clarke hyper-promotes the Creator State in the *Tribune*. That's why Alex left tonight. I mentioned the whole desire-to-be-immortal aspect, and she dropped out on me. Completely shut down."

Peter lit a cigarette. "Nah, she'll be fine. She just had a hard day, that's all. It's a lot to digest between her break up and the *Trib* showing up on her doorstep. Once she sees how good it will be for her to expose this thing a little, she'll come around."

Thomas leveraged the situation. Peter's secrecy couldn't outweigh his own. He could trust Peter with what he wanted to disclose, and he had to share it before Bob started poking around the State group. Thomas scanned the bar and assured their conversation went undetected. Miles was busy entertaining Lisa and Chris, and their laughter filled the space. Most of the regulars dispersed just after midnight. Charles was the only one who observed their presence in the corner. He detected the chat was not for the rest of the group's ears. Like any bar owner worth his salt, Charles knew to wait for a break in the private conversation before interrupting with a drink order. He delivered Thomas' second martini to their table, and respectfully placed it down without attracting attention. Charles nodded when Thomas showed his appreciation by giving him a heavy tip, and then he smoothly returned to behind the bar.

Peter sucked on his Marlboro, and appeared to be satisfied with the previous exchange. Thomas took a hit of his martini and lit a cigarette with shaky fingers. Peter noticed his jitters. "Hey man, what's the matter? You look a little tweaky. Sorry if the Alex thing is upsetting, I only meant to help her out."

"No, it's not that. There's something I have to tell you about Alex and me." They surveyed the bar for eavesdroppers and found none. Thomas whispered. "The Tuesday sessions aren't the only time when Alex and I get together to explore the Creator State. We meet in private two or three times a week." Peter looked hurt, but attentive, so Thomas went on. "There was an element that Alex thought was missing from the group work; a stronger feeling, a higher level of intensity which she thought could be attained if she and I got together without the others. We worked with our best material, moments when we experienced the State on stage." He paused and summoned the courage to tell his friend everything.

Peter frowned. "What the hell is it, man?"

"We kept experimenting with the State and one night we decided to direct our energies into creating a change. We tried to use the theory that Alex extracted from John's research, the whole tapping into the field of creativity thing, and we experimented with it. We weren't sure if anything would come of it, so we chose an improved attitude, a better outlook."

Peter tried to follow. "I don't get it. Why would you want to change yourselves?"

"No, we didn't want to change ourselves, we wanted to help someone else. Someone with an attitude that seemed to be burdened by negativity, someone who we thought would benefit from some good intentions."

Peter's mind raced through the population of people who surrounded them over the summer. He tried to think of who was so negative that they thought the poor fool needed assistance. And furthermore, who in the past two months had a changed attitude or better disposition. Then it hit Peter like lightning. There was someone who had drastically changed in the last few weeks. He gasped. "Joseph!" Then he quieted. "Is it Joseph?"

Thomas smiled, thankful that Peter recognized the transition in their subject. He whispered excitedly. "Yes! Does it really show? Because I'm so involved, it's hard to believe that the guy has actually changed right before our eyes."

Peter sat transfixed by the possibility until his cigarette burned into his fingers. He dropped it, crushed it into the ashtray, and held his forehead in his hands as if his mind was about to burst. "That's crazy, man. What the …? Jesus. For once I'm at a loss for words."

Thomas reached for his martini and took a long gulp. "That's why I had to tell you. I can't keep this under wraps anymore. It feels too important."

"So that's why Alex dumped John, so he wouldn't find out about the experiment?"

"Maybe," Thomas shrugged. "John may have been able to provide a few scientific answers, but he's no support system for her emotionally. I don't think she ever told him about Joseph."

"How could you not tell us, man? How could you not tell me?"

"How could you not tell me about arranging for Alex's job?" Thomas settled down again. "Besides, creating change in a person is a lot to handle. It's electrifying, but it also makes you feel alienated from the outside world. It's more like an inside world."

"So how do we tip-toe around this for the *Tribune*? This is major news and you guys won't even talk about it with your friends? This is your big opportunity, man. Get on the soap box and tell people that you found something extraordinary in your art."

Thomas agreed. "I know it's vital to share this. I'm just paranoid that when the time comes to demonstrate, it won't work."

"Performance anxiety?" Peter guffed.

The two of them laughed together, which attracted Lisa's attention. She jolted toward them, but Peter waved a hand and indicated Thomas' business was private. He delivered the gesture with finesse, and Lisa returned to her barstool. She winked back as if he would tell her about it later. Peter returned to the conversation. "How are you going to keep this under your hat when Robert Clarke is poking around the Andrews? What are we going to say to him?" Peter lit another cigarette and pointed at Thomas, "We gotta be careful, that guy is a first-class weasel."

The prospect of exposing this too soon began to trouble Thomas. "Fight or flight," he mumbled under his breath. A wave of laughter from the bar smothered his speech, and Peter continued with his commentary on Bob.

"I hear they want to fire him over at the Trib, so he's gonna be desperate for some hot information." Peter's dramatic tone prompted a laugh from Thomas, which made Peter even more emphatic. "This isn't a joke, man. This is your nice little local career on the line. If he wants to find a bunch of lunatics residing at the Andrews, he's going to pry until he gets what he came for."

Thomas looked incredulous. "He's not after that. That doesn't make sense, you're being paranoid. He just wants something to talk about for one column, one week. Something that isn't a review so he can prove he can still do investigative reporting."

"There's more to it. There's always more to it. Why would he pick on us? Why now? No one knows about the experiments except you and Alex, right?"

"Yeah, unless she told John, but I can't imagine why she would do that. She made it sound like they weren't that close."

Peter put his head in his hands. "Jesus, she probably told him. She always makes her relationships seem lighter than they actually are. If she did tell him, what if John squealed to Bob after they broke up today, like a revenge thing? It's a bit coincidental that Bob shows up at our door on the same day, don't you think?"

Thomas tried to let it go, but Peter had a good point. It was wise to prepare for the worst. "Let's get our group together and update everyone. That way Bob has nothing on us. No surprises."

Peter asked the obvious for confirmation. "And if Bob brings up the experiments?"

Thomas downed the rest of his martini and decided. "Then we tell him the truth."

9

Difficulty arises in the state of illusion; reality pales beside the opulence of its imitation. But these are reflections of the finest fragments of reality. We conjure the truth of human consciousness and its capacity for love and compassion. These emotions may be trying tasks for the population, but they are also its greatest contribution.

—*The Magic Mobile*

Alex rolled over in bed and winked lazily at the Sunday morning sunlight. She awoke to a feeling of freedom. There would be no calls from John today, no lunch dates to prepare for, no clever words to exchange with him. Her day was clear to do as she pleased, but the sadness of loss still lingered. The city was quiet, her voices were quiet, and the *Mobile* was quiet. A respectful silence surrounded her and allowed her to heal. She took advantage of the peace, avoided a morning run, and wrapped herself in the comfort of her aloneness. She suppressed thoughts of the *Tribune* article, the State, or a new *Mobile* message. The morning was calm and perfect, and she gently drifted back to sleep.

A dream manifested in her slumber. A lush hillside landscape appeared. Tall blades of grass in vibrant shades of jade and aqua flowed in the breeze. One hill met another and another, as far as her dream's eye could grasp. A single tree shined under a cloudless sky. Its colorful limbs sprawled umbrella-like up to the sun and back to the Earth below. A tinkling sound came from its direction as it sparkled in the distance. She walked through the deep grass toward the tree, and the source of the musical tones was revealed. The perennial was covered with strands of crystals in every color which glimmered in the sunlight. It was dazzling to behold. Silently the tree called to take a strand from its branches. When she lifted one, several new strands were revealed beneath. Its bounty instantly regenerated. She removed handfuls of the multicolored jewels, and the tree provided more in their place. The gleaming colors hung from her hands as she looked out over the landscape. She gazed back and the tree vanished. She became the tree. Her view stretched far beyond the rolling hills. She felt a connection to all living things, from the core of the Earth to the edge of the universe and beyond. It was the phenomenon of being everywhere all at once. A feeling she experienced in meditation, but stronger, more vibrant. She realized what it was and woke up, flushed with the familiar sensation of the Creator State.

Alex blinked at her ceiling. The morning glow had grown to full daylight. She lay motionless and interpreted the vision. The tree represented the source of all creativity. The crystals were every shape and facet of its expression. Creative talent was inexhaustible. When she accepted the gifts as her own talent, she connected with all things. She drank in the details of the dream's final moment. She became the tree, rooted to the source of creation. She persevered her line of thought: could she become a source for others by sharing her ideas on creativity? She knew if she trusted the State, there would be enough resources to draw upon during this journey. Alex felt a change stir within her soul: her fear of exposure was nonsensical. There was no wrong way to share these ideas. The theories were as natural as the Earth itself. A single article in the *Tribune* meant little; it was a stepping stone on the way to a grander mission. She trusted her intuition when she said yes to Bob. Now she would trust herself to express everything she had within her, regardless of the reaction it might produce. This thought brought her back to Thomas. He challenged her, and she fell short of expressing herself by walking out on him last night. That was a temperament better suited for Lisa. She wondered if Thomas would appreciate the dream and her interpretation of it. She got up to call him and apologize. Her hand touched the receiver just as it rang. It startled her and shattered the lazy morning vibration in her studio.

She tried to clear the shock from her voice. "Welcome to *Sun*day."

"Alex, what are you doing today?" Lisa's impatient tone slashed the peaceful silence. "I want to get together. Just us."

Alex heard agenda in her friend's request and almost declined, then she felt the tug of her new mission. Share everything. She would confess the Joseph experiments to Lisa. Maybe she could vent her guilt about leaving John too, and all within the time span of a languid Sunday brunch.

"Why don't you stop by in about an hour?" Alex grinned at herself in her bathroom mirror. She knew Lisa hated her studio.

"Nah, c'mon, don't make me come over there. It's so tiny and all those scribbled notes and papers everywhere give me the creeps." Alex looked around the space and saw evidence. There were papers, notes, and pieces of *Magic Mobile* messages scattered on every surface. She hadn't noticed it before. A nice casual patio meal would start the day well. She agreed to meet Lisa at the Night and Day Diner up the street.

New possibilities tingled in her veins. She picked up the phone again, dialed her voicemail, and recorded her message without her usual script. She trusted the words would be encouraging as she opened her mouth to speak.

"I dreamt of a cypress tree hung with strands of crystals. Heavy with the sparkling colors of creativity: oranges, purples, blues, and pinks. It waited patiently in a new silent dawn. The twinkling of these treasures whispered for me to partake of its bounty. Each time a strand was lifted, ten more were revealed beneath. Our creative gifts are inexhaustible and they call for us to utilize them!"

Lisa was already seated at a wobbly resin table on the Night and Day Diner's patio when Alex arrived. She hopped over the temporary rails which fenced in the outdoor seating area and joined her. The outdoor section would be taken down in less than a month, as Chicago typically had three months of heat and then the frost of fall set in. An autumn chill couldn't compete with the ice in Lisa's stare. Alex sat down and expected condemnation for her treatment of John. But Lisa had other topics in mind.

"Why didn't you tell me about your experiments with Thomas? Why did I have to hear about it from Peter?"

Alex wondered how Peter found out and hoped Thomas told him directly. She could handle unrest in their little foursome until the others gathered on Tuesday. Alex wanted to share her elevated mood, but was wary of Lisa's nasty disposition. "I wanted to tell you about all of this earlier, I just couldn't find the right moment. But something changed for me today. I have a new confidence about everything that I've been working on, everything that I've always wanted to do with my art. I feel I open to my life at last, and I'm giving myself permission to express everything."

Lisa shooed the waiter away when he approached. She quivered with anger, offended by her friend's sudden enlightenment. Rather than be selective about her argument, Lisa dug into the mound of resentment swelling within her, and tossed a shovelful directly at Alex.

"*Now?* You're ready to do something *now?*" Lisa seethed and tried to keep her voice low enough so she wouldn't attract attention. "We've been friends for five years, Alex. Don't you think I can read you? All summer long I've been waiting for you to bust open with what is really going on with you. But I was patient. I thought all of those meetings were making you shy or maybe you were intimidated by John's intelligence, or you were keeping yourself on the outside of the circle so you wouldn't get hurt. I kept my mouth shut and let you have enough room to figure it out for yourself, and now I discover that it's *me* who has been on the outside through this whole thing. And I have been *so* supportive and *so* patient with your commander attitude. When were you going to tell me about any of this? And why wouldn't you tell me right away? Why not *me*? What the hell?"

"Are you upset because I didn't tell you about the experiments, or because Peter found out before you did?"

"Leave him out of this. It's bad enough you've parked this situation between Peter and me. You're finally ready to reach a new level and you don't share it with me first? Do you know how that makes me feel? I've been the one following you around, accepting your whims and ideas for years, never expecting anything useful to come out of your antics other than a good friendship."

Alex stopped her friend's tirade and bit back. "So you're not mad about me reaching a new level, because you never thought I would accomplish anything to begin with?"

Lisa fell silent, and that silence told all. Their waiter cautiously approached and took their orders. Alex wasn't sure if Lisa would last through lunch. She always made a dramatic exit when they had arguments and typically left Alex with an empty seat across the table as well as the check. Alex offered a truce. "It was wrong to keep these secrets from you, but you must know that I have everyone's best interests at heart."

Lisa taunted her sardonically. "Yeah, especially John's best interests. I bet he's thrilled that you have such deep consideration for him."

Alex didn't want to talk about John. "Being honest with someone isn't being inconsiderate."

"And dishonest? What is that?" Lisa accused.

"I don't know what you are driving at this morning. I'm sorry Thomas spilled this to Peter before I had the chance to tell you. I'm not a saint, and I wish you would stop expecting me to be one. It's too difficult, and it's definitely not me. I'm a complex woman, and you know that. I want to give my ideas my best effort. But I'm not always going to be perfect for you. I'm sorry I didn't divulge everything that happened this summer. Can we please put all of this behind us?"

Lisa rose abruptly. "Yes, I can put all of this bullshit behind me." She grabbed her purse to dash away, but the strap yanked her back to her chair. Alex had slipped her hand through it before she stood up. Lisa looked confused as Alex pleaded with her.

"That's how well I know *you*, Lisa. You always find an exit line."

Lisa jerked her purse away and stormed out of the restaurant, visibly shaken that her dramatic getaway didn't have the impact she anticipated. Alex watched her fly down the sidewalk. Lisa's blonde hair whipped side to side with each angry step, until she was out of sight. The waiter brought their lunches and placed the check down. She sighed. *Always left with the check.*

She sipped her coffee and tried to dismiss the quarrel. There would be another chance to reconcile with Lisa, as there had been many times before. But she wondered if the lengthy quarrel that was their friendship had finally come to an end. Perhaps all of their relationships were changing, just as her attitude was. She considered her dream. From the view of the tree, everything seemed continuous; everything seemed to go on forever, regardless of daily interference. The tree was never concerned with using up its resources. It knew it was never-ending. Everything was always now, everything was doubtless.

"Yes," she mumbled aloud. "Without doubt. That's definitely the key."

She paused mid-thought. Eyes observed her from an adjacent table. They belonged to a well-dressed man who dropped his gaze to his newspaper when she looked at him. He glanced back up and they smiled at each other. Alex shrugged in self-deprecation for talking to herself. She began to nibble at her lunch, and searched her pockets for a pen to write down her latest thought. She usually repeated herself until she found a writing instrument. But the handsome spectator made her too self-aware to speak aloud again. She reconsidered in favor of her new attitude. The creative impulse was more important than temporary embarrassment. She whispered, "Without doubt, without doubt, in the absence of doubt, in the absence of doubt." She waved to ask the waiter for a pen. Her whispers were interrupted by the sudden approach of the well-dressed man, whose build cast a long shadow across her table in the morning sun. He swept by her and placed a hefty pen on her tabletop as he passed. She watched him leave, but he exited without turning back for a goodbye. She grabbed the pen to write her words onto a napkin, and noticed an inscription on the mahogany wood wrapped around its barrel. Written in block letters were the initials HIP. She put it out of her mind and wrote quickly.

Anything can be achieved when we eliminate doubt. In the absence of doubt we are all God. Purity of intention is a natural conductor of creation.

Alex leaned back and stared at the flimsy paper napkin, now covered with deep navy ink. Memories of businessmen who recounted stories of napkin scribbles that turned into lucrative ventures came to mind. So customary were those tales that a few claimed a business idea was guaranteed success if its inception arrived on a cocktail napkin. She thought of her situation, alone at a diner with a stranger's pen, and laughed off any notion of impending financial success. She studied the words carefully. Tuesday's interview would require her to reveal many secrets. She understood the concept, but was concerned about explaining them to others. She rehearsed it in her head.

When we enter the Creator State, there is a crossover to another level of consciousness. When self awareness is removed, we feel the sensation of being connected to everything in the universe. The joy of being everywhere and everything all at once. Interconnectedness in the absence of time. Surrender within this state of consciousness allows for manifestation of new realities.

Alex returned to her thoughts from the night before: if she and Thomas were able to alter Joseph's behavior, what could a larger group of artists create? Her thoughts were interrupted by the waiter who ascertained Lisa was not coming back. She asked him to wrap the abandoned lunch, which she planned to give to the homeless man who had ordained himself their corner evangelist. The rumpled vagabond dwelled on the same section of sidewalk since long before Alex moved to Lakeview. She named him "Homeless Max" during her first weeks in the neighborhood. From his pulpit of cement, Max called out to all who passed within earshot. His repertoire was nonsensical, but he did have a commanding voice that attracted ears. Alex used the HIP pen to scribble her latest revelation on top of the takeout box. *In the absence of doubt we are all God.* She handed the box to the thankless man as she passed him on her way home. He ignored the message and tore into the meal inside.

She strolled back to her building and received a warm hello from her elderly neighbor in the lobby. The tiny woman promised to visit tomorrow. She often stopped by on Saturday mornings and offered Alex fresh scones in exchange for an hour of chitchat about art. Alex's cell phone began to buzz at her waist. She gave the frail woman a nod of confirmation and checked her cell display. She saw Thomas' number and hoped there was no static between them from the night before. She had some ammunition if he wanted to argue, since he was so loose-lipped with Peter about their summer experiments. She wanted the group to get its act together before the interview. First impressions would weigh heavily on Bob's perception of the collective. Thomas was of the same mindset and agreed to get together. Her luncheon with Lisa tainted her outings for the afternoon, so she asked him to come to her studio.

Thomas hastily grabbed a cab and scooted across town. He tried to calm himself on the ride over. He opened his backpack which contained a new stash of Artist Exchange letters and studied them carefully. In his possession was new evidence that the Creator State was a widespread phenomenon. Web site links from

New York City to the West Coast revealed broad support. E-mails arrived from artists in all walks of life, in all mediums, which bore witness to the Creator State. It was just what they needed to present to Bob. He clenched the pile to his chest and mouthed a "yes" to himself, then noticed the taxi driver eyeball him in the mirror. Thomas gave him a grin and another "yes" out loud. The man scowled and returned his eyes to the road.

Thomas' short cab ride gave Alex enough time to appraise her disarrayed apartment. She took Lisa's earlier critique to heart and stuffed a few strewed belongings into drawers to tame the clutter. She covered her daybed, fluffed the pillows, and realized it might be wasted effort. Thomas might not notice. When he visited in the past, he appeared unshaken by her note-littered living quarters. She cleared the kitchen table for business and placed a pair of glasses out for iced tea. Her last effort to tidy the papers was interrupted by Thomas' arrival.

He gave a cautious hello at the door. She reciprocated by telling him Lisa revealed his discussion with Peter. All was forgiven between them and they sat down to discuss the impending interview. He complimented how nice the place looked. She smiled and poured the iced tea. There was a different feel to their friendship when he came over, something she couldn't put her finger on. Most of the time they met at the Andrews, or at Thomas' spacious loft. She thought it might be the size of her studio, and she aimed to make it a comfortable meeting. Thomas pulled out the new e-mails as if he had gold in his backpack. She diverted him before they got to business.

"I had a wild dream this morning."

"Yeah, I got that from your *Mobile* message today."

"It gave me a feeling I've desired for a long time. It urged me to say whatever I am experiencing or thinking, without worrying about people's reactions. I feel like I've been given a green light to throw caution aside and express everything. The key is to have an open heart and mind."

He studied her face as he swallowed his desire to express everything he hid from her all summer. It would be a blissful release, but he repressed his private sentiments. "I think you should definitely say what's on your mind." He gulped his iced tea to quench his burning tongue as she spoke.

"That means no more withholding information from our friends or from Bob. If I have to censor myself, then I'm hanging in the wrong circle. If we don't tell the *Tribune* everything that we've discovered, then we'll never find the kindred spirits and support that we need to continue."

"So we should reveal our little experiment with Joseph?" He anticipated a yes.

She contemplated the best way to present their information to the meticulous Robert Clarke. They would need someone outside of the art world to make him feel a little insecure. "We need some back up. Someone to confirm that our experiment wasn't just a guy changing his attitude without our influence."

Thomas knew where she was going with this and challenged her. "We need John, don't we?" He teased. "Good timing on the break up, Alex."

"Yeah, well, that bridge hasn't burned yet. Maybe he would be willing to help us out. Let me call him and see if he'll do us one more favor."

Thomas witnessed an unwelcome sight as she crossed to the phone. She was all too eager to give John a call. He felt his opportunity to approach her slipping away. Silently he coached himself to get up and tell her, right then, right there, how he felt. He took a breath to speak and John answered on the other end of the line. Alex paced with the phone and cautiously addressed the question with John. It wasn't bad for a day-after break up dialogue. She sounded centered and caring. She proposed his assistance at the *Tribune* interview and gave Thomas an o.k. signal. John agreed to do it. As she tied up the call, Thomas realized she must have told him about their efforts with Joseph. The indiscretion weighed in his chest as they settled down to sketch an outline of the interview.

Thomas prompted. "Peter thought we should get straight to the experiment and skip any niceties."

Alex ignored his attempt to reveal who discussed what with whom. She drummed her pen on the table as she spoke. "Bob will want to schmooze his way to something juicier, so he'll be on his best behavior. We should make him feel welcome. He wants to feel more like an artist than a reporter. We can work him from that angle first." Alex stopped tapping and nudged a distracted Thomas. "Are you okay with this?"

Thomas shook himself free of his preoccupations. "Maybe we can share the e-mails, the Artist Exchange responses, the Tuesday meeting notes; make him feel like he's one of the gang. If he understands the reasons behind our actions, he may find the experiment a natural progression of our growth."

Alex beamed and rolled the pen to him. "Write that down, Thomas! That is perfect. We can introduce our curiosity with the State and its possibilities, and John can assist with the scientific backup. Bob will really go for a technical point of view. I'm so glad John said yes. It will really help us. I'm glad he isn't pissed at me. He's a great guy."

Thomas gave her a warning glance out of reflex, which he immediately tried to drop. But it was too late; she saw it and assumed an interpretation.

"What the hell is that look for? Do you have a problem with John now? Ex-boyfriends aren't welcome in the clique? It's important that you treat him well at this interview. We have to be professional."

Thomas put his hand up to stop her efforts. "You misunderstood my look. I am not mad at John. That's the farthest thought from my mind."

Alex saw something else in Thomas' stare. He locked gazes with her and finally allowed his true emotions to be witnessed. The moment seemed to span a hundred lifetimes. She didn't need to voice her interpretation of the look. It was evident that he had some kind of crush on her. She leaned back in her chair and kept her eyes across the kitchen table. She repressed asking how long it had been, or why he didn't tell her, or what they were supposed to do now. That kind of talk wouldn't suffice for the level they had reached as friends and colleagues. They sat staring at each other as the moment went on.

Fortunately, Thomas started to laugh. The laughter was contagious, and she joined him in an uncontrollable fit of giggles. It seemed the kitchen was suddenly transformed into an absurdist play. After a minute the amusement subsided, they caught their breath, and returned to the interview outline without further discussion of his disclosure.

Thomas reviewed the agenda. "So John talks science for a bit, blah blah blah, and then what?"

Her face lit with panic. "Bob will want to talk to Joseph! He's going to have to interview Joseph and ask him if he knew about us, what happened to him, all of that. What do we do when that happens? I have no idea how Joseph will react!" She pulled at her blonde locks. "Crap, I'm going to get fired!"

"Calm down, you're the one who wants to reveal all. That means accepting the consequences. Joseph is bound to find out sooner or later. But we should approach Joseph before Bob does, just to cover our ass." He saw that she was anxious. "Hey, have faith, he'll understand. He's a better person these days. He's not going to suddenly become the old tyrant he used to be. And if he does, then we'll know his changes were just a fluke. But we have to get to him before Bob does. Is Joseph around the theater on Sundays?"

"He'll be there this afternoon, there's a lecture renting the space today."

Thomas beamed and gathered the papers from the table. "No better time than the present. Let's do this thing." She grabbed her things and met him at the door, where he paused. He looked into her eyes and smiled again. "I feel much better. Thanks."

The duo arrived at the Andrews as the lecture let out. Joseph remained in the loft, so they pretended to search for a forgotten item in the office until the crowd dispersed below. Joseph was about to excuse himself when Alex asked him to stay a while, that they had something important to discuss. He seemed uneasy, so they maneuvered him into a position of power on the high stool of the lighting table and planted themselves in lower chairs. Thomas spoke first.

"We are going to be interviewed on Tuesday by the *Tribune* arts reporter, Robert Clarke. He wants to talk to us about the artist meetings we've been holding." Joseph seemed to be fine with it and congratulated them. Thomas continued. "Part of our group has been experimenting with a new facet of performance, something we call the Creator State."

Joseph seemed unphased by the information. "Yeah, that thing Alex talks about on your Web site." He smirked at their surprise. "What, like I don't check out what you guys are up to?" He put them at ease. "I think it's cool what you guys are doing. Sounds like a lot of people are having the same feeling about their art. Don't worry, I'm cool with it, I won't say anything negative to your reporter. Is that what you're worried about? Hey, don't sweat it, I'm supportive."

They exchanged a look and Thomas kept on. "Thanks for your support. We do think we're on to something with our work. We, that is, Alex and I, have been conducting a little experiment this summer, trying to use our creative talents for something absolutely new. We're very excited about the outcome, and we wanted to talk to you about it." Joseph's interest peaked. He appeared to be flattered that they would share their secret with him.

Alex took the lead. "We thought if we felt a positive energy during our performances, that perhaps it could be directed somehow. We thought maybe the same energy could transform negativity. So we attempted to direct our energies toward improving a person's life. It's like when people meditate or pray for someone; sometimes the thoughts attract good things to that person. We proposed the Creator State would allow us to send a surge of positive energy toward a specific man."

Joseph looked curious. "So what happened? Did it work? Did the person know you were doing it, because that might wreck it right there. Because how would you know if it was really effective if they were forewarned? Did you tell them first?"

Thomas shook his head. "No, we didn't tell him."

Joseph liked the idea. "Cool. So what happened to the guy?"

"He had a rapid transformation." Alex encouraged. "Remarkably, his outlook started to change almost immediately after we began. Where he used to be disagreeable, he was suddenly kind. He offered help in instances where he used to be stubborn. The changes may seem subtle to outsiders, but to people who know him, there is a marked change in his attitude."

Thomas emphasized the change. "His positive energy is contagious. It affects everyone he comes into contact with; he's a pleasure to be around. Before we began, he seemed to be blocked from living a happy life. It's as if he was given a chance to be his true self."

The more they explained, the more it dawned on Joseph that the person they were speaking about was him. He rose to his feet, crossed to the back window, and threw open the curtain. A shock of afternoon light surrounded him as he swallowed hard and calmed himself.

"A few months ago I would have thrown your asses out of here." He turned back with melancholia in his eyes. "But now everything is different. I knew I was changing, but I thought maybe it was just being away from David. Or maybe that Alex's messages were rubbing off on me. I didn't suspect anything else." He leaned on the window sill. "Whatever it is you guys have done, I'm at a loss for the right thing to say about it."

They were dumbfounded by his acceptance. He looked up at them again and saw their surprise, which made him laugh out loud. "Don't worry guys, I'm saying thank you!" Alex embraced him. He hugged her in return and asked, "Just don't mention me by name in the interview, okay?"

They agreed to his confidentiality, and discussed the details of their private summer sessions. They calculated the more he knew, the more enthusiastic he would be if Bob wanted to question him. By the end of an hour, Joseph decided he would speak to Bob on the condition that he would remain anonymous in the article. He asked them to leave him alone to think. They left him in the loft, surrounded by the glow of sunlight and revelation.

Outside on the sidewalk, Alex felt as if the conversation with Joseph was a dream. It all went so smoothly. Thomas sensed her disbelief and confirmed his own. "That was most unexpected. Maybe we'll have to expect the unexpected from here on."

She let him see that she wanted some privacy for the rest of the afternoon. Thomas knew there would be no more discussion of his love for her today, so he left for home. She walked away and then turned back to watch Thomas. She hoped that seeing him again would confirm the day was not an ongoing dream. She saw him climb the stairs to the L. He caught her observation of him and waved. She returned the gesture and proceeded home as she reviewed the day's events. The calm of the morning, the waking dream, the quarrel with Lisa, the mysterious man at the Diner, a congenial call with John, Thomas' secret crush revealed, and a confession to Joseph. All of it oiled the cogs of the Creator State machine, which seemed to be gearing up for full operation.

As she approached her corner, the unmistakable voice of Homeless Max peaked above the din of city noise. She slipped by him and retreated toward the anonymity of her home. He shouted the words she wrote on the takeout box, over and over again as if chanting a mantra.

"In the absence of doubt we are all God! In the absence of doubt we are all God!"

10

○ ○

A clean slate is needed today for new beginnings, new challenges, and new visions. Clear your plate for better feasts. Empty the closets and drawers and corners to welcome the new guests. They will be staying for a while.

—The Magic Mobile

Alex waited in the late night air across the street from the Andrews and looked at the stars mounted on its roof. After two exhausting days of preparations for their meeting with Bob, the interview night was upon the group. Most of them had already arrived. They were forewarned about Alex and Thomas' experiments, and eager to participate. The event was a litmus test for her newfound confidence; it was a chance to fearlessly express herself. As she star gazed, she reminisced about her first meeting with David in the spring. His call that fateful morning had been an answer to a request for a next step. She now tempted fate with another silent request. She wished the interview to be a major step in the Project's progress.

Her appeal was interrupted by the approach of two gentlemen on the opposite side of the street. Thomas came from the west, and John came from the east. They grew closer to the theater and noticed her across the way. She gave them a wave from her position on the sidewalk, which they took as an indication to give her a minute alone. The two men exchanged an uncomfortable handshake and disappeared into the Andrews.

She inhaled a deep cleansing breath and quieted her inner voices. She caught sight of a man parallel parking a BMW just up the block, and recognized their special guest behind the wheel. Just beyond him a couple hustled down the sidewalk, which the streetlights exposed to be Peter and Lisa. They slowed at the sight of Robert Clarke getting out of his car and greeted him. The three of them spotted Alex as she crossed Belmont. She reached a hand out to Bob as he neared, but he gave her a quick embrace instead. Lisa silently watched them with insolence. She remained on her best behavior at Peter's request.

Robert Clarke entered the Andrews Theater with a well-worn leather bag slung on his shoulder and a sparkle in his eye. He was delighted by the reception he received in the lobby. Everyone made introductions while Joseph poured a round of wine; they wanted to warm up their guest before the big interview. Bob received the gallantries with ease. Thomas and Alex knew he would be true to his agenda, and they remained alert to their own. Peter approached them and spoke candidly.

"This reception before the interview was a brilliant idea. Look at him, he's eating it up. Probably isn't used to this kind of attention."

Thomas agreed. "Poor guy always has to slip in and out of performances undetected. I suppose we take all the receptions and after-parties for granted."

They watched as Bob was introduced to different members of the group. Rashan bent his ear for a while and represented the musicians, then Bob moved on to the dancers. All facets of the collective jewel were present, and Alex glistened with the good attendance. Actors, writers, filmmakers, directors, and performance artists from every faction made themselves available; a gathering of about fifty altogether. Thomas updated them about the experiments on Joseph prior to the meeting, so there would be no surprises or illicit reactions. He garnered support from most of the artists, and discouraged those who had mixed feelings to attend the interview. He realized it swayed the opinion in his favor, but considered his manipulation forgivable given the circumstances. Bob seemed impressed with the turnout. With each conversation his enthusiasm grew. He felt like part of the collective, and that was just what they wanted.

John quietly waited his turn until the right opportunity arose to meet their guest. As Kona and the painters departed, he approached Bob and introduced himself. They chatted for several minutes, until Thomas asked everyone to move into the theater for the interview. Bob sauntered over to Alex with a tongue-in-cheek grin and commented on his brief conversation with the scientist. Apparently John disclosed the breakup with Alex in the course of a five minute exchange. Bob beamed with delight at the ex-boyfriend's behavior.

"Two months of bliss and you break up?" Bob curled a shady smile. "Well, I guess that's the theater for you."

Alex tried to remain professional. "No, Bob, that's just life."

He laughed and pushed for information. "He seems like a bright one, but what's a scientist doing hanging out with you guys?"

Alex smirked and indicated that his answer would soon be revealed. Bob laughed again and threw his arm around her shoulders as they entered the house. "Let's see what Alex's little club has been up to. Let's have some fun, shall we?"

The house doors closed behind them with a vault-like thud. The empty lobby waited in silence as the interview proceeded.

Two hours later, Robert Clarke emerged with a thick pad of notes, a lengthy tape recording, and an even brighter spark in his eye. He hurried out of the Andrews, eager to pour the contents of the encounter into an article. He jogged down the sidewalk with his bag in tow, and huffed with the ballast of his new discovery. He tossed the bag into his car and scrambled to start the engine as his impending story bubbled behind his wide eyes. Thomas dashed to the front doorway to watch the BMW pull out, and gave Bob a polite thank you wave goodbye. When the coast was clear, Thomas reentered the house and shouted, "We did it!" The group cheered with relief.

"Holy crap was I nervous!" exclaimed Peter as he fumbled for a cigarette.

Joseph shouted over the crowd. "You were nervous? How do you think I felt?! It was like being interviewed by *60 Minutes*!" This sparked an outbreak of laughter.

Thomas hushed the group and began the congratulations. "Joseph, you were noble in the face of fear. We thank you." Joseph gave him a knightly bow. Thomas turned to their resident scientist. "John, you were informative, eloquent, and your references were perfection. We thank you." John tipped his head in acknowledgment. Thomas lit a sober look. "Alex, you could make a believer out of the darkest skeptic. You really shined tonight, my friend."

The group applauded earnestly as Alex turned down their requests for a speech. She finally gave in and spoke from the heart. "Everyone is a hero tonight. This has been a nerve-wracking few days for all of us." She suggested, "The article is going to be published Thursday, with the first edition hitting the newsstands at 3:00 a.m. Anyone willing to burn a little post-midnight oil and wait up with me tomorrow night?"

The group enthusiastically agreed to meet at the Night and Day Diner to await the arrival of the morning paper on Thursday. John lingered behind as everyone left and waited until Alex was alone in the theater. She noticed his hesitation to exit. He eventually approached her.

"Sorry for mentioning our breakup to Bob, that was unprofessional on my part. I'm still a little bewildered by it. Our break up, that is."

"No need to apologize. It's understandable, it's only been a few days. For what it's worth, I miss talking to you." She hadn't realized the emotion until she spoke it aloud. She did miss his companionship, not to mention the exceptional love-making. But she knew they couldn't rekindle a relationship, especially when everything was starting to pick up with the Project.

He knew she had regrets about leaving him, but he calculated they would never outweigh the importance she put on her personal goals. Her casualness indicated she got over him much faster than he got over her. But it didn't sway him to care for her any less.

"I don't see any reason why we can't keep in touch from time to time, Alex." He saw the loss of him finally reach her; a subtle reaction in her placid façade. Perhaps there was still some hope that he meant more to her than just a scientific reference. He added, "Good luck with the article, I think Bob enjoyed the evening. I know I did." He tried to exit graciously, but she wasn't willing to let him depart.

"Are you coming to the Diner on Thursday morning? Your input was so important to this interview. It gave us an edge we desperately needed."

John heard his importance to the process, but found no romantic inklings in her words. "No thanks. I'm done with middle of the night meetings for a while." He gave her a peck on the cheek and walked out.

Alex solemnly locked the door after he departed. She wandered around the Andrews and reviewed the interview in her mind. Everyone seemed satisfied that they wouldn't be portrayed as foolish, lofty or crazy. Perhaps a good review was all they could hope for. She sat center stage and listened. Her voices were quiet tonight. She sat in the stillness of the Andrews and strained to receive some wisdom on her personal life. The weekend troubles circled: she let Lisa go, she let John go, and she hadn't said a word to Thomas about his supposed crush on her. Here was a magical three, but she found no harmony in their purpose. Lisa cooperated on Peter's behalf, even though it meant faking her faith in the Project. Thomas turned his Creator State into an emotional state and Alex resented it; she believed crushes during an intense endeavor were insubstantial. Then there was John. She wanted to separate herself from his analytical notions about the State. But she needed his support to suppress the public's apprehension with their artistic theories. If she fed these three dramas with the fuel they desired, they would spin into needless quarreling or band-aid fixes on the deeper problems of their relationships.

As she evaluated her three recent turns of fate, she considered John to be the most revealing. She wanted information from John rather than romance. She used her sexuality to draw him closer, establish trust, and ultimately, get what she desired. She lay back on the stage and blinked at the dim work lights above her.

She wondered if she wanted the romance, too. She was genuinely attracted to him, enjoyed the sex, loved the companionship, the laughter, the sensuality of the relationship, all of it. Then she realized the two parts of John, John the lover and John the needed scientist, were woven together in her view of him. Her artistic views clashed with his established order of science, but when science-John was dismissed, she had dismissed lover-John as well. She questioned if art and science could be intertwined without difficulty. Alex disembarked from her train of thought and sat up. She spoke aloud to the empty house. "Enough discussion for tonight!" She shouted. "This is a theater, let's have a performance!"

She stood up, stretched her arms and mouth wide, and paced around the empty stage. "What would you like to see? Ibsen? Shakespeare? Chekhov?" The silent house seemed to discuss its choices among the vacant seats until an answer came.

"Williams!" Alex delighted. "An excellent choice!"

The Andrews settled in as she prepared Blanche DuBois. Slowly the timeless femme fatale materialized within Alex. Soon afterwards, Blanche delivered her classic monologue of lost love at the Moon Lake Casino. As the poetic scene came to a close, the house held its breath and savored the last words as they lingered in the air.

Twenty-four hours later, the Creator State group slumped in various positions of sleepiness at the Night and Day Diner. The 3:00 a.m. hour was wearisome as they waited for the impending *Tribune* delivery truck. Twelve members camped out; the rest called or e-mailed their support for the first morning edition at a more reasonable hour. Lisa stayed at home, snug in bed. Thomas was present and alert due to the Diner's bottomless cup of coffee policy. Every large vehicle that hummed up Broadway was suspect, and Peter went to the window each time a rumbling engine approached.

Time dragged its heels as Rashan tried to keep the group entertained by reading comical stories from the *Onion*. Eventually this lost its humor and dwindled to tediousness. He then picked up his harmonica and improvised a song with lyrics entitled *Kopy Kat Blues*, but the tune received groans of agony from Thomas. Rashan recognized that he was going to get the hook, bowed out gracefully, and returned to his table with a sigh. Another truck clambered by and Alex felt her anxiety get the best of her.

"It's like waiting for a review of my life!" She shouted.

Thomas chuckled. "No kidding, I'm wondering how many stars we're going to get." The troupe stirred with laughter and perked up a bit.

Peter paced and put on his best Robert Clarke imitation. "The Andrews has spawned a collective of nut jobs, all living in a delusion of grandeur." The group laughed again, so he continued. "Fascinating and tragic to behold."

Thomas began to sing, "Dance ten, looks threeeee!" The rest of them joined in on the fun, danced around the empty restaurant, and screeched off key. Since they were the only customers at that hour, the kitchen staff emerged to watch this bizarre floor show. Before the artists reached the big finish, a *Tribune* truck slammed to a stop out front. They froze, then applauded as Peter ran outside and greeted the delivery man. Fifty cents later, Peter returned and fumbled through the sections as he searched for the article.

The group sat in anticipation. Some held hands, some clenched their fists. Thomas buried his face in his hands, as if he was about to witness a lynching. Peter finally found the arts section. He pulled it out and exposed a large photo of Alex on the cover of Section D. She flinched when she saw how big it was, then peered over Peter's shoulder as he silently read the title. He raised a fist and shouted, "Yes!"

The group burst into objections and pleaded for him to share the article out loud. Thomas instructed from behind his hands. "C'mon man! Read it straight through without commentary, please."

Peter calmed himself, cleared his throat, and announced the title. "The State of Chicago Theater, by Robert Clarke." He looked up and saw that everyone liked the titled as much as he did. He continued.

"It's easy to respect Alex Davis. She is a smart woman, performs with depth and confidence, and in the past two months has turned the Andrews into one of the most talked about spaces in town. Her enthusiasm for the theater is contagious. But recently her views on creativity have left me wondering what they've been putting in the Lakeview water. Last Tuesday I investigated rumors on the street of secret meetings taking place after-hours at the Andrews. According to a few of my sources, an artistic collective had been kicking around some new ideas about changing the world, headed up by the luminous Davis. As I am a cynical old skeptic, I surmised they would not stand a chance of showing me anything new. But I had to know what was stirring in those old church walls, so I attended one of their late night gatherings.

"I was greeted like an honored guest, wined and chatted up by nearly fifty artists from different mediums. Painters, dancers, musicians, actors, authors, and filmmakers welcomed me into their sacred abode. The collective was formed through a sister project to these meetings, the online Artist Exchange. These artists responded to a posting which claimed to be looking for 'something more in

art,' that timeless ideal that seems to plague every generation of our creative people. However this group promised they discovered something different. I was
escorted into the Andrews house for the real show.

"While it's difficult to centrifuge nearly two hours of exceptional conversation
into a brief article, let me highlight a few key points. At the foundation of their
collective is a belief that all artists represent a tiny replica of the original creative
energy which made everything we know of. They propose that artists, as creative
microcosms of a universal creative source, tap into this energy every time they
create. Whether they do it consciously or unconsciously, they channel this creative power through their chosen method. Davis elaborated, 'Many artists have
felt the presence of a higher power or an inspiration flowing through them when
they create their best work. We are hypothesizing that it isn't a force working
through the artist, but rather the artists themselves who are the creative source
when they eliminate doubts, fears, or self-conscious awareness of being creative.'

"I proposed they may be portraying the greatest role of their careers; that they
are attempting to play God. The group objected and justified they are simply utilizing the essence of the natural order which is creation. They even have a name
for this point in consciousness, and call it 'The Creator State.'

"From the back of the group, a man rose to support their theory. I am surprised to discover they have a scientist among them, John Mitchell of Northwest-
ern University. He is an unlikely member given the artistic exclusivity of this elite
bunch. Mitchell explained, 'Quantum Physics has determined that a single unified field connects all aspects of the universe, including everything which makes
up our reality. Our minds have a direct link to this field. Thought can affect particles of matter, light, and water through this unified field of consciousness. Many
experiments have documented these effects. When a performer taps into their
creative ability to alter their own reality, it in turn alters the reality of those
observing the art form. For example, when you witness a passionate performance,
your reality is being altered by the creative thoughts emanating from the artist
themselves. They change their reality and it affects your own in turn. The performer's consciousness alters the observer's consciousness.'

"Mitchell added this is not exclusive to live performance. A painting, novel, or
film can have the same affect. It alters your reality during the time you are a witness to it. Davis then turned the conversation toward their purpose. 'Everyone
has the ability to create this way. Artists just happen to utilize it more effectively.
We believe artists hold the key to creating a better reality for our world.'

"And therein rests the progression. This group thinks they can change the
world into a more peaceful place by using the Creator State. Being a reporter, I

have my doubts about the effectiveness of world peace missions, and I ask for validation of their theories. I am shocked to find that they have carried out an experiment to test its effectiveness. For the past several weeks, Davis and her right-hand Creator Stater, Thomas Maxwell, have privately performed a very secret script in the wee hours of the night. This short play is cast with characters they portrayed when they encountered the Creator State. But this script spotlighted a change in the attitude of one of their colleagues, transforming him from negative and nasty to positive and polite. If that isn't strange enough for you, picture them doing this without the guinea pig present. The entire script is written as if the change takes place offstage, within the course of the play. They talk about his transformation in this well-meaning piece, send goodwill and positive energies his way each night for weeks, until lo and behold the guy starts to behave differently in the real world. Sound like witchcraft? It may appear to be voodoo on the surface, but physicist Mitchell steps in to clarify.

"'They used their absolution within the Creator State to create change in the reality around them. The power of intention has proved effective many times before. This is no different; they simply utilized the positive force of creation to manifest a positive reality.'

"The subject of their experiment, who was present but wishes to remain anonymous, has disregarded any wrongdoing. He is jubilant about the effect and claims, 'My perspective was altered. Maybe they activated things that already existed within me. It's possible that it just took some outside help to release it.' According to sources outside of the group, the changes in this individual are dramatic. Apparently the man used to have a monstrous chip on his shoulder and threw attitude wherever it would stick. They described his transformation as surprising and uncharacteristic.

"So what are the Creator Staters doing with this new information? And who is next on the list for a life-altering change? Davis proposed, 'We seek a broader goal of rejuvenating our art and its influence on society. Changing individuals one by one is not our target. We experimented because we wanted to provide evidence to justify our theories. Our goal is to utilize our creative gifts to spread world goodwill.'

"World peace wasn't the new idea I sought when I entered this meeting of professional artists. In fact it's an old idea, and I voiced my suspicions on its effectiveness in the past. Maxwell responded, 'We realize the idea is not new, but we feel our ideas are viable. This isn't the sixties. No one is aiming to provide freedom from the harshness of the world. We would like to explore how altered perspectives could make marked changes in the world view.'

"Maxwell disclosed their plans to gather an online network of artists to experiment with the Creator State. While their e-mail list has grown, it is not yet near the numbers they need to make a real difference. Davis emphasized, 'We have thrown the idea out there and so far it has been magnetic, attracting people who have experienced the same phenomenon and want to know more about it. If artists can master the true power of their talents, the possibilities for using the Creator State are infinite.'

"Currently we live in a world where violence, terrorism, starvation, disease, poverty, and abuse of the natural environment are the everyday norm. Change appears to be so unreachable it seems impossible that anything different could exist within my own lifetime, or for lifetimes long after I am gone. After listening to this group, I realized that I dashed the idea of change before giving it a fair shot. That realization made me think this group may have reached me already. Davis may not be able to convince everyone to open their minds, but she has my utmost respect for trying."

Peter lowered the paper. "It gives the Artist Exchange Web address at the bottom." The tables remained silent for a moment and contemplated the article. He urged, "This is good, yes?" The group erupted with pleasure and quoted bits and pieces of the article. Rashan and Lucas high-fived. Thomas lowered his hands from his face and heartily agreed with Peter.

"Bob is definitely a good ally. The way he said he was a cynic at first, and how we swayed him, that will help us. Don't you agree, Alex?"

She had moved to a corner table during the reading and didn't respond. They investigated her silence, and discovered she was crying.

Peter stood astonished. "Those had better be tears of joy!"

Rashan went to her side to comfort her. "Hey sistah, this is the good moment, you crying for the love of it?"

"It's unbelievable," she sniffled. "As cliché as it sounds, I can't believe this is happening to us. Maybe we should have someone outside of the circle read it, get some feedback, see if it's as good as we think it is."

Rashan laughed at her. "Woman, thousands of people gonna read it today. Don't worry, you'll have your answer." He raised a glass of water. "But for now we celebrate our little victory!"

Everyone raised a glass of whatever they could find and toasted with Rashan. He swallowed the water and looked disappointed. "Hey, I don't know about you other artists, but we musicians know how to do a moment some respect. Anyone interested in properly celebrating with a private party? My home is open to everyone."

Peter agreed first. "Libations on me!" He reconsidered his wallet. "Okay, libations on Thomas."

They hustled into the street and waved down the few cabs on Broadway. Alex felt her confidence return with the support of her friends. She grabbed Thomas' hand before he entered the taxi. "Thank you, Thomas. I wouldn't be here, doing this, entering this phase of my life if it wasn't for you. I want you to know I appreciate everything you have done for me."

He looked at her and gave her hand a squeeze. "Don't get sentimental on me, Alex. Can you show me a little more respect than that?"

She blinked at him and realized he was absolutely right. She shouldn't trivialize this milestone with tears of joy and thank-you-for-everything. She quickly promised, "Won't happen again."

Thomas held the taxi door open as she hurried inside. He mumbled under his breath. "Good. We need a clean slate."

11

These talents enshroud our waking moments and fly uninhibited in our dreams. To deny their existence is futile, and to live without utilizing our true purpose is wrong. Deny creation and we deny ourselves.

—The Magic Mobile

The celebration continued well past dawn. In the comfort of Rashan's home, the group drank and congratulated themselves for hours. All appeared victorious in the protective company of friends. By 7:00 a.m. Alex's cell phone buzzed repeatedly with good wishes. Its constant vibration urged her to leave the sheltered apartment festivities and go outside where she could experience the reality of the event. She voiced her concern to Thomas.

"What if the article is interpreted differently by the average *Tribune* reader?"

Thomas sloughed off her pessimism. "Don't overanalyze, it's all good this morning."

"It makes me anxious being in here, surrounded by my friends. I have no perspective."

"Then get out there," Thomas encouraged. He gave her a shove. She obeyed and wriggled her way out of the merriments.

With a few hours to spare before the Andrews demanded her presence, she opted for a long walk home rather than a cab ride. From the sidewalk she studied coffee shops and bus stops, anywhere a *Tribune* patron flipped through the day's print. The local cafe had a few papers scattered about on the tables. As she passed she saw her photo propped in front of a few morning readers. It gave her a chill. Her image was used before for publicity purposes, and it never bothered her because she was photographed in character. This morning's use was different; it showed Alex Davis alongside her personal views on art. For the first time, the intimacy of a thousand observers made her uncomfortable. She shivered and moved on to the next observatory: a crowded Starbucks at the corner. She turned off her busy cell phone and stiffened as she entered the establishment. Her own eyes glared at her from across the room, in the hands of a faceless reader hidden behind the interior of Section D. The businesswoman lowered her paper, spotted Alex in the coffee line, and did a double-take on the image in her newspaper. Alex looked away and modestly avoided recognition. After ordering a latte, she glanced back at the woman, only to find an empty chair. She was startled when the woman suddenly spoke from behind her.

"Alex Davis?" The woman had a smooth voice with a hint of East Coast dialect. Alex smiled humbly, and didn't know what to expect from the designer-clad urbanite. The distinctive scent of Chanel Number Five wafted from the woman as she thrust a business handshake toward Alex.

"Victoria Winston," the woman gleamed. "I've just read about your work at the Andrews. Just fascinating."

Alex returned the firm grip with a smile. "New York?"

Victoria looked flattered. She confirmed she was a Manhattanite who was visiting Chicago that morning for a meeting. When Alex questioned what business she was in, she skirted the inquiry and popped open her briefcase on a nearby table. She produced a card and whispered. "This is what I do; don't let the Prada suit throw you off." Alex smiled again, embarrassed to be caught admiring Victoria's impressive ensemble. She took the card and glanced at the contents of the woman's briefcase. Before she had a chance to register what it held, Victoria snapped it shut again and was on her way. "If this article generates the kind of interest I think it will, I'll be contacting you." She extended an exit handshake. "Nice meeting you, Alex."

Alex was called at the counter at the same time Victoria said her name. They shook hands again and Victoria darted for the door, off to her appointment. As Alex retrieved her beverage, a seated man connected the face at the counter with the face on his morning newspaper. He waited for her to turn around and waved her over as he leaned back in his chair. His suit jacket widened with the gesture and exposed a blue striped shirt which stretched over a span of untamed belly. He wore a flashy red tie adorned with a well-polished tie bar. Alex laughed to herself: any man who waved a woman over as if she were wait staff had some lessons to learn. She waved back as if he said hello and turned her eyes to Victoria's business card. The portly individual became agitated and yelled out, "C'mere!" which disturbed everyone in their morning routines. All eyes volleyed from the yelling man to Alex, and waited to see how she would handle the oaf. She motioned for him to join her at a table with two chairs, which perturbed him even further. The

Starbucks manager appeared silently at the edge of the counter, which indicted this man had a history of disturbing the mandatory franchise peace.

The aggravated man got to his feet, raised his Section D, and slapped it with his opposite hand for dramatic emphasis. "It's all bullshit, girlie. You 'real' artists with your 'creative unity' are all gonna be extinct in a few years. Reality TV stars and supermodels are all we're gonna need. Wake up to the future, kiddo. You got a hot body and a cute face; don't wreck your shot at fame by trying to be noble. If you want people to pay attention to you, you'd better learn to take your clothes off!"

He crushed his paper into the trash can on his way out, and leered back at Alex as he walked down the street. The crowd politely returned to their routines, and a few rustled through their morning paper for the article in question. The manager apologized to Alex and settled her at a table before he returned to his duties. She tried to mask her shaken nerves and reached for the closest thing available to calm her: her *Magic Mobile* journal. She flipped to an empty leaf, looked at the blank space, and listened for words of wisdom. She scribbled a drawing of the angry man, complete with popping buttons and electrified hair, with his words in giant letters above. "TAKE YOUR CLOTHES OFF!" She giggled at the humorous sketch, and then wrote the day's *Mobile* message below it.

If I had a dollar for everyone who told me I was too close to my work, I'd be rich. If I had taken their advice and distanced myself, I would be very, very poor.

She studied the simplistic words, grateful she hadn't allowed Bob to print the *Mobile* number. She surveyed the room and noticed a few eyes on her. The exposure felt much different than a review or pre-show write up. She had to defend herself. Endurance and grace would have to prevail in the face of adversaries such as the angry man. She tried to rationalize his viewpoint. Maybe, for someone who didn't subscribe to culture, it appeared that the higher arts weren't needed anymore. Maybe he didn't know what he was missing, or maybe he was one of those people who had seen an awful performance in his youth. One bad show witnessed in high school can ruin a lifetime of attendance. Or perhaps he was right, and higher art was slipping into a thing of the past. She expelled the thought and shooed negativity from her exciting day.

She sipped her latte and studied Victoria's business card. The heavy matte stock was a deep orange, with black letters printed in a simple font. Alex grinned because it looked like a Monopoly game "Chance" card. She wondered if it was intentional, which would make it terribly clever. She read the type:

HIP
Victoria Winston
Client Liaison, East Coast

Alex reread the card, stunned by the connection. She searched for the pen she received from the Night and Day Diner patron, dug it out of her bag, and held it aside of the business card. HIP. Same font type, same company name. Her heart quickened with the combination of synchronicity and caffeine. Suddenly she wanted to be home, inside her little protective pod of a studio. A young man recognized her from the photo on his paper. She felt his eyes on her, but gathered her things and hurried for the door. He gave her a thumbs up and she reciprocated with a faint smile as she left.

She turned on her cell as she walked, and it displayed several received calls. She would have many messages to retrieve when she reached her apartment. Her voices commanded. *Don't hide. Express everything. Let them see you, talk to you, hear you.* Alex slowed her pace as she entered the solace of her neighborhood. She scanned for friends and familiar faces. There was no one recognizable in immediate range, so she pushed the issue and stopped in at her corner market. Behru, the shop's owner, greeted her with warmth and excitement.

"Alex, you are my famous customer!" He held out his copy of Section D and a pen. "You must sign. Please sign my paper and I will hang it on our wall."

Flattered by his endearing behavior, she signed the paper with a flourish. "That's the first autograph I've ever given."

He tacked it on his bulletin board as she watched. He hung it with familial pride, as a Father would hang a good report card on the refrigerator door. Behru turned around, leaned over the checkout counter, and motioned her to move closer for secrecy.

"I believe it, you know." He glanced toward his stock boy to assure the teen wasn't listening. "There is more to art than art. It has powers most cannot see. If you can see the power within, you have the power of the goddess. Use it wisely."

He lurched back as a couple entered, and acknowledged them with a loud welcome. He winked at Alex to indicate she should heed his proper advice, and strolled away to assist his customers. Alex gave the article a last look as it flapped in the breeze of the counter fan. It was time to get home and prepare for her work day. She disputed how long it would take for the article to reach David. Maybe he still read the *Tribune* online, just to keep up on things. Or maybe Chicago was far from his mind. One step out of the kingdom and it disappears.

From the opposite corner of the street, Homeless Max gave his midmorning sermon. His wild eyes landed on her and delivered no recognition whatsoever. Her words were long gone from his tongue, thrown away with the takeout box. She flashed on the angry man at Starbucks cramming her article into the trash. If this day held her fifteen minutes of fame, she calculated she had about nine minutes left. She had better get home before they were all spent prior to noon.

Both her studio answering machine and cell voicemail were full. Friends she hadn't heard from in years called to voice their support and surprise at her summertime activities. It was just what she needed after the eventful walk home. She knelt in her studio as the voicemails played on, and her passion to express herself reignited. Before she spoke with anyone else, she wanted to call one person.

Bob's voicemail chimed in at his *Tribune* extension. She thought he might be receiving the same flood of communications, so she left him a heartfelt thank you to pick up later. She looked at her writing from the coffee shop and prepared to record the day's message. A simple twist of words about money wouldn't work for today; she knew she could do much better. She picked up the phone and let the words flow as she improvised.

"My wish for you is simple. Love, peace, happiness, compassion. For many these ideals appear distant, like a mysterious unattainable goal. But for you this is simple, because all of these elements are present each time you create. So I suppose my wish is more for our community's sake: how lucky we are to have artists."

Satisfied with the message, she decided to get herself to the Andrews. If the morning was any indication, it was going to be a very interesting day.

The Andrews house was empty and eerily quiet when she arrived. She heard rustling in the loft, and discovered Joseph hard at work underneath the lighting board. He seemed distraught, as if he worked to avoid a confrontation. When she greeted him, he silently pointed toward her office. On her desk stood a giant spray of roses in a large crystal vase. She eyeballed John's sentiment and let them sit.

"Never mind those, did you see the article?"

"Yes," he sulked. "I don't mean to be grumpy on your big day, but I'm thinking that I should have revealed my name." He sat upright and confessed. "Your phone has been ringing all morning. And that's just at the Andrews; I can't imagine what you're getting hit with today. Everyone's interested in this Creator State thing." He lowered his eyes to the floor. "I wish I would have had the guts to reveal myself."

She squatted next to him and considered her own trepidations when it came to disclosing all to the world. She recognized his need to be involved and proposed a solution. "Maybe you can help me out with something? David is eventually going to find out about all of this. When he does, I could use your help justifying our summer activities."

He brightened, eager to assist. She crossed to the flowers in the office and called back to him. "What do you think, is David going to freak out?"

He loosened a laugh. "It's not like he's reading the Chicago paper in L.A. There's plenty of time for all of this *Tribune* excitement to settle down before he gets back."

Alex read the enclosure card from the roses and blanched. She extended the card to him. He got to his feet, perplexed that she would let him see John's missive, and he read the card aloud. "Congrats on the positive review. Best, David."

"Well that was easier than I thought it would be," she said. Joseph looked to her with concern and she cocked her head. "I thought the arrangement looked a bit funereal. This isn't a good sentiment, is it?"

He shifted in his boots and joked weakly. "He, um, just wants you to know that he knows?"

Neither of them could decipher David's reaction, and both were too excited about the day to concern themselves with someone two thousand miles away. For the time being, they felt untouchable in their fortress of the Andrews. Joseph returned to the light board, while Alex tended to the red flashing light on the office answering machine. When she hit the play button, a warped automated voice garbled, "You have fifty three messages." She yelped, jumped into the desk chair, and braced herself for the onslaught. "Okay folks, this is not a drill!"

By evening the Artist Exchange Web site was loaded with visitors. Many e-mails of support and a few of beratement poured in, the latter of which was expected by the group. Thomas became agitated with the negative responses, but Alex reminded him that positive missions were often met with resistance. The nastiest of the protesters objected to the location for the Project. The conservative critics labeled the experiments as "sacrilegious" because they took place in a former church. Thomas wanted to give the protesters a good scolding, but he let the missives flow for a day without response. He abused his Kopy Kat privileges and printed out numerous e-mails of interest, while Alex logged in the phone calls. By 10:00 p.m. that night, after a sold-out show at the Andrews, Alex received the most disappointing voicemail of the day. Their Web master informed them that the increased traffic overloaded their server. The Artist Exchange Web site had crashed.

After the long and exciting day, Alex and Thomas wanted to review the feedback in private. Both of them were too tired to go out with the others, but too wired to let the day end, so they decided to go to Alex's studio. A hot evening thunderstorm brewed over the lake as they hit the pavement, and they raced it toward Lakeview. The thick air broke into a downpour at the corner of Belmont and Broadway, and saturated them before they reached her door.

They howled with exhaustion as they entered her studio, dripping wet from the deluge. The windows flashed with the storm, and a deafening crash of thunder plunged the neighborhood into darkness. The two of them laughed harder, too tired to care, and too overwhelmed by the day to complain. She lit a few candles, which were outshined by the storm's ferocity. Thomas stood at the window and observed the display as he swabbed himself off with a dishtowel. She emerged from the bathroom in a plush spa robe.

He caught a glimpse of it in the next flash of lightning, and noted the crest on the pocket. "When were you at the Canyon Ranch?"

She crossed to the kitchen with a candle and disappeared into its cove. "Like lifetimes ago. I'll make some tea. There's another robe on the bathroom door." She urged him from behind the kitchen wall. "We're all friends here. Don't get modest on me, Thomas."

He tried to unstick his clothes from his skin to no avail. The idea of hanging around in a comfy robe sounded good to him after the day's craziness. At the very least it sounded dry. He reappeared from the bathroom and did his finest Cary Grant as he tightened his robe sash. He delivered a few lines to Cleo as if the ivy was his Judy. Alex carried in two steaming tea cups and appealed to Mr. Grant to "sit his manly ass on the floor." They riffled through the e-mails and voicemails by candlelight and looked for anything outstanding. Thomas paused and gazed at Alex. He waited for her to stop and take notice of him. She appeared sleepy yet determined to make the day last, like a defiant child at bedtime. Thomas relished being this close to her again. He wondered if their lives would be drastically changed after today, but it didn't matter to him. Tonight they were their simplest selves in the snug comfort of her studio. The storm rumbled again and Alex's eyes remained on the papers.

"Thomas, I can hear your wheels turning over there." She avoided looking at him, fearful the candlelight and terry cloth put him in a romantic mood. He confirmed her weariness and placed his hand over hers as she grasped another e-mail. She playfully shook him loose and raised her eyes to speak. "Sweetie, this has been a remarkable day for us. Let's not muck it up with anything we'll regret."

He laughed faintly. "That's not what I'm doing! Don't be so patronizing. All we ever do is work when we're together. I need our friendship tonight. This day is the start of huge things for me, I can sense it. I need to share it with a friend, and you probably should do the same. Can't we just chill for a while? Visit? Drop the Project for a moment? You used to treasure a good thunderstorm: you're not even watching it tonight. You're going to burn yourself out if you don't recharge the batteries once in a while." He noted that she softened. "The Web site is down and the *Mobile* is off. Let's shut down for the evening and hang out together." He added, "As friends."

She knew he was right. She started to stack the e-mails when an all-caps subject line caught her attention. THE *READER* WANTS AN INTERVIEW. She scooped up the paper and held it near a candle for inspection. "Just a sec, look at this one. 'The *Chicago Reader* would like to do an article on the Creator State Project, with a pitch on how it could affect the local artistic community.' This would be good for us, Thomas! A lot of artists pick up the *Reader*, this would reach so many people!"

He took the e-mail from her hand and set it back on the pile. "I'm sure it's all going to be wonderful. Can we please just drop the P.R. for the evening?"

She leaned back in frustration. "This day has been huge for me too. I don't know how you can be so nonchalant about it."

"I need to take in the day a little. Check in with my best friend, and not get obsessed with the exposure." He smiled. "Believe me, I'm not going to try anything stupid." She chuckled and blew lightly across her tea. He saw her relax. "I was at work today, which was extremely tedious given the circumstances, and my mind starting wandering. How was I going to handle the *Trib* feedback, my feelings for you, and the Project all at the same time?"

The lights jumped back on. Alex got up, flicked them off again, and resumed her position on the floor. He appreciated the gesture and resumed his train of thought. "I'm not saying that I couldn't juggle all of it, but I found that I didn't want to. I started thinking about what you said to John, how the work had to take precedence, that this was a unique opportunity. And I decided that you're right. My art, the Project, and our friendship are all more important than a love relationship, especially one that might have a better shot in the future." Satisfied with his new agenda, he relaxed, and took a few gulps of tea.

Alex stared at the distorted cityscape in her window panes. The exterior light cast shadows of rain which drizzled across her face. At first it appeared to be projections from the storm, but Thomas soon realized that tears slowly drained down her cheeks. The sight of her crying again confused him.

"Hey, you usually save all of your tears for the stage. What's with the water-works today?" He tempted, "Am I wrong about putting my feelings on hold? I thought taking your advice would flatter you."

"It's not that." She rubbed her eyes. "I'm just not sure that I did the right thing with John. I always preach about opening ourselves up to love and taking the risks involved. And I did that with John. Well, I tried anyway. But I think I may have cut it off too quickly. Maybe I should have trusted my own ability to handle more than a few things at once. It's not like he was high-maintenance." She looked to Thomas, who had his eyes locked on her. She desperately wanted Thomas the friend to listen to her, not Thomas the romantic. Then something in his face gave way to the circumstances. He adapted well in the wake of this emotional day.

He collapsed to his side, propped his head up with one arm, and emanated the casual appeal of Thomas the friend. "Is it more than the Project that's got you overloaded? You've always been the tough one, Alex. I can't imagine you not being able to handle anything that came your way. So what else is going on?" He coerced her to confess all. "C'mon, let's just talk like old buds, okay? Forget everything else. What's got you bursting into tears like this?"

She rounded up all of the events which brought her to this night on the floor with him. She could use the release of a good conversation, and chose to dash any inhibitions while Thomas was in friend mode. "You know the feeling you get the last year in college? As if everything you worked for was about to blossom into something you couldn't see, but imagined as exciting, unknown, the 'real' life that you had been aiming for?"

"Actually, college wasn't that way for me. I graduated and wandered aimlessly for two years, eventually landing at the Kopy Kat because I desperately needed a job." He smirked. "But go on, I get your analogy. You feel like you just graduated. I get it."

"No," she corrected. "It's as if I'm in the last year of school, finishing my thesis on how I'm going to live my life, and preparing as best as I can, but I sense the people who surround me and my way of life are about to be lost to the past."

"Oh, okay. I can follow that. Is that why John is on the hit list?" Before she could protest, he held his hand up in surrender. "Sorry, that was a bad choice of words."

"That's alright, I prefer you uncensored." She pressed her point. "There's a sadness in knowing that your life is going to change. And I know it will. The past year has been leading up to these changes, and it's not over yet. The voices, the *Magic Mobile*, the Artist Exchange, the Andrews, the Creator State Project, John;

all of these are stepping stones to my future. But I feel most of the familiar, comforting things are going to be discarded with my new choices. Like the final year in college. You start saying your goodbyes to friends, everyone scatters, and you move on. Old habits start to die off; things that used to seem important get pruned for the new growth to survive."

Thomas agreed with the analogy. "I see similarities in my own life. I have almost nothing in common with my roommates anymore. My day job seems laughable in light of what my nighttimes have been revealing. Friends have been dropping off. Susan moved to New York, Lisa is distancing herself from all of us." He lowered his voice for dramatic emphasis. "And Peter is full of surprises."

Alex enjoyed the distraction. "Do tell, Mr. Maxwell!"

He wanted to tell her about Peter all week long, but he held back because of the *Tribune* write up. Now it was time to reveal the gossip. He enjoyed himself as he blurted it all out. "Peter's uncle in L.A. got David's screenplay to be seen in Hollywood! That's the only reason David was invited to go out there this summer, and the only reason why they have kept him there for so long!"

Alex fell back against the daybed. "No way! Why would Peter bother with David? What's in it for him?"

"David's uncle may be a hot shot within the City Government, but he couldn't keep covering David's ass when it came to the new building codes that have been closing every other theater north of the loop. So he pressured David to come up with something outstanding, something new that would keep him justifiable in the City Council circles. David, as you know, is a decent director, but he's a bit limited in the creative thinking department. So he found himself in a tough spot and began to write screenplays, hoping to get out of town before he had to face the embarrassment of closing the Andrews." Thomas took a breath for affect.

Alex shoved him to reveal the clincher. "C'mon, spill it!"

"So Peter is watching a friend of his preach all of these new ideas for the way people perform, and he thought, 'Hey, if I could get David out of the way, we could save the space from the wrecking ball, give my friend a shot at managing a theatre, and have a new home for my artistic buds to hang out in.'" Alex looked stunned. He enjoyed it and revealed. "So Peter makes a deal with him. David is to take the summer off and go to L.A. where his screenplay will get reviewed and possibly picked up. Peter's uncle will keep David out there for at least four months. During that time, Alex will take over management of the Andrews and attempt to make it the new place to be in off-loop theater."

She sat with her mouth open. "What happens to me after four months? Holy shit, that's in September, that's like two weeks from now. What's the plan for when David comes back?"

"I don't really know. David probably plans on stepping back into his theater and reclaiming his title, with the added glory of running the new hot spot in town." He saw Alex squirm and consoled her. "But that's not possible because the success of that space is attached to you now, so if you leave the Andrews, the glory goes with you. I don't think David is prepared for that."

She was dumbfounded by the unseen manipulations, but there was a piece missing. "What does Peter get out of all of this? What's his motivation to do all of this?"

Thomas gave her a Cheshire cat smile. "The oldest motivation next to money, my friend. Love."

"Lisa? He wanted to be with Lisa? But that doesn't make sense, she was all over him."

"Lisa isn't the greatest actor. We both know that. And Peter, well, he's the kind who *has* to date an actor. So he wanted to make sure that Lisa would keep performing. Circle Rep probably wouldn't have her back after *Dylana*, and she's grown too dull to audition well. He was concerned that she would drop out of acting altogether. That's why he resisted her for a while; she was always talking about leaving the theater."

She remembered Lisa used to talk about that all the time. "But why didn't he just date somebody else? Another actor?"

He replied with an air of personal insight. "He is in love with her. He sees a future with her. He knows they are supposed to be together, and he didn't want her to feel lost if she wasn't performing. So he made it possible for her to stay in the game by getting her best girlfriend a job at the Andrews. Then Lisa would be a shoe-in for the summer show."

It was a lot to process after such a long day. Alex wanted to mill over the details, but felt the impact of fatigue hit her hard. "I'm not sure if his plan is going to play out the way he expected. Lisa isn't speaking to me, and if David kicks me out of the Andrews, there won't be any easy casting opportunities for her." She stretched and tried to hide a yawn. Thomas took the hint, collected the cups, and crossed to the kitchen. The thunder picked up again and he knew he had to get home soon.

"Alex, we can't predict how David will react to all of this. Maybe the roses you received today are a good sign. Maybe he's going to stay out in L.A. We just don't know." He sat down next to her. "The Andrews isn't going to be important. I can guarantee that. What was that message you had earlier this year? 'Release anything extraneous. Everything you need is carried within you?' Well, you should take it to heart and forget about the day job. If things change and you leave the Andrews, you'll have more time on your hands. Then maybe you can give John another try."

She looked deep into his eyes. He was hard to read. He manipulated his own emotions for the stage so regularly that he mastered masking them offstage. But he was open with her tonight, and it was honest advice. She showed her gratitude for the evening's talk by embracing him on the floor.

"I'm so grateful to have you in my life, Thomas. We have a magical friendship. Everything we touch turns to gold."

He squeezed her with the compliment and watched the storm turn to heavy rain through her window. He reluctantly noted, "I should get on my way. We both need some sleep or tomorrow will kick our asses."

She held him by the arms. "You can't go out in that storm. Stay here. I have a pop-up unit."

Thomas was flattered. "Uh, is that some kinda new term for ..."

"It's a roll-away mattress under the day bed!"

"Okay. But no funny stuff. And no snoring."

They readied themselves for sleep and tried to deploy the pop-up mattress. After a ten minute battle with the unit's bear trap style legs, it stood solidly and covered the entire floor next to the day bed.

"Haven't you ever set this thing up?" Thomas wisecracked.

"I never have overnight guests. This is its maiden voyage."

He looked at the two mattresses on their separate bases. "What if just push them together, make one giant bed, and we stay on our own sides."

"Alright, but I don't have pajamas for you to sleep in, so keep it clean, Mister."

The two finally settled into bed, joked around like two kids at a slumber party, and giggled under the glow of the plastic stars on the ceiling. After a brief blanket tug-of-war and good nights, both of them fell soundly asleep.

The next morning Alex stirred and looked at the clock: 8:00 a.m. A good night's rest. Thomas remained in dream-land, so she tiptoed into the kitchen nook to make some Saturday morning java. The gurgle of the coffee maker didn't wake her guest as she sat at her table and leafed through the e-mail stack. She tried to find the *Reader* e-mail she spotted the night before. She paused and thought about the night's conversation. By the light of morning, Alex saw she didn't want to rekindle the relationship with John. The Project took priority. She decided to remain true to it until it reached fruition. She wondered if she could express this to John. He was still involved in the Project, by his own choice, but he probably hoped for their reconciliation. Feelings for him drifted through her mind, but were interrupted by a light knock on her door.

Accustomed to her elderly neighbor's Saturday morning visits, she answered without checking the peep hole. She swung the door wide open with a smile. Her breath stopped as her eyes landed where the woman's face should have been. A silver mantis pendant shined in its place. John took three glances: one at her, one at Thomas asleep in her bed, and one gravely disappointed look back to her. He turned on his heels and quickly walked away.

She stepped into the hall, shocked speechless by the circumstances. He bolted into the stairwell. Before she could vocalize an explanation, he was gone.

12

Art and love take courage. Failure at either one is inevitable from time to time, but our pleasure and progress come from throwing ourselves out there to take the risk. We toss our hearts in harm's way, and know courage alone can be reward enough.

—*The Magic Mobile*

The *Chicago Reader* pursued an interview with Alex, and printed a feature story which emphasized the Creator State group's peaceful motivations. It closed with a persuasive remark: "A collective of true artists with the health of the future as their objective cannot fail on any level." The comment spurred a fortune of local supporters to join the online membership. The *Reader* also printed the *Magic Mobile* number without Alex's permission, which generated a landslide of calls to the little machine and burned it out within three days. It was replaced gratis by her local cell phone dealer, who deemed Alex's use of their service as the most interesting to date. They negotiated with her to use the *Magic Mobile* name on a series of local print ads throughout September. Alex agreed to it when they offered her free service and all the cell phones she could burn through. She selected a stylish black model which shimmered like a miniature Batmobile parked at her waistline.

One of the first calls to ring the new contraption came from Victoria Johnson. Apparently the group attracted enough attention to warrant HIP's interest. Alex researched the mysterious HIP entity and discovered they weren't obscure at all. She simply wasn't high enough on the performance ladder to know about agencies of their stature. HIP represented some of the boldest and most successful talents on the planet. They also maintained an inner circle of philanthropists who supported unique creative organizations around the globe. Top rung talent donated anonymously to groups or individuals they deemed fit for financial backing. Victoria offered Alex any kind of help she needed to get them up and running. Alex humbly asked for Web site support. The Artist Exchange site had been unstable for weeks and she was desperate for a permanent fix. Victoria made a few calls which resulted in a new Web service and complete redesign of the site at no cost to the group. Her generosity revealed ulterior aims; she wanted to shine up her newfound treasure before she pitched them to her portfolio of philanthropists.

The slick appearance of the site gained the attention of a few curious HIP clients, who saw an opportunity to get in on the ground floor with the ambitious troupe. Victoria skillfully maneuvered the interested investors to generate a grant which would fully fund the first year of the Creator State Project. The endowment covered everything they needed: salaries for Alex and Thomas, Web support, computers for the staff, and a marketing budget to gather a larger population of artists. The Project had one year to collect a membership and devise programs to implement their theories. If they succeeded, the anonymous donors would renew their grant for the following year. It was a symbiotic marriage of artistic integrity and disposable wealth.

The growing membership demanded action. People shared their experiences, which was easily accomplished via the new chat boards, and learned more about Alex and Thomas' application of the Creator State. Artists recognized the common feeling of the State and wanted to mobilize. As the Artist Exchange morphed into the Creator State Project, performers expressed their awareness that the State was not merely coincidental, but purposeful.

The Chicago community was curious about the group, and invitations to speak on local media programs started to materialize. Alex and Thomas gave a few good TV and radio interviews, and Victoria determined they were ready for bigger and better exposure. She arranged for the group to give their first lecture by mid-October. Alex wanted to host the lecture at the Andrews where the experiments originated. She asked David and he turned her down over the phone from L.A. The exposure surrounding the project didn't please him, primarily because he felt left out of their success. The distance that grew between Alex and David amounted to more than mileage.

Crown Circle Repertory theater was selected as the space for the lecture. Thomas and Alex starred in the first fall show and the box office benefited from their presence when the season began. Curious audiences filled performances, hoping for a glimpse of the Creator State in action.

The challenge of juggling the Andrews, her performances, and the Project began to wear on Alex. Her daytime hours were congested with responsibilities, but her evenings still belonged to the stage. She savored the escape of performing each night. Her manic schedule was relieved by David's unannounced return to Chicago in early September. His screenplay was viciously rejected after months of studio foreplay. He flew in on a Sunday afternoon, and within twenty-four hours he fired Alex and reclaimed his title at the Andrews. It didn't take long for him to discover that many things had changed during his absence. By mid-week he called her and tried to collect the details of what occurred while he was away.

"Alex, I owe you an apology. Everyone is raving about how well you handled things while I was gone. I may have jumped to conclusions. I thought you were trying to take over, or take my place, or show me up. Hell, I'm not sure what I was thinking. Regardless, I want it on the record that I'm sorry for firing you without notice. That was rude of me."

She listened as she sat at her kitchen table and checked her e-mail. She smirked at her new HIP laptop and scrolled through the day's correspondences as he rambled on. David's apology sounded empty, more formality than genuine regret. Apparently he didn't regret firing her, he regretted the way he did it. She longed to share this observation with Lisa, who would appreciate the irony of David's narcissism in the wake of what occurred at his theater. She knew she was untouchable since he fired her.

"David, are you feeling guilty?"

He hesitated. "Yes, I suppose. I just got a call from the *Reader*, and they made it sound like I fired you because I couldn't handle your success at my job."

"Wow, it's only been a few days. How did they find out that I was gone?" Her mind clattered with connections. The *Reader* fished for a follow up story, and David's behavior would make a perfect topic. Peter might have dropped them a tip, as several staff members at the paper were drinking buddies of his. Perhaps Peter decided to craft some payback for her dismissal. Her suspicions were justified when David responded nervously.

"This town is even smaller than when I left." He tried to bow out gracefully. "Alright. Well I just wanted to get things straight with you." He gave her a compliment which sounded more for public consumption than for their private conversation. "Thanks again for doing such a fine job while I was away."

She gave him a sound bite in return. "Thank you for the opportunity, David. It really was a pleasure managing the Andrews; I learned so much." They exchanged polite goodbyes and ended the call abruptly.

Even though the Andrews position was behind her, she felt David was a threat. He despised her accomplishments in his position. Hearing about it from the community fueled his resentment. She closed her eyes and inhaled deeply, then exhaled his negative energies from her day. She reminded herself that she was free from him, the Andrews politics, and the secret deals made on her behalf. She made her mark and moved on. All old bets were off.

She escaped David's petty wrath until a story in the *Reader* hit the streets the next day. The title boldly asked, *Is there no room in the City for the State?* The *Reader* portrayed David as a power-hungry diva, whose past successes were made possible by the support of his familial City connections. The article spun Alex's termination into a classic struggle of old versus new. David represented the old guard, intolerable of the capable and forward-thinking Creator State group. They also mentioned the Project's anonymous funding and questioned the motives of the mysterious grantors. Thomas read the closing sentences aloud from Alex's kitchen table.

"We have to wonder if this elusive powerhouse of an agency has the group's best interests in mind. Backing a media darling is easily justified. We only hope that the goals of the Project will remain intact." He folded the paper under his arm, stuffed his hands into his pockets, and contemplated a reaction. Alex waited patiently for him to respond. He appeared to be apprehensive and finally spoke.

"They might be right about our best interests. What if HIP decides to cut us off if we get unpopular? I don't like them having control over us."

"They haven't said a word about anything we're doing." She discarded his suspicions. "We have an entire year to prove ourselves, and then they'll decide if they want to fund us again. Don't fall for this conspiracy angle. The *Reader* just wanted to spice it up a little. I think their sights were set on David, not HIP."

"Yeah, you're right. This gift horse doesn't need an inspection." He shook it off. "The David slam sounds like Peter's doing. Perhaps we should have a word with him, let him know we don't want this kind of help anymore."

She agreed. Too many manipulations fogged their goals. "There is something I'd like you to consider. I know you're still concerned about the reliability of this grant, but you may want to think about leaving Kopy Kat, rather than taking vacation days until they finally realize your mind is elsewhere." The week dragged on her endurance. "Hey, it's Friday. Want to grab some lunch and lay in the park while we still have pleasant weather and peace of mind?"

"Lunch, yes." He sighed. "The peace of mind is already lost."

They ordered a Thai takeout feast for a well-deserved Friday break. The two spread a blanket on the Lincoln Park lawn, kicked off their shoes, and basked in the last days of lakeside warmth. Senses were heightened in the calm of the park. Food tasted better, the city noises faded in the distance, and the breeze blew problems out to sea where they dissolved in the lake's afternoon sparkles. Thomas reclaimed his peace of mind and turned his thoughts to art. He spoke to the beautiful view around them.

"I wish I felt the freedom that I have on stage during my offstage hours. Why is that so hard to do?"

Alex set her takeout carton on the blanket. The same question circled in her since the summer began. If they could achieve pure creative freedom when they lived someone else's life on stage, why weren't they able to find that abandon in their own lives?

Thomas saw he interrupted their afternoon delight. "Sorry, did I wreck your appetite?"

"No, just the opposite." She brightened. "I am hungry for more experimentation. I feel like there is another life surrounding me that I cannot get to. It's as if the real me, my real life, is a transparent entity, existing in the same space and time as myself. But the only way to live that real life is to discover some fundamental key to my creativity. I know my life is supposed to be lived as a creator. I just want that real life to be mine."

He didn't allow her insecurities to faze him. "You've said that to me before. Personally, I see you as the most connected artist I know. You live openly, you take action on your ideas, and your performances move people. How can you think you're not living your best life?"

"But life is constant desire, we always want more out of it. I still expect something more to be revealed; there's a corner of this garden that hasn't received any light yet."

Thomas slumped backwards at her poetic description. She kicked him lightly with her bare foot and he straightened up again, ready to hear her proposal. She spoke point by point, as if she delivered a closing argument in a very important trial.

"What if our Creator State is a connection to a place where everything is born? What if at the root of every kind of creativity is the infinite mind of the universe, the place where we all exist as fellow creators? What if, when we surrender to the State, we are connected to the origins of creation? What if there is a key in the Creator State to channel the creation consciousness?" She checked, "Are you with me?"

"Sounds like you hung out with a scientist all summer."

"This isn't John's research I'm spouting here. These are ideas I tried to share with you the first time I mentioned the State, that first night we got together at the Andrews. I want it to be clear that these ideas didn't grow out of John's studies. That was the main reason John and I broke up. I wanted to keep my intuition pure and unaffected by outside information. I wanted my creative ideas to be mine, to grow out of my own intellect and my own reality, not some scientific study." She tried to suppress her emotions. "Sorry, I'm trying to keep a grip on these ideas before they dissolve into John's observations on quantum physics. I'm interested in the creative aspect, not justifying if they have validity. Art doesn't need an explanation, it should be natural and unaffected by scientific examination." She caught her tongue. "You're not the one who should be hearing this. These are leftover arguments intended for John."

"Does that mean you do or don't want to hear my response?"

"Sure." She pushed her lunch aside, flipped over on her stomach, and challenged him to say something important. Thomas hid a smile and knew she was not going to like what he was about to say. He spoke as lightheartedly as he could. "Your ideas are unique, Alex, but you have to take into account that many, many people have been mulling around the same problems for centuries. We have to consider the collective consciousness. We all feed off of each other's thoughts and ideas. The collective is providing information to us all of the time. The Field research has taught us that we're all in this together. So regardless of who is saying what, at any hour, there is a shared purpose in all of this." He tried to soften the blow. "Your application of artists as natural creators of reality is the new twist in this cocktail." He grinned at his Alex-like verbiage. "You should run with your ideas, stretch them as far as you possibly can. But try to see the influence of other people's ideas as a good thing. Just like your ideas will influence others. It's one giant conversation, spoken or contemplated. You should be proud that we've made a forum for these ideas."

She didn't question his wisdom. She silently reprimanded herself for forcing John away from her process and wished for a chance to apologize. She changed the subject before Thomas noticed her train of thought.

"If we can use the Creator State to manipulate positive energy to a single person, like what we did with Joseph, then why can't we create original material?"

He brushed the idea off. "Nothing is original anymore. It's all been done. The universe is expanding out of boredom; it wants to get away from itself."

"I'm serious. What if we are really meant to be creators and our talents include creation of new life? What if these revelations are surfacing now because there is more universe to fill? Since the universe is growing, maybe it is activating our natural creative energies, because there is so much creation taking place out there? Like an awakening of our creator-selves by the universe?"

He wanted to respond, but not before he fully grasped what she said. "Give me a minute." He lay on his back and looked up at the clear cloudless sky. A breeze drifted over him as he calculated the possibilities of her words.

Alex turned her gaze to the gleaming lake and tamed her impatience. She knew his style of repartee. He often paused during their discussions to gather his thoughts. After a summer with John where conversation played like a pro tennis match, the contemplative style of Thomas seemed tedious. Memories of John surfaced as the blue-green waves lulled in her vision. She repressed her discomfort and submerged thoughts of him into the lake. Her voices began to whisper. *We are creating a new reality for humanity.* She reached for her journal. Thomas remained deep in thought as she wrote: *This is when we stand on the rubble of misguided purposes and begin to rebuild human beings. When societies crumble, art always endures.* She reread the lines and noticed her pen. It was the one the man gave her at the Diner last month. She ran her thumb over the HIP monogram and wondered if the mystery man was one of their anonymous funding sources. She considered the encounter: he noticed her too easily at the restaurant. Perhaps it was his influence which pushed Victoria to speak with her the morning of the *Tribune* article. Alex hoped the *Reader* was wrong to suggest the grantors had ulterior motives.

Her thoughts spun around the HIP group. They represented many big celebrities. Perhaps Victoria's job was to find the little people, the smaller groups to balance their portfolio. Regardless of the reason, Alex gratefully accepted HIP's generosity. Thanks to their funding, she had the chance to reach as many artists as possible. The marketing plan included ads for the Project in all of the major performance magazines, and direct mailings to theaters, galleries, dance troupes, film studios, and music venues. E-mail blasts went out to their growing member list and encouraged them to sign up their colleagues. They explored every avenue to the arts community as they accessed the creative culture across the nation. The support of their peers would enable their vision of a larger Creator State experiment. Alex looked to Thomas, who continued to mill over the thought of being a creator. She laughed to herself. If everyone took as long to process information as Thomas Maxwell, it would take a lot longer than a year to reach people. He felt her gaze and let his eyes drop from the blue above him.

"What? I'm still working it out." He turned on his side. "There's something missing in the logic. We know we can affect others by directing energy to enable something positive in them. But if we think we can create, oh, let's say a bird; the bird doesn't exist on the physical plane yet. We would have to create new matter. So how did the original creator make the original bird? Is it an image first, then matter? And is that knowledge within us, lying dormant, just waiting for us to summon it up? And is it just a matter of creating without self-doubt like you've mentioned? If you eliminate any doubt, then it just happens? Is that the key to creating new things?" He rolled on his back, exhausted by his questions.

"Maybe there is another kind of creation that is waiting for us. We already have birds and people and material things. Maybe the Creator State is leading us to the invisible, to the essence of creativity. The universal force of life."

"What's the universal force of life?"

"Love," she answered. "Probably love. No matter where we search for divine meanings of life, we always get the same answer. Love."

Thomas felt some truth in her words. Something stirred within him at the thought of universal love. But his habitual sarcasm repressed the exploration of it. "We keep looking because it seems inadequate," he objected. "The universe isn't expanding because it loves."

"Maybe it loves to create, and creation is the force. Maybe that's why the State works. It has the true essence of love in it: creation."

Thomas sat up and surveyed their lunch. "Sorry, I'm burned out for any more discussion. We seem to be closing in on the answer. Someday we'll have it." He grabbed his carton of curried chicken. "Meanwhile, I'm just going to eat birds, not make them."

She picked up her carton and wondered if vegetable creation was any easier. She knew they followed the right path, but they had to learn these lessons carefully. She sighed. "The joy of the journey."

"You make a lovely traveling companion." He witnessed a subtle flinch in her and defended himself. "Just an observation, take the compliment." She relaxed, lounged on the blanket, and gazed out over the water. Thomas allowed his *Grande Jatte* fantasy to swirl into his thoughts, undetected by his leading lady beside him. The seaside scene painted itself around them as a breeze caught Alex's skirt hem. He pictured her in the flowing white gown, but resisted the temptation to imagine their kiss. A long silence followed as the two dined. At first it felt uncomfortable, but after smiles were exchanged at the blissful break in their routine, it eased into enjoyment of the fine afternoon. Dragonflies whizzed by their picnic, shore birds patrolled the lake edge, and giant oaks lazily played with the wind. Alex's cell phone interrupted the bliss.

"Mind if I check this message?"

Thomas objected. "Sometimes it's better to be unavailable. Let them wait."

"I'm not as important as you are."

Alex checked her voicemail as Thomas silently probed her comment; what did she mean "not as important as you are" when she was the one with the overflowing answering machine?

She summarized the message as it crackled in her ear. "It's Joseph; he just got an offer from Circle Rep. He's leaving the Andrews!" Thomas urged her to play it back on speaker phone.

"Hey Alex, it's Joseph. Just wanted to thank you for mentioning me at Circle Rep. We had a meeting and they made me their new Technical Director. Less money than the Andrews, but it'll be good to get away from David. I have a whole new perspective on him thanks to you guys. Thanks again for everything. I owe you another one."

Joseph became a trusted partner after they revealed the source of his changed heart. Having him at Circle Rep would be like a family reunion. Alex, Thomas, and Peter were all in the first show together. Lisa wasn't selected for the Circle Rep season. She covered her disappointment with a veil of nonchalance and denied it bothered her to be uncast. Meanwhile, David was left high and dry at the Andrews. They tried not to gloat. They finished their picnic, excited by Joseph's new appointment.

"We should see what kind of reaction the *Reader* article is brewing," Thomas prompted.

She wanted to linger in the park and procrastinated for a while. Eventually she gave into the day's agenda. She reminded him on the way back that he shouldn't trust people's reactions. "People will forget about these fleeting articles. Keep the larger view in mind, not the petty agendas. They only distract us from our work."

"It's good to have people's favor, though. We need that kind of support right now."

"We don't need to be likable. We need people who trust their intuition, not those who blindly follow the press. They are not our audience." She repeated, "No petty agendas."

"Speaking of agendas, how about we work on that upcoming lecture?"

She threw an arm around him. "I was thinking we should get the group together at the last second and see what we're made of. Just wing it!" She waited for him to catch up to the joke. When she realized her touch distracted him, she jerked to a halt on the sidewalk. He slowed to a stop and guiltily turned back to face her.

"I don't want to wing it, Alex."

He didn't mean the lecture. She waited for words to come to her, dismayed that his crush issue had resurfaced. Then, like an answer to a private request, her cell phone began to ring. She looked to its display, saw John's number, and wondered if she should tell Thomas who was calling. She gave him a flat stare. He interpreted her nonresponse, invented urgent business to take care of before the show, and hurried away toward the West Side. He mumbled as he sped down the sidewalk. "Nothing ventured, nothing gained." He lit a mischievous smirk. "Can't blame a guy for trying."

He knew Alex watched his departure. He turned back, gave her a cheery wave, and spun around again. She sighed relief that he wasn't upset, and hurried home to return John's call.

John's call was well timed. The October lecture was to be an introduction to the State by a panel of select Tuesday nighters. They were unable to solicit a scientist to replace John at the lecture. Most of his colleagues viewed the group as cult-like, and thought John stretched the facts to meet his needs. It may have been the professional rejection which made him call Alex and ask to rejoin the Project. The group unanimously agreed to accept John's return. One short month later, the group was poised for their first public lecture on the Creator State.

13

*As man exercises his power to challenge the empty chair of judgment,
we must seize our opportunities to be good. The consistent amending
of laws to detail what should be obviously ethical is no match for the
speed at which the population is exploring evil. Society's acceptance
of tragic events is quickening. We are taking the bullets and living
with them buried deep inside; soon we'll all be made of metal.*

—*The Magic Mobile*

Alex spied through the curtain at the crowd filtering into the Circle Repertory Theater. The house rumbled with various levels of conversation as she surveyed the scene for familiar faces. She found no one she recognized. Typically she could spot a few friends or acquaintances in the crowd before the show. This lecture was unexplored territory for her, and the people gathering at Circle Rep that evening were of a different stock. Her eyes finally landed on Miles, who sashayed into the back row. Joseph negotiated with HIP to save a seat for his fellow ex-Andrews crew member. Miles quit right after Joseph left, and the Playhouse Theater snatched him up, eager to hire the best Stage Manager in town. It caused a chain reaction: Chris and Lucas found new employment, anxious to distance themselves from David's worsening temperament. Alex felt bad about breaking up a ten year team, but she also understood their need to move on.

She watched Miles hum with delight at the size of the lecture audience. He looked like a proud parent waiting for the dance recital to begin. Earlier that day he called to give her a pep talk and inquired about what she planned to wear. He was shocked that she hadn't considered her wardrobe, and escorted her to Marshall Field's that afternoon. He insisted a new ensemble would boost her confidence. As she waited behind the curtain, she knew he was right. She needed all the confidence she could get. Underneath her fresh attire, nerves caught hold of her chest. She pulled back into the wings and took a deep breath.

The moment provided butterflies in her stomach. She cautiously returned an eye to the slice of light and studied the personalities present. The audience was a sea of black turtlenecks, lengthy scarves, embroidered tunics, and dramatic accessories. Some of them emphasized their artistic flamboyance for the media as the event would be taped by HIP for later broadcast on the cable arts channel. There was also the possibility that a few high-end HIP clients might see the program; who wouldn't want to look their best for a close up or two? Alex shivered, backed up from the curtain, and bumped into Joseph in the dark.

"Shit!" She whispered harshly. "Don't sneak up on me like that!"

Joseph covered the mouthpiece to his headset. "Sorry, just wanted to give you a twenty minute warning and remind you to sit halfway back in those big chairs they set out there. If you sit all the way back in them, they'll swallow you on camera."

Alex read the stick-on badge the organizers slapped on his chest. "Joseph Bancroft, Technical Director." She snickered. "Doesn't the headset make it obvious that you're in charge?"

"Evidently this crowd wants to know exactly who is who." He peeked at the audience through the drape. "They're labeling everyone as they come in. So and so, Painter; what's-his-face, Musician. They think it'll help to show off the different professions involved."

"Involved?" Alex hissed. "They wouldn't even save a row for our Tuesday night group. I've never seen most of those people out there."

"Hey, calm down." Joseph placed a hand on her shoulder. "They just want it to look good on the tape. You're going to do fine, stop worrying about it. No doubts, remember?"

Alex patted his hand in thanks. "Guess I'm a little nervous. Has John arrived?"

"He's in the dressing room," Joseph confirmed. "You should go back there too. Get away from the curtain and regroup with the team before the big game."

Alex jiggled his headphones as she left the stage. "Thanks, Coach Bancroft!"

Nervous artists choked the hallway. Rashan bounced in place and chattered at Peter who sat vacant-eyed. He took no notice of Peter's obliviousness and kept talking to him. As they exercised their preshow coping devices, Lisa smoked in the alley near the open doorway. The group chose its representatives for the panel, and Lisa was not on the list. Her eyes met Alex's and they exchanged a polite smile of encouragement. Lisa knew the panel selection was out of Alex's hands, but it wasn't easy to see her that night.

Alex heard Thomas in the men's dressing room. He boasted the infamous *Dylana* teapot story to an enthusiastic Lucas and John. She listened in the doorway as he described the moment when Phil began screaming over his deflowered antique. Lucas enjoyed the narrative and rolled with laughter. Thomas waved Alex in to complete the story. She took her cue and finished the tale. "I grabbed Thomas and we bolted out the door like lightning and tore down the alley!" She added, "We could hear him yelling from half a block away!"

The men shared a long laugh, fueled by their nervousness. Alex studied John and remembered the story took place the same week he entered their lives. So much had occurred since June; a few months and everything had changed. Thomas broke her spell. "I was surprised they forgave us after our bad behavior." Thomas grinned and knew Alex would hear the real intent of his words. She gave him a rebellious glare in return.

Lucas was still amused by the story. "They must like you more than that props dude." He repressed his laughter. "Hey, did you check out the crowd? This place is packed with arr-teeests." The backstage speaker crackled as Joseph gave the ten minute warning.

Alex fidgeted. "They're almost ready to get started. Break a leg everyone." She gave John a quick smile and exited. In the hallway a familiar sight greeted her: ten feet away stood the gleaming duplicate faces of the Brothers Slim. Their appearance backstage caused a slight commotion. They worked outside of the city, so their visits in town were cherished. The boys decided to listen from backstage since they couldn't get a seat out front. They sandwiched Alex in a good luck squeeze and took a seat on the hallway floor.

The members rounded up for a last circle of hugs and handshakes before the panel left for the stage. They had much to share with the world tonight. Alex felt another marker burn itself into her personal timeline; the evening materialized from a predetermined sketch somewhere in the book of Alex. The audience suddenly quieted and Victoria welcomed their host. The panel filed into the wings for introductions.

The moderator for the evening was the astute Baxter Hayes; a perceptive film and theater critic, art collector, and outstanding painter in his own right. HIP selected him because he gave the evening an air of importance. His power emanated from the influence he carried in the art world. Most knew his reputation but few had seen him in person, which made first glances of him intriguing. His rectangular face danced behind tortoise shell eyeglasses, and his perfectly coiffed brunette hair shined in the downstage glow. He wore impeccably tailored brown silk pants, which fell into a cuff above tasseled mahogany loafers. Pale yellow socks flecked with red flashed at his ankles and complimented his pale yellow cashmere sweater. His thin neck sported an ascot-style scarf, which would have looked fey on a less stately man. His enthusiasm for all things new betrayed his regal looks. Baxter would look properly placed in an old English library, with volumes of leather-bound books as his backdrop.

He started by reciting an introduction for the video, a short synopsis of the Creator State group's brief history. HIP prepared it for him, gathered from information which the group submitted. Alex listened as Baxter read the well-polished summary of their backgrounds and discoveries. It sounded impressive coming from him, which was certainly HIP's intention. As he began to introduce the panel, Alex's heart sped up. She would be the last to enter. She tried to steady her trembling hands and heartbeat as one by one the members left her in the blackness of backstage. Her thoughts raced in the moment. How did she get to a moment when Baxter Hayes was about to introduce her? She wondered if she had "arrived" or perhaps Baxter and HIP were stepping stones on a long trail of appearances and interviews. She tried to quiet her questions. *Regardless of where this leads, this is my introduction to the world. This is where I expose the things that matter most to me as an artist. That in itself has validity.* She heeded her own advice. Then Alex realized she heard her own inner voice, and not the many whispers of her clairaudient voices.

Baxter's smooth tenor resonated from the stage. "Last but never least, a fine actor and the head of our panel tonight, Alex Davis."

Alex was greeted by a rush of applause as she parted the curtain and crossed to her seat. She gave a hello wave to the crowd on the way. When she saw the perfectly groomed Baxter glowing in the stage lights, she silently thanked Miles for insisting on her new outfit. She settled into her chair and scanned the beaming audience. She recognized no one.

Baxter opened with a sly compliment. "We are at capacity tonight at Circle Repertory Theater." He tried to warm up the audience and turned to Alex. "Looks as if we could have used a bigger house for this discussion, like the Andrews?"

Alex grinned politely. Everyone knew she had been fired, everyone knew David had been a prick about it. She answered calmly. "The Andrews wasn't worth the price we had to pay."

The audience enjoyed her comeback. Baxter seemed surprised at her wit and toyed with her. "Maybe David Cooper could use a little attention in your next experiment."

The crowd tittered appropriately. Alex remained in check. "We're not interested in manipulation."

Baxter registered she had business on her mind, and led directly to the core topic. "What exactly is the Creator State Project interested in?"

Alex surveyed the panel members for permission to speak for them, and they nodded consent. Earlier that day she rehearsed a few answers, but those words were suddenly absent. From deep within her, she felt a clear voice rise to her lips. "The Project is interested in finding artists who have experienced the heightened awareness while creating or performing which we call the 'Creator State.' This lucid creative consciousness is the common denominator of our membership, which to date is ..." She turned to Peter. "How many members do we have now?"

The attention pleased Peter. "Currently we have three thousand members in the Chicagoland area, with an additional one thousand or so outside of Illinois who have sent in e-mails of support."

Baxter seemed shocked by the numbers, mirrored by gasps of surprise in the audience. "You've had thousands of people sign up already? In a matter of months? How did they find out about you?" He leaned in with a sly turn of his head. "Is there a fee to become a member? Because if there is, I may consider starting my own little club."

Thomas sat forward, bothered by Baxter's little jabs, and explained. "The membership is merely a collective roster, a list of people who support our theories because they have experienced similar connections in their work. After the *Chicago Tribune* article last August, we had hundreds of e-mails pouring in every day. We invited those people to become members of what we hope will be the largest collective of artists working for a worldwide cause."

Alex watched Thomas as he spoke and peripherally checked out the crowd. The fourth wall was down tonight and it made her uncomfortable. She examined the audience, who usually didn't watch her, but her character. She laughed to herself and thought; *Tonight they're still watching my character, aren't they?* Her eyes drifted to a middle aged woman in the front row. The woman dressed for the occasion in a rich rust velvet suit, complemented by strands of tiger eye that glittered in the light spilling over her seat. She gave Alex a smile of approval when they locked eyes for a second. The gesture assured Alex that she was in the company of a few friends.

Baxter shifted in his chair and crossed his legs, which exposed more of his well-selected socks. "Let's get straight to the plan, Thomas. Throughout the centuries, artistic types have aspired to change the world. Most of them failed to make a difference. What makes your group anticipate success?"

Thomas cracked a smile. "Well Baxter, it's not a matter of artists making a dif-ference in their own lifetimes. Art has endurance; its power resonates well beyond the lifespan of its creator. Each creative action influences another, so the subtle changes they inspire appear invisible to the less observant eye."

This rebuttal put Baxter on the defensive. "I'm very aware of the influence of art in religion, politics, and culture. But what subtle changes does the Creator State seek? Eliminating negative attitudes one by one across the United States?" He smugly added, "With a two to one ratio for creators to victim, you might have about one thousand happy people by the end of your grant." The audience didn't react as Baxter anticipated. His sarcasm fell like a stone. Apparently people were interested in what this group had to say. He shifted his style to accommo-date. "What I'm asking is, what are you hoping to accomplish with a lengthy e-mail list?"

The panel exchanged glances. The moment had arrived to reveal their plan. Before the taping, the group agreed Alex would speak first. Her eyes landed on the woman in rust velvet again. The woman gave her a slight nod, as if urging Alex to tell it all. Alex crafted her address to the crowd and cameras as if it was an intimate conversation.

"Activating creative energies within us can be an effective way to make bril-liant works of art. We have seen this notable brilliance in many performances, both on stage and in film, on the dance floor, on the canvas, through the instru-ment, and on the page. Many artists think this brilliant state is the product of a higher source. We are asking artists to consider that this state of consciousness may be a natural creative energy which exists within them." She directed her attention to the front rows. "It may be difficult at first to perceive this as a per-sonal power. Try to visualize the Creator State as a channel within you which leads to the truest essence of creativity. Our creative powers are merely a micro-model of the powers encompassed within the universe."

Baxter grew pale as Alex spoke. HIP didn't familiarize him with the esoteric portion of the State, and for good reason. His speechless face spoke volumes. Alex realized he wouldn't interject, so she passed the conversation to John who was primed to continue her line of thought.

"If I may offer another perspective." John inquired of their host. Baxter cleared his throat and gave him a please-do. All eyes turned to the scientist and hoped for a rational explanation of Alex's statements. John pushed up his glasses. "Creativity can be a powerful tool. When the boundaries of creative activity are expanded, such as the instances of the Creator State which we have seen, new possibilities are revealed for the power of creative thought."

Baxter furrowed his brow and challenged, "Is this uncharted territory?"

John laughed lightly. "Not at all. Quantum physics has shown the reality of matter is merely a result of observation, or the effect of our own thoughts on matter. Particles are simply rearranged to please our reality-addicted minds. All things are made of the same energy, reorganized at the whims of thought patterns." He smirked. "We are all 'uniquely' the same substance." John felt the complete attention of the house. "It is quite possible that the power of mind over energy is limitless. Our thoughts tell subatomic particles what to form, or what to mimic over and over again. This is reinforced by the population's collective thought processes. The creative level is where everything begins."

Baxter was enamored with John's intellect, and turned to more studious conversation. "That's fascinating. Can you explain for us how Alex and Thomas' experiment managed to alter their subject's reality?"

John obliged. "Everything we see boils down to energy, an active energy that interacts with a background of electromagnetic force called the Zero Point Field, or the 'Field' for short. We are all connected to the farthest reaches of the cosmos through the Field. Not figuratively, but literally connected to this field of energy. We constantly carry on a dialogue with the Field through our thoughts, consciously or unconsciously. Since we are always plugged into the Field, our thoughts affect others regardless of physical location." John addressed the room, confident with his research. "Studies have been conducted with groups of individuals who directed their thoughts to a common purpose. It created a kind of super-radiance, documented by instruments which measured the energy around the group. The results were proven. A Transcendental Meditation group in Washington back in the nineties decreased violent crime in their location by 24% during their meditations. It does work, and from a scientific point of view, remarkably well. Alex and Thomas tapped into the Field through their craft, where their talents allow for a strong shift in thought patterns, and the result was a shift on the physical plane."

Baxter remained intrigued. "So the intention to change the man is what did the trick?"

"The focus of their thoughts toward a common goal. The Field seems to register similar thoughts and execute them in our reality. The more we learn, the easier it is for others to follow in our footsteps due their imprint on the Field. So we can build on prior knowledge acquired by others. It is also possible that our higher cognitive processes are merely an interaction with the Field: intuition, creativity, or bursts of inspiration. They are not things happening outside of us. We are tapped into the Field whether we acknowledge its presence or not. The Creator State, or let's say, a brilliant performance, may be an example of coalescence in the Field; a coming together of creative energy in an instantaneous moment."

"Brought on by the intention of the artist to create." Baxter comprehended. He gave Thomas another chance to speak. "So Thomas, is this why so many artists are responding to your search? Are artists experiencing the Creator State because some kind of coalescence is occurring?"

Thomas was impressed by the idea. "Well, history has revealed periods of infectious creative activity, such as ancient Greece, or the Renaissance, or the movements in the Sixties, when poetry, music, and art rushed into the collective consciousness. If the Field accounts for intellectual synchronicity, then bursts of creative synchronization cannot be far behind. The Field is interpreted by the brain through waves of energy. Humans can manipulate this energy to our own wills, because our brains are capable of rational thought."

Baxter couldn't resist the opportunity to make a political slam. "That ability is not evidenced in our current politicians." The crowd agreed with a few claps.

John suddenly took the floor again and pressed on. "The Field is a recording medium for everything in the universe. It provides a means for everything to communicate. Conscious creatures are not isolated entities. Human beings can communicate with the Field and change our world into whatever we desire."

Thomas read the audience's reaction and fidgeted in his chair. Someone would have to explain their application of this research before John lost the crowd with scientific interpretations. He saw an opening and jumped in. "What John is so eloquently explaining is that through the Field, what exists and what does not exist is dictated. So we want to take the next step in exploring our artistic minds. We think it is possible to alter reality through creativity. As artists, we exercise our creative muscles all the time. It enables us to be stronger candidates for using the power of creative thought."

Thomas looked to Alex and saw her yearn to explain their intentions. He forfeited the spotlight. "Alex, this is your territory, if you would explain."

"Thank you, Thomas." She smiled in appreciation. "When an artist creates a work of art, they express it as reality. They can do this easily because they exercise this skill regularly." Alex scanned the audience and felt confidence rise in her chest. "We plan to attempt an experiment during a specific point in time. If peaceful, positive intentions are simultaneously projected on the collective consciousness, we may be able to alter the world's reality."

The audience registered the proposal with smatterings of discussion.

Baxter quieted the room and turned to her. "So many issues need our attention. Hatred, violence and greed are so prevalent in the world today. It all seems like unstoppable madness. How can you stop any of it?"

"By knowing that it is possible. The Creator State exists when doubt is absent, when fears are eliminated, and truth is allowed to align itself, uninhibited, with our artistic expression. We plan to take the reality of peace and worldwide compassion for granted, as if it already exists. It's the same idea as art: when you perform as if your creation is real, and it affects the reality of the observer. During a single event, pure doubtless peace and compassion will exist on the creative plane. It cannot help but influence all other energies within the universal consciousness. Creation cannot be denied when doubt is nonexistent."

"So what you are proposing to do," concluded Baxter, "is gather as many artists as you can and have them execute the same experiment that you performed this summer, only on a grander scale."

Rashan seized an opportunity to speak and moved to the edge of his chair. "May I provide some insight from those who weren't involved in the first experiment?" Baxter seemed pleased that the musician had something to say, and nodded to him. Rashan flashed a smile and began.

"The house of truth exists in our brain. It has been untouched, unopened for a long time. I see the Creator State as a window in that house. Sometimes the curtains part on that window and the occupant peeks out and entices us to come inside. Sometimes my music feels trance-like, and I think that is when the occupant is calling to me to enter the house." Rashan's eyes wandered through the audience and made sure they followed his analogy. His warm persona and rhythmic dialect won their attention. "When the window is open, and we see clearly what is inside, we realize that house is actually our own home." Rashan turned to Baxter. "Do you follow? There is no mysterious man in that house. When we see the house is ours, we can create whatever we want from inside. The home within us becomes the world, a place where we can create whatever is our own truth. I believe the ultimate truth is love, and love can grow within a peaceful world." Rashan laughed and exposed his wide mouth of white teeth. "I try not to use the word 'peace' too often. People look at my dreads, hear me say 'peace' and stop listening."

Baxter enjoyed his self-observation as the audience tittered. "Well Rashan, you could say the world is still suffering from hippie-phobia. A limiting stereotype, but we'll not get into that this evening. Thank you for your lovely metaphor." Rashan sat back in his chair, satisfied with his part of the conversation.

Baxter glanced at the ceiling as he formulated his next question. "I am curious about implementation. How do you get a few thousand artists together?"

"Free beer!" exclaimed Peter. The audience and panel broke into laughter. It energized the mood and Baxter ran with his questioning.

"I'll be there!" Baxter shot back. "Seriously, it's going to take a good deal of coordination to get your membership aligned for your special night." He turned to Thomas. "It is just for one night, yes?"

"Yes, just for one night." Thomas glanced at Alex, who was supposed to make the HIP acknowledgment per the arrangements with Victoria. She saw her segue and took over.

"HIP has generously coordinated a year's worth of funding for the Creator State Project. Within the next eight months we will attempt to collect artists who have experienced the Creator State to join us for that one night. Our aim is global participation. With HIP's marketing expertise and influence in arts management, we anticipate the number of artists participating that evening to be in the hundreds of thousands." The audience reacted and she added, "Yes, it's going to be very big."

Baxter shook his head again and resisted their certainty. "I still don't see how you're going to convince people to drop everything and participate."

Alex leveraged some patience with him. "Honestly, if a fellow artist approached you about the thing you hold dearest in life, your art, and asked you to be part of an event that might influence the course of the world by doing what you do best, wouldn't you do it? Wouldn't you be curious to find the true purpose of your creative talents?"

"Do you think this is the real purpose behind being an artist? Using our talents to create global balance?" Baxter scanned the panel for responses. Thomas caught his gaze and offered one of Alex's *Magic Mobile* quotes.

"Living life as a creator flatters the universe."

Baxter followed up. "So we flatter God by imitating him as a creator?"

Alex and Thomas gave each other a glance. They privately agreed to keep Alex's expanded ideas on the power of creation confidential. Alex geared the line of conversation toward the present agenda. "We want to concentrate our intentions on worldwide awareness." She spoke humbly. "Our understanding of the creative process may allow us to create healing, peace and goodwill on our earthly plane. It may be as simple as one grand connected evening of art." She smiled. "Or at least we hope so."

Baxter seemed satisfied with her explanation. "We're nearing our time limit, so if you will allow me a last round of questions." He adjusted in his seat and pulled at the cuffs of his sweater as if he had another appointment to get to. "Kona, we haven't heard from you this evening. How is this worldwide creative event going to be executed?"

Kona swallowed hard. Of all the panel members, she was the one who had no stage experience, no live performance history to quiet her thundering heartbeat. Her leg bounced nervously at the sound of her name. Alex gave her a reassuring smile and Kona's jiggling leg slowed to a stop. She cleared her throat and tried to smooth her South Side dialect as she responded.

"Well, the actors are going to have a script about the existence of a peaceful world community. They're supposed to alter it, and use their favorite characters from when they felt the State the strongest. Musicians will play their favorite music, with the intention of generating world harmony. Dancers, performers, anyone who gets in front of a live crowd is supposed to color their performance with the intention of world unity as reality. The rest of us, um, 'fixed' artists, people who paint, write, sculpt, anything without a live audience, will follow the same idea. Painters like me will try to express world balance. Filmmakers will work on creating images of a peaceful planet. Dancers will dance their most joyful pieces; writers will compose tales of compassion." Kona ran out of breath as her stage fright got the best of her. She looked to Thomas for help and he came to her rescue.

"All of us will use our talents to express world peace as truth," he explained. "I mean the truth as we want it to exist, like a piece of art: we make exactly what we want to exist. Absolute knowledge, without any doubts. From within the Creator State, we will know a better world. Knowing a better world will magnetize energy to the intention."

Thomas stopped talking. Kona inhaled as if she hadn't taken a breath during her speech. She scooted back in her chair and crossed her legs. Baxter looked as if he had a follow-up question for her, so Peter jumped in to distract him and reinforce their point.

"Everyone is to use the strongest creative experience that they can bring to the table." Peter chopped the arm of his chair for emphasis. "We know anything is possible in our art. Our creativity is made of the same stuff as what created the universe. Whatever we direct our clear, direct thoughts toward will be changed."

Baxter cleverly concluded, "So it is indeed the thought that counts." The audience enjoyed his summation. It brought him seamlessly to the closing statements. "This is an ambitious experiment, to say the least. I admire all of your noble efforts. When will this momentous occasion occur?"

Alex answered. "The next summer solstice. It's a symbolic day for many historic rituals, so we concluded it would be good enough for us." She realized the taping was almost complete, and tied up the conversation with a flourish. "We don't want people to surmise that this is some kind of protest, or march, or meditation. This is creative action. Focused action toward a positive outcome. Artists have always been powerful people. This is an opportunity to let our creative souls demonstrate their effectiveness."

Baxter graciously thanked them. "Well it has been a grand pleasure meeting you and hearing your plans for the future. I truly wish you success."

The audience applauded as the lights dimmed slightly on the stage. The camera crew director yelled, "That's a wrap! Thank you everyone." The crowd clapped again as the lights came up in the house. The panel stood up, congratulated themselves, and thanked Baxter. He reciprocated by bolting off to a private gallery show. He did manage to give Alex a "good job" compliment before he exited. The panel milled with the audience, shook hands and answered questions about the Creator State. This went on for over an hour until the crowd thinned to a few stragglers. Thomas and Peter slipped into the alleyway to have a much needed smoke.

Peter sucked deeply on his Marlboro, and exhaled a lengthy breath as he relaxed. "That went extremely well. I have to say, I am impressed with all of us. Y'know, I didn't think we would sound as good as we did. Alex was really on target. You too man, good work."

"Thanks. I'm sure HIP is pleased. And you're right, Alex was very good tonight." He stared down at his feet. Peter suspected something was amiss.

"Hey man, something bothering you?"

"I didn't realize this until tonight. I'm not really in love with Alex per se, I'm addicted to the feeling we have on stage when we're performing together. Until tonight my stage time with her was spent living as other people, other characters. But this evening we were just ourselves, and it was different. I felt a different kind of love for her." He took a last drag of his cigarette. "I love our creativity and the way it makes me feel." He dropped his cigarette to the ground and smashed it underfoot. "The rest is just a waning crush."

Peter encouraged him. "Maybe pure love exists in creativity, like we talked about tonight. Maybe that's what you're in love with, the love in your work with her."

"Or maybe I've been tapping into the Universal love. Maybe my love for the world is larger than I thought. All these years I thought I hated the world. I guess I was wrong." Thomas' face relaxed as the discovery lightened his weary heart. He looked to Peter, who acknowledged his friend's relief with a smile. Thomas sighed. "Well, that's a load off."

"Hell yeah." The two friends laughed and hung in the alleyway. They joked and smoked until the rest of the members escaped the post-show chitchat.

Inside the theater, Alex finally managed to wriggle out of the conversations. She finished her obligatory duty to HIP and wanted some cool fall air. As she entered the empty backstage hallway, she grinned as she remembered her fine performance as Alex Davis that night. Every word was genuinely hers, not the echoes of her voices. After a year of hearing inspirational strangers, the change was significant for her. There was a transition happening. She wondered if her nerves had simply chased the voices away during the panel discussion.

John stepped into the hall and walked toward her. She noted the pep in his step. He was proud of himself, and rightly so, as he had done a great job. The confidence gave him extra appeal, and Alex took note of her attraction to him. They gave each other a polite congratulations, and after some trepidation, a quick hug. Alex seized the chance to inhale a little essence-of-John. He was still the best smelling guy she ever encountered. John said farewell and exchanged goodnights with Thomas and Peter as he passed them in the alleyway. She watched him leave and felt a tug of loss. Lisa broke the spell and barked a question at her as she approached.

"Hey I listened to your *Mobile* today, and you know what I thought?" Lisa was confrontational. Her tone held the anger of a jealous lover. "I was thinking, when is Alex gonna drop the *Magic Mobile* thing and just speak for herself, y'know, just admit that the words are hers and not some spooky mystery voices in her head."

Alex was surprised by the choice of topic. She was dismayed because the panel discussion turned out well. Congratulations were in order, not criticisms. She attempted to speak, but Lisa cut her off.

"Y'know," Lisa projected a little too loud for the hallway. "You're speaking for a large number of people now. It's time to drop the creepy voice charade and realize that you are the one expressing all of those beautiful thoughts. Apparently *you're* the eloquent one." She headed for the exit and shot over her shoulder, "Good job tonight." She pushed through the back door. Alex watched her grab the cigarette from Peter's mouth and storm down the alleyway. Peter shrugged at Thomas, and jogged to catch up with her.

Thomas saw Alex look in his direction and he motioned for her to come out. She hesitated and he mimed drinking a cocktail. She yelled a goodnight to Joseph who was still inside. When Joseph didn't respond, she poked her head in to the house. Joseph was in a deep conversation with Victoria. Their body language indicated they were flirting. She backed out of the room unnoticed. The sight made her giggle as she walked into the alley.

Thomas asked, "What's so amusing?"

She linked arms with him and grinned as they walked away. "Thomas, this is going to be a very successful adventure."

14

Ah the moment one finally surrenders to their art. The craft becomes you, you become the art, and the experience of trusting creativity becomes its own reward. Giving ourselves over to that ever-changing entity is our ultimate challenge. Submission to it brings such brilliance that all else seems to be in shadow. The moment is nothing short of seeing the face of God.

—The Magic Mobile

The eight months of preparation for the solstice event rushed forward at full speed. HIP utilized their film industry connections and produced a sharp hour-long television program from the panel discussion. They interspersed Baxter's interview of the Creator State group with clips of private comments from some of HIP's top clients. The addition of celebrities and renowned artists gave the Project the mass appeal it needed, and encouraged important artists to get involved. It was a dynamic calling card which HIP quickly expedited for national and international distribution.

"It's the thought that counts" began to pop up everywhere the Creator State group was mentioned. HIP adopted Baxter's clever remark for the Project's ad campaigns, against the objections of the group who perceived the phrase as too catchy for their endeavor. The publicity plowed forward despite the collective's apprehensions.

The television piece garnered excellent results. The membership numbers doubled each month. By Christmastime, the Creator State Project enlisted over one hundred thousand artists from all over the world. Interest in the final event thrived on all levels; financially, artistically, and theoretically. Clearly the idea ignited a fire in the creative population. The magnitude of the Project demanded additional event coordination at various local sites. A call for volunteers went out and was answered around the globe. A main office was established in Chicago, with satellites in several cities. Supportive Web sites linked to the Creator State site, while advertisements and interviews flooded periodicals. As the experiment date drew closer, a promotional television campaign began.

When interviewed about the strong support for the experiment, Alex humbly denied credit. She insisted the idea of the event existed in the creative consciousness; the group merely enabled it into action. This justified the incredible response they received. Others in the group felt that the simplicity of the experiment was the key to their success. It didn't require money or sacrifice, it only called for an evening of doing what they loved most. Regardless of the reason, it looked as if the experiment would occur as planned. The membership was projected to be in the hundreds of thousands by the longest day in June.

Meanwhile, Alex received a request which she hadn't anticipated. Victoria discreetly asked her to silence the *Magic Mobile* until after the experiment. The HIP media-savvy staff concluded the *Mobile* didn't fit the image they desired for their Project's super girl. HIP asked politely if she would "shut the *Mobile* down for a while" and alluded to a conflict of interest. Alex recognized the veiled threat, and conceded to disconnect that part of her life until the following year. The absence of the *Magic Mobile* troubled her for weeks, but she realized the Project grew out of her control. The little group at the Andrews activated a force of creation within thousands, and it would need the guidance of an entity like HIP to execute the solstice event properly. She set aside her pride and surrendered to the cause. Privately she kept writing her missives into a journal, and planned to resurrect the *Magic Mobile* in the future. Each day she searched the messages for traces of her own voice, and wondered if Lisa's post-panel criticisms were valid. If Alex accepted the clairaudient observations as her own voice, then she would have to accept herself as a true communicator. Despite her ability to raise thousands of people to creative action, she still wondered if she was a leader. She remembered her conversation with Thomas on the green lawn of last September; the open creative life they imagined. Something would need to occur to achieve that reality. But these ponderances would have to wait for the moment; the Project demanded her complete attention.

She relieved *Mobile* withdrawal by occasionally calling her friends with messages of the day. This activity excluded Lisa because her criticism of the *Mobile* still burned in Alex. Tension lingered between the two of them until the holidays arrived. Alex finally confronted Lisa at a swanky high rise Christmas party, which was thrown by a wealthy sculptor friend of theirs. After a few vials of champagne, the two velvet-clad friends began to argue, and took their tempers on to the host's balcony. They took no notice of the stunning city views from the thirty-fifth floor as they quarreled.

Lisa wrapped her beaded scarf tightly around her upper body as they fought in the blowing nighttime snowfall. Her first comment was as cold as the wind. "The *Mobile* is self-important and preachy!"

Alex thought the now-silent messages were the least selfish of her habits. She stood in the freezing ankle-deep accumulation and defended herself. "The messages were free for anyone who needed some inspiration. I didn't preach, they were just beautiful words I wanted to share with my fellow artists. I didn't do it to draw attention to myself."

"Oh right, just like the Project." Lisa sneered. "You definitely don't want any personal publicity from this whole thing."

Until that moment, Lisa tiptoed around her resentment of Alex's newfound notoriety. She hid it under wisecracks and jabs at her circle of friends. Most of the group chose to ignore Lisa's behavior, since Peter was a full-time champion of the Project. Alex's patience wore thin with the ever-expanding demands of the solstice event, and Lisa's negativity was unacceptable.

"What the hell is your issue with the Project?"

Lisa cinched her scarf tautly across her chest as she blurted out months of distress. "I'm the only one in the group who can't get to the State and I feel like a hack and the only reason I'm still part of this crazy group is because I love Peter! I've had to watch my best friend turn into some kind of guru thanks to some huge arts organization, and I don't know what my role is in all of this, and I'm fucking jealous of all of you! Why can't I get there? Am I so fucking mediocre that I can't get to the State?"

Lisa's sobbing stopped her tirade. She grasped the railing and cried cathartically in the freezing night air. Alex gave her a moment and wrapped her arms around her. Lisa surrendered to the consolation and wept into Alex's gown. Alex watched the traffic below snake along Lake Shore Drive. A chain of headlights lit the drifting snowflakes. Alex pondered what the world would be like after the experiment: would it be suddenly different, or would the changes be more subtle, more internal? If many of the members were involved for bragging rights, or because a friend required them to participate as in Lisa's situation, would there be any changes at all?

Lisa's tears slowed enough for her to speak again. She withdrew her face from Alex's shoulder, riffled a tissue from her pocket, and attempted to rescue her evening makeup. She took a deep breath.

"So enough about me. How do like my dress?" She wiped her tears as they laughed together. They felt renewal in the brisk snowy air. Lisa raised her eyes and surveyed the neighborhood. "Jesus, look at the view from up here."

Alex admired the skyline and asked the inevitable. "Why didn't you tell me that you couldn't feel the State?"

"Jealousy." Lisa answered flatly. "Insecurity. All the wrong reasons to hide something from your best friend." She turned toward the night sky. "I have wanted something more from my art for a long time now. Being involved with this group hasn't helped me. I know I'm faking the entire experience just to save face, and maybe to save my relationship."

Alex advised and tried not to sound preachy. "Perhaps you haven't felt the State because you've been trying too hard?"

"Thanks Alex, but we both know that my intentions aren't in the right place. It shouldn't be this hard. I'm doing it for the wrong reasons."

Alex didn't disagree, but she reassured her. "It is never too late to try. Maybe you should try a different art form. You've secretly despised acting for years. How about trying another way to express yourself? You know you're a creative person."

Lisa turned and revealed a deep hurt behind her eyes. She had something to tell her, but was afraid of retribution. She lowered her eyes. "Peter likes actors. Not painters or musicians or dancers. He likes actors." She halted any protest. "I know what you're going to say, I know how wrong and twisted and shallow it is. I know how wrong I might be, but I'm not willing to risk it, Alex. I love him too much. Way too much. I have never felt this way before. Maybe art doesn't have what I need. I know it's everything to you, Alex. I know it brings you some kind of sacred level of joy. But right now, I have to follow what makes me happiest, and that's Peter."

Alex fabricated an analogy to help her friend feel better. "We're having opposite experiences. You've traded art for love, and I've traded love for art. How did this happen to us?"

Lisa seemed to brighten with Alex's acceptance of the situation. "There's a lesson in there, I'm sure." She laughed. "But maybe we can ease off the interpretations for now? I'm fucking freezing."

Alex laughed and slid the balcony door open for her. "Hey, maybe you should try sculpture. Look at this place. What is he, like a gazillionaire now?" They giggled and joined the party again. They agreed to disagree, which rescued their friendship. Alex urged Lisa to privately explore another outlet for her creativity. Lisa promised to do so. Shortly afterwards she enrolled in a modern dance class which led her to a fresh expression of her soul's longings. She told Peter that dancing was just a way to keep in shape, an exercise class to maintain the body he loved to love so frequently. He was oblivious to her new infatuation which had her absent three nights a week. Before long, she experienced the creative fulfillment she sought, as well as the unmistakable euphoria of the Creator State.

In the swirl of excitement surrounding the Project, there were a few people who intended to give the group as difficult a time as they could conjure. David Cooper was at the top of the list. Throughout the fall, the repeated airing of the panel discussion worked David's nerves. The opening remarks about the Andrews and himself were not edited out. It reinforced his bad behavior with each broadcast. When it began to affect his box office, he called on his uncle again to keep the Andrews open. Each nepotistic favor increased his resentment of the Creator State group. He needed the support of the locals to release him from the City's watchful gaze. People would rally for a space to stay open if you were in their favor. The City learned to avoid the theaters with outspoken audiences. David's thinning crowds were mostly transient. He depended upon the tourists who filtered through town, people who were unaware of current local events. He crushed any chance of involvement with the Creator State Project when he fired Alex so harshly. He was blinded by ego when he prematurely judged the group; he hadn't anticipated their success. Amends would not be made, and David remained steadfast in his negativity toward the Project.

"This solstice event is nonsense," read David's quote in the *Tribune*. "The Project is a bunch of fabrications that will embarrass every artist the day after the experiment." He went on to claim the original experiment never took place, that it never happened at all. The paper pressured Thomas for a name, and he pleaded with Joseph to reveal himself. A week later, Robert Clarke satiated everyone's curiosity with an article about Joseph Bancroft, the experiment's mystery man. In the weeks that followed, Joseph gave an overwhelming number of interviews. Afterward, he told HIP he was a shy man, and would prefer to be left alone. They obliged, but not before they made sure David's derogatory observations were removed from public opinion. After the release of Joseph's name, David was unusually quiet and made no counterattack at all. Alex felt his silence like a slow burn. She knew his style too well, and anticipated they hadn't heard the last from him or his City connections.

The disclosure of Joseph's name brought a collection of naysayers to the forefront. Irritated conservatives criticized the group's methods and accused the members of cult-like rituals. They labeled the upcoming experiment as a large-scale publicity stunt. HIP countered the negative press with articles written by John, who quoted his resources and references to support their theories. His scientific viewpoint appealed to many publications, and his schedule filled with speaking engagements. He also acquired a few new comrades along the route to solstice. The panel discussion attracted the interest of a few local scientists who wanted to study the measurable affects of the State. John decided to lead a scientific collective to document the experiment. The attention of his colleagues and the media's infatuation with his comments pleased him. John enjoyed the glow of the Creator State spotlight.

The scientists planned to monitor the experiment before and after solstice. They tracked violent actions and various environmental, economical and behavioral factors worldwide for three months prior to the event. Three months after solstice, they would report any changes in worldwide activities. Parameters would compare prior years to dispel coincidental variables. The team of scientists were excited to document the facts of the event. Once the data was collected and summarized, the *Tribune* would publish a special report, written by John. The *Tribune* received exclusive rights to the report as gratitude for Robert Clarke's article last summer. HIP was unhappy with the deal. They had larger papers and periodicals which would pay top dollar to be the first to publish the report. Technically, John's group wasn't part of the Project. He found his own funding through a private source and was beyond the reaches of HIP control. The report truly belonged to him and his colleagues. Alex and John shared a private victory over the controlling forces at HIP, and they celebrated into the early hours one cold January night.

Their ongoing attraction to each other pulled them into bed three times since the fall, but this three wouldn't seem magical to Alex. Their lovemaking provided evidence of higher possibilities and strengthened the unspoken ties between them. The winter sunrise found them bound by the June deadline, while their past disagreements tore them apart. Neither could find a solution to their relationship in the flurry of activity. They rarely crossed paths as they scrambled from lecture to meeting to interview. But occasionally in the center of the whirlwind there was calm; a few quiet nights when they shared each other's company.

John and Alex nuzzled under her daybed comforter when the phone interrupted their afterglow. She hesitated to break the January morning spell and missed the call, but retrieved the voicemail just after the ringing ceased. She let the message play on speaker as she hustled back to the warmth of the bed. John engulfed her with the covers as they listened. It was Thomas. Robert Clarke suffered a heart attack and died.

Alex felt her own heart drop at both the shock and the premonition of it. She foresaw his funeral when he first came to her at the Andrews. It was January, just as she imagined it. John held her as she wept for their advocate. She chose not to tell anyone about her vision. It seemed everything she did was examined and reexamined by the press. The media might find out, and their conjectures would distract attention from Bob's memorial.

After a two-day wake, the funeral of Robert Clarke arrived. It was attended by both friends and colleagues. Newspaper folk from many publications paid their respects, as well as performers who dubbed him an artistic champion. His elegant mahogany casket was placed in the cemetery for final services. It rested beneath a pale gray winter sky; a blotch of glossy red-brown amongst the barren trees, colorless tombstones, and glistening white groundcover. Alex stood graveside in the icy snowfall after the ceremonies ended and contemplated Bob's impact on her life. She quietly thanked him. Thomas came to her side and stared down at the casket. The beautiful box sat just above where Bob's grave would be in the spring. He murmured, "What do they do with him until the ground thaws out?" Alex didn't answer right away and he put his arm around her. He felt bad about his comment and realized he should be a bit more sensitive. Thomas tried to make up for it. "He was a great journalist."

Alex stifled a laugh and whispered, "He was a manipulative bastard."

Thomas joined her in a giggle and feared karmic retribution. "But he was the best damn manipulator that the *Chicago Tribune* has ever seen."

This comeback sent them both into a giggling fit. They hurried away from the grave site as they tried to control themselves. The two friends dodged behind a private mausoleum and muffled their hilarity into gloved hands. Alex recovered a little and took a few breaths of wintry air.

"I haven't laughed that hard since you said you were in love with me." They both broke into another fit of hysteria. Thomas had to sit on the frozen ground as his knees collapsed beneath him. Alex joined him and they backed themselves against the cold stone of the crypt which hid them from public view. They slowly recuperated from the spell as the laughs burst and retreated for several minutes. The stress of the Project and the death of a friend dispelled in the cemetery breezes.

Thomas spoke at last. "Hey, for the record, I never actually said I was in love with you."

"That's just like you to cover your ass."

He changed the mood. "I had a realization after the panel discussion. I wasn't in love with you. I was in love with the energy we create together. I discussed this with Peter again last week. My view on love seems to have changed. He had some good advice for me."

"Peter had good advice?"

"Yeah, we discussed universal love as being a part of creation, the creative energy. A kind of love for everything, a love that's connected to everything. Like the State, it's a loving-everything-at-once kind of feeling. Maybe that's what my crush was all about; feeling that universal love every time I was with you."

"So what did Peter have to say that was so wise?"

Thomas reached for his cigarettes which were buried in his thick wool coat pockets. "He said that love should be like that slogan 'think globally, act locally.' Honor the one you love, but don't wall yourself up in it, stay connected to the big picture at the same time."

"Wow, that is wise." She reflected. "I really hope he and Lisa work out. During my argument with her last month I mistakenly said that I had traded love for art, and she art for love. I knew it was wrong the second I said it. There's no sacrifice needed, we can have everything we want."

Thomas sat with his lighter and cigarettes on his lap and pressed a point he tried to make earlier. "You should take your own advice one of these days. Lisa is learning to get what she wants. If you want both the universal love and the local love, then you should start acting locally yourself."

She knew he meant John, but she wasn't about to forfeit her independence just yet. "Someday I'll find a way to balance it all. Even the *Mobile* is on hold for the moment. Who knows, it may never come back; maybe I'm done with that part of my life. But I can't fret about the way things used to be or what I'm missing along the way. This might be the most exciting year of my life, and solstice may be the biggest event of my life. I want to put everything I have into it. I'm overwhelmed by reaching out to the world. It's everything to me. This may be my big shot at making a difference. How can I think about anything else?"

He knew what she meant. The world did seem more important than anything that could happen personally. "I keep sensing that things are going to change. I wonder if my intuition is detecting world change or personal change."

"Probably both, but let me do something locally today." She grabbed his cigarettes and lighter, raised herself up, slip-slided along the frozen ground to the trash can, and disposed of his bad habit. He chuckled as she shuffled back. She offered him a hand to stand up. They brushed the snow off their coats and started back toward the road. He sulked in jest. "Can we at least have a drink in Bob's memory?" She looped her arm in his and agreed.

As the spring approached, an outreach campaign of what HIP coined as "warm-up" events began. The exhibits and happenings reminded people to put the experiment on their artistic agendas. The general public gawked at the advertising campaign in print and on their televisions, but HIP wanted to reach the working artists who felt the State. The warm-up campaign urged the membership to produce events, shows, or exhibits which would demonstrate the Creator State in action. By the beginning of June, warm-up events were en vogue. Galleries showed paintings, sculptures, or multimedia installations from State supporters. Poetry slams and literary readings were hosted by writers who believed their best work existed in the open consciousness of the State. Lectures assisted creatives to find their deepest connection in preparation for the upcoming event.

As solstice neared, the membership finalized their plans. They designated a three-hour window as "prime time" for Creator State activity. This time slot would be the high point of the evening, when as many artists as possible would enter the State with the intention of creating peace. It was anybody's guess as to when the "best" time would be. Since New York had a long-standing history as a center for live performance, it seemed reasonable to work from their schedule. The experiment was slated to start at 8:00 p.m. eastern standard time.

Groups of various sizes would perform together on the big night, while some individuals would make solitary efforts. It depended upon how they reached the State. The Brothers Slim resided at their new artistic home out in Galena, and they convinced their cast and crew to participate in the State event. They, like thousands of others, would have a live audience to entertain during the hours of the experiment. Audiences anticipated a few added lines during the performances on solstice night. Many theaters altered entire acts to appease the solstice cause.

Rashan and Lucas planned a large group effort at a downtown warehouse. Their music would be complimented by a local modern dance group, which included the newly discovered Lisa Harris. Peter would deliver his favorite monologues in the middle of this rhythm and movement from a raised platform center stage. Kona decided to paint a giant mural of a peaceful planet during Rashan's event. This collaborative performance art piece would be witnessed by a selective audience. A friendly crowd would motivate the players through a glorious evening of creativity.

Alex and Thomas decided to break off on their own. They had a very special atmosphere in mind, and chose to execute a private endeavor. Everyone had the option to participate with or without an audience present, whatever allowed for the most freedom of thought. Lisa accused Alex of hiding behind a veil of mystery once again, but Thomas noted Joseph's results were achieved without spectators. Lisa wanted Alex at the warehouse performance, but she accepted Thomas' defense and backed down.

Thomas selected the Playhouse in North Ravenswood for their solstice venue. It was the theater where he and Alex first performed together. The Playhouse was the also the theater which hired Miles last fall, and it was dark for the summer months. The owner gave them permission to use the space as they pleased. He knew he would receive publicity if the event did what it supposed to do. Miles helped them set up for the experiment and filled the space with what Alex called "magical objects." These included candles, incense, and crystals from Rashan, along with representations of the worldwide participants. Paintings were propped on easels about the room. Musical instruments and scripts were scattered in the house and on stage, with a clear area at the center. The night sky was projected in tiny white dots of light onto the black ceiling above. Below the stars rested a globe on a black base, washed with a rosy light which made it appear suspended in the dark space of the stage. It was an elementary way to convey the worldwide reach of their efforts through simple symbols. Thomas and Alex would perform segments of their best scenes together, then migrate to a script written specifically for the evening.

The day before the solstice event, stages were set all over the world in anticipation of change. Expectations ran high within the membership, while skepticisms surfaced outside of it. It seemed as if the world chose sides, pro and con, as to whether the experiment would have any effect at all. Alex encouraged the creative population to engage their own sense of the State during the experiment. The *Tribune* quoted her the day before the big event: "Any creative action during the solstice will strengthen our energy. A positive shift will occur if we have vast numbers generating the genuine desire for change. If you haven't felt the Creator State, open yourself to it. Let the energy flow through you. Enjoy it, celebrate it; this is a worldwide initiation of change."

Alex couldn't sleep the night before the event. She flipped through her *Magic Mobile* journal in the early morning hours and reread the missives which paved her path. Some of them brought a smile to her face, and some of them were so beautiful that she reaffirmed her interpretation of them. These voices must circle in the ether, in the Field; they couldn't be her own voice. As the morning light warmed the windows in her studio, she scrambled into her running clothes for a sleepy-headed jog.

She treaded along and admired the sunrise colors which grew over the city. Her pace slowed to a walk as she felt a rush of whispers. *This is the last day of an era. What lay in slumber beneath the weight of man's foolishness is about to be awakened. The cloak of negativity will be cast off, and every moment will be penetrated by the new light of creation. For creation is selfless compassion, and compassion is universal love.*

She hopped up on the wave break wall and stretched her arms wide to the city. She felt connected to a larger system, an endless system of energy. A strong surge of joy and power flowed into her, like a blessing from the master creators. Within her heart she felt an intuition: the creators who manifested this enormous artwork called Earth sent their love to her, sent good wishes for the task ahead.

She turned and faced the lake with her arms still spread to the horizon and let out a yell. It was a simultaneous release for preparations completed and a welcome to solstice. Whatever today held, she was already a part of it, already past it, already victorious because of her intentions. She inhaled and called to the morning sun as loudly as her stage voice could carry. "It *is* the thought that counts! We're already there! We've already made the change! Now let's go and *live* the day!"

From a half mile down the track, she heard an early jogger yell something back. She cheered in reply, jumped down and flew down the path on weightless feet. The life she anticipated, the feeling, the connection, had finally arrived.

The members began to stir all over town. Thomas' eyes shocked open and looked to his alarm clock: 5:30 a.m. The big day was upon him. He felt anticipation hum in his head and he rose to his feet. The sunrise sent a pale light through loft. He stretched and faced the lake.

"Morning Alex." He knew she was out there, already running, already taking in the moments of the day. Thomas could feel the collective connection as artists awakened to their solstice. He spoke to the clear June sky. "Morning everyone. Let's do this thing."

Further north, Peter awoke with the same start. He slid an arm toward Lisa and found her side of the bed empty. He called out to her with his broken morning voice and she answered from the living room. He swung out of bed. He crossed to his robe, winked at the plaid flannel, and dressed himself in it before he went to Lisa. He found her propped in the bay window, sitting cross-legged in meditation. Peter apologized, as he always did when he discovered her in this position. His discomfort with her meditations never wore off. He couldn't do it himself, but he respected it. Lisa reached an arm to him. He wrapped himself around her and they faced the sunrise together. Peter watched the glow on her hair and skin as they sat in the radiant silence of the morning. He squeezed her for a long while and they felt the presence of the day.

"It's here. Can you feel that?" she said. He agreed by squeezing her tighter. "So much is going to happen tonight, Peter. It's like it's already happening."

Peter watched her eyes as she felt the faraway connection. He felt it swell within him. "Yes, so much is going to change today." He slipped himself off of her and backed away.

"Lisa." He waited for her to turn around. She did, and discovered him bent down on one knee as he searched in his robe pocket with his hand. Her heart began to pound as he produced a black velvet box and popped it open. A diamond flashed at her from within it and mimicked her wide stare. Before he had a chance to speak, she tackled him without hesitation. She knocked them both to the ground as she repeated, "Yes!" over and over again. They tumbled in happiness on the floor and Peter fought to place the ring on her finger. When he succeeded, they rolled again in a flurry of kisses. Two comments were made in between their lip locks. Lisa said, "I don't want to be an actor anymore," and Peter responded, "I don't care."

The Project office bustled with activity as Alex arrived. Last minute questions were answered and details confirmed. The hustle in the office brimmed with the purpose of the day. Everyone could feel it. Energy fluttered around the rooms as volunteers zoomed to get everything in place for the evening. Alex handled many calls from the media. They repeatedly inquired if the Project began the experiment already. She confirmed it had not, and offered that the power of thought was the energy people felt. The intention of change unmistakably graced their agendas.

By 4:00 p.m. the phones went eerily quiet. It was 5:00 p.m. on the East Coast, which meant preparation time had begun for many. Most of the volunteers left for their own Creator State activities, but a few remained. A small group of painters offered to man the office that night, in case any last-minute questions came in. They also wanted to be the first to hear reports of any results, so they planned to spend the next twenty-four hours camped out at the headquarters. One of them walked by Alex's doorway and pointed to her watch. Alex finished up a last call with Victoria, who wished her all the best. It had been an extremely busy few months for both of them, and they congratulated each other on their endurance. Victoria wanted to make sure that Alex enjoyed the final experiment, and asked her to leave the headquarters in the capable hands of her staff. She agreed and thanked Victoria for all of her efforts on their behalf. Once officially relieved of responsibilities, Alex wanted to get to the Playhouse where Thomas planned to meet her. She was late, but Thomas knew she would have to stay at the office until the last minute. The last minute arrived, and the volunteer returned and begged her to leave.

"Miss Davis, I think you should go *now!*" the girl demanded. Alex grabbed her things as the girl guided her out the door. They hit the sidewalk, which was mobbed with people headed north. Alex paled at the sight and instantly realized what was happening. There was a Cubs game at Wrigley Field.

"I'll never get a cab in this crowd! And the buses and L will be packed. Oh my God, this can't be happening. It'll take me an hour to get out of here!"

The girl grabbed her panicked leader by the arms. "Hey, it's ok. My car is right up the street." The girl handed her the keys. "I think you should take it for the night. You can return it tomorrow."

"Are you sure? I can walk a few blocks and try to get on the subway."

"Miss Davis, it is 5:30 p.m. already. You have to get to the Playhouse, you have to get into the State." She urged, "Please, you have done so much for me, it's an honor to help you out."

Alex appreciated the girl's generosity. "What's your name? Have we met before?"

"Susan," the girl smirked, "and I think it's very important to help you right now."

Alex squeezed the keys in her hand. "I used to have a friend named Susan." She accepted the offer. "I'll have it back first thing tomorrow."

The girl looked relieved, escorted her to the car and waved goodbye as she drove away. Alex glanced at her in the rear view mirror, thankful for the unexpected favor. She turned onto Lake Shore Drive where traffic crawled. Just past the ballpark, the congestion thinned to typical rush hour. She thought of Thomas, and felt him wonder where the hell she was. "On my way," she whispered. "Just a few more minutes."

Once on Montrose, she noticed a police car behind her that kept pace with her vehicle. She added a bit of caution to her driving and slowed down as she turned onto Clark. The cop car followed. She was five blocks from the Playhouse when the police turned on their lights and motioned her over. Alex promptly obeyed and speculated what she did wrong. She reviewed her driving and found no offense. When the cop approached the car, he seemed agitated.

He asked for her license, which she provided. "This your car?" the officer demanded.

She cleared her throat nervously. "No, it's a volunteer, um, it belongs to a friend of mine. She let me borrow it just now."

The officer gloated in disbelief. "We have a report of this car being stolen. Please step out of the vehicle." He opened her door. "Hands on the roof, ma'am. You're under arrest."

Alex obeyed, stupefied as the officer recited Miranda and handcuffed her. Her mind raced as he escorted her into the police car. She pleaded with the officers to call the headquarters and let the girl who lent her the keys explain. There had to be a mistake. But her requests fell on deaf ears; they were numb to that kind of chatter. She paused and collected her thoughts. It was 6:00 p.m. The experiment was at 7:00 p.m. This arrest was a wild misunderstanding. She calmed herself. She would be out and at the Playhouse soon enough. No need to panic. She asked, "Have you heard about the Creator State experiment?"

The officer turned to his partner and laughed. "Yeah, big bunch of art weirdoes gettin' freaky tonight." His eyes seared at her in the mirror. "What about it?"

She realized what was happening. This was not a misunderstanding; someone set this up to keep her from the event. Her blood boiled at the thought of it, and her face must have shown her discovery, because the cop laughed again.

The second officer turned to the one driving and scoffed, "It's the thought that counts." They both joked cruelly about solstice on the way to the station. Once they arrived, the jailer abruptly put her in an empty cell across the walkway from a drunk they impounded. He was the only other captive at the station and leered at her with bloodshot eyes.

As the jailer walked away she yelled after him. "Why aren't you booking me? What about fingerprinting and paperwork? What the hell is going on?!"

The white-haired stocky man turned back and studied her for a second. "I don't know what's up with your case, sweetheart. Just sit tight and I'll find out, okay?"

She appreciated his kinder tone. "Thank you. What time is it?"

He pointed to the wall clock behind her. "It's 6:30 p.m." He smiled flirtatiously at her. "You got a date?"

She smiled back and tried to sway him to her defense. "Kind of, I'm Alex Davis. I'm the Creator State girl everyone's been talking about."

The man frowned. "Hey isn't that solstice thing happening tonight? Don't you have to be there?"

She heard his words echo in her head. The arrest was so unbelievable, so wrong. "Yes." She broke into tears. "I'm supposed to be at the Playhouse."

The officer rolled his eyes at the drunk to cover his sympathy for Alex. He handed her his handkerchief. "Well you'll get there. What did you do anyway?"

"Nothing!" she demanded, then quieted herself for the only reasonable ears in the place. "A volunteer gave me her car to get to the theater tonight. The officers who pulled me over said that she reported it stolen. It's just a misunderstanding.

It can't be the same car, she gave the keys willingly. She begged me to take it." The look on the jailer's face indicated she wasn't going anywhere soon unless the girl dropped the charges. There was only one thing she could do. "Don't I get a phone call, Officer …"

"Jenson. Gimme a minute, I'll check it out." He gave the drunk a warning look to leave Alex alone, and left.

She ignored the lurid remarks from the drunken man across the hall and closed her eyes. *Don't wait for me, Thomas. If it gets to 7:00 p.m. and I'm not there, don't wait for me.* She could feel the members prepare. The event was happening, with or without her. A swell of frustration popped her eyes open and she reeled to look at the clock: 6:45 p.m. "Shit!" she said aloud, which attracted comments from the drunk again. Officer Jenson barked at him to shut up as he approached her cell.

"Got you a phone call." He glanced toward the front desk. "But, uh, you're gonna have to use my cell." He whispered as he passed the phone to her. "I don't know who got you in here, but the guys up front are dead set on keeping you here for the night." He smiled. "Keep it quiet, okay?"

She nodded and thanked him. She crouched in the corner, flipped open the phone, and called Thomas.

The Playhouse waited quietly. Candles flickered, the night sky glistened above, and the Earth waited in suspended silence. The space lingered timelessly, charged for the evening's purpose. Thomas paced for a while after he called the headquarters for Alex's whereabouts. When 6:00 p.m. passed, he decided to get on with his preparations. He assured himself that nothing would stop Alex from getting to the theater. He lit more incense and his cell phone rang. He dashed to it and heard a frightened voice on the other end.

"Thomas, I'm in jail!"

He laughed as if she was kidding. She emphasized, "I'm serious! This volunteer lent me her car and then reported it stolen. I'm sure there's more to it but I wanted to call you." She started to cry, swallowed her tears, and tried to keep quiet.

"How could this happen *tonight?*" He calmed his voice and rationalized the situation. "Okay. Are you going to get out anytime soon?"

"I have no idea. Whoever did this is probably going to make sure I'm in here all night." She felt acceptance sweep over her. There was no escaping the circumstances. Thomas felt it too.

He made a decision. "Okay, so we do it from different locations." She started to cry again and he explained, "We have everything set up here, just be here with me. Are you alone?" She confirmed with a whimper she was. He advised, "All you have to do is your part of the scenes. Talk to me, be with me, it won't matter if you're physically here by my side. We'll be in the State, in the Field. It's the same thing as being here, understand?"

Alex sniffed. "Yes, like being there. It isn't the location, it's the consciousness." She felt hope rise within her. "Okay, I'll do my part, you do yours, and I'll see you in the State." She looked at the clock. "It's almost time. I'll start at 7:00 p.m. sharp." Her spirits lifted again. "Thank you, Thomas. No one is going to block us tonight. Sorry I panicked."

He sighed. "No problem, jailbird. Are you safe, I mean, are you okay?"

She looked at the opposite cell and saw the drunk passed out. "I'm fine. Actually I'm more than fine. Oh Thomas, can you feel them beginning? It's here! The event is here!"

He backed her enthusiasm. "Yes! Let's get to it, eh?"

Alex called for Officer Jenson. She returned his phone and asked for one more favor. He agreed and winked before closing the hall door behind him for her privacy. The echo of it subsided and the cells quieted. She looked at the clock: 6:55 p.m. She inhaled a few cleansing breaths, closed her eyes, and let the Playhouse stage appear around her. Slowly the stars began to twinkle above, the circle of candles glowed, and the incense lingered sweetly in the air. After a few moments of concentration, Thomas materialized in her vision and stood aside of the globe at center stage. She breathed in the scene and strengthened its reality. She was with him. She breathed in Dylana and felt familiar emotions flow through her. Dylana pulsed in her veins as she felt Thomas transform into his role, and they began their first scene.

Their dialogue flowed from one scene into the next; effortless transitions gained from years of performing together. The anxieties and doubts of the physical world faded into the distance as they succumbed to the excitement. The Creator State enveloped them, and they began the special script devised for the evening's purpose. Words of compassion lifted from their mouths and expressed world peace as a reality. Their portrayals spoke words of kindness and understanding and happily discussed the camaraderie among all living things. As their reality morphed into the reality of the script, art became life, performance became truth, and imitation became a command for change.

Thomas opened himself to the farthest reaches of the Creator State's energy. He felt something in his consciousness which he hadn't encountered before. A rush of pure universal love filled his existence. It both exhilarated and frightened him. When he rejected any doubts about the feeling, it flowed openly into his awareness. It allowed him to experience the fullness of joy coalescing in the ether, a joy which tapped untouched abilities in the human race. The high of universal compassion surged in his cells. Alex felt the overwhelming joy run through her and knew Thomas felt it too. The moment contained more energy than their previous experiments. The echo of thousands of artists reverberated in the background, all with the intention to shift a worldwide population to positive action. Threads of unified purpose connected the creative acts of every soul who participated that evening. Alex and Thomas could sense the connected population at work.

A similar experience unfolded at the South Side warehouse performance. Rashan and his musicians crossed over to the State through their rhythmic interpretations of a joyous world view. They played and sang tirelessly, confident their participation was crucial. Peter delivered his monologue with a chant-like pace as he stood above the ecstatic flail and twist of the dance troupe below him. Lisa felt her mind and body give way to the dance, which was a piece choreographed to represent compassion for all creatures. At the back of the stage, Kona's zealous brush strokes dazzled a giant canvas and synchronized with the energy of the performance. The audience at the warehouse applauded and cheered. They reinforced the artists' expression of peace, and became part of the message to the universe to create a new reality.

The collective creative consciousness expanded as artistic souls from around the world entered the Creator State. They intertwined in a vast interconnected creation. Music swelled, images flashed, colors danced; the rapture of performing gave way to the pure essence of creation itself. Alex sensed the height of the experiment approach, and her command simultaneously called out with thousands of others. *It's so wide, it's so vast! We are all here, make the change! Make the shift! Use the intention! Make this reality!*

As the collective thought of change occurred, a brilliant rush of energy raced through the creative consciousness and flashed through the Field. When it reached the utmost edges of interpretation, a second wave of energy began, with greater intensity than the first. It sped through the collective and the Field a second time. The artists stayed focused as they performed. The flashes were both physical and metaphysical, both felt and envisioned. Everyone maintained their activities throughout the surges of brilliance; voices lifted, music sustained, chords and choruses, brush strokes and key strokes, exalted bodies and dialogue streamed through the creative population and universal mind.

A third stream of energy grew as the collective expedited the intention of a peaceful reality. The brilliant force flooded the universal consciousness and magnetized energy to its cause as it made a request of creation. An order directed every particle in existence to comply: peace is the natural order, let all energy and substance express this truth. In the silent space of universal thought, the Field quivered at the command.

The lengthy moment began to pass. Accomplishment replaced urgency and one by one, artists released themselves from the Creator State. They knew something extraordinary had happened. Thomas slowed his words to a stop and sensed Alex did the same. He sat center stage and listened. He didn't know what to expect next.

On the South Side, Rashan's musicians quieted their instruments. The dancers slowed and panted from the frenzy of activity. All paused and waited for someone to make the first observation. Lisa caught her breath and shouted, "Did anyone else feel that?"

Rashan's mouth widened into a broad smile. He raised his guitar in both hands high above his head in a victorious stance and began laughing. "Ha, ha! Euphoric!"

The room erupted with affirmations.

"Light?"

"Brilliance!"

"Did you feel the connected energy?"

Conversations boomed until Peter gave a piercing whistle for their attention. "Hey, y'know, we're supposed to keep going, but, I think we may have done it already." Voices rose in agreement. Rashan stood on his amplifier and hushed the group again.

"We all felt that! Let's play to celebrate now, keep the energy flowing, yes?" Everyone agreed. They started up again.

Alex knelt in her cell as the event's energy pulsed within her. She remained on the floor for a long time, overwhelmed by what had just occurred. She tried to detect any changes, any feeling of change around her, but was too stunned by what she encountered. Such an enormous, connected, universal feeling; she wondered if everyone felt it, or if it was her own mind which conjured the visions. Joy swelled within her. She knew it was universal. She could sense the happiness of her fellow creatives and celebration twitched in her cells.

The hallway door cracked open and Officer Jenson appeared. Across the way, the drunk stared at her wide-eyed, apparently sobered by her strange actions that night. She looked to the clock.

"It's ten o'clock," Jenson confirmed as he rattled the cell keys at her. "Everything, uh, go alright?" Alex nodded and he looked relieved. "You're a free woman. There's a guy here who demanded your release." He unlocked the door and whispered to her as they walked down the hall. "Careful, I think he's in cahoots with whoever put you in here. The other cops seem to know who he is."

Alex squeezed his forearm before they reached the door. "Thank you so much for your help."

His cheeks flushed as he responded. "Hey, anyone who wants to make my job a little easier has my support." They entered the front office where her releaser waited for her. She couldn't believe her eyes.

"David? What are you doing here?" She raised her voice as she realized the answer to her question. "How did you know I was here?!"

David paled and gave the policemen a nod of thanks. He escorted her out of the station. She faced him and demanded an explanation. His eyes dropped and his face weakened with shame.

"Alex, I am so sorry." He wasn't sure how to explain so he blurted, "This whole Creator State thing has been a thorn in my side, and it just ate away at me. I couldn't figure out how to get back at you. Then I thought, well, if I keep her from the experiment, that would be my revenge. So I had my uncle call in a few favors to the cops, and well, here we are." David looked horrible and on the verge of tears. "I am so very, very, sorry Alex. I had no right to keep you from solstice." He started to weep and looked away from her. "I had no right, I am so sorry."

Alex's disappointment melted in his tears. She knew he did a horrible thing, but it hadn't affected the experiment. In fact, it strengthened her understanding of the State. She watched him try to snuff his tears, but it appeared therapeutic for him. David never apologized for his actions in the past. This was the first time she saw genuine emotion from him. She marveled if this was a result of the event. She walked over to him and held his shaking form. He softened to her touch after a few moments and wept. He confessed between sobs. "I've been an idiot, Alex. All this time wasted on manipulation and petty grievances, just for control's sake, for my own ego." He sniffled and asked, "I don't deserve a request, but can I beg you not to tell anyone about this?"

She wondered if he meant locking her up, or bawling his eyes out on Clark Street. She promised without confirmation of the details. "I won't tell anyone. It didn't matter anyway. The experiment went on, and I was present for it."

He lightened to her forgiveness and turned his face to her. "You mean you got there?"

Alex beamed. "Yes, David. I got there." She put a hand to his tear streamed face. "And so did you."

15

John dashed into the Night and Day Diner and held up a copy of the *Chicago Tribune*. The shoulder-to-shoulder crowd of artists and scientists cheered at his entrance. He searched the first morning edition for the anticipated report, pulled out a section of newsprint, and cleared his throat theatrically before he commenced. He propped himself on a table top and read from the top edge of the paper. "*Chicago Tribune*, September 21." Everyone hushed.

"State of the World, by John Mitchell." He smiled at his own name in print and read on. "Everyone knows that something peculiar happened a few months ago. Be it subtle or obvious, there is one fact dwelling in our daily lives as of late: something good has occurred, and we want to know how it came about. Three months ago an ambitious experiment was conducted to provide insight into the creative thoughts of artists around the world. This experiment, entitled the Creator State Project, was an effort by creative people to shift the global consciousness toward a more peaceful existence. Utilizing their creative gifts, the subjects involved set their intentions on worldwide change. During a three hour window of opportunity, all involved exercised their brightest talents and unified their creative thoughts. The chronicles from this event are astounding, and some unbelievable. Thousands of participants reported visions of brilliant energy during the experiment, which remain unexplained. Others described an expansive feeling of connection, as if the entire collective met on another plane of existence. While the experiment is celebrated as a success by the membership of the Project, it is the factual results which interest the scientists. We gathered data from a three month period prior to the experiment, and for three months afterward. We accounted for the previous year's variables and many control factors, which my team would be happy to share outside of this brief summary of the results. We are both amazed and pleased to report the following worldwide statistics since the Creator State experiment which took place on June 21 this year.

"Violent acts including murder, rape, shootings, stabbings, and domestic violence have decreased by 23%. Gang activity has decreased by 33%, which is astonishing, considering that three months prior to the experiment we noted a steady increase of 4% per month in gang related crime. Violence related to war has decreased by 21%, meaning less people died at the hands of religious unrest, territorial disputes, and politically motivated violent action. Drug traffic arrests were significantly lowered, dropping by 42%, which may be the result of an estimated 30% decline in drug traffic itself.

"We also monitored other worldwide activities, and discovered a few interesting shifts in consumer choices. A 52% increase in sales of environmentally friendly products was noted, and solar and alternative energy product sales increased by 43%. Enrollment in environmental protection causes also increased by 56%. Membership and financial support for programs related to AIDS relief, poverty relief and human rights is up by 47%. These are areas that were gaining at a barely measurable 1.3% in the three months prior to the experiment.

"The measurable impact is evident, but the real results of the solstice experiment are witnessed in our everyday lives. As a scientist, I am wary to admit any belief that is not backed by solid evidence. While the percentages don't lie when it comes to worldwide activity, there is definitely more to these results than meets the eye. A shift in consciousness has occurred. We can all sense it, we live it each day when we find a kind word or smile for our fellow man, lend a hand where a fist used to serve, or take action against negativity in our communities where apathy once thrived. It is this scientist's opinion that regardless of the evidence noted above, the experiment was indeed successful. We have all become more aware of the world we exist in. We stopped mocking a peaceful world vision and began to meet the demands of unity, which is more than you can ask any group to accomplish. While coincidence may be a factor, we recognize the changes in individuals around us. That is the most significant result that my panel of scientists will report, and we thank the Creator State membership for their dedication to all of us. Perhaps it is now up to the population to expand on the possibility the event created. Each individual can now implement their own actions from this generated energy of peace. Recovery has been activated for a shift in world attitude. In the future, violence may be a thing of the distant past, and we will remember the early summer day when the artists led us to peace."

The crowd erupted into applause and gave John, and themselves, a standing ovation. They honored his report of the results and the long journey they endured to achieve them. Everyone at the Diner felt accomplishment. The experiment left a path wide open for the world population to explore, as well as an altered perspective on the power of art. The din at the Night and Day Diner escalated with celebration.

Thomas crossed the sea of elations and finally reached Alex. They held each other for a lengthy interlude, overjoyed by the results of their hard work. Thomas broke their hug and gripped Alex by the shoulders. He gave her a direct gaze. She saw the love he strove for in his eyes; the universal love for all beings. He glowed with it, and was prepared to live that best life they discussed one short year ago. Gratitude surged in both of them as they recognized the value of their friendship. She smiled at him. "Well what do we do now? What's our next step?"

Thomas knew they had more plans to make, especially with the release of the experiment's results. For the moment, he brushed off plans for the future. He swallowed back tears of happiness, tilted his head toward the other side of the room, and indicated she should reconcile with John. "Act locally," he advised. She knew it was time to attempt her own experiment and tell John how she felt. Trepidation danced across her face, and Thomas took action. He gave her another hug for luck and sent her weaving through the celebration toward her future.

John was surrounded by a mob of well wishers. Everyone thanked him for his glowing report and indispensable assistance throughout the Project. He spotted Alex over the crowd and reached for her, unable to move from the crush of people around him. He squashed his way to the empty breakfast bar counter, the only clear space between them, and hopped up on it. Alex followed suit, wriggled through the mob, and climbed onto the counter. The restaurant owner dismissed any wrongdoing. He grew to love this crowd, and all was fair during their celebration. John and Alex met halfway on the counter top and embraced as they stood above the festivities. Alex knew it was time to gather her nerves and ask him for a second chance. She shouted over the commotion as they hugged each other. "How are we going to celebrate this momentous occasion?"

John yelled back over her shoulder. "I thought we could follow our intuition today; let the energies take us where they may!"

Alex realized they met halfway on more than the counter top. She gave in to his science and recognized its value, while he accepted the freedom of possibility into his everyday life. She pulled back from their embrace and looked deep into his eyes. She knew what she was about to say was long overdue. She parted her lips to speak, but he placed his finger on them to keep her from talking.

He wrapped his arms around her again, held her tight, and whispered in her ear. "It's the thought that counts."

Epilogue

○ ○

As the stars gain momentum again, past, present, and future melt together. All the prejudices, judgments, and skepticisms fade into the illusions they have always been. After all of the war, struggle, and examination, the history of civilization and the true meaning of life are left in one seemingly inadequate word: Love.

—Alex Davis

978-0-595-45237-8
0-595-45237-X

Printed in the United States
103374LV00005B/73-96/P